FOUR
SUMMONER'S
TALES

FOUR SUMMONER'S TALES
IV

KELLEY
ARMSTRONG

CHRISTOPHER
GOLDEN

DAVID LISS

JONATHAN MABERRY

GALLERY BOOKS

New York   London   Toronto   Sydney   New Delhi

G

Gallery Books
A Division of Simon & Schuster, Inc.
1230 Avenue of the Americas
New York, NY 10020

First Gallery Books trade paperback edition September 2013

GALLERY BOOKS and colophon are registered trademarks of Simon & Schuster, Inc.

For information about special discounts for bulk purchases, please contact Simon & Schuster Special Sales at 1-866-506-1949 or business@simonandschuster.com.

The Simon & Schuster Speakers Bureau can bring authors to your live event. For more information or to book an event contact the Simon & Schuster Speakers Bureau at 1-866-248-3049 or visit our website at www.simonspeakers.com.

Designed by Kyle Kabel

Manufactured in the United States of America

10 9 8 7 6 5 4 3 2 1

Library of Congress Cataloging-in-Publication Data is available.

ISBN 978-1-4516-9668-4
ISBN 978-1-4516-9675-2 (ebook)

Contents

Summoning
AN INTRODUCTION

Whenever writers come together, ideas are born.

In July of 2011, Christopher Golden and Jonathan Maberry sat in a Chinese restaurant in Rhode Island, discussing the nature of story and of plot. It has been said that there are only seven basic plots, and that each and every story can be reduced to fit within the parameters of one of those fundamental structures. While the authors of *Four Summoner's Tales* could debate that assertion for eons, that dinner conversation brought Golden and Maberry into a tangential discussion about diverse works that share the same root plot, and how the quality and value of a story comes in the details and in the approach of the individual writer.

In other words, it's all in the execution.

Wouldn't it be interesting, they mused, to give a group of very different writers the same short, simple premise—just a single sentence, without any other parameters—and see what the result would be?

Long before the fortune cookies arrived, musing turned into planning, and not long thereafter came the single-sentence premise from which the authors would work:

A strange visitor comes to town, offering to raise the townsfolk's dearly departed from the dead—for a price.

It was agreed that the authors could interpret "strange visitor," "town," and "raise" any way they liked. The stories could be set in the past, present, or future, in a fantasy world or the real one, and be based on science or magic.

The novella form was chosen as the best platform for this endeavor, long enough for plots to be fully explored and brought to fruition, but short enough to still be collected side by side. At novella length, four seemed the perfect number . . . thus, *Four Summoner's Tales*.

The only question that remained was who would pen the other two novellas, but Maberry and Golden found themselves in swift agreement, quickly enlisting Kelley Armstrong and David Liss, both renowned for their talent and imagination. Soon, the ideas began to coalesce . . .

FOUR
SUMMONER'S
TALES

IV

Suffer the Children

KELLEY ARMSTRONG

ADDIE

Addie slid through the forest as silent as a lynx, her beaded moccasins muffling her footfalls. The young stag wasn't as quiet. When it vanished from sight, she could track it by the crackle of autumn leaves under its hooves. Finally, it stopped to feed and she closed the gap between them until she could see it, small antlers lowered as it tugged at a patch of grass not yet brown and withered.

Addie eased the bow from her back, notched an arrow, and took aim. The buck's head jerked up. She loosed the arrow, but it was too late—the buck was in flight. Addie fired a second but too quickly, spurred by frustration and anger, the arrow lodging in a nearby maple.

When the crash of the fleeing deer subsided, she peered around the dawn-lit forest. Something had startled the beast and it hadn't been her. She would never have been so careless.

Addie pulled her coat tighter against the chill. The jacket was too small for her now—she'd grown nearly a half foot in the past year—but she refused to let Preacher and Sophia buy one from the traders. She wanted to make one exactly the same way, doing everything from killing the deer and mink to curing the leather to sewing the cloth. There was not another twelve-year-old in Chestnut Hill who could claim the same. Not a girl of any age. Her parents may not have given her much, but they'd taught her to look after herself.

They'd also taught her—unintentionally—how to sense danger. So now, after the buck had bolted, she went still and listened. She paid particular attention to noises from the north, upwind of the deer, presuming it was a scent that had startled it. After a few moments, she heard the tramp of boots on a well-packed path.

Addie eased her bow onto her shoulder and pulled her skinning knife from its sheath. Then she slunk soundlessly through the woods. She knew exactly where to go—there was only one trodden path in the area, used by the villagers to get to the lake. When she was near enough to see figures, she crouched behind a low bush.

It was two men. One middle-aged, perhaps thirty, the other so ancient that even with a cane and the younger man's arm, he shuffled along. Neither was from the village. A hundred people lived in Chestnut Hill and Addie knew every one. The only travelers they saw were trappers and traders, and precious few of either so deep in the forest, three days' ride from Toronto. These men were neither traders nor trappers. Settlers, then? Lured north by the promise of land or work on the railroad or in the mines? Settlers needed supplies, though, and these men carried only packs on their backs. No wagon. No cart. Not even horses.

And where had they come from? The road lay on the other side. The men headed toward town on a path that only led from the lake. Trappers did come through the forest, but she saw no sign of such gear on these men. They hadn't come *across* the lake—it was too small, with no settlements nearby save Chestnut Hill.

Addie slipped through the forest to get a closer look. Both men had short hair and neatly trimmed beards. Though they wore long coats, she could see their clothing underneath. White shirts and black trousers. They looked as if they were heading to church.

Missionaries. That's what they had to be. Perhaps they'd been traveling on foot from Greenville, ten miles away, and gotten lost in the forest, taking the first well-trodden path they saw. It didn't matter *where* they had come from, only that they were heading to Chestnut Hill.

How would Preacher feel about other men of faith in his town? She ought to warn him. With any luck, they'd just be passing through. Chestnut Hill might not even allow them to stay, given that it still reeled from the tragedy that had Addie out in the woods, avoiding the glowers and glares of villagers, blaming her for the simple fact that she lived. That she'd survived.

She was about to start back when the younger man looked straight at her. She froze, telling herself she was mistaken; there was no way he could have heard her, no way he could see her now, dressed in brown behind the dying leaves of a cranberry bush. But he didn't simply glance her way. His eyes bore straight into hers, and when they did, she swore her heart stopped.

"You there," he called. "Girl."

How could he tell she was a girl? She was dressed as a boy, in trousers, her dark hair pulled back.

"Girl," he called again. "We're heading to Chestnut Hill. Is this the way?"

Her parents had taught her to look after herself because no one else would do it for her. She knew now they'd been wrong—

and so she did try to be kind, to be helpful as Preacher and Sophia counseled. Yet even as she spurred herself to step from behind the bush and lead this man to Chestnut Hill, she looked into his eyes and she could not move, could not speak.

The man released his grip on his elder's arm and started toward her.

"We're here to help, child," he said, his voice low and soothing, like Preacher coaxing Sophia's cat from under the porch. "We know what Chestnut Hill has suffered and we wish to—"

Addie bolted from her hiding place, running back toward the village like she had a black bear on her tail.

PREACHER

Preacher was taking confession behind the village outhouse. As the wind sliced through the weathered boards, bringing a blast of the stench from within, he reflected that this might not be the place to conduct such a holy endeavor.

He also reflected that it was rather a fitting choice, given the astounding inappropriateness of the entire situation. He was as suited to the position as the location was to the task.

He'd come to Chestnut Hill to teach, along with his wife, Sophia. They'd been doing so in Toronto together, and when this offer came, Sophia begged him to consider it. They'd been wed six years, and she'd had yet to conceive, a situation that bothered her far more than it did him. She'd begun to wonder if it was the noisy and noisome city affecting her health. The job in Chestnut Hill seemed the best way to test such a theory. Preacher didn't care much where they lived, as long as she was happy, and off they went.

They'd arrived in Chestnut Hill to find the local priest had been taken by the same influenza as the schoolteacher. So the council had made a decision. Two teachers was a luxury, one they were willing to bestow on their beloved children, but it seemed equally important that they be reared as proper Christians. Sophia would teach and her husband would take the priest's place.

Preacher had argued most strenuously against this arrangement. He was not a man of the cloth. That was all right, the council had replied—they'd never really wanted a papist anyhow and the good father had simply been the only man who'd take the position. Preacher could obviously read the Bible. That was enough.

It was not enough. He knew that, felt the deception in his gut every day. He was not a God-fearing man. He wasn't even a God-loving man. Sophia was the churchgoer, though he'd attended when he could, to please her. She'd offered to take the position instead, but the council had been aghast at the suggestion. Men taught the word of God. Even, it seemed, wholly unsuitable men.

So, from that moment on, he was Preacher. Despite his best efforts to retain his name, only Sophia called him Benjamin. To everyone else, he was Preacher. The false prophet of God.

Now he sat straddling a wooden bench, his back to old Millie Prior, listening to a litany of offenses too trivial to be called sins, as he tried not to inhale the stench of the outhouse. As for why he held confession here, it was the village's decision—not a commentary on his ability but based, like all their choices, on simple convenience and expediency. Even if it was a papist custom, the people still expected confession, and the outhouse was discreetly removed from the village, used only when folk were out and about and couldn't get home to utilize their own facilities. It had a bench, in case people had to wait their turn during a festival or such. It made sense, then, to have the priest—and now the preacher—hold confession there.

As he listened to Millie admit to envying her sister-in-law's new dress, a commotion sounded in the woods behind him. When he saw who it was, he had to blink, certain his vision was impaired. His foster daughter never made a noise, and here she was, barreling toward him like a charging bull, dead leaves and branches cracking underfoot.

"Preacher!" Addie said, stumbling forward. "There's men—"

As Millie glared over, Preacher said, "I'm sorry, child. I'm hearing confession. You'll need to leave." Then, behind Millie's back, he motioned for Addie to simply step to the side and pantomime the news, which she did, mouthing that she'd seen missionaries heading to town as he gave Millie two Hail Marys and absolved her of her sins.

"But I'm not done, Preacher," Millie said. "I still—"

"We ought not to take up too much of the Lord's time, Miz Prior. If you need to unburden yourself of more, we can do it at your next confession."

She grumbled, but there was no rancor in it. Everyone knew God was a busy man—she simply thought she deserved more of his time than others. Once she was gone, Preacher strode over to Addie. She was obviously agitated, but he knew better than to offer any of the usual parental comforts, like a hug or even a squeeze on the hand.

When he was a boy, he'd found a dog half-dead in an alley and though he'd nursed it back to health, it was never quite right, always wary, always expecting the worst. His mother said someone had beaten it when it was a pup, and he ought to do his best to be kind to it, but he ought never to expect too much. It would always cower at a raised hand, anticipating a beating, no matter how often it got a pat on the head. Addie never cowered, but she had that same look in her eyes, always wary, always expecting the worst.

"Missionaries, you said?" he whispered as he walked over to her, hiding in the forest until Millie was gone.

"Two men. I don't like the looks of them."

"Indigent?" he said. When she seemed confused, he said, "Vagrants?"

"No, they were dressed as fine men. I just . . . I didn't like their looks. They said they were coming to help us. After . . . what happened."

Preacher sucked in breath. "Snake-oil salesmen."

"Yes!" Addie said. "That's what they put me in mind of. Peddlers. We had some a few years back, when they were thinking of putting the railroad through here. They sold my ma a cream that was supposed to make her look young again and it didn't work and my pa got so mad at her for wasting the money . . ." She trailed off, her gaze sliding to the side. "It wasn't good."

No, Preacher was certain it wasn't. Not much had been "good" in Addie's young life. Sometimes, the wilderness did things to people, especially those like her folks who stayed out there, away from the villages. People weren't supposed to live like that. It was as if the forest got into their blood, leached out the humanity. He'd been there, when they'd found Addie's parents. You'd have thought a wild creature broke in. That's what they told Addie anyway. Whether she believed it . . .

Preacher looked down at his foster daughter, holding herself tight as she peered into the forest, watching for trouble. No, he hoped she'd believed them, but he doubted it.

"I'll go warn the mayor," he said. "No one needs the kind of comfort they're selling. Perhaps we can stop them before they reach the village. Can you run home and tell Sophia? She might hear a commotion, and she ought to stay inside and rest."

"Is she still feeling poorly?"

He nodded. "But if anyone asks, she's busy writing lessons for when school starts again."

Addie gave him a look well beyond her years. "I know not to tell anyone she's unwell, Preacher."

He apologized and sent her off, watching her go, bow bobbing on her thin back. Their house was across town; it was quicker cutting through the village, but she always took the forest. Once she disappeared, he headed into town.

Sophia was indeed unwell, yet it was no grave cause for concern. Celebration, actually. After three years in Chestnut Hill, her dream had been realized. She was with child. And it could not have come at a worse time.

Preacher strode toward the community hall. That's where the mayor and his wife would be. Where *he* ought to have been, even though it wasn't Sunday. For the past month, he'd spent more time in the hall—which doubled as the church—than he had at home. Tending to the living. Tending to the dead.

So many dead.

These days, the only villager as busy as Preacher was the carpenter, building coffins. Tiny coffins, lined up in the community hall like props for some macabre play—a tragedy unlike anything the Bard himself would have dared put to paper.

Thirty-six dead in a month. One-third of the entire village. Eight elderly men and women had passed, but the rest were children. In September, twenty-four children had trooped back to Sophia's class for the year. When they reopened the school, she'd have six. And there would be no little ones starting for years after that. No child below the age of five had survived.

Diphtheria. Not that anyone other than Preacher and Sophia used the word. Here, it was simply "the sickness," as if there were no other that mattered.

What had Chestnut Hill done to deserve this? How had they offended God?

They had not. Preacher knew that. He'd gone to university. He knew about Louis Pasteur and the role bacteria played in disease. That was why Sophia had disbanded school as soon as they realized it wasn't merely children's coughs and colds. That was why they had urged the town to quarantine the sick. They had not listened, of course. Everyone knew the way to treat ailments of the chest was with hot tea, a little whiskey, and plenty of prayer.

Except that God was not listening, and the more their preacher insisted that this tragedy was not a punishment from on high, the more they became convinced that Preacher himself had done something wrong. Displeased the Lord. Failed to make some proper . . . Well, they weren't sure what—only heathens offered sacrifices, but they were convinced he'd failed to do something.

Or perhaps he had done something . . . for his foster daughter. Addie had lived, hadn't she? Preacher could point out that Addie had been on one of her hunting trips when the diphtheria broke out, and as soon as she returned, they'd sent her back into the woods with supplies, to stay another week. Also, she was twelve, past the age of most victims. It didn't matter. The preacher's daughter had lived where their children had perished. And now his wife was pregnant? That would only seal the matter, which was why Preacher and Sophia had agreed to not breathe a word of it until they had to, hopefully months from now.

"Preacher?" a voice called as he stepped into the village lane. "Where are you off to in such a hurry?"

He turned. It was Mayor Browning, helping his wife into the community hall, where their son lay in one of those small coffins, the last victim of the outbreak.

"May I speak with you?" Preacher said. "I know it couldn't be a worse possible time but—"

A commotion sounded at the end of the road. Someone calling a welcome. Someone else ringing a bell, telling the town that visitors had arrived, an occurrence rare enough to bring everyone out, no matter how dark the mood.

He was too late. The strangers had arrived.

ADDIE

Addie raced home through the woods. As she did, she tried not to look at the houses that backed onto the forest, tried not to remember the children who'd lived there. She hadn't known most of them very well. She'd not even gone to school until her parents passed and she came to live with Preacher and Sophia. Still, she had known the children, and there'd been many times she'd come this way and seen them. Sometimes, if Addie felt Sophia's invisible hand prodding her, she'd even call a hullo.

When she reached the mayor's house, she circled wide into the forest, so she wouldn't need to see it at all. Not that it helped, because her path ended up taking her by the fallen oak tree where she'd last seen Charlie Browning, the mayor's son. They'd been tramping around in the woods before her hunting trip, before the sickness came. Just tramping around and talking, as they usually did. Then they came to the fallen oak and sat and kept talking. It'd been night, and she'd leaned back to look at the stars, her hands braced against the log. Her hand had brushed his, and he'd laid his on hers, and when she'd looked over, he'd given her a smile that was shy and nervous and not like Charlie at all.

She'd seen that smile and she hadn't pulled her hand away, even if she thought perhaps she ought to, and now . . . Now she wasn't sure if she wished she had or not. She thought of that summer night, and she was glad he'd been happy that last time they'd been together, but . . . perhaps it would have been easier if he hadn't been. If she hadn't been. If they'd fought and now she could look back and say she hadn't liked him very much, that they hadn't been very good friends after all. It hurt too much otherwise.

They hadn't even let her see him after he'd gotten sick. Preacher and Sophia said it was all right, if it was a short visit and she didn't touch him. But Mayor Browning and his wife wouldn't let her, not even when she heard Charlie in the sick-room, coughing and calling for her. Perhaps tomorrow, they said. When he was feeling better. Only there was no tomorrow. Not for Charlie.

Addie circled the mayor's house and continued on until she reached the little clapboard cabin she shared with Preacher and Sophia. It was one of the smallest homes in town, only four rooms. Addie had her own bedroom, and it didn't matter if it was half the size of Charlie's; it was hers, something she'd never had at her parents' house, where she'd slept by the fire. Sophia assured her that when the baby came, it would sleep in their room, and they'd build a new house before it was old enough to need its own. Addie had said it didn't matter, not really. It did, though, and she was glad they understood.

Addie went in the door and found Sophia at the kitchen table, composing lessons. Sophia wanted to reopen school in a week. She said the children needed to be reassured that life would return to normal. But Addie had heard people saying they weren't going to send their children back. Perhaps next year. Getting an education wasn't all that important in Chestnut Hill. It wasn't as if you would do anything with it. Wasn't as if you were going anywhere else.

Addie didn't plan to tell Sophia there'd be no school. Her foster mother needed to get back to normal too, perhaps more than anyone else. Each death had been a blow that Addie swore she could see on Sophia's fragile body. There'd been days when it was all she and Preacher could do to make Sophia eat. That's when Preacher told her about the baby, so she'd understand how important it was for Sophia to be healthy. Addie had already known. Her mother had lost three babies after Addie, and she'd recognized the signs of pregnancy. She'd kept quiet, though, until they'd seen fit to tell her. Now she guarded that secret as ferociously as a bear with a single cub. It was theirs, and it made them a family—truly a family, trusting one another with their deepest secret. No one was going to take that away from her.

"Addie," Sophia said, rising with a smile. "What did you catch?"

"Nothing."

Alarm filled Sophia's pretty face, and Addie could have laughed, as if returning empty-handed portended the end of the world. Sophia knew she always caught a deer or a few rabbits and if she hadn't, then something was wrong. Having a person know you that well . . . it felt good.

"There's men coming," she said. "Preacher says they're snake-oil peddlers, on account of the deaths."

The alarm on Sophia's face grew. "Oh my."

"It's all right. Preacher will stop them. He just wanted me to tell you. Are you feeling poorly?"

A wan smile. "Better today. Let me make you some breakfast—"

"I already ate. Took biscuits this morning before I left." Addie paused, still just inside the door. "Can I go back? Help Preacher if he needs me? He seemed mighty worried."

"Go on, then. I'll stay inside. Last thing anyone needs is hearing me tell those peddlers where they can put their wares."

"You can tell me," Addie said with a grin.

Sophia laughed. "Go on, now. Tell Benjamin I'm feeling fine. I'll make a hot lunch for both of you."

When Addie headed back out, she could hear a hullabaloo down the road and knew Preacher hadn't been able to stop the peddlers.

Addie blamed Millie. True, the old woman had left as soon as Preacher asked, but Addie blamed her anyway, for taking up his time with something as silly as confession when he had so much else to attend to these days. Addie believed in God; Sophia said she ought to, so she did. She just didn't figure He had time to be listening to old gossips confess their sins. Not if He obviously hadn't had time to listen to Addie's prayers and save Charlie.

Addie stayed in the forest as she circled around to the commotion. People were spilling out of their houses now. Eager for the distraction. As she drew close, she could hear the whispers starting already. The men were doctors. No, they were undertakers. No, they were from the government, putting the whole village under quarantine.

The advantage to moving through the woods was that Addie could get a lot closer to the situation than those who'd just come out their doors. Someone had brought the two men straight to Preacher and the mayor, down by the community hall, so she was able to creep alongside it and hear everything unfolding.

"We'd like to have a word with you, Your Worship," the younger stranger was saying, and Addie figured that meant Preacher, but it was the mayor who answered.

"Whatever you're selling, we aren't interested."

"I'm sorry," Preacher said. "It's been a very hard month for us. We really would prefer to be left alone in our time of crisis. We'll certainly provide a hot lunch, though, and replenish any supplies you need before you go on your way."

"I understand your hesitation," the younger man said. "But I can assure you that we did not come to profit from your tragedy. Instead, we offer . . ." He cleared his throat. "I hesitate to say more in public, Your Worship. Please, grant us a few minutes of your time. After hearing what we offer, if you wish us to move on, I assure you, we will, without another word to anyone."

Mayor Browning clearly wanted the men to leave. He was a

brusque man by nature. Now his only child had just passed, and he had no patience for intrusions, no more than he'd had when Addie tried to visit Charlie. Yet Preacher took him aside, pulling him closer to where Addie hid.

"Let's allow them to have their say," Preacher said. "They're here now. If we refuse, they may try to sell their snake oil on the side. We'll hear them out, refuse their offer, and escort them, politely, from town."

Mayor Browning allowed that this was probably the most expedient way to deal with the situation. When he went back and told the strangers to have their say, though, they insisted on having the whole town council present at the meeting. That led to more discussion, but finally the mayor broke down again. There were only two others who made up the council and they were there, anyway, listening in. He'd bring them all inside and get this over with, so he could return to his grieving wife.

Addie went in the back door of the community hall. It led to a small kitchen, where they would lay meals for a festival or other special occasions. Now the table was covered in food brought for the bereaved, most of it left untouched for days and starting to stink.

She could hear Mayor Browning in the next room, asking his wife to leave for a few minutes. She argued—her child would be in the ground soon enough and she wanted to spend every last moment at his side. But the mayor was firm. She ought to go, but only briefly. Leave out the back door and take some air. He'd call her back when he could.

Addie quickly retreated and hid herself under the porch as Mrs. Browning left. Then she crept inside again.

The hall had two main rooms with a wall between them, which could be removed for large gatherings. During the funerals, they'd kept the wall up—bodies would be laid out in the back room, while the service for one victim would take place in the front. From the voices, Addie could tell that the men were holding their meeting in the front room, so she slipped into the back one.

As soon as she saw the open coffins, she went still. She'd just finished thinking that this was where they kept the bodies and yet she hadn't really thought about it at all.

He's here. Charlie's here.

I won't look. I won't. I'll just walk—

Walk across to the other wall. Where his coffin lay. She couldn't see Charlie, nestled too low, but she could tell the coffin was his by the items laid on the table. All the parents had done that, set out small personal belongings that would be laid to rest with the child. Things that mattered to them. Things that mattered to Charlie.

An American coin from a trader who told wild tales of life in the south. A ribbon from a parade in Toronto, on his trip there five years past. A drawing of a pure black Arabian horse, the sort of fine mount he dreamed of owning. Finally, an eagle feather, from last summer, when they'd climbed the bluffs together. He'd wanted her to have it, but she'd found one for herself. Now she wished she'd taken his gift. Something to remember him by.

She could still take it.

Steal from the dead? What would Preacher say?

Addie swallowed and yanked her gaze from the feather. She could hear voices settling in the next room as the introductions finished. This was what she'd come for—to hear what the strangers wanted. Not to lose herself in grief and wicked thoughts.

She hurried to the wall and pressed her ear against it.

PREACHER

Preacher tried not to pace as the other members of the town council introduced themselves. It was not a quick process. While

there were only four, including himself, explaining their positions took some time. No one in Chestnut Hill held a single
occupation, not if they participated in public life. The village was
simply too small for that.

To supplement his own income, Preacher hired himself out
as a scribe, composing letters for the largely illiterate population.
He helped Sophia with the garden and chickens. He rode four
hours a week to retrieve the village mail. And he'd begun letting
Addie teach him to trap, though that was primarily an effort to
participate more fully in his foster daughter's life.

The mayor also ran the trading post out of a room in his
house. The blacksmith covered any issues of law enforcement.
The doctor raised cattle and hunting dogs. And, of course, when
each explained his council position, he had to make it sound
more important than it was, necessitating further pointless delay.

"And my name is Eleazar," the younger stranger said as the
council finally completed their introductions.

"Eleazar? Is that French?" the blacksmith—Dobbs—asked.

"It's biblical," Preacher said. "The first son of Aaron."

"Yes," Eleazar said. "It is a foreign name to you, I'm sure, but
my family has been in this country since before the war with
the Americans. My colleague's roots go back even further." A
smile flickered on the man's face. "Rene is indeed French, though
I hope you will not hold it against him."

The old man gave a creaky laugh. Preacher marveled that he
managed to stay on his feet, let alone that he had traveled here
on foot. Rene had to lean against Eleazar even now, and as much
as Preacher hated to draw this meeting out any further, he could
no longer watch the old man teeter.

"Please," he said. "Have a seat. We don't have much time to
spare, but your walk must have been long. Rest your feet."

"Thank you, Benjamin," Eleazar said.

Preacher stiffened at the use of his Christian name. He could tell himself it was too familiar and they ought to use his surname. But the truth was that after three years of lamenting the fact that he seemed to have lost his name, lost his identity, he took offense now. It felt disrespectful, as if the man was refusing to acknowledge his place as the village's spiritual representative. Which was ridiculous, of course. Preacher was just being testy.

Eleazar continued. "I understand you have suffered a great tragedy. Diphtheria, wasn't it?"

The men nodded.

"And, if I may ask, how many were lost?"

"Thirty-six," Preacher said. "We lost thirty-six souls."

"Most of them children?"

Preacher tried not to squirm. None of the men sitting here needed each fact recited, every reminder thrown in his face. He could tell by Eleazar's soft tone that he didn't mean it that way, but that was what it felt like. Each of these men had lost someone—the blacksmith his eight-year-old son and toddling daughter, the doctor two grandchildren, and the mayor his son. The pain of waking daily to a world without them was reminder enough.

"Yes," Preacher said. "Mostly children. I'm sorry to be blunt, but if you would like a fuller explanation, I would happily provide that in private. I don't think we all need to be part of such a conversation, not when Mayor Browning's boy lies in the room behind us."

Preacher kept his voice low, but he would admit that was a little sharper a rebuke than a man of God ought to give.

"Your Worship," Eleazar said to the mayor. "I apologize. I did not realize—"

"There was no way you could," Preacher said. "However, under the circumstances, you can see why we're being more abrupt than is Christian. If you could please tell us what you want, so we can return to grieving for our children . . ."

"What if you didn't have to grieve?"

Preacher's head whipped up as his eyes narrowed. "What?"

Eleazar leaned forward. "We are here to offer life, my friends. Renewed life. The resurrection of your children."

Preacher shot from his seat so fast that it crashed over behind him. "You would dare——" He struggled to get the words out. "I have seen peddlers prey on the fears and misfortunes of others, but I have never, in my life, heard anything as outrageous or egregious——"

"We are not peddlers, Benjamin. We are, like you, men of God——"

"*You are not.*"

"Preacher," the doctor murmured. "Let the man finish."

Preacher glanced over at Doc Adams, normally the most level-headed and reasonable of the group. The old sawbones held himself very still, giving no reaction, but deep in his gaze Preacher saw something terrible. He saw hope, and he wanted to stamp it out, no matter how cruel that might seem, because this was the wrong sort of hope, the absolutely wrong sort.

"There's no harm in letting him finish," Mayor Browning said, his voice uncharacteristically quiet.

Yes, Preacher wanted to say. *There is harm. Great harm. He's offering you the thing you want most. The thing you know you cannot have. You must resist the temptation by refusing to listen.*

Yet how could he say that? These were grown men, not schoolchildren to be lectured by a teacher—or a preacher. If he suggested that they were not capable of seeing through lies to truth, he would insult them. Which he'd gladly have done, to be rid of these hucksters, but it was too late. They'd already heard the insidious whisper of the serpent. They would find a way— any way—to listen to the rest.

"Please proceed," Preacher said stiffly as he righted his chair. "Forgive my interruption."

Eleazar waited until Preacher was seated again. Then he folded his hands on his lap and said, "This is no snake oil, my good men. I would not exploit your tragedy that way. When my ancestors came from the old country, they brought with them special knowledge. Great knowledge. Passed on from God Himself."

The man glanced at Preacher, as if expecting another interruption. Preacher clenched his teeth to keep from saying anything. He'd not give Eleazar the satisfaction. He had to trust that the village men were not fools. Let them listen and recognize lies.

"You are familiar, I'm sure, with the story of Lazarus? Raised from the dead by the Holy Son, Christ Jesus?"

"I can assure you we are," the mayor said.

"Mr. Dobbs mentioned that my name seems odd. It is my family name, and it has a meaning that is indeed biblical. It's another form of Lazarus. My ancestor was that poor man, raised from the dead, taught the art of resurrection by Christ Jesus himself."

"No," Preacher said, rising. "I'm sorry, gentlemen. I can't countenance this. To say this stranger is descended from Lazarus is one thing. Even to say he can raise the dead is merely preposterous. To claim that Jesus taught his ancestor the skill? That is blasphemy."

The others had to know that. They took their faith more seriously than he. All of them, as much as it pained him to admit it. Yet not one even looked his way. They kept their gazes averted, and when he saw that, he knew that they recognized the blasphemy. And they chose to ignore it.

"Is it not . . . possible?" Doc Adams said.

Preacher turned to stare at him. The doctor? He was the most educated among them. The one who made his living following the natural science of the world. Who knew that dead was dead.

"It can happen, can't it, Doc?" Dobbs asked. "I mean, I've heard of things like that."

Doc Adams nodded. "And I've seen it. A man on the dissection table at the university. We cut into him, and he started awake."

"Because he *wasn't* dead," Preacher said.

Mayor Browning turned to him. "Are you saying that the doctor who pronounced him so was wrong?"

"Yes, that is exactly—"

"I am surprised you would be the one arguing most vehemently, Benjamin," Eleazar said in his soft voice. "A man of faith ought to believe in miracles. In the mercy of God." He paused and looked Preacher in the eye. "Unless you are not such a man of faith."

Preacher blanched. He was certain the barb was thrown wild, that Eleazar did not truly see into his heart, and yet, with his reaction, he confirmed it. And in Eleazar's response, a faint smile, Preacher knew he was lost.

"Our preacher is a good man," Doc Adams said. "If he is skeptical, it's because he . . ." The doctor seemed to struggle for a way to put it.

"He doesn't have a dog in this fight," Dobbs said.

The doctor flinched and Dobbs flushed. "That didn't sound right," the blacksmith said. "But they know what I mean. He hasn't lost anyone. His wife lives. His daughter lives."

"Foster daughter," Doc Adams said, correcting him.

"It's the same thing," Preacher said. "While you all know how I feel about the loss of our children, I would not dare match my grief to yours. So I take and concede the point. However, my having not lost anyone means that I'm the only one who can see this clearly and—"

"Preacher?" Mayor Browning turned to him. "I'm going to ask you to step outside. We want to hear what these gentlemen have to say."

Preacher forced a nod. "All right then. I will remain silent—"

"No." The mayor met his gaze. "I don't believe you will. I am asking you to leave. Please don't make me insist."

Preacher looked into the mayor's face, the set of his jaw, the flint in his gaze. Dobbs rose to his feet, squaring his thick shoulders, as if he were a tender of bar, ready to throw an unruly patron through the door. Doc Adams shrank back, taking great interest in a mark on the wall.

No one here would take Preacher's side. They wanted to hear what the men had to say. They needed to. His job was to counsel them to make wise and spiritual decisions, but if their ears were stopped, he must leave them to make their own mistakes. He could hope they'd hear the lies for what they were but, at worst, they would lose only coin and pride.

"All right," Preacher said. "If anyone needs me, I'll be home with my wife. Good day, gentlemen."

BROWNING

Preacher left without argument. Which the mayor took to mean he wasn't as strenuously opposed to the idea as he pretended.

Their preacher was an odd duck. A fine enough man—he just had odd ideas. City ideas. Dobbs thought him soft, and while it was true that he wasn't like the men who'd lived out here all their lives, the preacher held his own. He just spent more time in his head than a man ought to. Worried more than a man ought to.

That was, Browning decided, what had happened here. Preacher felt obligated to object to anything that might smack of dark arts, but it was only a perfunctory objection. A strong perfunctory objection, Browning would give him that, and yes, the man had seemed genuinely upset, but . . . well, he'd left,

hadn't he? If Browning wanted to see that as a sign that his protest lacked conviction, then he could and he would.

Besides, this wasn't the dark arts. It was faith. Eleazar was
right—the Lord Jesus Christ had raised a man from the dead. It
was right there in the Bible. That made it a miracle. A gift from
God, not the Devil.

"Go on. Tell us more," he said when Preacher had left.

"Thank you, Your Worship. We can return the living, but only
if they have been dead four days or less, like Lazarus. I presume
there are children that meet that criterion?"

"My son," Browning blurted.

There were others, of course, but in that moment, he did not
even pause to consider them. They did not matter. His son—his
only child—lay dead twenty feet away, behind the wall. What
would he give to see the boy alive again? There was part of him
that dared not even ask the question because the answer terrified
him.

"And my granddaughter," Doc Adams said. "And Mr. Dobbs's
son and—"

"My daughter died five days ago," Dobbs said. "Is that—"

"No," Eleazar said softly. "It is too long."

"Like my grandson," Doc Adams said. "Gone a week now."

Eleazar nodded.

"My daughter was wee still," Dobbs said. "My wife can have
others. My son was growing into a strong lad. If you could return
him . . ."

He said it so casually, Browning marveled. *If you could return
him.* As if asking for a simple favor. *If you could bring a pie on
Sunday, that would be lovely.* Browning knew Dobbs loved his boy.
But it was not the same as his own situation. Dobbs had two
other children and apparently planned others to replace those
lost. Browning's wife had lost their first two in infancy, to
influenza. She was past the age of bearing more. Without their

son, they had nothing. No child. No grandchildren. No great-grandchildren. Only the two of them, growing old in their loneliness and their grief.

"Tell us more," Browning said again.

"There is a price," Doc Adams said. "Surely there must be a price."

Eleazar looked uncomfortable. "Yes, I fear there is. I cannot perform this miracle often. That was the stricture given by the Lord Jesus Christ. We must be very careful imparting our gift, so as not to disrupt the natural order of things. I search out trage-dies, such as yours, where it can be of most use. That means, however, that there is a cost, to allow my assistant and me to live frugally and continue our work."

"How much?" Dobbs asked.

"My normal rate is a thousand dollars for a resurrection."

Doc Adams inhaled sharply. Dobbs looked ill. Browning began quickly calculating. He had money and a few items he could sell. Yes, he could manage it. When he looked at the faces of the others, though, he felt a slight pang of guilt. A thousand dollars would be near impossible for them. Men at the mines bragged of earning that much in a year.

"Most of us would not be able to afford that," Browning said, quickly adding, "though a few would scrape it together."

"Understandable," Eleazar said. "And while that is my fee, normally I am performing a single resurrection, so I require an exorbitant amount, as it is all I may earn for a year or more. However, as there are multiple resurrections required here, I did not intend to charge so much for the good people of Chestnut Hill. How many children would there be, if price were no object?"

"Seven," Doc Adams said. "I pronounced seven poor children dead in the last four days."

"Then my fee would be three hundred dollars apiece."

Doc Adams exhaled in relief. Browning knew he could afford that with ease. He glanced at Dobbs as the younger man counted on his fingers.

"Would you require cash?" Browning asked. "Or would goods be sufficient?"

"If they are easily transported goods—horses, jewelry, furs—yes, we would take them for market value."

Dobbs nodded, a slow smile creasing his broad face. He could absolutely manage that. Most could. It was not a small amount—one could purchase three good horses for as much. But at least half of the families would be able to get by and there were enough wealthier folks in town to lend the rest. That would be important, Browning realized. He could imagine the rancor it would bring to Chestnut Hill if there were parents unable to afford the fee. Best to lend it to them, at a reasonable rate.

"We could manage it," Browning said. "For all seven."

"But we'd need the children back first," Doc Adams cut in. "What you're offering is, as you said, a miracle, and those are few and far between. We cannot simply trust you can do as you claim."

A kernel of panic exploded in Browning's gut. He wanted to shush the doctor. Tell him not to insult this man, who was offering a dream come true, lest he take that dream and vanish whence he came.

As soon as he thought it, though, he was shamed. Was this not what Preacher had warned of, when he said the men were coming? *They'll want to prey on our tragedy, Mayor. They'll offer us impossible things for our hard-earned cash, and I fear the village folks are too grief-stricken to think straight.*

Browning had agreed wholeheartedly . . . when he thought the men might only be selling some elixir of youth or happiness. Instead, they offered something even more unbelievable, and here he was, ready to leap on it without a shred of proof.

"The doctor is right," Browning said. "We'll need the children resurrected before we pay the full cost. We can arrange something, of course—a contract or such."

Eleazar smiled. "I doubt any court would recognize a contract to raise the dead, but yes, of course I do not expect you to pay us without the children. In fact, I do not expect you to even agree to pay us without proof. That is why I will resurrect one child first, free of any charge. In demonstration." He turned to Browning. "You said you had a son newly passed?"

Browning's heart pounded so hard he could barely force a nod.

"May I ask his age?"

"He just passed his thirteenth birthday."

"A boy on the cusp of becoming a man. I am particularly sorry for your loss then. I know the disease usually affects only the very young and the very old."

"He was the eldest of the victims," Doc Adams said. "He'd suffered a cold this summer—a serious one that affected his lungs. While he seemed quite recovered, I believe it must have made him vulnerable."

"Indeed." Eleazar glanced at the old man, Rene. "Then with my assistant's aid and the mayor's approval, I will return this boy to life."

"When?" Browning blurted.

Eleazar smiled, indulgent. "He will be back in time for your wife to serve him dinner." The smile faded, his gaze growing troubled. "There is, however, one other—"

Eleazar stopped, looking sharply toward the door at the back of the room.

"Sir?" Doc Adams said.

"I thought I heard something. Is anyone back there?"

Browning shook his head. "My wife left that way before we began. The room was empty."

"So there is a door?" Eleazar rose and walked to it, swinging it open fast and peering in as the others scrambled to their feet.

As Eleazar strode through, Browning hurried after him. He found the man in the back room, looking about. Browning could see into the kitchen, where the rear door was closing.

Someone *had* been there. Eleazar hadn't noticed it, though, and Browning didn't point it out. Browning was not about to do anything to upset him. Not after what he'd just said about . . .

Charlie.

Browning's gaze swung to the coffin, the largest in the room, two chairs placed in front of it, where he and his wife had spent the night.

His wife. Dorothy. What would she say? Her heart might break with joy.

Eleazar strode over, scattering Browning's thoughts.

"There's no sign anyone was here," Browning said. "Perhaps mice? Or coons in the eaves."

"I'm sure it was nothing," Eleazar said. "I'm a touch anxious about what I have to say next. My fears likely got the best of me."

"What you have to say?" Browning paused. "Yes, you were saying there was something else." His heart thudded anew. *No, please, nothing else.* Nothing that would stop this man from bringing Charlie back.

Eleazar was walking again, moving to Charlie's coffin.

"Is this him, then?" he asked. "Your boy?"

Browning stayed where he was. He wasn't looking in that coffin. If there was a chance he could see his son alive, he didn't wish to see his corpse.

Was there a chance?

Dear God, let it be possible. Let his boy rise from that coffin, not the pasty-faced child with the mottled lips and eyelids, that sick child, that dead child. Let him rise as Browning remembered him.

Browning cleared his throat. "Yes, that's Charlie."

Eleazar smiled. "He's a fine boy. Well-formed. Don't you agree, Rene?"

Browning had not even noticed the old man there. Rene leaned over the coffin, and something in his face made Browning go cold. He wanted to leap forward. Yank the old man back. He swallowed hard. Rene nodded, jowls bobbing.

"You have a fine boy, sir," Rene said, and there was nothing in his clouded old eyes but kindness.

"Thank you." Browning turned to Eleazar. "You said there was more?"

Eleazar nodded. "Another price, I fear. One that cannot be negotiated." He walked back to Browning. "I said earlier that I use my powers sparingly because that is the Lord's will. There is another reason. The second price. Unlike our Lord, I am but a mortal man. I cannot return the soul to a body for nothing, as he did. There must be an exchange."

"Exchange?"

"A soul for a soul."

Browning blinked. "I . . . I don't understand."

"I do," said a voice behind him.

Browning turned to see Doc Adams in the doorway, looking ill.

"Yes," Eleazar said. "Our good doctor understands. I cannot steal a life from heaven, like a base thief. I take a soul for you, I give a soul to Him. For a child to live again, someone must die."

PREACHER

Preacher was poring over a Latin book with Sophia. The words . . . well, as he'd joked to her, they could have been Greek for all he understood of them. He knew Latin, of course. At this moment, though, his mind was otherwise too occupied to translate them to English. He was trying to distract himself from what was happening at the community house and it was not working.

His wife was also trying to distract him, and had been since he'd explained when he came home.

"You can do nothing about it," Sophia said. "They must make their own choices and their own mistakes."

Which is what he'd told himself. Yet he could not shake the feeling that he ought to have done more.

"You cannot," his wife said, as if reading his thoughts. "You dare not, under the circumstances."

Again, she spoke true. His position was precarious enough of late, worse now with the baby on the way. If he were to argue against listening to these men when his daughter had survived and his wife was with child . . . ? Who knew of what they might accuse him.

"I'm going to start teaching Latin to the younger children," Sophia said, thumbing through a well-used book. "Simple words, as I do with French. The names of animals and such."

What younger children? he wanted to ask. The three below the age of eight who'd survived? He knew they could not think like that. Better to focus not on the loss but on those that remained, on how the smaller class would mean more attention for each pupil, more work they could do, such as starting Latin sooner.

Preacher was saying just that when the front door banged open, Addie rushing in, words spilling out so fast that they couldn't decipher them. Both Preacher and Sophia leaped from the table and raced over, thinking she was injured.

"No," Addie said. "I'm well. It's the men, what they're offering. To bring back the children."

"Yes, we already know," Sophia said, leading the girl inside. "It's terrible and—"

"Terrible?" Addie pulled from her grasp. "They say they can resurrect the children. It's wondrous."

Sophia winced.

Preacher moved forward, bending in front of the girl. "Yes, it would indeed be wondrous . . . if it was possible. It's not. They're taking advantage of our grief. Promising the impossible because they know we're desperate enough to pay the price."

"You're wrong," Addie said, backing away.

"So they aren't charging a fee?" Preacher asked softly.

Addie said nothing.

"Adeline?" Sophia said, her voice equally soft but firm. "Did they say there would be a cost?"

"Yes, but they're reducing it, on account of there being so many children—"

"How much?"

She hesitated. "Three hundred apiece."

"My Lord," Sophia breathed. "That's . . ."

"Exactly the right price," Preacher said grimly. "As much as they can charge and still have people pay it . . . with everything they have." He turned to the girl. "You see that, Addie, don't you? These families have lost their children and now they may lose everything else, in a desperate and hopeless attempt to regain them."

Addie shook her head. "It's not like that. He's going to do a demonstration. Free of charge."

"What? That's not poss—" Preacher began.

"It's a hoax, Addie," Sophia said, laying her hand on the girl's arm. "Swindlers have many of them. They'll conjure up some trick and—"

"And what if it's real?" Addie said, crossing her arms. "You don't know that it isn't. You don't."

"Yes, we do, sweetheart. They cannot—"

"You're wrong," Addie said. "They're going to do the demonstration. They'll bring Charlie back. And I'll be there to see it."

She turned and raced out the door as Sophia and Preacher stared at one another.

"Charlie?" Sophia said finally. "Oh, Benjamin. Of all the children . . ."

"I know," he said. "She does not need that. I'll go and be there for her when she's disappointed."

"Not disappointed," Sophia said. "Heartbroken. I'll go with you, too. I'm well enough, and I ought to be there for her."

He nodded and gathered her bonnet and coat.

BROWNING

Someone must die.

You knew there was a trick, Browning told himself. *There had to be.*

No, it wasn't a trick. It was a hitch. He ought to have known it couldn't be as easy as paying cash on the barrel. A life given for a life returned. That was how it worked, and he ought to have been relieved, now that it made sense.

Relieved? Someone has to die for Charlie to live.

His wife would do it. That was the first thing he thought, even as the idea horrified him. Dorothy would gladly give her life for her son's. Yet that didn't help at all. What would the boy do without his mama? What would Browning do without his wife? Their family would be torn asunder as much as it was now.

I could get another wife. I can't get another son.

Again, his mind recoiled, but again, it didn't quite drop the idea. Dorothy was a good housekeeper and a fine cook. He would not wish to lose her. But if he had to choose . . . and if the decision was hers, made on her own, without his prodding . . .

"You cannot expect us to do that," Doc Adams was saying. "While there are those who would give their lives for the children, we would again need proof before such a decision could be made. No one will sacrifice himself on such a chance."

Browning turned sharply on his heel, to motion for the doctor to be silent, not to give offense, but again Eleazar seemed to take none, only nodding in understanding.

"The good doctor is right," Eleazar said. "Normally, there would be someone near death willing to offer his or her life—eager, even, to leave this world of pain and pass into the kingdom of heaven. But you have lost all your elderly and infirm in the same tragedy that claimed the lives of the young. There is but one elder remaining."

"No," Doc Adams said. "I fear there is not."

"Oh, but there is." Eleazar motioned to his assistant. "Rene has offered himself for this demonstration."

"What?" Dobbs said, stepping forward.

Browning made a move to shush him as his heart filled with hope again.

"It's all right," Rene said in his creaking old voice. "A man as young as your blacksmith cannot understand what it is to wish his life done. I pray that he may never know the horrors of age. My body has failed me, and yet it stubbornly clings to life. I cannot end it myself or I would be damned. So I offer it to this village, to the mayor's young son. I will die so he may live."

That was the end of the discussion. It had been decided, apparently, even before the men arrived in Chestnut Hill. The old man would die so the younger one could prove his skill. With Charlie. Browning's son would live again, and there would be no price to pay. None at all. Of course, he would not tell the others that. He'd pretend that he'd paid his three hundred to help cover the cost of others. As for the other price . . .

How will I tell them? Where will we find volunteers?

Did it matter? Charlie was coming back. The others could deal with that choice themselves when the time came.

Eleazar killed his assistant in the back room.

There was no hesitation, no preparation. He didn't even say what he was doing, only asked Dobbs and Browning to take Charlie's coffin out the front, where the villagers could see. They were not to say what was to come—it must be a surprise. As they'd told him, they didn't want to raise hopes unnecessarily. Take the coffin out and make some excuse, and he'd be there in a moment. Doc Adams ought to speak to anyone still outside. With that, Eleazar and the old man disappeared into the back.

Browning was still carrying Charlie's coffin to the door when Eleazar appeared.

"Rene has passed," he announced.

"What?" Dobbs nearly dropped his end of the coffin.

"It was swift and merciful. Doctor, could you please confirm it is done? He's resting in the back."

Doc Adams did as he was asked, while Browning and Dobbs carried the coffin outside.

Most people had gone home now, content to wait and hear what the mysterious men wanted. Some had lingered, though, and when they brought out the coffin, a gasp went up.

"All is fine," Doc Adams assured them as he came out. "All is fine. The men have asked us to bring one of our dearly departed into the sunlight, so they might better see his condition."

Whispers snaked through the smattering of people. The men were doctors then, or scientists. A few left in disappointment.

As Browning stepped away from his son's closed casket, he caught sight of a man striding along the road, a slender woman beside him, her blond hair pushed up under a bonnet.

Preacher. Bringing his schoolteacher wife to chastise them.

He's going to stop this. Take away your chance. Take away your Charlie.

The warnings seemed to slide around him, whispers like . . .

The voice of God. That's what it was. Resurrection was God's work, and now this "preacher" thought he'd stop it. The preacher who hadn't stopped Charlie from dying. The preacher whose own daughter lived. A girl who'd wanted to see his son before he passed.

The voice whispered, *You know there's a reason she lived. And a reason your son died. A strong, healthy boy, older than the others, contracts the disease after the rest? It's unnatural.*

Browning shoved past the villagers, ignoring their grunts of surprise. He bore down on Preacher. The schoolteacher started forward, chin raised, eyes flashing, but her husband pulled her back with a whispered word. He strode forward to meet Browning.

"If you dare—" Browning began.

"Dare what? Dare stop you from something we both know will fail?" Preacher said, lowering his voice. "If I thought it would do any good, I'd try, but your course is clearly decided. Nothing will help now but for you to *see* failure, however hard that will be for all of us."

Browning clenched and unclenched his fists. The rage still wound around his gut like a cyclone.

Hit him. Show him who's the mayor.

But he's given me no cause.

Hit him anyway. Drive him off. Tell him begone. He's a doubting Thomas. He'll spoil everything.

"If you'll excuse us," the schoolteacher said, elbowing between the men. "Addie is here somewhere, and we'd like to find her."

Browning looked down at the woman. It took a moment for his gaze to focus, the rage still nearly blinding him. He felt his fists clench again. Felt them start to rise. Then he realized what he was doing, whom he was about to hit, and they dropped quickly, and he stepped back.

"Thank you," the schoolteacher said.

"Your Worship?" It was Eleazar, calling to him. "We're ready to begin."

ADDIE

Addie could see Charlie's closed coffin, out in front of the community hall. She could also see Preacher and Sophia, searching for her in the small gathering. She started scooting around the building, but her foster parents were splitting up now, one heading for each side, knowing if she wasn't in the crowd, she was still in the forest.

She raced to the back porch and swung onto the railing, then up to the roof.

Like Charlie taught me to do.

While Addie was an expert tree climber, she would never have considered using those skills to sneak around town. Spying on folks wasn't right. As Charlie said, though, "when you're a child, no one tells you anything, so you need to eavesdrop sometimes, to know what's going on." They'd tried listening in on the town meetings through the chimney, but it didn't really work. So they mostly just climbed up here to get a better view of anything taking place in the village square.

Like bringing a boy back to life.

Bringing Charlie back to life.

She crawled across the roof carefully, slipping a little as she went but always catching herself in time. Below, she could hear Preacher asking someone if they'd seen Addie. They hadn't. No one had.

If Addie went down there, she wasn't sure that Preacher would stop her from watching. He probably wouldn't. He and Sophia really were teachers, right down to their bones. They'd explain why she ought not to watch, but if she insisted, they'd let her, believing it was always best to see a thing for yourself. To learn a lesson for yourself.

She didn't care. She wasn't going to watch this with them standing beside her, suffocating under the weight of their disapproval. Even recalling their expressions when she told them made her want to scream. Made her want to charge back home, grab her belongings, leave, and never come back.

They'd betrayed her. That's what she felt, and it hurt worse than any of her dead father's beatings. Eleazar had promised to bring Charlie back, and they wouldn't even consider that he might be able to work miracles. Sophia and Preacher—the very people who'd taught her about God.

She took a deep breath and calmed herself as she crept to the front. She stretched out there, then inched forward until she could peer down.

Below was Charlie's coffin. Still closed. Eleazar knelt beside it. Addie couldn't see the old man—Rene. He must have stayed inside, where it was warm.

Mayor Browning stood at the foot of the coffin. Dobbs and Doc Adams flanked him. All three stared at the coffin as if mesmerized. The other spectators milled about, peering over and then whispering to themselves, as if wondering what the fuss was about. They hadn't been told. Good. If people knew, they'd all come running and they'd crowd around and Addie wouldn't see the miracle. Wouldn't see Charlie rise.

If she listened closely, she could hear Eleazar talking. She couldn't understand what he was saying, though. It wasn't English.

Because Christ didn't speak English. That's what Sophia told her when she'd asked why the Bibles were translated. Jesus spoke another language and so did the people who wrote the Bible. Hearing Eleazar speaking in a foreign tongue only proved he was no fraud.

He finished the words, and then he reached for the coffin lid. Addie held her breath, her heart beating so hard it hurt.

What if Preacher and Sophia were right?

When were they ever wrong? When had they been cruel to her? Misled her?

"No," she breathed. "They *are* wrong. They must be."

As Eleazar opened the wooden lid, Addie squeezed her eyes shut, prayed as hard as she could.

Please, God, let him live. I know you didn't listen before. I know why—

Addie's heart clenched, and she couldn't hold her breath any longer, panting for air as pain filled her.

I know why you didn't listen. I was evil. I was wicked. I . . . I . . .

She couldn't even form the words in her head. What she had done. The sin for which God had punished her.

I deserve that punishment. But Charlie doesn't. Please let him come back.

She heard a gasp from below and her eyes flew open. *He's alive. He's really . . .*

Addie stared down. Charlie's coffin was almost exactly under her perch, and when she opened her eyes, she saw his face. His pale, dead face. His sunken, closed eyelids.

No, he is alive. That's why they gasped.

Only it wasn't. She looked at the faces of the villagers, the women shrinking back, and she knew the sound came from them, a simple reaction to seeing the poor dead boy. She had but to see Mayor Browning's expressionless face to know Charlie did not live.

Yet the mayor's face *was* expressionless. It did not crumple with grief and disappointment. He stood there, resolute. Waiting.

Eleazar bent over the coffin. He lifted his fingers to Charlie's face and traced them over his pale forehead. When he pulled them back, there were three red lines left there.

"Is that blood?" someone whispered.

"Of course not," another hissed back.

Eleazar spoke again, in that foreign tongue, touching his fingertips to Charlie's eyelids, his nostrils, and then his lips. When he reached the lips, he held his fingers there, his head bent, words flowing faster until . . .

Eleazar stopped abruptly, as if in midsentence. His head jerked up. His fingers pulled back and . . .

Charlie's lips parted. Or they seemed to, opening so little that Addie was certain she'd blinked, certain she was seeing wrong, that his lips had been like that already or were moved by the man's fingers.

Yes, moved by the man's fingers. A trick. Isn't that what Sophia warned of? Charlie's lips moved by chicanery and—

His eyes opened. Addie stopped breathing.

Trick. It's a trick.

Charlie sat up and looked about. His gaze lit on Mayor Browning and he smiled, and Addie knew there was no trick.

Charlie lived.

After Charlie sat up in his coffin, the village erupted like a volcano in one of Sophia's books. Some people ran shrieking that the dead had risen. Others fell and gave thanks to God for his infinite mercy. And still others barely drew breath before demanding to know why Charlie had been resurrected—why him, why not their child.

"Charlie was returned to us as proof of this man's holy power!" Browning's voice boomed over half the town. "I offered my own child to be tested, as is only right. As your mayor, I must take that risk for my family, before asking you to take it for yours!"

"Is he truly alive?" Millie Prior pushed through and peered at Charlie as Doc Adams examined him. When she reached to poke him, Eleazar grabbed the old woman's hand hard enough to make her shriek.

"Please," Charlie said, his voice low and rough with disuse. "She meant no harm."

"He speaks," Millie breathed.

He speaks, Addie thought. *But he doesn't sound like—*

She bit her lip, as if that could stopper her thoughts.

"Yes," Charlie said. "I can speak, but barely. I feel . . ." He gripped Eleazar's hand for support.

"He's very weak," Eleazar said. "I'm sorry if I startled you, my good woman. I do not wish him to be poked and prodded about during his recovery. Your doctor is examining him now."

Doc Adams rose. "The boy lives. He breathes. He speaks. His heart beats. His blood flows."

Millie dropped to her knees. "Praise be. Dear Lord, thank you . . ."

As she continued, Doc Adams explained which children could be resurrected. Eleazar took Charlie's hand and helped him from the coffin. He told Mayor Browning to fetch his wife and then announced that he would take Charlie inside to rest. Addie waited until they were gone, then scampered back across the roof.

Addie eased open the back door to the community center. Inside, she could hear Eleazar talking to his assistant. She closed the door silently behind her. While Eleazar was occupied, she'd speak to Charlie. Yes, he was weak, but she'd take up none of his time or his strength. She simply wanted to . . .

She didn't know what she wanted. What she expected. Only that she'd been robbed of the chance to see him before, and she would get it now. No one would take that from her now, and if something went wrong—

It won't. He's back.

If something went wrong, at least she wouldn't lie awake, wishing she'd seen him one last time. So she crept into the community hall while Eleazar spoke to Rene.

She hadn't even reached the kitchen door, though, before the conversation stopped.

"I need to rest now," Charlie said, and she realized Eleazar hadn't been talking to his assistant, Rene, at all.

This would make things more difficult. Eleazar and Charlie were both in the front room, and the assistant was here somewhere, too.

It didn't matter. She *would* see Charlie.

She peered into the back room before she slid through. There were three coffins now, the fourth gone. Something caught her attention on the floor. An eagle's feather, under the table where Charlie's coffin had lain. When they'd picked it up, they'd let his treasures scatter.

Anger darted through her. Those things of Charlie's had been so important to his parents after he'd died. Now they were as they'd been in his life—useless clutter. How many times had his mother tried to throw out that eagle feather, saying it was filthy? It was treasured only after he was gone, like Charlie himself. His father had paid him no mind when he was alive—

Addie wiped the thoughts from her mind. *Unchristian*, Sophia would say.

She paused again, caught on that new thought. Preacher and Sophia. She hadn't even seen them after the resurrection. They'd been there, lost in the crowd. Were they regretting their hasty judgment? Looking for her to apologize?

Stop thinking. Start moving. Or you'll lose your chance.

She stepped into the room, gaze fixed on that feather, to retrieve it for Charlie. She picked it up and as she rose, she caught sight of a figure and stifled a yelp as she wheeled. It was Rene. He sat in front of one of the other coffins, with his back to her. His head was bowed. Asleep.

Addie exhaled in relief. She ought to be more careful. She'd been checking the room for him when she'd gotten distracted by the feather. She tucked it under her jacket now and silently tiptoed to the door joining the two rooms. He never stirred.

The adjoining door was closed tight. Addie turned the handle as carefully as she could and then eased it open. Through the crack she could see Charlie. He sat in a chair, leaning back, his eyes closed, looking like . . .

Well, looking like Charlie. Exactly like the Charlie she knew, his color coming back, the swelling fading. His dark hair hung in a cowlick over one eye, and Addie smiled, expecting him to reach up and push it impatiently aside, as he always did. He seemed too tired for that, though, and just sat there, slouched in the chair.

Eleazar was across the room, rummaging in his pack. He muttered to himself as he did, doubling the noise.

"Charlie?" Addie whispered.

No response.

A little louder. "Charlie?"

His eyelids flickered. Then they opened, and she was looking straight into those eyes she knew so well, gray-blue, like the sky on a windy day. She looked into them and saw . . .

Nothing. Not a flicker of recognition.

Because he can barely see me through this crack in the door.

She glanced at Eleazar. He was still retrieving things from his pack, turned away enough not to see her. She inched the door open until her face fit in the gap. Then she grinned at Charlie and, in her mind, she saw him grin back, as he always had, ever since the first time they met, when her ma brought her to town for supplies. Charlie had been in his father's shop room, and he'd snuck a licorice whip from the jar for her. That's who Addie saw in her mind—that boy, that grin—and it took a moment before she realized she wasn't seeing it in front of her.

Charlie wasn't even smiling. He looked right at her and that expression in his eyes never changed.

He doesn't know me.

Because he's tired. He's confused.

She lifted the eagle feather and waggled it. He frowned.

Addie glanced at Eleazar. He was reading a book, muttering to himself as he turned the pages. Addie opened the door a little more and slipped through. Charlie sat barely three paces away. She crossed the gap and held out the feather. He only stared at her. She laid it on his blanket-draped lap.

"Here," Eleazar said. "I've found that—" He looked up and saw her. "Who are you?"

"I-I'm Addie. Adeline. I came to see—"

"He's not ready to see anyone. Begone, girl."

She backed up to the doorway. Charlie didn't look down at the feather, as if trying to remember where it came from. He didn't look at her either. He closed his eyes as if she'd already left.

"Charlie?"

His eyelids flickered open, and he glanced over with annoyance.

"He needs his rest, child," Eleazar said, striding toward her. "He's not himself yet. You need to leave."

She retreated through the door into the rear.

"No!" Eleazar said, raising his voice. "Not that way."

But she was already through, already racing across the room. As she reached the kitchen door, she heard Charlie's voice, and she thought he was calling her back, telling Eleazar he remembered her now. She turned, and as she did, she saw the assistant, Rene, saw his face now as he sat there, head bowed. Saw the bruises around his neck. Saw his eyes. Open. Bulging. Dead.

Addie spun and bolted out the kitchen door.

BROWNING

Mayor Browning's wife was home now with Charlie. When he'd left, she'd been sitting at his bedside, watching him sleep, looking very much as she had the night before, sitting at his coffin's side. She'd even had the same look on her face, anxious and afraid.

When he'd first told her the news, she'd shouted at him, for the first time in their marriage. She'd even thrown something—a plate she'd been washing, shattering it against the wall as she cursed him. She seemed to think he was pulling a prank. Yes, he'd been known to make them. Yes, sometimes, perhaps, they bordered on cruel, but this was not one he'd ever have attempted. He'd struck her, another first for their marriage. Struck her full across the face, bellowing at her that she was an ungrateful wretch, that he'd done this for her—brought back her boy—and this was how she treated him.

She'd raced out of the house then, not even pausing for a bonnet or a cloak, gathering her skirts and running like a girl through the streets, graying hair streaming behind her.

Now they were home. Her boy was home. Yet she was not beside herself with joy. Not falling to her knees to thank the Lord. She hovered over Charlie, pushing his cowlick aside, tentatively, as if the slightest touch might send him back to the other side. It was not what Browning expected. Not what he wanted. But he supposed it might take time for her to accept the miracle as real.

Eleazar had summoned him back to the community hall. Yes, *summoned* him, as if he were a common innkeeper. That rankled, but Browning reminded himself of the incredible debt he owed the man. Eleazar wished to speak about the other children, and he had a right to be somewhat abrupt—time was wasting, the children were wasting.

So Browning returned to the community hall. Doc Adams and Dobbs were already inside with Eleazar.

"How is Charlie?" Dobbs asked.

"Tired. Sleeping."

"That's to be expected," Eleazar said. "I fear he will not be his usual self for several days. He will require sleep, and he may be somewhat confused. His memory is weakened also. Do not overtax him."

"We won't," Browning said.

"Now, on to the matter at hand—the rest of the children. Doctor? As I was saying, I'll ask that you go round the parents up now. I'll need them all here to discuss my fee."

"About that," Doc Adams said. "I've been thinking on the . . . other part. I-I'm not certain how to tell—"

"You won't. Just bring them here. I'll discuss the rest with these two gentlemen."

As the doctor left, his words repeated in Browning's mind. *The other part.* How would they tell people that to bring their children back, they had to pay a life? Before Charlie was resurrected, it had seemed simple enough. Of course people would pay that price, terrible though it was. This was their children. His own wife would have gladly given her life for their son.

Except, now, having seen Charlie return, Browning wasn't as certain. No, in fact, he was quite sure that if he'd told Dorothy the cost, she'd have flown at him like a harpy, as she'd done when he said Charlie was back. She'd never have believed him. She certainly wouldn't have offered to die for the chance to resurrect their son. She'd have thought him mad.

It is madness. Desperate madness. How had they ever agreed—

No, not madness. Charlie was alive.

"How're we gonna do it?" Dobbs asked, and when Browning looked over, the blacksmith was sitting down, his face pale.

"Strangulation," Eleazar said. "That is the swiftest and cleanest way."

Dobbs raised his gaze to the man, his eyes filling with horror. "I only meant finding volunteers. We don't need to . . . to . . . *take* them, too, do we?"

"Do you expect me to?" Eleazar's eyes flashed with annoyance. "I took Rene's life because I owed him as much, for his years of service. He trusted me to be swift and kind. It is still an unpleasant task, one I don't intend to repeat six times."

Dobbs looked as if he might be sick. Browning's mind reeled. *Six times. Strangle six people. Take six lives.* How had this seemed simple before?

"Now, you must do it quietly," Eleazar said. "You cannot announce this price or you will have chaos. Even if you get your volunteers, there will be resentments and rancor for years."

"*Even if we get our volunteers?*" Browning turned to the man. "I thought . . . You've done this before. People must have volunteered."

"Certainly. If, as I said, they are ill or elderly and wish to escape this life. Sometimes, though, that is not the case, which is what it seems here."

"Then how . . . ?" Browning swallowed. "You brought Charlie back in front of them. Now the doctor is out telling them they can have their children back for three hundred dollars. If they arrive and we say it's not true . . ."

"It damned well better be true," Dobbs said, pushing to his feet. He turned on Browning. "You tricked me."

"What—"

"Your son was the demonstration. He's alive, and you didn't have to pay anything for it. No money. No life. Now my boy lies in his coffin, and you're telling me he's not going to come back unless I kill someone?"

"I never said— I didn't volunteer Charlie. Mr. Eleazar asked for him. You were sitting there when he did. You heard everything."

Browning turned to Eleazar and the man nodded, but his agreement seemed a moment too slow.

"You two made a deal," Dobbs said to Browning. "On the side, before Doc and I arrived."

As Browning sputtered, Eleazar rose, shaking his head. "That's ridiculous. His Worship heard the plan when you did."

The words were the right ones, but something in Eleazar's tone didn't properly support them. Browning could see it as Dobbs's meaty face mottled with fury.

They won't believe me, no matter what Eleazar says. They'll think I used my position to get a bargain.

"I'll pay," Browning said quickly. "I will offer my three hundred to help anyone who falls short, at no rate of interest."

"And the rest?"

"I had nothing to do with the rest. Mr. Eleazar offered his assistant. Everyone else will have to find a suitable volunteer."

"How?" Dobbs's voice rose. "My wife? Myself? Bring back one child and leave the rest with no one to raise them? No one to support them? Another of my children? Pick the one I like least? How is a father supposed to do such a thing? There is no one else. We have no other family in Chestnut Hill."

Perhaps you ought to have thought of that before you agreed. That's what Browning wanted to say as his guilt turned to outrage at the injustice of it all. He hadn't offered Charlie. He hadn't brokered a special deal.

Browning squared his shoulders. "If you cannot pay, then perhaps—"

The mayor never saw the blow coming. He felt Dobbs's fist hit his jaw, sending him reeling back. He recovered and swung at Dobbs but missed, the younger man grabbing his arm and wrenching, sending him flying into the wall.

"Gentlemen," Eleazar said. "Really. Must it come to this?"

He sounded almost bored, and Browning turned on him, the outrage filling him as pain coursed through his jaw. They were turning on each other now, and Eleazar was to blame. Eleazar had brought this to Chestnut Hill. He'd—

Resurrected Charlie. This was the man who'd granted his fondest wish.

Browning's fists dropped to his sides.

"There are other ways," Eleazar said. "They may be distasteful, but given the alternative of not returning the children . . ."

"What do you propose?" Browning asked.

Eleazar took a seat again. "In every village, there are . . . those who are not fully contributing to community life."

The blacksmith's face screwed up in confusion. "What do you mean?"

"I mean those who live on the outskirts, both physically and metaphorically. Those living outside the village. Those who drink more than they ought. Perhaps aren't quite as intelligent as others. Perhaps not as mentally sound. Perhaps don't fit in—the native population and such. Are there any of those around Chestnut Hill?"

"Some," Dobbs said. "There were little Adeline's parents, but they're dead now. There's others, too. Old man Cranston and his wife. They're crazy, both of them. Trapper Mike. He's half-Injun, with a squaw wife. Timothy James, another trapper, when he's not too drunk to remember to empty his traps."

"See, there's five, with only a few moments of thought. I'm sure there are more."

Dobbs nodded, thinking it through. Dear God, was he really thinking it through? No, he couldn't be. Not that way. He was seeing a solution and seizing it, with no thoughts except how this brought his boy back.

"You're . . . you're suggesting we commit murder," Browning said slowly.

"Hardly. I'm suggesting you remove an unproductive segment of the local population. A potentially dangerous segment. Have any of these people ever caused problems for you?"

Dobbs nodded again. "Timothy James went after one of Millie Prior's granddaughters a few years ago. Grabbed her in the forest and touched her before she got away. Old man Cranston shoots at anyone who steps on his property. He doesn't even *have* property. No one knows what he considers his, on account of him being crazy. And Trapper Mike? Folks around here swear he steals from their traps. Never caught him, but he's sneaky. I don't doubt he does it. Then there's Paul over by the lake. Won't tell nobody his last name. I hear he's a fugitive. I've been trying to get an accounting from the Mounties, but they haven't come by Chestnut Hill in near on a year."

"Because you aren't on the railroad route," Eleazar said. "The authorities are ignoring you. Leaving you to defend this town all by yourself . . . Sheriff. I'd say it'd be your God-given right to go talk to those folks, and if they give you any trouble, well, I think you've had enough trouble from them. Who knows what they'll do next? You need to look after your town."

Dobbs nodded. "I do. Look after my town and its children."

"Now, you, Mayor Browning." Eleazar turned to him. "I'd say it's your responsibility to accompany the good sheriff." He paused. "If your people don't get their children back after you got Charlie . . . ? I've seen some ugly things in these wilderness towns. Folks can go a little wild themselves out here. A mob is a wicked thing, Mayor."

Browning looked from Eleazar to Dobbs. And he knew he didn't have a choice. This was the cost of bringing his boy back. The real cost.

ADDIE

Addie raced all the way home. She got there just as Preacher and Sophia arrived. Any other time, walking together, they would have been talking or whispering, and Preacher would have had his hand on Sophia's arm. Today it was as if each walked alone, silent and stone-faced with shock.

Preacher saw Addie first. He seemed to take a moment to recognize her. Then he said, "Adeline," and Sophia started from her stupor.

"You were there," Sophia said. "You saw."

Addie nodded.

"I—we don't know how to explain it," Sophia said. "It is . . . beyond reckoning."

"There must be something to it," Preacher murmured, as if to himself. "Some science. Perhaps the boy was not dead. I've read of such things. Perhaps it's not diphtheria but some new disease. These men pretend to raise the dead, but they know the children were never truly gone, so . . ." He shook his head. "No, I don't see how that's possible. Doc Adams would have noticed."

They reached the porch. Preacher ushered them inside. Neither seemed to have noted that Addie hadn't breathed a word. As soon as the door closed, she said, "Something's wrong with Charlie."

Preacher blinked, as if waking from sleep. "Wrong . . . ?"

"Besides the fact that he's been raised from the dead?" Sophia stopped and her cheeks flushed. "I'm sorry, Addie. I don't mean to be sharp. I'm still trying to reconcile what I saw. That a boy could rise—"

"It's not Charlie."

She got them into the living room, prodding them along as if they were the children. "I went inside to see him. Whoever—whatever—is inside Charlie, it's not him. Or he's wrong. Very wrong. He didn't know me at all."

Preacher lowered himself into a chair. "Eleazar said he'd be exhausted—"

"It was more than that. He had no idea who I was. He didn't recognize a feather that he wore in his cap for half a year. He didn't care to try to recognize it. Or me. It was not Charlie."

"But that's . . ." Sophia trailed off and shook her head. "I'm not sure if that's more or less incredible. How would it not be him? Who would it be?"

"*What* would it be," Addie said, correcting her. "Eleazar has summoned a demon into Charlie's body. He is possessed."

*   *   *

Preacher and Sophia didn't much like Addie's possession notion. It seemed quite reasonable to her. She'd grown up in a world where monstrous things happened, and rather than run from the idea, she'd always embraced it. Nothing thrilled her so much as stories of hags and squonks, loup-garous and wampus cats.

She knew all about possession. It was right there in the Bible. And it was real, too. Millie Prior's cousin up in North Bay had been possessed, and they had to bring a priest all the way from New York City to exorcise her. If priests did it, then it must have been real. Addie didn't see how you could argue with that. Preacher still did.

Eventually, they seemed to accept that something might be wrong with Charlie.

"If he was brought back, it would make sense that he'd be . . . not right," Sophia said. "It's unnatural. It's not the work of God. I know that."

"The work of the Devil," Addie said.

She could tell Sophia didn't like that idea much either. If Addie found herself pulled toward demons and evil, Sophia sought out angels and goodness. That's the way she was. As for Preacher, Addie figured he didn't quite believe in angels or devils—he just knew this was wrong. The dead ought not to come back, however much one might wish it.

"His assistant is dead, too," Addie said.

Sophia stared at her for a moment, then managed to say, "His . . . ?"

"Rene," Preacher murmured. "Or Mr. Rene. I'm not sure if it was a Christian name or family."

"There is no Christian in these men," Sophia muttered. "You mean the old one, then? He was the assistant? And you say he's . . . he's . . ." She couldn't seem to finish.

"Dead," Addie said. "I saw him at the hall. I thought he was asleep, but his eyes were open and . . . he was dead. I'm sure Eleazar has killed him."

"But why?" Sophia said finally. "Why bring him here, only to kill him?"

"I'm going to find out," Preacher said, rising. "Addie? Stay with Sophia and watch over her. I'll return as soon as I have answers."

PREACHER

When Preacher said he was going to get answers, he didn't mean to find out why Rene had been murdered and what was "inside" Charlie Browning. The first step was confirming that what Addie said of Rene was true. Not that he suspected her of lying. She'd never do so on such a grand scale.

No, Addie believed what she said to be true. While he could not take her claims as truth, he had been a teacher long enough to know that you did not doubt a child to her face. Few things eroded her confidence more—or were more likely to turn her against you. You accepted the truth of what she said and quietly investigated on your own. As he was doing now.

When he arrived at the community hall, Doc Adams was coming out. Preacher stopped on the road, behind a cluster of people. Through the open door, he could catch a glimpse of Eleazar with the mayor and Dobbs.

Another meeting. He wouldn't be welcome there. He watched Doc Adams hurry away, fending off questions from those gathered outside. Of the other council members, the doctor would be most likely to speak to Preacher, but he was clearly on a mission. Preacher was too—a mission that involved finding answers, not asking for them.

Once the doctor had left, Preacher retreated two houses over and cut through to the forest. He came out behind the community hall and entered through the back door. As he walked through the kitchen, he could hear Dobbs shouting about something, but the walls were too thick to allow him to hear more than angry, unintelligible words. By the time he opened the door into the back room, the dispute was already over, the voices low again.

He slipped through the doorway and—

There was Rene. Preacher had been so caught up in the voices that he'd forgotten why he was really here. One glance in Rene's direction and he knew Addie was right. The man was dead. Still, despite what his eyes told him, he had to check.

He pulled off his boots and crossed the floor silently. When he reached the old man, he put his fingers to his neck and then checked for breathing, and the whole time, a voice in his head was saying, *The man's eyes are open. He has bruises around his neck. His skin is cold. Do you have to question everything?* Yes, apparently, he did. So he checked, and he confirmed that Rene was indeed deceased.

As Sophia had said, why bring the old man here on foot, a difficult journey, only to kill him? There was something missing here.

Preacher stood there, puzzling it out, until he remembered that the men were still talking in the next room. He ought to have been listening in. When he got to the door, though, he could hear the mayor and Dobbs leaving. Preacher left quickly and ducked through the kitchen doorway as Eleazar walked into the back room.

"Now, what am I going to do with this?" Eleazar mused aloud. "I ought to have had the blacksmith carry it out back to the woods." He sighed and crossed the room, and Preacher could hear him lifting the old man, testing the weight.

"Let's get this over with," Eleazar muttered.

Preacher hurried out the back door.

When Preacher got to the road, there was no sign of Dobbs and Browning. He asked those gathered which way they'd gone. They pointed, but the two men were already out of sight. Had they gone into a house? Gone home? No one seemed to know. They were all waiting for Eleazar.

Preacher caught sight of Doc Adams at the far end of the road. He started that way but didn't get far before someone hurried out to stop him. Maybelle Greene, a widow whose two children had both survived the outbreak. He'd have liked to see that as the grace of God, but it probably had more to do with her having been ten miles away visiting her sister at the time.

"Preacher," Maybelle said as she hurried up to him. "I heard what they're saying. Is it true? That man brought Charlie Browning back?"

"Seems so."

She stopped, her face clouding as she looked both ways. No one was nearby, but she still leaned in as she said, "I ought to be happy. Thanking God for his mercy. But . . ." She looked up at him. "They say it's God's work, but I can't quite reckon that. Why would God take our children, then send this man to bring some back? Why not just take fewer? Or none at all?"

That was the question, wasn't it? Along with "Why would God take them at all?" but few dared ask that one. In his heart, Preacher believed that God simply didn't concern Himself in the daily affairs of man. He'd given them the tools they needed to survive—the intelligence to discover things like the causes and cures of disease. It was up to them to use those tools against forces of nature that sought to keep the population in check. It was not a popular answer. So instead, he'd babble about God's plan and God's wisdom and the book of Job and such.

To Maybelle, he only said, "This man—Eleazar—claims to do God's work."

"Does he truly do it?" Maybelle asked, her dark eyes searching his.

"I hope so," he murmured. "But that's what I'm trying to find out."

She nodded, seeming satisfied. As he took his leave, he saw Doc Adams coming out of the house down the road.

Preacher broke into a run, garnering a few askance looks from passersby. He reached the doctor as he still stood on the porch, talking to the Osbournes, who'd lost a child three days past. When the Osbournes saw Preacher, he expected them to want to talk, seek spiritual guidance. Surely Doc Adams had been there about their child. But they caught one glimpse of him and immediately withdrew, cutting the conversation short and closing the door.

The doctor saw Preacher then and went still.

"I'd like to talk to you," Preacher said.

"I'm very busy." Doc Adams started to scurry off. "I can speak to you later—"

Preacher swung into his path. "I'll only take a few moments of your time. Were you telling the Osbournes that their daughter can't be returned?"

"No, I was telling them that she can."

"For three hundred dollars."

Doc Adams tried to pass. "You ought to speak to the mayor—"

"He's gone."

The doctor paused. "Gone?"

"He left with Mr. Dobbs. On some task, it seems. So . . . three hundred dollars is the price of a child's life?"

"Yes, and the Osbournes will pay. We will make sure everyone can pay. Now, if you'll excuse me—"

"Three hundred and what else?"

Preacher hadn't honestly expected any "else"—it was an arrow fired wild—but when he saw the other man's expression, he knew that arrow had struck home.

"I heard there was something more," Preacher said. "Something you aren't telling the families."

Doc Adams's face went bright red. He blustered, asking who'd told Preacher and insisting it was merely rumor, people talking, that there was no other price. Finally, when he seemed to see that Preacher wasn't going to back down, he started down the street.

"I have work to do," he said. "Other families to inform of the wondrous news."

"And families to tell that they will not have their children returned. You yourself admitted they cannot all be returned. Has Mayor Browning set you on that task as well? Deliver the good news and the bad?"

"It was not the mayor—"

Doc Adams clipped his words short and kept moving, shoulders hunched, as if against the cold, but there was no more than a light breeze.

Preacher strode up beside him. "So it was Eleazar who sent you on this mission. Then he sent the mayor and Dobbs on another, one that ill suited you."

Doc Adams glanced over, eyes narrowing, then quickly looked away. "I don't know what—"

"I was there. Outside. You left. They kept talking. Arguing, even. Then Browning and Dobbs left. Eleazar wanted to discuss something with them out of your earshot. I'm sure you know it. He sent you away, just as the mayor sent me away when I balked. What did you balk at, doctor?"

The doctor's expression told Preacher he had not balked. Not openly.

"He knew you would," Preacher said. "That's why he sent you off before the subject was raised. Because, like me, you are a fellow of conscience and—"

Doc Adams spun on him. "Good God, man. Do you never stop? You're like a hound with a bone. Leave it be."

"I will not. I'll ask until I have answers. What's the other cost? What else must we pay for our children's return?"

The doctor turned and resumed walking.

"The old man's dead, you know," Preacher said.

Doc Adams glanced back.

"Rene. Eleazar's assistant. He's dead."

Again, it was the expression that gave the doctor away. Preacher had expected shock. He didn't see it.

He's not surprised. He's not horrified. He knew, and however it happened, this man—this good man—has no compunctions about it. How is that possible?

The cost.

When the idea hit, Preacher brushed it aside. It was as wildly fantastical as Addie's claims of demons and possession. And yet it clung there, like a burr, prickling his mind as he caught up and walked alongside the silent doctor.

"That's the price, isn't it? To return life, you must give life."

The older man's shoulders slumped and when he looked over, it was with an expression Preacher saw each week . . . in the face of a parishioner at confession.

"Yes," Doc Adams said. "That is the price. But the old man gave his life willingly. He volunteered."

"And now you need to find a volunteer for each child? Is that what you said to the Osbournes?"

"No, I was told not to tell them."

"Then how does Eleazar expect to get volunteers, if no one knows they're needed? He requires . . ." Preacher trailed off. "That's what they were discussing without you. How to fulfill that part of the bargain. And whatever Eleazar suggested, he knew you would not countenance it. That's why he sent you off."

Doc Adams shifted. "I don't know anything about that."

"I know, which is why I need to find the mayor and Dobbs."

Preacher took off before the doctor could say another word.

ADDIE

Addie had been anxious when Preacher set off in search of answers. Now, almost two hours later, she paced the house, glancing out the windows, stepping onto the porch, and peering down the street. At first, Sophia would tell her to rest, find something to occupy her, not to worry about Preacher. The last few times she'd gone outside, though, she'd come back in to find Sophia standing inside the doorway, waiting for a report. Addie would say she could not see him and Sophia would deflate, only to rouse herself with assurances that Preacher was fine, he could look after himself.

Finally, as the second hour drew to a close, Addie said, "I want to go look for him."

Sophia said nothing, which Addie knew meant she wished to say yes but knew she oughtn't.

"I'll be quick," Addie said. "He's probably down at the hall, talking to the mayor and Eleazar. I'll find him, and then I'll come straight back."

Sophia nodded. Addie gathered her things and went.

Preacher was not in town. Neither was Mayor Browning nor Mr. Dobbs. As Addie learned, Preacher had been asking after them, and someone had last seen Dobbs and Browning heading into the woods, and Preacher had gone off in pursuit.

Addie followed. They'd taken the main trail out of town, which made tracking difficult. She looked for small signs—a broken twig, a boot print in damp ground—and kept her ears attuned. She was no more than a quarter mile from town when she heard Browning and Dobbs returning. She snuck into the forest to watch as they passed. Soon she saw them, trudging along, faces grim, not speaking. There was a purpling bruise on the mayor's jaw. She stared at that, then began drawing back farther to let them pass, when she spotted something on Dobbs's boots. They were light brown, tanned leather . . . and one was speckled red.

Addie crept hunched over through the undergrowth, until she was close enough to see the glistening specks. More on his trouser leg. Blood. There was no doubt of it.

Addie tried to inhale but couldn't force the air into her chest. Her heart pounded too hard.

Mr. Dobbs is speckled with blood. Preacher is missing. Preacher, who dared argue against their plan. Dared suggest it was not the work of God.

She held herself still until they were gone. Then she dashed onto the path and broke into a run.

Addie tore along the path, convinced she would at any moment stumble over Preacher's dead body. She did not, which only made her more panicked, certain it was out there in the forest, where she would not find it, where scavengers would feast—

She took deep, shuddering breaths to calm herself, then began retracing her steps along the path, slower now, searching for any sign that someone had left the path. When she reached the first fork, she heard something. She stopped, eyes squeezed shut as she listened. Then she tore down the secondary path, branches whipping her face, until—

"Addie?"

Preacher's voice. Preacher's footfalls, pounding along the path. Then he was there, standing in front of her. No blood to be seen.

"Addie? Are you all right? Is it Sophia? Is she—?"

"Sophia is well." She bent, catching her breath. "All is well."

She hiccuped a laugh. *All is well? Charlie is possessed by some demon monster. All is not well. But right now, it is. Preacher is fine. Unharmed.*

Preacher came over, face drawn in concern, hand resting on her arm as she found her breath.

"It's all right," she said. "We were only worried about you. Me and Sophia."

"Sophia and I," Preacher said.

Addie burst out with a real laugh then. No matter how dire the situation, he could not fail to correct her grammar, as gently as if they were at the supper table, saying grace.

When she laughed, Preacher gave a crooked smile and shook his head, murmuring an apology before saying, "Well, you've found me. And I did not find what I was looking for."

"The mayor and Mr. Dobbs? I saw them a ways back. Returning to town."

"They've finished their mission then," he whispered beneath his breath.

"What mission?"

He looked startled, as if he had not meant to speak aloud. "They were out here for something. I know not what. Come. Let's go back to town."

As they began to walk, Addie thought about the blood on Dobbs's boot. He had not hurt Preacher, but he had hurt something. Some animal? She recalled stories of dark magic, with animals sacrificed to the Devil.

"Perhaps we ought to find where they've been," she said.

"That's what I was trying to do."

"No, you were trying to find where they *were*. I can track where they've *been*."

He hesitated. "All right then. I don't want to leave Sophia for long, but if we can discover what they were doing, we ought to."

PREACHER

Addie was indeed able to track where the mayor and blacksmith had gone. And when she found out, Preacher wished to God she hadn't. He wished he hadn't asked. Wished he'd found this on his own, before she'd arrived. A merciful God would have made sure of that.

She'd tracked Dobbs's and Browning's footsteps back to where they'd left the main trail. It had taken time, but she'd eventually determined that they'd taken a secondary one, little more than a half-cleared path through the trees. Preacher had not known where the trail led. Addie had. He was certain of it. But it was not until they saw the cabin ahead and he said, "What's that?" that she said, "Timothy James's place."

Timothy James. An odd creature, like most who made their living in the forest. Preacher had heard whispers about Timothy James, that he'd come here fleeing the Mounties, that he'd been caught with a little girl. Preacher had been furious—if there was a man like that in their midst, they ought to warn the children. But Dobbs said it wasn't true. Timothy James was merely odd. Preacher had always wondered if Mr. Dobbs's reluctance to drive the man out had anything to do with the fact that he brought in good furs and he accepted less than market rates for them.

Now, seeing that cabin ahead, Preacher knew where Browning and Dobbs had been going. What they'd done there. He'd told Addie to wait while he ran ahead.

He found Timothy James behind his cabin. Lying on the ground. Rope burns around his neck. His shirt covered in blood.

"He must have fought."

It was Addie's voice. Preacher wheeled to see her standing there, looking down at the body.

"They tried to hang him," she said. "Or strangle him. Like Rene. But he fought and they had to stab him."

She stated it as a matter of fact, and for a moment, he was frozen there, unable to react. Her thin face was hard and empty, her eyes empty, too. He'd seen that look on her once before. That horrible day two years ago, when Addie had shown up on

Preacher's doorstep in her nightgown, her feet bare and blood-ied and filthy from the two-mile walk.

Something's wrong with my parents, she'd said.

They'd gone back, Preacher and Dobbs and Doc Adams. Rode on the horses, Addie with Preacher, dressed in someone else's clothes, her thin arms wrapped around him. They'd gone back to her parents' cabin, expecting they'd taken ill, and instead found . . .

Preacher swallowed, remembering what they'd found. Re-membering Addie beside him, her face as empty as this, hollow and dead, looking at the terrible bodies of her parents.

Preacher strode over, took her by the shoulders, and did what he'd done two years ago—turned her away from the sight and bustled her off. She let him take her around the cabin, then dug in her heels and stopped.

"Why did they kill him?" she asked.

"I don't know."

"Yes, you do. That's why you made me stay on the path. You knew he was dead."

Preacher hesitated. She was right, of course. She wasn't a child. That was the problem. He wanted to tell her not to worry, not to think on it. She didn't require an explanation. He was the adult, and he could make that decision, as parents did for their children. Yet he knew that to do so was to loosen his already tenuous grip on his foster daughter. Treat her as a child, and he'd earn her disdain. He would have taken that chance if he thought it would truly stop her from learning the truth. It would not. She'd proven already that she was as curious—and as dogged—as he.

"They killed Rene, too," she said as he tried to decide what to tell her. "Is it the same thing?"

"Yes, it appears so. Eleazar claims that to give life . . ." He struggled for the kindest words.

"They must take it," she said, again as if this were a simple matter, one that anyone ought to be able to see. "They killed the old man to bring back Charlie. And now they've killed Timothy James . . ."

He didn't hear the rest of what she said. He knew the rest. They'd killed Timothy James to bring back another. Then, once that child was raised from the dead, there were five more . . .

"We must go," he said. "Back to town. Immediately."

Preacher heard the weeping before he saw the town ahead. Wailing and sobbing and crying out to God. That's what he heard, and he ran as he hadn't since he was a boy. Ran so fast he could no longer hear anything but the crash of sound, like the ocean's surf, rising and falling.

From the end of the main road he could see the crowd. The entire village it seemed, gathered down at the hall, the mass of them blocking the road. People sobbing. People on their knees. People standing in stunned silence.

He looked back for Addie, but she was right there.

"Go to Sophia!" he said.

She hesitated, but she seemed to see the fear in his eyes, nodded, and veered off in the direction of the house. Preacher kept running. When he reached the crowd, he prepared himself for what he might see. The horrors that could cause such wailing.

On a normal day, if the villagers saw him coming, they'd make way. He was the preacher. But now, even when he nudged through, they resisted, pushing him back until he had to shove past, as if he were at a cockfight, jostling for a better view.

Finally, the villagers seemed to see him, to recognize him. Or they simply realized he would not be held back. The crowd parted. There, at the front, he saw . . .

Children. All six of them. Sitting up in their coffins, looking about, as if confused, their parents grabbing them up, hugging them, wailing.

Now that the thunder in his ears had died down, he realized what he was hearing. Sobs and wails of joy. Praising God. Thanking God.

He looked at those six children and those six families, and there was a moment when he wanted to fall to his knees with the others. To say, *This is a miracle.* To accept it as a miracle.

Then he remembered the body in the woods. Timothy James, lying in the dirt, covered in blood, staring at the sky.

Six children alive. Six people dead.

Dear God, who else did they take? Who else did they murder?

He reeled, stomach clenching, gaze swinging to Dobbs, embracing his child, his big body shaking with joy. Preacher glanced down, about to back away. Then he saw the blood on Dobbs's boot. Timothy James's blood on his boot. Timothy James's murder on his hands.

"What's going on?" a voice cried.

Everyone went still. The voice asked again, and it was a high voice, a reedy voice. A child. Preacher turned to see one of the resurrected—six-year-old Jonas Meek—pushing his mother away as his gaze swung over the crowd.

"Who the bloody hell are all of you?" the boy asked.

Eleazar leaped forward as the crowd gasped and the boy's mother fell back, crossing herself. Jonas began to push up from his coffin, his face fixed in a snarl as he said something Preacher didn't catch.

"Restrain him!" Eleazar said. "Quickly!"

Two men leaped in to do it as Eleazar strode forward, cloth in hand. He pressed it to the boy's face, ignoring his struggles. Preacher caught a whiff of something vaguely familiar from his college science classes. Chloroform.

As Jonas went limp, Eleazar's voice rang out over the stunned crowd. "I warned you that this might happen. I will sedate them all now, to prevent further injury. They are confused and will act most unlike themselves for a day or two. But all is well. Your children are returned to you and all is well."

Preacher stepped forward, but before his boot even touched down, Dobbs was there, moving unbelievably fast for a man of his size. He planted himself in front of Preacher.

"You don't belong here, Benjamin," he said.

"I know—"

Dobbs stepped forward. "I said you don't belong here." He lowered his voice. "I would suggest you run on home, preacher boy. Back to your wild brat and your pretty wife. You ought not to leave your family alone."

Preacher looked up into the man's eyes and his gut chilled. There was nothing there. No compassion. No compunction. Perhaps there had been, when he'd undertaken his task, but now that it was done, Dobbs had severed any part of himself that might have felt guilt. He'd done right, and if Preacher dared suggest otherwise . . .

"He's right," another voice said. It was Mayor Browning, moving up beside Dobbs. "Go home, Benjamin. You aren't wanted here."

"But, Preacher," someone said. It was Maybelle, pushing through the crowd. "What do you think of this? Can you speak to us about it?"

"No," Browning said. "He cannot. This isn't your preacher. It's a false man of God, one who would deny this miracle, who would tell you it's wrong, sinful."

Behind Browning, Eleazar stood watching, lips moving, and that chill suffused Preacher's entire body.

It is as if he is putting words in their mouths. As if they are puppets to his will.

"This preacher would take back our children," Browning said. "Steal them from us again."

Preacher started to argue, to say that was not it at all, but there seemed to come a growl from the crowd, and when he looked about, he felt as if he were surrounded by wolves, scenting a threat in the air—a threat to their young and to themselves. He saw that and knew what he must do. The only choice he had.

He closed his mouth, backed away from the crowd, and raced home.

ADDIE

Addie was arguing with Sophia when they heard Preacher coming up the steps. Sophia wanted to go out, to see what was happening. Addie had to block the door to keep her in.

"You ought not to see," Addie was saying. "Preacher doesn't want it."

"I'm not a child, Adeline—"

"But you are with child. You cannot be upset. You might lose the babe."

That had stopped her, as Addie knew it would. Then Preacher's footsteps clattered up the steps, and he threw open the door and said, "Pack your things. You're leaving. Now."

Sophia argued, of course. She often did. Addie had never seen a woman who felt herself so free to dispute her husband's word. Or a husband who allowed it. Certainly, in her own home, her mother had only to issue the smallest word of complaint, and she'd be abed for days, recovering. To actually argue? Addie had only seen that once. And when it was over, her mother would never argue again.

But Sophia did. And yet, even as she disputed her husband's word, she did not stand there and holler at him. She could see how agitated he was, and she immediately set about packing as he asked, while arguing about leaving.

Preacher wanted them to go. Her and Sophia. Immediately.

He told Sophia what had happened, in the gentlest terms possible, but they still shocked her into a near trance, gaping at him as if he'd gone mad. Addie confirmed it was true, all of it. Rene and Timothy James had been murdered to bring back the children, and there was something very wrong with the children, and they had to flee.

"But . . . but the villagers," Sophia said. "They are almost all innocent in this. We cannot abandon them—"

"I'm not. I'm sending you and Addie on ahead. I need to find out precisely what has happened here and warn those who will let themselves be warned. Then I will join you."

Sophia pulled herself up to her full height—which barely reached Preacher's chin. "I am not going anywhere without you, Benjamin."

"Yes, you are. You and Addie and the baby. Dobbs has already made his threat against my family. You will leave, and I will do what I can here, which I cannot do if I'm worrying about you."

"Preacher's right," Addie said.

She walked up beside Sophia and took her hand. It felt odd, reaching for another person, voluntarily touching another person. But she took her hand and squeezed it.

"You need to go," Addie said. "For your child."

Sophia looked down at their hands, then at Addie.

"All right," she said. "I'll go. For my children."

PREACHER

What had Eleazar done? Dark deeds, Preacher was sure of that. Murder. Inciting others to murder. And more. But what more? What exactly was wrong with Charlie and the others? That was what he had to discover.

Of the children who'd been raised, only Charlie was awake.

The others had all been sedated. Deeply sedated. He confirmed that by paying a visit to the Meeks. They were a God-fearing couple who'd always been kind to him, and he'd seen the look on Ella Meek's face when her son started spewing such venom after the resurrection. She was frightened. So Preacher spoke to her.

Jonas had not stirred since he'd been chloroformed. Eleazar had told them that if he did, and he said anything untoward or concerning, they were to give him another dose, from a small bottle he'd left. The boy was fine, simply not himself. Not yet.

"But he's only six years old," Ella Meek said to Preacher. "He doesn't even know those words he was saying. He's a good boy. A quiet boy."

And so he was, one of the quietest in the town. All his family was, prompting the joke that they truly earned their surname. Meek and mild.

"And the others have been told the same?" he asked.

She nodded. "All of them."

All except Charlie. Who was, by all accounts, resting comfortably at his home. It was time for Preacher to pay the boy a visit.

ADDIE

Addie had lied to Preacher. She would, perhaps, eventually feel guilt about that. But not today. Today did not count by any proper reckoning. Sophia knew of the promise and had participated in breaking it, which proved the world had, indeed, turned upside down.

Addie had promised to stay with Sophia. To ride through the forest, where they'd not be seen, then over to the road and high-tail it to Greenville. That was not what she had done. She'd gathered the horses—they had two—and met Sophia on the wide main path. It was quite impossible to hide the taking of the horses, but no one seemed to pay her much mind. In truth, no one had even noticed. She took them and they rode them until they had to dismount and steer them along the secondary path to Timothy James's cabin. Then Addie ensconced Sophia there, shotgun in hand, and went back to town. For Preacher. To keep him safe.

PREACHER

"I've come to apologize," Preacher said, standing on Mayor Browning's front porch, hat in hand. "I was wrong, and I see that now. My lack of faith blinded me. Mr. Dobbs is right. I am not fit to be a man of God. I will be withdrawing from my position immediately."

"What?" The reply came from deep within the house. Dorothy Browning pushed past her husband. "Quit? No. Our town needs you, Preacher, perhaps now more than ever—"

Browning nudged her back. "We'll talk on this later, Benjamin. It's a poor time."

"I know. I didn't come here to resign so much as I came to apologize. I was wrong. I misspoke. A miracle has occurred in Chestnut Hill. Seven miracles."

The whole time he spoke, Browning nodded absently, as if urging him along. *Finish up and begone, man.*

"Charlie is well, then?" Preacher asked.

"Well enough."

Dorothy made a noise, but a glare from her husband cut her short.

"May I see him?" Preacher asked. "Addie is most anxious to speak to her friend again. I've told her this is, as you've said, a poor time. However, she asked me to give him this."

He pulled a stone from his pocket. It was a pretty one, veined with fool's gold. He'd found it two doors down, by the roadside.

Preacher continued. "She says it will lighten his spirits. It's hers, and he always admired it."

"He's not—" Dorothy began.

"I'll take it and give it to him," Browning said.

"May I?" said Preacher. "It would mean so much to Addie if I could tell her his response."

"He's gone," Dorothy said. "With that—" Browning glowered at her, but she squared her thin shoulders and said, "He's gone with that man. They went a-walking a while back. He says Charlie's weak, and then he takes him a-walking. The boy has—"

"That's enough, woman," Browning cut in.

She continued. "The boy—my boy—has scarcely said two words to me. Too weak to converse, that man says. But Charlie can walk and converse with him, easily enough."

"Well, I'll leave the stone, then," Preacher said. "And I'll leave young Charlie with Eleazar. The man does not wish to see me, I'm certain, so I will stay clear."

Preacher found Eleazar and Charlie. They had not gone far, just deep enough into the woods that they wouldn't be overheard, and far enough off the path that they wouldn't be seen. Preacher snuck up as best he could. It would not have satisfied Addie, but the two were in such deep conversation that they did not notice him.

"Are you certain that is enough food, boy?"

"I am, sir."

"I don't think it is. My instructions were clear. We will be walking in this forsaken wilderness for at least two days. We need more food."

"I have enough, sir. Much of it is dried."

Preacher paused, shaking his head as if he was mishearing.

It was not the content of their conversation. While he was startled to hear they were leaving together, that paled against surprise of the voices themselves. Of who was delivering which lines. He was hearing wrong. He must have been.

He crept forward until he could see the two figures. Charlie was bent on one knee, examining the contents of a pack, while Eleazar stood behind him.

"This money and these goods are not the full accounting," Charlie said. "There's eleven hundred dollars and perhaps two hundred more in goods. That's five hundred short."

"Yes, sir," Eleazar said. "I imagine it is. But this is not a wealthy village. They are gathering more, but I presumed you wanted to be gone before the children fully woke."

"Don't be smart with me, boy," Charlie snapped.

Eleazar cleared his throat. "Given the situation, sir, I might suggest you'll want to stop calling me that."

"In private, I'll call you what I want. How long would it take to get more from them?"

"Too long. And that was not the primary purpose of this trip. We got you something far more valuable than money, did we not?"

Charlie snorted. "A child's body is not particularly valuable. Now, a strong young man's . . ."

"It will be such in a few years. We ought to count ourselves lucky that there was a boy of goodly age who died. You'd not have wanted to be brought back as a toddling child. Or a girl."

More grumbling. When Preacher had first heard them speaking, his mind had reeled. Then something in his gut steadied it, saying, Yes, this makes sense. Of course, in the larger scheme of things, the fact that an old man's soul had been put into the body of a dead boy did not make sense, but given all that Preacher had seen, it was more sensible than any explanation he'd considered.

The soul was the essence of life. Charlie's was long gone. In heaven, he trusted. And if one believed that, and one believed the scriptures, then a merciful God would not allow a child to be stolen back from paradise. The body would need to be returned to life with a soul still wandering this world. The soul of someone recently departed.

It had seemed odd that Rene had been Eleazar's assistant, but the man had been so doddering that it would have seemed more shocking to realize the situation was reversed. Now it seemed it was indeed the case. The old man—the leader, the teacher—had been in need of a new body, and they had taken it here, in Chestnut Hill.

As for the other six children . . .

Dear God. The other six.

Timothy James's soul. The souls of five others. Murdered, only to awaken in the bodies of children . . . children whose parents they would hold responsible for their deaths.

Preacher turned away from Eleazar and Rene. What they had done was a horrible thing, deserving a terrible punishment, but right now, there were others about to be punished even more terribly, others who'd known nothing of the murders, who'd only wanted their children—

"You do realize we are not alone, I hope," Rene said, his voice as easy as if he were discussing the possibility of rainfall.

"What?" Eleazar said.

"Someone watches from the woods. I trust you plan to take care of that."

Eleazar let out a curse. Preacher began to run, not caring how much noise he made, only that he got back to the village in time to warn them before—

Something grabbed his legs. He did not trip. He was certain of that. He felt the pressure, something wrapping about them as he ran, and there was no time to stop. He fell face-first to the ground.

"Preacher Benjamin," Eleazar said, crashing through the forest behind him. "You are a persistent man. I will grant you—"

"No, you fool," Rene exclaimed. "Not him. I meant—"

"Preacher! Run!"

It was Addie. Eleazar spun toward her voice, back toward the clearing where Rene stood. Preacher clambered to his feet. He could see no sign of Addie, but he had heard her. He had very clearly—

The twang of a bow. He saw the arrow. Saw it heading straight for Rene. Saw it hit him square in the throat.

Eleazar let out a howl of rage and ran for the girl, now standing ten paces away, stringing her bow again.

ADDIE

Addie couldn't ready her bow fast enough. She ought to have been able to—she'd made sure she would have time to fire two arrows. One for the monster that had stolen Charlie's body and one for the monster that had helped him. Yet as she strung the second arrow, the ground seemed to fly up under her feet, as if by magic.

She toppled backward, and Eleazar was on her, wrenching the bow away with one hand while grabbing her coat with the other. She went for her knife, but before her fingers could touch the handle, he'd grabbed it himself. Then he whipped her around, knife at her throat, shouting at Preacher to stop.

Preacher halted in midstep, and stood there, his eyes wild with fear, breath coming so hard she could hear it.

I'm sorry, she thought. *I ought to have shot Eleazar first. Let you escape. But all I could think about was Charlie. That monster in his body.*

The monster that was dying now. Lying on the ground, wheezing its death rattle, arrow lodged in its throat.

"Let her go," Preacher said.

"I cannot," Eleazar said. "I need—"

"I know what you need. And I know that what you have isn't satisfactory. What you had wasn't either. So I'm offering you a trade."

"Are you? Interesting . . ."

"Take it," Preacher said. "It's what he'd want. You know it is."

Addie struggled to figure out what they were talking about. Preacher was making sure she didn't. She could tell that, and a knot of dread in her gut grew bigger with each passing moment.

"Take it," Preacher said. "Quickly."

Eleazar seemed to be considering the matter, but then, without warning, he grabbed Addie by the hair and whipped her against a tree. Her head hit the trunk hard, blackness threatening as she fell. She lay there, fighting to remain awake, as she heard them continue.

"You did not need to do that," Preacher said.

"Oh, I believe I did. She's a feisty little one, and I don't think she'll like what I'm about to do."

"Just get it done. Quickly please."

Addie managed to raise her head and saw Eleazar walk to Preacher. She saw his hands go to Preacher's neck, wrapping around it, and she understood what he'd meant. That with Charlie's body dying, the monster—Rene—needed a new vessel. Eleazar had been going to take hers. Preacher had offered his instead.

"No," she whispered. "Please no."

She could see her bow there, only a few paces away. She dug her fingers into the dirt and pulled herself toward it and—

And she passed out.

PREACHER

As Preacher watched Addie lose consciousness, he had a sudden vision of her death, of Eleazar killing him for his master and then walking over, kneeling and wrapping his fingers around the girl's neck. Preacher's hands flew up, catching Eleazar's, stopping them as they squeezed.

"Wait!" he said.

He held the man's hands still as he looked at him.

"You'll not hurt her," he said. "After it's done."

"I have no cause. You'll have given me what I want."

"It was not a question," Preacher said, locking eyes with the man. "You are accustomed to bodies where the soul is long departed. If Rene's soul still lingers now, then so will mine, for a time. If you hurt the girl . . . I cannot lie and say what I will do, because I do not know what I *may* do. But I am certain I can do something, and so I will, if she's harmed."

"As I said, I'll have no cause once Rene has his new body. A girl child is no threat to me. As for telling anyone, I'm quite certain that by now, your village has already realized something has gone very, very wrong."

The village. The other children.

"No," he said. "You—"

Eleazar's grip tightened. Preacher tried to stop him, to say more, but the man squeezed with inhuman strength and then—

Darkness.

Preacher jolted upright. He was lying on the forest floor, Charlie's body beside him. He scrambled to his feet and looked around, but there was no sign of Eleazar.

Something had gone wrong. He'd been tricked.

Addie.

Preacher whirled, searching for his foster daughter, seeing no sign—

No, there she was, across the clearing, still on the ground. He raced over and dropped beside her. He put his hands to her thin chest and—

His fingers passed through her. He stumbled back, falling on his rear. Then he looked down at his hand, the grass poking through it, undisturbed.

Nothing has gone wrong.

I'm dead.

He gasped, the sudden realization as agonizing as a bullet to the heart.

I'm dead. I'm gone.

Sophia. Dear lord, Sophia. I'll never see her again. Never see our child. Never see Addie grow up.

Addie.

He hurried to the girl again. She was breathing. He could see that. As he rose from her side, a scream split the night.

The village. The villagers. The resurrected children.

Preacher ran toward Chestnut Hill. At first, he weaved around trees and bushes, then realized there was no need and tore through them. He could hear more now, shouts and screams and cries for God.

Soon he could see the houses in the distant darkness. Lights flickered. Doors slammed. Shots rang out. And the screams. The terrible screams—of shock, of pain, of horror.

He came out of the woods behind a house, following some of the worst cries. A woman lay on the grass, not screaming now, but making horrible gurgling noises. Atop her was a boy covered in blood, his face contorted and wild as he raised a stone, hitting her again and again, smashing her face until she couldn't scream, until Preacher could only tell she was a woman by her dress.

He ran toward them, shouting for the boy to stop, please stop.

As he drew near, he could see the child under that mask of blood. Jonas Meek. Little Jonas Meek. And the woman below him, gurgling her last? His mother.

"No," Preacher whispered. "No."

The boy flickered, as if *he* were the ghost, beginning to fade. So too did his mother and the blood-soaked grass below them. Something tugged at Preacher. He tried to fight it. Tried to stay, to help, to do whatever he could, but the pull was too great, and as he scrambled for a hold, feeling himself lifting, he caught sight of something moving at the end of the woods.

He saw himself. Standing there, with Eleazar, watching Jonas Meek beat his mother to death and laughing. He was laughing.

ADDIE

When Addie woke, Eleazar and Preacher were gone. It was growing dark, and she knew she wouldn't find them, but she still raced down the path they would have taken, only to get a quarter mile along it and realize she wasn't even sure this was the way they'd gone. She made her way back to the clearing and tried to search again, to no avail.

And what good would it do if I found them? It's too late. He's gone. Preacher's—

She couldn't finish the thought. Her knees buckled, and she fell to the ground, weeping as she hadn't wept when Charlie died, hadn't when her parents died.

Preacher was gone. Dead. Possessed by that thing, and if she found him, all she could do was what she'd done for Charlie— set his body free. Did that even matter? Their souls were gone. In heaven, she hoped. In heaven, she prayed.

Preacher had given his life for her, and she wasn't even his child. Now he'd never see his real child, because of what he'd done for her, a stranger who'd come into his life and slept in his house and eaten his food. He'd let her in and he'd given her everything. Absolutely everything.

There had been, she realized now, always a part of her that

didn't quite trust Preacher and Sophia's motivations in adopting her. They were good people. The best she knew. But surely no one could be that good, no one could voluntarily take her, not when her own parents had begrudged every morsel she took from their larder.

She'd always suspected that there was more to it, that the town paid Preacher and Sophia to care for her. That still made them good people—of all those in the village, she'd known them for the shortest length of time, and yet they were the ones who'd taken her in. But surely they were receiving some compensation. They ought to have been.

Except they weren't. She knew that now. They'd taken her because they'd been worried for her. They'd kept her because they cared for her. And now Preacher had given his life for her because . . . well, perhaps because he loved her.

Addie picked herself up then. She dried her eyes, and she walked to Charlie, and she said her good-byes. He wasn't there. He hadn't been there for three days. But she said them anyway, hoping he'd hear, wherever he was.

Then she gathered her bow and her knife, and she set out. She had a job to do. A job for Preacher.

There was death in the village that night. Addie could hear it as she walked back toward Chestnut Hill. Screams. Horrible screams, as the "children" awakened and everyone learned the truth. They'd murdered people outside the village and put them into the bodies of children, and now the children had awakened, possessed by those vengeful spirits.

This was what Preacher had been running to stop when Eleazar caught him. He'd known what was coming, and he'd wanted to warn them. If he were here now, he'd race to that village and save whom he could.

Addie decided he'd done enough for the village. They'd

brought this on themselves, and even if Sophia would say there were many who were innocent, Addie disagreed. They'd let Eleazar into their town. They'd ignored Preacher's warnings. Now they should face whatever wrath their actions had unleashed.

They would not all perish. Likely only a few. She supposed that was terrible enough, if they were innocent of murdering Timothy James and the others. But she did not think as Preacher and Sophia did. It wasn't how she'd been raised, and there were parts of her that all Preacher and Sophia's goodness could not heal.

Addie had spent the last two years haunted by the grave sin she had committed the night her parents died. What she'd done. Or, perhaps, what she'd failed to do.

She'd heard the fight. A dreadful one. The worst ever. She'd listened to her father beating her mother. That was nothing new, but this was not like any other time. Her mother's screams were not like any Addie had ever heard.

Addie had lain in her tattered blanket by the fire, feigning sleep as her father beat her mother to death, and she had done nothing to stop it. Her mother never stopped the beatings he gave to Addie, so why ought Addie to interfere and risk turning that rage on herself?

When it was over, the house had gone silent. She'd risen then, and seen her father sitting in his chair, shotgun in hand. Her mother's body lay crumpled and bloody on the floor.

"You'll hang for this," Addie had said, and what she'd felt, saying it, was not horror or fear but satisfaction.

"No, I won't," he'd replied, and put the gun between his legs, pointed it at his head, and pulled the trigger.

For two years, Addie had lived with that. With listening to her mother die and not intervening. With telling her father what she thought and making him splatter his brains across the room. It was her fault. Her sin. For two years, she'd regretted it, and now she did not. Now she realized they had brought it upon themselves, and had she interfered, she'd only have been lying there with them. They had not raised her to interfere, so she had not. As she would not now.

So she circled wide around the village, ignoring the screams, and continued on.

Addie found Sophia in Timothy James's cabin. She told her that Preacher was gone. Sophia wept as if she'd break in two, so much that Addie feared for the child.

She told Sophia what had happened. Or part of it. That Eleazar had returned the old man to Charlie's body. That he'd returned the souls of the murdered to the children's bodies. But there Addie's story for Sophia changed.

In Addie's version, Preacher had made his escape. He'd run to the village to warn them. He'd arrived too late, the children reawakening, but he'd fought for the villagers. He'd warned who he could and then he'd helped fight off the threat. He'd fought for his village, and he'd lost his life doing it. He was a hero.

That part was true. He *had* sacrificed his life—for Addie. And she would never forget it. He'd given her a family, and now she'd protect that family with everything she had, in every way she could.

So she told Sophia the lies that would set her heart at rest, and then she gathered her up, got her on the horse, and took her away from that place of death, off to find a place where she could bear and raise Preacher's babe, and where she could be happy.

Where they all could be happy.

Pipers

CHRISTOPHER GOLDEN

1

Ezekiel Prater drove his ancient Ford pickup along Doffin Road, enjoying the cool night air that streamed through the open windows. His daughter, Savannah, had never understood why he had spent the time and money to restore a sixty-year-old vehicle, but she sure liked riding in it.

"Turn it up, Daddy," she pleaded from the passenger seat, barely turning from her open window. "I love this song!"

He smiled and obliged her, though it was one of those bubblegum pretty-boy songs all the young girls seemed to love and anyone over the age of sixteen wanted to scrub from their brain. Zeke felt eighty years old when such thoughts entered his head, but he couldn't help himself. Savannah's preferred entertainment might have had rhythm, but it didn't sound much like music to him.

"So, who's going to be there tonight?" he asked.

The wind blew through the cab of the old pickup and carried his voice away. Savannah put her head back against the seat and closed her eyes, letting the breeze whip her hair across her face. His heart melted just looking at her. Savannah had gotten her big blue eyes and the spray of freckles across the bridge of her nose from him, but the copper skin and dark brown hair and lovely, sculpted features had all come from her mother, Anarosa, who'd found the lump in her left breast too late.

Zeke felt the familiar pinch of grief, but by now it had become his bittersweet friend, his reassurance that he had found love in his life. Seven years had passed since Anarosa's death and he still missed her constantly. Once in a great while he would find himself realizing that he had gone an entire day without thinking of her and the guilt would nearly suffocate him. Savannah always saved him with some bit of prattle about her day, a fight she was having with a girlfriend or a boy who had paid her some special attention.

He turned down the music.

"Hey, bud," he said when she shot him her patented irritated-teenager look. "Who's going to this thing tonight?"

"Most everyone, I guess. We talked about this already."

"Refresh my memory. Terri, Vanessa, Abby . . . ?"

"Abby can't make it," Savannah said, twisting slightly in her seat to face him, the seat belt fighting her. "She went to Austin to visit her brother."

Zeke flexed his fingers on the steering wheel. "Her parents are okay with her sleeping in her brother's college dorm room? She's thirteen!"

"She's fourteen."

"Oh, well, that's so much better."

He laughed and shook his head, watching the road for the potholes that had played hell on his gorgeous whitewalls a few months before. The October moon was so bright that it suffused the ranchland that rolled away on all sides with a golden glow. Zeke had known people from up north who believed they had a claim on autumn, and on October in particular, because they believed folks down south never had a proper autumn. But the moonlight in South Texas this time of year had a certain quality to it—a kind of soft, tender magic—that made the world seem a kinder place, rich with possibility. Nights like this made the threats of an uncertain economy and the dangers of living so close to the border seem far away indeed.

"Daddy, please. You know Daniel. It's not like he'd let anything happen to his little sister." She rolled her eyes with a huff.

"I just don't want you gettin' ideas in your head, is all. You're not sleeping in any boy's dorm room, even when you get to college!"

She smirked and cast him a sidelong glance. "And how will you know if I do?"

"Twenty-four-hour surveillance, kid," he joked. "Three hundred and sixty-five days a year."

"Better be careful, Daddy. One of these days you're liable to see something you don't want to see." She waggled her eyebrows in a way that seemed goofy rather than suggestive, and that silly, innocent part of her warmed his heart. "Besides, one of these days you're going to want grandchildren. You can't keep me away from boys forever."

"Slow down there, girl. I'm not halfway old enough to be a grandfather."

"Oh, don't have a heart attack. I'm not in any hurry." Her voice grew quieter, though he could still hear her over the wind. "You've got nothing to worry about, anyway. The boys I like never like me back, and the ones who do make my skin crawl."

Zeke swallowed hard. Nothing pained him more than hearing the hurt in her voice.

"I'm sure that ain't true, Savannah. Maybe it seems that way—"

"It seems that way because it is that way, Daddy. I know it won't always be, but for now, that's my life."

"What about that Marco boy? I know he's been flirting with you. He texts you often enough."

"Oh, he likes me all right. He just likes Kasey Mason more."

Zeke scowled. "That'll pass, honey. A boy that age, why, he's just mesmerized by how much faster Kasey's filling out her bra. The rest of you girls will get there."

Savannah gave him an amused look, one corner of her mouth lifted in her trademark smirk. "Well, there you go," she said. "Right there is a stretch of conversational road I hope we never traverse again."

"What's the matter, bud? You uncomfortable talking about bras with the guy who pays for yours?" he teased. "Or is it just me talking about Kasey getting boobs that—"

"Ding ding ding! We have a winner! Daddy, *please*—"

"Boobs. Breasts. Knockers—"

"'Knockers'? Wow, you're old."

"—titties—"

"Ugh. Now you're just gross."

"Next I'll start talking about nipples or pubic hair or—"

"Okay, Daddy, okay!" Savannah cried, her whole body cringing as she covered her ears. "Enough, enough. I surrender!"

They shared a laugh and Zeke couldn't wipe the grin off his face. Embarrassing his daughter always felt like a triumph. Slowly, though, his smile slid away.

"Listen, honey, I know you don't like talkin' about this stuff, but—"

"Daddy," Savannah said sharply, her tone turning serious. "I know, okay? We went through this when I was ten, and again when I got my period, and again and again. Without Mom around, you had to step up and have some talks that most fathers probably avoid like the plague. And you did great. I'm not kidding. Sure, sometimes it got weird, but I don't know . . . I feel kind of lucky to have a father I can talk to about anything."

"You can, y'know."

"I know. Really, I do." She took a deep breath. "But I'm thirteen now—"

"And you've acquired the wisdom of the ancients."

"No!" she snapped. "I'm not saying that!"

They fell silent for a moment, cast adrift on a sea of shared awkwardness.

Then Zeke let out a breath, all trace of amusement gone. "Sorry, honey. I really do understand. And I trust you. Hell, I wish I'd been half as smart and savvy as you when I was thirteen. It's just that you not needing me so much is gonna take some getting used to."

"Don't worry, Daddy," she said. "I'm always gonna need you. I'm sure some boy or other is gonna break my heart soon enough—"

"Well, it *has* been at least a couple of weeks."

Savannah smacked his leg. "—and I'm gonna need a shoulder to cry on."

"Well, I'm good for that much, at least."

"Always," she promised.

Savannah turned the music back up and Zeke smiled and sat up straighter behind the wheel, a sly smile on his lips. His daughter was growing up to be one hell of a young woman.

He studied the road ahead, enjoying the rattle of the ancient Ford and the thrum of the wheel in his hands. His day-to-day truck was less than a year old, a red beauty he used both on the ranch and on longer drives. But on a lovely fall night when the temperature had fallen to the midsixties and they could have the windows open to let in a breeze that was actually chilly for once, he hadn't been able to resist the F1. He'd done most of the restoration himself, including repairing a sizable dent in the clunky metal grille, which he'd painted white to match the whitewall tires. The rest of the truck was a crayon-box blue that had just seemed right. Bright enough to satisfy the little boy in him, who had thrilled at the idea of restoring his grandfather's old pickup when he'd rescued it from the crumbling ruin of the ranch's original barn, and yet manly enough not to draw ridicule from his friends, who'd been envious as hell once all his hard work had paid off.

"Daddy?" Savannah ventured.

Zeke glanced at her. "Bud?"

"I just want you to know that I'm okay," she said. "I wish Momma had been here for all of this. But even if she had, I'd be saying the same things to her now. I'm almost fourteen. I know about sex and I know boys are pretty much like puppies who'll piss everywhere and hump your leg unless they're properly housebroken."

A wonderful pride swelled Zeke Prater's heart, and yet it was also melancholy. An end-of-an-era sort of pride.

"You've got that right," he said.

His little girl smiled and reached over to take his right hand off of the steering wheel. He squeezed her hand and she held on tight for a minute, and then they were approaching the turn onto Hidalgo County Road and he wanted both hands on the wheel.

He slowed at the corner, waited for two cars to pass—high traffic for the area—and then turned right, traveling parallel to the new fence Bill Cassaday had put up along the eastern edges of his ranch. A couple of horses grazed in a pasture and Zeke frowned at the foolishness of leaving the animals out this far from the barn after dark. They were two miles from the Rio Grande here—two miles from the Mexican border—and while

old-time horse thievery was a thing of the past, there was never
any telling what might happen to people, property, or livestock.
That was the whole reason the Texas Border Volunteers had been
formed—Zeke and Cassaday and Alan Vickers and a bunch of
others taking it upon themselves to improve the policing of the
border, at least in Hidalgo County. They'd installed lights and
hidden cameras and had been reporting drug- and human-
trafficking activities to the government for half a year, leading
to a flurry of deportations and drug seizures. Just five nights ago,
they'd caught a trio of hikers coming through the well-trodden
paths at the back of Vickers's acreage, each carrying a hundred
pounds of cocaine from the Matamoros cartel. They'd come
across the river on a raft and would have been long gone if the
Volunteers hadn't picked them up on video and reported them.
The border patrol had caught them before they'd made it to the
highway.

It was hard on the younger folks, living out here. Their elders
all knew it, and over the past few years had been dreaming up
one program after another to give them alternatives to sneaking
off into the fields to drink beers or have sex. Dances and clubs
and outdoor movies projected on the back of the Praters' barn.
Tonight was the best of all, the first annual Lansdale Music Festival. People had laughed at first, mocking the idea that a town
as tiny as Lansdale, Texas, could draw enough people to warrant
such an event, but every roadhouse in the state had a band or
two dreaming of bigger things, and right there in Lansdale they
had Annie Rojas and Jesse McCaffrey, both of whom were gifted
musicians and had lovely voices.

Lansdale had been founded in 1912 and only then because
of the five huge, sprawling ranches that surrounded it—
thousands and thousands of acres. The ranch families had wanted
a post office closer than the one in Hidalgo and then it had
seemed only natural to have a grocery and a hardware store and

a gas station, and soon enough Jesse McCaffrey's grandmother had opened a dress shop and the saddlery had been replaced by an auto mechanic's shop and someone had the bright idea to open a bookshop. Decades had passed, and there still wasn't much more to Lansdale than that. They'd never had a movie theater or anything as precious as a florist; the grocery had rented videos when such things were still of interest, and the hardware store had a garden center these days. Not long before the twentieth century gave up the ghost, a medical equipment company with its factory in Hidalgo had moved its home office to Lansdale, bringing an influx of out-of-towners. Half a dozen border patrol officers called it home, as well. There were only a few hundred houses, but the ranch owners and workers and their families were all a part of the Lansdale community, swelling its ranks.

When Zeke was growing up, it had been a nice little town.

Now it lay squarely in the path of drug smugglers and the coyotes who guided illegal immigrants across the border, and Zeke Prater wore a gun belt that made him feel like an idiot, as if he were some kid playing cowboys. Tonight he had left the gun belt and his Smith & Wesson 1911 back at the ranch . . . but he had a high-powered rifle in the backseat of the rattling old pickup, just in case.

Around his daughter, Zeke wore a mask of confidence, doing everything he could to cast an illusion, but he kept vigilant at all times in order to assure her safety and the safety of all of the people who worked on his ranch.

He glanced over at Savannah just as she pushed her hair away from her eyes, and the gesture caused his heart to stumble. *God, she's so beautiful*, he thought. *Too beautiful*. He knew that all fathers must have similar fears, but he worried about his daughter not only because she was pretty, but because she looked older than her age. She often drew the attention of older boys and even young men who misjudged her years, and like most girls, she relished the attention. Young girls were apt to be persuaded to do almost anything to maintain a constant stream of such affections.

Not Savannah, he told himself. *You've always been blunt with her, always open and fair. She's too smart.*

But Zeke figured lots of fathers told themselves the same things about their daughters and ended up being dead wrong.

"I assume Ben Trevino's going to be there," he said, keeping his eyes on the road. He had attempted to keep his tone neutral and hoped that he'd succeeded. Savannah was in the eighth grade, but she liked the older boys just as much as they liked her; the Trevino boy was a sophomore at the high school in Hidalgo.

"I assume Skyler's going to be there," Savannah said.

Zeke shook his head. "Touché, kid. Touché." He'd been on half a dozen dates with a waitress at a diner in Lansdale called the Magic Wagon, and Savannah knew that he'd fallen hard for her.

Rounding a corner, they came in view of the lights of Lansdale and Savannah sat up straighter. Zeke smiled as he took in the multicolored bulbs that had been strung from lamppost to lamppost, like Christmas had come early. With the windows open, they could hear the discordant jangle of instruments tuning up.

"Wow, this is going to be loud," Zeke said.

"You really are getting old," Savannah replied.

He couldn't argue. Forty-one didn't feel old, but if his first reaction to the volume of the speakers set up for the music festival was something other than excitement, maybe he truly had gotten ancient before his time.

They found a parking space behind the post office and Zeke locked up the pickup, hoping he wouldn't regret having brought the antique to town. He patted his pockets to make sure he had his wallet and phone and keys, and then they set off, walking out to the main street and joining the flow of people moving toward the park in front of the town hall, where a stage had been erected just for the event. Zeke glanced around, admiring the size of the gathering even as he searched the crowd for Skyler, who'd told him that she'd be wearing a yellow hat.

Beside him, Savannah bumped into a thirtyish woman Zeke didn't recognize, and he realized that she'd been looking down at her phone, texting someone.

"Hey, bud, pay attention," he said, gently pushing her arm down. "Why not put the phone away?"

"Terri just texted me. She's here. I'm just trying to figure out where."

Zeke took a breath and decided not to fight her. They weren't used to having this many people downtown at once, and it would be hard for Savannah to find her friends in this throng without texting them.

"Just watch where you're going," he said.

They were half a block from the town hall when the first band began to play. People howled and applauded and groups of young people put their arms around each other and swayed together. Zeke figured there must have been six or seven hundred people—not exactly throngs, but a massive gathering for Lansdale. Glancing around, he saw faces and the backs of heads, sweatshirts and T-shirts and jackets, and then a quick flash of yellow glimpsed between moving bodies.

Skyler?

"Daddy, I see Vanessa!" Savannah said, tugging his arm. "Can I go hang with those guys?"

"Just a second," he said, rising to the tips of his toes and moving around, trying to get another glimpse of that yellow flash, hoping to find that it had been Skyler's hat.

"They're just over there in front of the bookshop," Savannah said. "I have my phone. Can I just catch up with you in a bit?"

There! Another glimpse of yellow.

He hesitated, turning toward Savannah and then glancing over at the little bookshop across the street, its windows dark, the CLOSED sign on the door. A group of kids clustered on the sidewalk there and he thought he did recognize Vanessa amongst them.

"All right," he said. "But don't leave this block. I'll text you in—"

"Thanks, Daddy!" Savannah cried in triumph, waving at him as she pushed away through the crowd.

The band's first song ended. In the moment between the last chord that rolled out of the speaker system and the beginning of the audience's applause, Zeke heard the roar of car engines coming fast.

He turned and saw the headlights, frowned as he saw the pair of dust-coated, jacked-up pickup trucks with their blacked-out windows—

—began to shout as he saw the figures that crouched in the beds of the pickup trucks and the guns they held in their hands, a rainbow of multicolored festival lights gleaming off of the barrels and the truck hoods and the windshields.

The band charged into their second song, a country-rock anthem everyone in the crowd knew by heart, but people had already begun to shout, and when the first gunshot split the night and echoed off of the storefront windows, they began to scream.

"Savannah," Zeke barely whispered. And then he shouted her name.

Hurling himself through the crowd, shoving people aside, he caught sight of her at the edge of the lawn, nearly to the sidewalk. She'd raised her hand in a wave to her friends across the street but stood frozen there as she turned toward the roaring engines and the gunfire that erupted in the very same moment, silencing the music but not the screams.

Zeke had his arm outstretched, reaching for her, no more than five feet away when the bullet punched a hole through her chest. Her white denim jacket puffed out behind her, the fabric tugged by the exiting bullet.

Savannah staggered several steps backward but remained standing for a second or two, a sad, mystified expression on her face as a crimson stain began to soak into the pale blue cotton of her top.

He froze, fingers still outstretched, still reaching for her as she lifted her gaze to focus on him. Zeke was sure of that. Savannah *saw* him.

And then she crumpled to the street, bleeding, her mouth opening and closing as if she desperately wanted to speak, until at last her chest ceased its rise and fall and Savannah lay still.

By then the gunfire had stopped and the sound of engines had faded, but the screaming went on and on.

2

On a Monday morning, the first week of February, Zeke Prater stood in his east pasture and stared at a job only halfway done. He'd gotten the gate off of its hinges and scraped the hell out of his knuckles in the process. The top hinge had rusted nearly all the way through, and over the weekend it had finally given way, the weight of it twisting the bottom hinge and wreaking havoc on the spring mechanism that swung the gate closed automatically. Of all of the hardware bolted into the wood, only the lock seemed in good working order.

"Son of a bitch," Zeke said with a sigh, stepping back and wiping the sweat from his forehead.

The dark red cotton sweater he'd worn this morning lay hanging over the pasture fence. Winter mornings had a special chill, even all the way down in Hidalgo County, but it had warmed up nicely. He'd worked at the hinges for half an hour before he'd managed to get the gate off. Now he had to remove the twisted hardware before he could install the new hinge set, and then he would see if the spring could be salvaged.

He turned and walked to his truck. His toolbox lay open in the flatbed of the F150 and he tossed the screwdriver into it. The drill case sat beside the toolbox, along with the new set of hinges. Zeke reached for the drill but paused as he noticed the blood dripping from his knuckles, surprised he had not felt it.

Swearing under his breath, he grabbed a rag from the toolbox and wrapped it around his right hand. As he leaned against the tailgate, he took a deep breath, trying to enjoy the feeling of the sun on his skin and the cool winter morning air. But he couldn't help glancing down at the rag, noticing the thirsty way the cloth absorbed his blood. He got lost in that moment, thinking of blood and fabric.

When he heard the sound of an engine he snapped his head up as if awoken from a trance, dropping his right hand—rag and all—to the butt of the pistol hanging at his hip. A plume of dust rose from the road to the west, and he recognized the battered old Jeep coming his way. Even so, it took a few seconds for him to move his hand away from the gun.

The Jeep skidded to a halt in the dirt a dozen feet from his truck and the driver climbed out, smile beaming beneath the shadow of his wide-brimmed hat. Lester Keegan had put fifty in his rearview mirror a couple of years past and never looked back. Wiry and tan, in his daily uniform of tan work pants and blue cotton button-down shirt, he'd have looked every inch the working cowboy if not for the hat. Zeke had an eye for hats and he knew a custom job when he saw one. Lester might have owned the smallest of the five ranches surrounding Lansdale, but he had the most money and the expensive tastes to match. Oil had done that, two generations back, and the Keegans had never squandered their windfall.

"I'm assuming there are still folks around here somewhere that you pay good money to do things like fix pasture gates," Lester said, surveying the scene with an eyebrow cocked.

"Sometimes a fella likes to get his hands dirty," Zeke replied, checking his knuckles, satisfied to see that the bleeding had stopped.

"Seems to me I recall you saying you were too old for this sort of thing."

Zeke narrowed his eyes. Something in Lester's tone troubled him. They were in the habit of paying each other a visit now and then, sharing a beer or a coffee. Lester's wife, Anita, had taken an interest in Zeke's widower status years ago and had been determined to do something about it. The Keegans had reached out to him many times in the past four months—since the night of the music festival—but he'd driven them away just as bluntly as he had everyone else, even though their own son, Josh, had been among the dead.

"If you're not too old to ride or to sink a fence post now and again, I guess I'm not too old to fix a damn gate. I just turned forty-two, Lester. That don't make me old; it makes me lazy."

Lester took off his hat and ran his fingers around the soft brim. "Well, now—"

"What brings you out?" Zeke asked.

Lester's smile slipped away and suddenly he looked his age. "Didn't have much choice. You're not answering your cell and you haven't returned my calls from yesterday."

Zeke wiped the back of his hand across his brow. "This doesn't sound like a lunch invitation from Anita."

"No," Lester said in agreement. "You're right about that. I need you to come with me, Zeke. We've got an appointment in town. Vickers said someone's gotta be there to represent everyone we lost, and Savannah doesn't have anyone but you to stand for her."

Zeke felt a trickle of ice along his spine. He stared at the ground, at a blade of grass growing up through the dirt road.

"This some insurance thing?" he asked without lifting his gaze.

"I asked Vickers the same question. He says no."

"Then what is it?"

"Asked him that, too. He says 'revenge.'"

Zeke stood a little straighter. Doubt and suspicion flooded him, but logic prevailed. Vickers had lost his wife, Martha, that terrible night. The cartel had killed twenty-three people in all, with Savannah the youngest of them. As much as the Keegans and some of Zeke's other friends might have wanted to see him leave the ranch for some human interaction, even just for a few hours, none of them would stoop so low as to hold out the possibility of revenge for bait.

"Feds say they're working on it," Zeke said. "We get directly involved, more of our people are gonna die. Leave it to them, they say."

Lester's blue eyes narrowed, the edges crinkling, and suddenly he looked older than ever.

"Leave it to them? We've tried that before and it didn't work. Hell, that's why we formed the Volunteers, ain't it? The Mexican government is too damned disorganized and too corrupt, top to bottom, to stop the drug war and all the killing that goes on around it. If you could call this an act of terrorism, maybe you'd get the funding it would take to launch an all-out war on the cartels, and to hell with Mexican sovereignty. But the Feds know it's all drug related, so what do we get? Exactly what we got the last time the media got up in arms about killings along the border: another fifteen hundred National Guard troops for additional patrols and promises from the FBI that they're infiltrating the cartels, working to dismantle them from within, 'cause they've had so much success in the past. Now even the media's forgotten about us, not that they were much help. All the spectacle they put on, all that mock horror, only lasts until the next tragedy comes along. That school shooting in Rhode Island knocked us right out of the news cycle."

Lester gave a slow nod, as if to affirm everything he'd just said. He glanced up at Zeke.

"They can send all the National Guardsmen they want, but if there's revenge to be had, nobody's going to go out and get it for us. Hell, I didn't get to be my age without learning at least that much, and neither did you."

Zeke felt an all-too-familiar rage burning in his chest. It had been there ever since that October night.

"You don't have to preach to me, Lester," he said. "I'm living this too, remember?"

Lester pushed his shaggy hair away from his eyes and slid his hat back on.

"I haven't forgotten," he said, and glanced away from Zeke, up toward the main house.

Zeke averted his eyes, not wanting to see his vacant windows for fear that his voice might betray him and he might speak aloud the question that concerned him the most. Did he even belong out here anymore? Without a wife or a child, with his sister up in Virginia and their parents dead in the ground, what was the point of this life, holding every breath an extra beat just in case the bullets started flying?

Zeke had spent four months trying to come up with a reason to stay. The only one he'd found was the promise he'd made to himself—the promise that he wouldn't leave until he knew the men with Savannah's blood on their hands had paid the price, in full.

He slid the toolbox and the drill kit off the tailgate and onto the truck bed, then slammed the tailgate.

"You drive."

As they made their way into town, Zeke spotted small clusters of people gathered near parked cars or milling about in front of shops. Victoria Jessup was in front of the post office with her two younger boys, and she looked to Zeke as if she were holding her breath. Sarah Jane Trevino, little sister to Ben, sat on the hood of her mother's Ford. Some of the people in Lansdale that day watched Lester Keegan's Jeep as it rolled through town and pulled into a spot across from the hardware store, but most of them ignored the new arrivals. They were all watching the front door of the Magic Wagon.

"What the hell's going on here, Lester?" Zeke asked as they left the Jeep and started across the street toward the diner.

"Your guess is as good as mine, amigo."

Bells jangled overhead as they entered the Magic Wagon. All around the diner, familiar faces turned toward them. Victoria Jessup's eldest boy was there, along with Ben Trevino's mother, Linda, and the pretty young wife of Tim Hawkins, the sheriff's deputy who'd been shot through the throat. Mrs. Hawkins looked about five months along with her pregnancy now, and as sorrowful as her loss had been, Zeke couldn't help thinking how lucky she was to have her new baby to remember Big Tim by. Now that he and Lester had arrived, there were more than two dozen people gathered in the diner, all but three of whom he knew had lost someone to the cartel's bloodlust back in October. Two of the three were employees of the Magic Wagon, a waitress named Deena Green . . . and Skyler Holt.

It shamed Zeke to see Skyler, though he'd suspected she would be there. She smiled tentatively at him and he could muster only a nod in return. She'd gotten blond highlights in her hair and the look suited her. Curvy and bright and charismatic, Skyler was ten years his junior and the first woman he'd met in his life as a widower who had brought a lightness to his heart. She had called a dozen times after Savannah's murder, but he had returned not a single one and had avoided her when he'd seen her in town. This was the first time he'd set foot in the Magic Wagon since October.

She nodded back, just a little tilt of the head. He would have liked to talk to her—had thought all along how nice it would be to see her smile again and hear her laugh—but he had nothing to offer in return. No joy to give.

Of all the faces that'd turned toward him and Lester as they'd entered, only one was entirely unfamiliar to Zeke. A stranger. The little man with the brown skin might have been thirty-five or fifty-five, depending on how many years he'd spent working in the sun. Perhaps five feet three inches tall and tipping the scales at a mighty one hundred and twenty pounds or so, he ought to have gone almost unnoticed in the room, but Zeke could feel an aura of intensity around him, as if he had everyone's attention though everyone studiously avoided looking directly at him. He wore loose black cotton pants and a white shirt that made his sun-darkened skin stand out even more starkly, and his eyes were wide and round . . . the eyes, Zeke immediately thought, of a man who sat in the last row on a bus, talking to people nobody else could see.

His eyes were unnerving, and Zeke lowered his gaze, discomfited by his regard.

Alan Vickers stood up from the stool where he'd been perched.

"Zeke, welcome," the white-bearded rancher said. "I'm glad Lester could persuade you to join us."

Zeke glanced again at the little man, and again he looked away.

"Well . . . yeah, I'm here, Alan. But I've got work to do, as I'm sure we all do, so why not say your piece, whatever it is."

"Of course," Vickers replied. He glanced around the diner. "Deena? Skyler? If you ladies would step out for a time, maybe go on down to the park, I'll send someone to fetch you when we're done. And thank Agnes for the use of the place."

Zeke watched curiously as the two waitresses took off their aprons, said quiet good-byes to several of those gathered, and then departed. Skyler walked within five feet of him and barely glanced up as she passed. For the first time, he noticed that the people in the Magic Wagon all seemed to have coffee or some other beverage, but not a single plate of food had been set before them. None of them had come here to eat. Whatever Vickers had in mind, the whole diner had been put at his disposal.

And why not? Zeke thought. *He's the landlord.*

Vickers wore the smile of a heartbroken man trying his best. Zeke figured his own smile must have looked like that and vowed to himself to try to avoid smiling ever again. It was a wretched, pitiful expression, but Vickers cast it about with the confused air of excitement and apology found in men who'd sought truths better left unspoken.

"I want to thank you all for coming," he said, his face reddening. "I'm not going to waste your time. I know most of you don't want to be here. Hell, looking around at each other, knowing there's only one thing everyone in this room has in common . . . it makes me want to scream."

Vickers paused and took a breath. To Zeke's surprise, nobody called out for him to get to the point. *Maybe because they recognize the pain in his eyes from the mirror,* Zeke thought.

Vickers went on. "I could give you a whole long buildup, folks. But I'd lose you halfway through, because no matter how long you've known me, you're gonna have a hard time believing a damn word I say. So here's the only preamble I'm gonna give you. Reality is a consensus. It is what we agree it is, and by 'we' I don't just mean the people in this room, I mean society. We all grow up with an idea of what's possible and what's impossible. Most of you folks believe in God, or you did, once upon a time. We spend—"

His voice broke, thick with emotion, and then he smiled that painful smile again and forged on.

"We spend our lives building up these walls between what we believe in and what we don't believe in, and it's never easy when one of them gets broken down."

Vickers gestured to the little man seated on a counter stool just beside him. The stranger had been sitting as still and silent as a monk in meditation, but now he blinked as if coming awake and glanced around at the mourners. His face held no expression and his storm-gray eyes were cold.

"This fella here is Enoch Stroud. His daughter, Lena, dated a small-time drug dealer out of Houston by the name of—well, his name doesn't matter, really; point is, he stole from the Matamoros cartel. They could've just killed this kid, but there's always some fool who thinks he's smarter, thinks he can get away with something, and the cartel wanted to teach a different kind of lesson. They took Enoch's daughter—"

The little man interrupted with a choking laugh that gave Zeke chills.

"Took 'er," Enoch said, glaring at the gathered mourners one by one, as if accusing them of the crime. "Raped 'er. Left pieces of her for the boyfriend to find, wrapped up like birthday gifts and set on his bed or in the backseat of his car. Hands. Feet. Teeth. Breasts. Then her head, just to make sure we knew she was dead."

"Oh, sweet Jesus," Alma Hawkins said, covering her eyes so nobody would see her cry.

Tommy Jessup swore under his breath, but in the silence between Enoch's words, they all heard it.

Enoch went on. "It was after we got her head that we buried her. Oh, we waited a week or so, but then we understood that the message had been sent and that we wouldn't be getting any more of Lena back."

Vickers had turned away from the man, and for the first time Zeke noticed that he was fiddling with something in his right-hand pocket, clutching it like it was some sort of talisman. For some reason it unnerved Zeke, as if he'd peered inside the man's secret sorrow. He'd known Alan Vickers for most of his life but they'd never been friends, never had much in common besides geography. Now they had pain.

Zeke shifted his gaze. He wanted to bolt from the diner, from Lansdale, from fucking Texas, and go somewhere he could watch the snow fall and sit by a fire and feel like a stranger to the world. Because something was coming; he felt that very powerfully. This moment was building up to something that clearly frightened Vickers. And Zeke would have run from it, would have gone north until there were only white mountains and warm hearths, except for the single word he'd heard out of anybody's mouth today that had tantalized him. The word Lester had used as bait to get him here.

"You want revenge," he said, surprising even himself by speaking aloud.

Every pair of eyes in the diner shifted toward him, but Zeke kept his focus on Enoch.

The little man did not smile. He nodded, just once. "Yes, Mr. Prater. It is Mr. Prater?"

"I'm Zeke Prater," he confirmed. *Though how you knew that, I'd like to know.*

"Here it is, then, Mr. Prater," Enoch said, then took in the others with a sweeping glance. "I know a way to have my revenge on the Matamoros cartel and if you will all cooperate, you can have your revenge as well. Revenge and more."

"What do you mean, 'more'?" Lester asked, arms crossed.

A chair squeaked across the floor as Arturo Sanchez shifted to look at Enoch directly. "The Lord has a poor opinion of revenge, Mr. Stroud."

"Not in the Old Testament he don't," Linda Trevino said. "Go on, Mr. Stroud. If there's a way to fix these sons of bitches, we're all ears. It won't bring my son back, but it'll ease my soul when I go to bed at night."

Enoch looked at her, head bowed slightly, dark shadows beneath his eyes. "Interesting that you should put it that way, Mrs. Trevino."

"What way?" she asked, and Zeke could see she was unsettled. "And how do you know my—"

Enoch clapped his hands on his thighs, still seated on the stool by the counter—so tiny in comparison to Vickers and yet somehow the focus of all attention.

"That's enough of what Mr. Vickers called 'preamble,' don't you think?" Enoch said, nodding as if in conversation with himself. "I think so. There's only one way you folks are going to listen to the rest of what I've got to say without laughing me out of town or maybe stoning me in front of the town hall, and that's if you see what I can give you with your own eyes."

Zeke frowned. His skin prickled with a dark sort of anticipation that he didn't like one bit. Whoever Enoch Stroud was, Zeke didn't want anything to do with the man. But when Enoch nodded to Vickers and Vickers produced the object he'd been fiddling with from his pocket, Zeke couldn't turn away. Several people muttered and Zeke saw the same unease he felt ripple through the diner.

"What the hell's that supposed to be, some kind of tin whistle?" Lester asked.

"I don't—"Vickers started, a strange combination of apology and relief flooding his face.

"Just play the tune, Mr. Vickers," Enoch said. "Just play the tune."

With a hitching breath, Vickers put the yellowed instrument to his lips and blew into it, one finger shifting across a trio of small holes on top. It was a kind of flute, strangely carved and with little streaks of dark brown along its shaft like war paint. The sound it emitted could not rightly be called music, but Vickers managed a sequence of discordant notes that had a certain melody when he repeated them a second and third time. It was one of the strangest displays of incongruity Zeke had ever seen, but something about the tune tugged at the base of his skull as if part of him remembered it, down in what Lester always called his lizard brain—the part that hadn't changed in people since cave days.

"This is stupid," Big Tim Hawkins's widow said. "What is this supposed to—"

The swinging door at the back of the dining room squeaked open, and Martha Vickers walked in from the kitchen, wearing the same dress she'd been buried in.

The bullet hole in her right biceps was still open, a dark, winking wound. Above her left eye, the missing part of her skull—the part blown out by the cartel gunman's kill shot—had been covered by a thin membrane of skin like a birth caul. Even from across the room, Zeke could see the pulsing beneath it.

Screams filled the Magic Wagon.

Alan Vickers kept playing the flute, tears streaming down his face. He would not look at his wife. His dead wife, now up and walking, pale and sickly and shuffling but alive, a slow, uncertain smile making her lips tremble.

Zeke felt sick.

"Stop!" Lester shouted, storming across the room to knock the flute from Vickers's hands. "Stop it!"

The bone pipe—for it was bone, Zeke could see that clearly

now—skittered across the floor. Vickers shoved Lester away and lumbered after it, shifting a table out of the way to retrieve it while his dead wife swayed in place, waiting for another note.

"What the hell is this?!" Lester demanded, rounding on Enoch.

The little man had still not risen from the stool.

"It's exactly what it looks like," Enoch said, not smiling, his lip curling with hate. "Resurrection. Mrs. Vickers has been up and around for three days. Another week or so and she'll be good as new, if I let her stay aboveground that long."

"What the hell do you mean if you let her?" Zeke snarled, feeling his own hate—and his own hope—rising like a cobra.

"It's all or none," Enoch said. "I can give this gift to all of you, bring back all of the folks the Matamoros cartel murdered back on October twelfth. If you want it. If you all agree. In exchange, you—and the dead ones, the ones you lost—will help me get my revenge. We will all have our revenge, as long as you all are in agreement."

Enoch rose and glanced around.

"I'll expect your answer by noon tomorrow."

"But what do we have to do for you?" Linda Trevino asked. "What do they—"

Enoch had started to move toward the door, but he paused and turned toward her. Zeke thought he caught a glimpse of the real pain inside the man, the loss and ruin.

"Does it matter?" Enoch asked.

When no one seemed to have an answer, he continued to the exit, people moving aside to let him out.

In his absence, the mourners could only stare at the resurrected Martha Vickers and her strange, lost smile, until her husband collected her and led her back out through the diner's kitchen.

3

Lester drove Zeke home in stony silence. The radio whispered, volume turned down so far that the music was barely audible. The sun had moved almost directly overhead and it felt too warm for February, even in South Texas. Zeke sat in the passenger seat and watched the fields rolling by, his heart numb and growing more so by the moment. He felt sick and hollow at the same time. Empty, as if he were the one who had died—and wasn't that the truth, in a way? Savannah had died just once, and he had spent the past four months doing the same, a little bit every day.

The thought made him cringe with self-loathing. *Fuck, listen to yourself. You get to watch the wind move the trees and the sun rise over the ranch. You get to breathe.*

If a small cry came from his throat in that moment, as he turned fully away so that his friend could not see his face, Lester had the decency not to remark upon it. His own son, Josh, had been thirty years old, married and with his first child—Lester's first grandchild—on the way. Grief had become like a secret they shared.

"Son of a bitch," Zeke whispered, pressing the heels of his hands against his eyes, as if he could drive the image of dead Martha Vickers from his memory.

He couldn't, and neither could he stop himself from imagining Savannah standing there in the diner in Martha's place, alive but not quite alive, the bullet wounds she'd sustained beginning to heal.

How is it possible? he asked himself. *How in the name of God . . .*

An icy knot formed in his gut. Maybe it wasn't in the name of God at all.

The big question was whether or not that even mattered. If Enoch had only been able to raise the dead, had them shuffling around looking the same way they had when they'd been buried, or worse, decaying . . . that would have been easier. Zeke would never have wanted Savannah to live that way, no matter how much the pain of her death gnawed at his insides. But if she could be fully alive again—really alive, restored to her true self—what then?

He'd never have believed it if he hadn't seen it with his own eyes.

Lester turned in through the gates of the Riverbend, which was the name Zeke's grandfather had given the Prater ranch in 1927, and drove back out to the pasture where they had left Zeke's truck ninety minutes and a lifetime before. When he skidded to a stop, clouds of dust rose up from the dirt road and swirled around them.

"What are we gonna do, Zeke?" Lester asked in a strangled voice. He looked pale and drawn, as if he'd aged twenty years in the past hour.

Zeke opened his door and put one boot on the running board. "What do you think we're gonna do? If there's even a chance, what else *can* we do? Go home and call Vickers, Lester, and tell him we're both on board."

Lester gripped the steering wheel, staring out the windshield as if the dusty ranch beyond the glass was the starry nighttime sky and he sought the answers to every question he had ever been afraid to ask.

"It's unholy, Zeke. It must be. One of these days, we're gonna come face-to-face with the Lord. What do I say to Him on that day if we do this now?"

Zeke turned to stare at him, unable to keep the snarl from his voice. "You say, 'Where the fuck were you on October the twelfth, you son of a bitch?' How does that sound?"

The main house was so quiet at night that Zeke felt like a ghost haunting his own home, but if he sat on the porch with a beer and listened to the wind, it brought him the sounds of laughter and camaraderie from the bunkhouse. Sometimes he welcomed those noises, but more often they pained him.

After Savannah's murder, the ranch hands had quieted down for a time out of respect. Most of them had been in Lansdale the night of the festival and somehow they had all come home unharmed, just as Zeke had. They had loved Savannah and doted on her like extended family, and her death left a wound in all of them, but in the end they weren't her family. Not really. They could move on and heal and Zeke could not, though he never blamed them for it.

When he heard a car door slam out in front of the house, he imagined it must be one of the hands getting up the nerve to approach the house to ask for an advance on his pay. Zeke tried to be as flexible as he could, as long as he didn't think the money was going to drugs or gambling and none of the hands borrowed too much up front. A couple of times it had bitten him in the ass, with guys who'd taken off for greener pastures still owing him days or weeks of work, but for the most part, he had found honest men for the ranch.

Zeke didn't answer the knock at the door. He didn't feel capable of holding a conversation tonight. How could he pretend there was anything else that mattered to him beyond what he had seen at the Magic Wagon that morning? He remained in the easy chair in his living room, an ancient Cary Grant movie flickering on the television. He had barely paid attention to a moment of the film, but it was a balm to his soul, allowing him to travel back to a simpler, gentler time.

The knocking ceased for only a moment before his visitor began to rap again, harder this time. Zeke stayed in his chair, admiring the stern lines of Myrna Loy's pretty face. As a boy, he had found a genuine comfort in classic cinema, inheriting the love of old films from his parents. Savannah had never understood his interest and had teased him about his boring taste in movies, but she had been sucked in the night he'd watched *Rear Window* while she did her homework on the living room floor, and Zeke had hoped to introduce her to other Hitchcock films, and then to Bogart, who'd always been his favorite. He had hoped to share so many things with her, to watch her grow and learn and turn into a young woman and maybe a mother someday.

Despite the terrifying, monstrous miracle he'd seen today, he dared not allow himself to hope for those things again.

His cell phone buzzed once, a text coming in. Exhaling, he shifted in the chair and tugged the phone from his pocket to discover that the message was from Skyler.

Open the damn door.

Zeke almost didn't get up. He had never wanted to hurt Skyler, but since Savannah's murder the idea of loving *anyone* made him want to lock himself in the cellar and never come out. Love meant pain and loss; better to be alone.

But he had known Skyler a long time before they had begun dating, and he knew she would not go away just because he ignored her—seeing her earlier today at the Magic Wagon confirmed that. She had come out here with some purpose in mind and as long as she believed he was at home—and his car out in the driveway had already given him away—she would see it through.

"Shit," he muttered, rising from his chair.

When he opened the door, Skyler barged in without an invitation. She had made no effort to pretty herself up for the visit; her hair was in a ponytail and the only makeup he could see was mascara. Her hooded burgundy sweater fit her tightly enough to show off her curves, but it was frayed at the cuffs and the laces of her boots were untied, as if she'd made the decision to come abruptly and hadn't paused even to tie them.

"Come in, I guess," he said, letting the irony into his voice.

Skyler spun on him, there in the foyer, stammering nonsense for several seconds, the words crowding each other to get out. She paused and took a breath, so furious with him . . . and she was so beautiful that it made him want to shove her back out the door. He loved the fire in her, the passion, but he did not want to love her.

"You guess . . . ? That's the greeting I get after you ignore me?" She looked as if she didn't know whether to cry or slug him. "I've given you all the space you could ever have asked for, Ezekiel. I've respected your desire to be alone even though I think it's the opposite of what you need. But I come and bang on your door and you ignore me—"

"I didn't know it was you banging, Skyler."

"—hush, now, I'm yelling at you!" she said, waving a finger, blue eyes alight with righteous fury.

Zeke couldn't help smiling. "I can see that."

Skyler faltered, the corners of her mouth turning upward, tempting a grin. Instead she punched him in the shoulder.

"Ow!"

"Don't try to make light," she said grimly, searching his eyes. She tucked a stray lock of hair behind her ear. "I figure you know why I'm here."

Zeke glanced out the still-open door, then slid it slowly shut.

"I'm guessing it's to do with the meeting at the Magic Wagon today."

"You know it is."

He narrowed his eyes, turning to look at her. "That doesn't concern you, Skyler. You didn't lose anyone that night—"

"I lost you," she said softly. Angrily. "If you think I'm overstepping, well, I don't know why I should care. You've already put me out of your life. But I care for you, Zeke, and that's not going to change. You're a good man. Don't let yourself be talked into this."

"Too late."

Zeke walked into the living room with Skyler trailing behind him.

"It's not too late," she said insistently. "Nobody's done anything yet that they can't take back except for Alan Vickers and his little hoodoo conjuror, or whatever the hell that Enoch fellow is."

He sat on the edge of the sofa with his arms crossed, staring at the knots in his pine floorboards.

"This about God?" he asked, not looking up.

"Partly, I guess. But it's more just about what's right. Up until today, I never gave a second thought to the rules I always thought the world worked by. Dead was dead. Maybe that's not so. Unless it's some kind of trick—"

"It wasn't a trick. It was Martha Vickers in there, I'd swear to it."

"Trick or not, it isn't natural, Zeke. You know that. Even if you can bring Savannah back, you'll never erase the truth from your mind."

"If she can come back, the truth'll be that she's alive," he said.

"The truth will be that you saw her get shot and you held her while her body went cold and she was dead, and the dead are not supposed to come back to us. You look inside your heart and you won't be able to run away from the fact that you're doing this for yourself, not for Savannah. You have no way of knowing what it means to come back from the dead, what she'll remember, or if she'll even be whole. All you have is this creepy little fella's word. Don't do this, Zeke. It's abominable. And if you bring her back, she'll be an abomination."

For a moment he could not breathe. He closed his eyes and ran a thumb over a spot on his temple that had begun to throb. Skyler only wanted the best for him; he knew that. And, in quiet moments, he had allowed himself to imagine a future with her. But how could she not understand?

She has no children, he thought. *She can't feel what you feel.* Skyler would never know the silent screaming that went on inside his heart, day and night. His wife, Anarosa, had been a God-fearing woman, but he had no doubt what she would have done if she were still alive. Hell, he figured if he gave up this chance, Anarosa would find some way to come back and haunt him, but Skyler would never understand.

To have lost his daughter, seen her die in front of him, and now to have a chance at restoring not only her life, but her lifetime—all the days the future still held in store for her—he would do anything. No matter how noble her intentions, Skyler wanted to rob him of that. For a moment, Zeke hated her for that.

He looked up at her. "You need to leave."

Skyler flinched. "Please, Zeke—"

"You announced that you'd be overstepping, and by God, you kept your word. Now you need to go, Sky."

"Ezekiel—"

"I don't want you here!" he roared, pushing away from the sofa, crowding her backward into the hallway. *"Get out of my damn house!"*

Skyler's hands were shaking and her chest rose and fell in short little breaths as she glared at him.

"You don't get to . . . ," she began, tears welling in her eyes. "I only wanted to—"

His face a mask, Zeke stared at her. *"Go. Now."*

Skyler nodded slowly, wiping at her tears, and then turned and left, slamming the door behind her. Zeke went to the door and laid his hand on the wood, listening to the growl of her engine starting up. The ice in his gut—in his heart—was the only thing protecting him, and he invited it deeper inside him, wanting to be cold. To be frozen.

He could hear her tires on the driveway as she turned the car around and he wanted to go after her, to kiss her and let her cry with him. But if he went after her, then he would have to admit that she was right, and then where would he be?

4

The following night, Enoch passed out the pipes.

Each of the bereaved who had gathered in the Magic Wagon—one mourner for each of the twenty-three people murdered on October the twelfth—received one; none had declined Enoch's offer. They gathered in a haphazardly formed circle on a gravel path that ran through what was called the New Field, the modern part of the cemetery where the recently dead had been buried. Enoch moved wordlessly amongst them, reaching into a burlap sack and producing yellowed bone pipes similar to the one that Vickers had played in the diner the day before.

Vickers stood at the edge of the road, not far from the crypt where his wife had been buried, but she wasn't inside that marble tomb any longer. Martha now stood with her husband, clad in a flowery dress and a light green sweater and wearing a wide-brimmed hat that hid much of her face from view. Somewhere between dead and alive, it was as if she were ashamed of herself, but she held her husband's hand, and though Zeke knew it might have been the moonlight, he thought that her skin looked less pale than it had the day before, as if some of the pink health had returned to it.

Enoch paused in front of Zeke and rooted in the burlap sack, which made a rasping noise as he drew out the next pipe. Zeke hesitated before accepting the instrument, but Enoch narrowed his eyes in suspicion until he took it. The pipe might have been human bone, but it had been carved and shaped so that it was difficult to know for certain, and Zeke chose not to examine it too closely. It had three holes in the top and otherwise had no markings.

Clutching the pipe in his hand, nursing the icy numbness inside him for his own sake, Zeke glanced around at the others—friends and neighbors and near strangers—and found that most of them wore expressions as blank as his own to mask their grief and hope and doubt.

Several yards away, Aaron Monteforte leaned against the trunk of a massive, dying oak tree with his arms crossed and an almost petulant air about him, as if he thought no one could understand his grief. With twenty-three dead in a small town, everyone in Lansdale had lost a friend or family member in that massacre. There was nothing special about Aaron's grief and, Zeke knew, nothing special about his own . . . except that it was his. His pain. His rage. His loss. His daughter, goddamn it.

Aaron tended bar at the Blue Moon but looked more like he ought to have been the bouncer, with a weight lifter's build and reaper and angel tattoos on his thick biceps, brown hair to his shoulders and a perpetual scruff that couldn't rightly be called a beard. Several years before, Aaron had spent the summer as a hand on the ranch and Zeke knew he ought to go over and say something. But what could he say that he hadn't already said four months ago to Aaron and everyone else who'd lost someone that night? That he was sorry? They were all fucking sorry.

Still, he managed to catch Aaron's eye for a moment and gave a solemn nod, just to say, *Hey, man, you're not alone.* After a second of recognition, Aaron returned the gesture. The kid had lost his sister, Trish, who'd been twenty-five and unmarried, and he had chosen to be her proxy. That was how Vickers had referred to them all, "proxies," just folks stepping in to do a deed on behalf of those who couldn't do it themselves.

When Enoch reached Aaron, the big man with the tattoos and the muscles took the pipe and knelt to pray with it clasped in his hands. When Enoch held a pipe out to Linda Trevino, she backed away, shaking her head.

"I can't," she said. "No, Jesus, I can't."

Lester strode over to her, took her firmly by the arm, and brought her to Enoch. "You will," he said. "You already agreed. It's all of us or none of us. Are you going to take this chance away from everyone because you're afraid?"

She spun on him, stared into his weathered face. "Aren't you?"

Only the wind spoke. Otherwise the cemetery was silent.

"We all are," Zeke said at last, quietly but clearly.

Linda stared at him with wild eyes. "But he won't even tell us—"

"Take it, damn you!" Mrs. Hawkins snapped. "Just take it or you might as well be killing them all again!"

Linda sucked in a breath as if she'd been punched in the gut. Shaking, she took the carved length of bone from Enoch, who moved on to young Tommy Jessup and then Arturo Sanchez and to a man Zeke knew only as Mooney, a salesman from the medical supplies company who had brought his new bride to the music festival and then lost her to a bullet only a week and a half after they'd been wed.

The last two pipes in the sack went to Lester and to Harry Boyd, the owner of the oldest of the five ranches that surrounded Lansdale. His boy, Charlie, had been twenty-one and the spitting image of his father, with ginger hair and a freckled face and a lanky, awkward build. Harry looked as if he might be sick when Enoch offered him the pipe, and the gathered mourners held their collective breath until he accepted it.

They had all agreed before, but this was the moment when it felt to Zeke that a bargain had truly been struck. The air around them turned cold, and when a gust of wind rustled the branches of the trees in the cemetery, he shivered.

I'm here, bud, he thought. And I'm not running.

It had almost been a prayer, and he wondered if Savannah could hear it, or if she felt the love he had for her.

Enoch moved to the center of their ragged human circle, ignoring those who wept or who had gone so pale that Zeke feared they might faint. The little man—*hoodoo conjuror*, Skyler had called him—glanced around the circle and then reached into his pocket, taking out a small metal tin, which he opened to reveal the glitter of metal and then passed on to Zeke.

"These are pins. Take one and pass them along until everyone has one."

Zeke did as he'd been told, giving the tin to Lester before looking at Enoch. "What now?"

"Now you stick yourself with the pin," Enoch said, his eyes a stormy gray. "Don't be gentle. When you're bleeding well enough, you can toss the pins aside, and then write the name of the one you've lost on the pipe in your own blood. It's got to be the name you called them, the name in your heart, not the name they were born with."

"Blood ritual," Arturo Sanchez muttered. "Blasphemy."

"What did you expect, Artie?" someone said.

Zeke glared at Sanchez. "Blasphemy is murdering twenty-three people, not loving them so hard you'll do anything to have them back."

Zeke tucked the pipe into his pocket and then thrust the pin into the index finger of his right hand, jabbing hard and giving the pin a little jerk to make sure the tiny wound would not seal itself up too quickly. When he'd dropped the pin, he took out the pipe with his left hand and scrawled small, crude letters onto the bone in bright crimson, turning it in his hand so that her name encircled the pipe and so that he could fit all of the letters.

Savannah.

He had a dozen nicknames for her, but her name was beautiful. In his heart, that was who she'd always been.

"I will show you the notes to play, the notes they'll hear,"

Enoch said. "I'll play my own tool, and the notes will weave together and call to them, and they will rise."

Zeke closed his eyes, feeling the trickle of his own blood along his fingers. Hope and horror were at war within him and he could not allow either to triumph, because either would defeat him. He thought of Anarosa and how beautiful she'd looked the first time she'd held Savannah in her arms. Anarosa had left this world behind, but it might just have been that the daughter they had both cherished was not yet out of reach. Holding the pipe with two fingers so his blood would dry, Zeke listened to Enoch go on.

"It'll take 'em eight or nine days to heal . . . to come back to themselves," the hoodoo man said. "They won't know you at first, but in time they'll start to recognize their surroundings and your faces. Till then, they'll follow your commands completely, as long as you play that pipe."

The words chilled Zeke. The dead of October the twelfth would be like puppets until they began the final stage of transition from dead to living.

"What is it you're going to ask us to do, exactly?" Harry Boyd demanded. "How the hell is my son supposed to help you get your revenge?"

Enoch shot him an angry glance. "Not only my revenge, but his own, Mr. Boyd. And I'll explain my price in due time. For the moment, just ask yourself this—is any price too dear?"

Boyd didn't look satisfied, and neither was Zeke, but they were in no position to argue—not if they wanted what Enoch had to offer.

"Now," Enoch said, "be careful not to smear the blood but put the pipes to your lips. Here are the notes you need to play."

The little man's fingers moved smoothly over the pipe, covering and uncovering holes. The tune was simple but it took Zeke more than ten minutes to master it, and others took even longer, muttering in frustration as they fumbled with the pipes. As Zeke played the tune over and over, perfecting it, Harry Boyd's question echoed inside his mind, followed by one of his own.

Enoch stood by Mrs. Hawkins, showing her the notes more slowly until she seemed to have the tune.

"It can't really be this simple, bringing them back," Mrs. Hawkins said.

"There is nothing simple about it," Enoch replied. "Now, all of you—play."

One by one, the pipers began. The music was strange and discordant and haunting, lifted up by the strangely chilly breeze and spread throughout the cemetery. The branches of the trees trembled, and when Zeke shifted his stance, the scrape of gravel underfoot was impossibly loud.

"What's to stop us from not keeping up our end of the deal?" he asked, raising his voice to be heard over the pipers.

Lester stood next to him, already playing, and he shot Zeke a glance that seemed to take him to task, not for the question but for its timing. Zeke knew he ought to have waited, that only an idiot would telegraph a double-cross before they had what they wanted. But he wasn't going to gamble with Savannah's second chance.

Enoch did not reply. Instead he produced another pipe, this one from inside his jacket and twice the length of the others and streaked with dried bloodstains; turned to look at Vickers and his dead wife; and played.

Half a dozen notes, and Martha Vickers dropped abruptly to the ground. Her hat fell off and tumbled off along the gravel path in the breeze. The pipers all halted their haunting music as her husband cried out in anguish and knelt beside her, her hat forgotten as he cradled her head in his lap and turned a rage-filled gaze upon not Enoch, but Zeke.

"Always the smart one, Prater. Always the one who can't just go along, you arrogant son of a bitch," he snarled. "This here . . . this is a miracle. You don't question it. And whatever we have to do in return, it's goddamned worth it."

Vickers twisted around to glare at Enoch.

"Now give her back, you bastard. Give her back to me!"

Enoch turned a questioning gaze upon Zeke, as if to say, *Is that enough for you?* Zeke nodded his assent. He would ask no more questions. A fist of anguish clenched around his heart. They had come too far along this damning path to turn away now. Enoch had them at his mercy, for no one would refuse him now. Not when they had seen the consequences. Whatever darkness might be hiding inside it, he would accept the miracle . . . and whatever it cost him.

"Play," Enoch said, and the chorus of pipes began again.

This time, Zeke played with them, and so did Vickers.

Martha, who lay on the gravel path beside him, was the first to rise.

She staggered to her feet and studied her husband for a moment, and then dusted herself off as if vaguely embarrassed . . . as if she had done nothing more than trip, rather than die again and be resurrected in front of them all in the space of a minute.

Big Tim Hawkins was next. He'd been buried only a dozen feet from the path in a plot that the Hawkins family had been using for years. His father had been laid there a decade ago and there were spots for Tim's mother and siblings and their spouses. A family grave.

The hands that punched up through the soil were huge and fish-belly white, nails torn and one finger broken from smashing through the top of the coffin and digging his way up through the dirt. Zeke shuddered at the sight, and at the thought of the inhuman strength required for such a feat. Whatever power Enoch had called upon, it had instilled within October's dead more than just a renewed spark of life.

There were screams and Mrs. Hawkins nearly fainted, one hand on her pregnant belly as Aaron Monteforte caught her.

"Play, damn you!" Enoch cried shrilly before going back to his own pipe, his notes different from the others, weaving in and out of the discord and creating an unnerving sort of order.

They played, and some of the dead rose. Some, but not all.

Five minutes passed, no more. Zeke could not look at their faces but he knew them. Ben Trevino was there, standing near his mother like a sleepwalker as she wept and kept playing the same ugly, maddening notes. The funeral home had done an excellent job with the bullet hole in his neck.

Enoch stopped, lowering his pipe.

"That's enough," he said.

"But . . . ," Lester said, looking around. "Where are the others? I count nine."

Enoch slipped his pipe inside his brown wool coat. "The others are buried in metal coffins. They're going to need your help. Mr. Vickers has shovels in the back of his truck."

Arturo Sanchez made the sign of the cross.

"Dig them up," Enoch said, his stormy eyes alight with golden sparks as whatever magic he'd wielded began to burn off.

As he turned, Zeke strode up and grabbed his arm. "The cost, damn it. What's the price?"

Enoch glanced at the lumbering, shuffling dead who were even now being embraced by the living who had summoned them.

"Tomorrow night I'm going across the border," Enoch said. "There's a compound, a house where the cartel lieutenant who oversees all their local business lives and works. The drugs. The murder. His name is Carlos Aguilar, and I intend to kill him and everyone who tries to stop me. Your people—he gave the orders to the men who killed them—your people, they'll come with me and help me do this, and so will you."

Mrs. Hawkins began to shake her head, covering her mouth as she cried.

Zeke thought of Savannah facing down cartel enforcers with guns, hardened killers. He steeled himself, knowing the bargain had been struck, the gift Enoch offered and the consequences of refusing.

"You need us to control them," Zeke said. "Pull their strings."

"That's right, Mr. Prater. And you'll be happy to know that no more harm will come to them. Right now they're dead, more or less. They're . . . recovering. Another bullet hole or a knife wound will add to their recovery time, but it won't hurt them."

"What about us?" Linda Trevino asked, horrified.

Enoch's gaze was hard as flint. "I suppose you'll just have to be careful."

Zeke went to get a shovel.

5

Late the next morning, Zeke stood on the scattering of hay and dusty horse shit that carpeted the floor of his stable, wondering if he had run out of tears. His eyes burned and he knew it was partly from the lack of sleep—he'd surprised himself by dropping off for a couple of hours just as the sun came up—but he thought the sandpaper feeling came from the unfulfilled need to cry. He felt empty in so many ways; the inability to summon tears was just one more.

"Come on, bud," he rasped. "Say hello to Jester. He missed you."

His voice cracked on that last bit, but Savannah didn't notice. She stood in front of the stall where her horse, Jester, snorted and chuffed and turned his back to her. From the moment Zeke had led Savannah into the stable, playing the ugly tune on his

pipe—which still had the coppery scent of his blood on it—
Jester had done his best to stay as close to the back wall of the
stall as possible.

Zeke clutched the pipe in his hand, forcing himself to loosen
his grip, afraid he might break it or rub off some vital part of
its magic.

Ain't magic, he thought. *It's a curse.*

What could it be but a curse that let him see his daughter
like this? Savannah still wore the rose-hued dress she'd been
buried in, a lovely thing she had persuaded him to buy her for
the fall dance at her school and that had garnered far more attention from the boys than he would have liked. The funeral
director had gently implied that the color might be too red, that
it might trouble him to see such a red on her, there in her casket
at the wake, but Zeke had insisted, remembering the smile on
her face when she'd worn it.

Now it seemed obscene. A party dress on a corpse.

He stared at her pale skin and noticed the way the warm
breeze through the barn stirred her limp, dead hair, and bile
burned up the back of his throat. He turned away, dropping to
his knees as his stomach revolted and he vomited in the sawdust
and hay. On his knees, trying to breathe, waiting for his stomach
to calm, he thought for sure he would weep then, but still his
eyes were dry.

After a few seconds, he rose shakily to his feet and looked at
her.

There were bruise-dark circles under her eyes and she had
the tallow complexion of old candle wax. Her blue eyes had
paled, faded like their color had been nothing but paint, left in
the sun too long. In the warm, late-morning light coming
through the open doors at the far end of the stable, the shadows
around her had acquired a gold hue. In that golden darkness it
would almost have been possible to believe she was merely ill,

were it not for those eyes, staring into a null middle distance, as if she could still see back into the land of the dead.

"Come on, honey," he breathed. "Do it for Daddy. Say hello to Jester. You love your Jessie-boy, don't you? He's right here."

It felt to Zeke as if something at the core of him was collapsing inward, a little black hole growing in his gut. An invisible fist clenched at his heart.

"Hey. I'm here, bud."

Something darted along the left side of his peripheral vision and he turned to see a furry orange tail vanishing into an empty stall. Tony was a marmalade cat who had been born in the stable. His mother had been a stray who had taken up residence there, and Zeke had never tried to drive her away because he believed that every stable and barn needed at least one cat to catch the mice who would invariably find their way in. The rest of the litter had been given away, but Savannah had kept the orange marmalade and named him after Tony the Tiger, the mascot of her favorite cereal.

The memory struck him hard—seven-year-old Savannah sitting on the floor of the stable, holding Tony and stroking him and giving him his name. She'd put a little bow in her hair that morning that nearly matched the color of Tony's fur, her way of making the moment into a sort of ceremony. The image led to a rush of others. Zeke closed his eyes and let them come, a sad smile on his face as he recalled nine-year-old Savannah's first ride on horseback, and the squeals of delight a year later when he brought Jester home and told her the new horse was hers and hers alone.

Mine forever? she'd asked.

He could still hear the little-girl voice in his head.

"Oh, Jesus," he whispered, though not in prayer.

Or maybe it is a prayer, he thought. *Maybe it always is.*

"Come on, Savannah," he said, slapping his hands together

and moving to stand only a foot away from her, face-to-face. "Come on, bud!"

His hands were empty. Frowning, he turned to search for the pipe. When he'd thrown up, he must have tossed it aside. *No, no. Where the fuck are you?* he thought as he scanned the floor until he located it. He'd worried that he might have broken it, but the pipe seemed intact. He stared at it, turning it over in his hands.

The night before, he had begun to experiment with the tune that Enoch had taught them. Lester had suggested that they work together, that he bring his son, Josh, over to Zeke's ranch and they practice how to influence their children with Enoch's pipes. Zeke had refused. What they were doing was both a miracle and an obscenity, and either way it was too intimate to share.

His hands and arms and back still hurt from digging up Savannah's grave. His muscles had burned as he'd thrown himself into the work, numbing his mind and heart so he would not let horror stop him, knowing she must have awakened down there in the cold ground along with the others. But he hadn't really believed it until he had used the shovel to smash the casket's lock and then pried open the lid and seen her moving, milky eyes staring blindly through the webbing of thread that had been used to sew her eyes shut. The thread had torn loose, her ripped eyelids almost instantly healing. A corpse, to be sure—she already looked so much better than she had last night—but a corpse resurrected.

Zeke had screamed, then, but not in fear or horror. He'd screamed out the pain and grief of her death and dragged her up into his arms and sat there cradling her inside her grave, whispering to her, promising her that he would do anything to bring her back to him, all the way back to him. She had been the light in his life, the sun around which his heart and soul revolved.

He would do anything.

Once he had more or less mastered the notes Enoch had taught them to play, he had put her into his truck and brought her home, cleaning her hands and face and feet but not willing to change her clothes. Eventually he would take off her dress and put her in a pair of jeans and a sweatshirt and boots, but not yet, because he didn't want to see the wounds on her chest and back where the bullets had entered and left her body. They'd have been sewn up, but he didn't want to see. Enoch said the wounds would heal, and so he wanted to give her a little more time.

"Time," he whispered now, standing in the stable. Zeke took a breath. Time was really the only thing of value in the world—time to live, time to be with the ones you loved.

Stuffing the pipe into his pocket, he turned away from Savannah's catatonia and went to the vacant horse stall into which he'd seen the cat disappear. Zeke unlatched the door and dragged it open. Tony had curled into a pad of hay in one corner and jumped up as he entered. As Zeke approached, the mouser tried to bolt past him, but Zeke had been wrangling cats in the ranch's old buildings since he could walk and snatched Tony up before he could escape.

The cat struggled, but Zeke carried him out of the stall and over to Savannah. He knew that he was supposed to use the pipe. Enoch had made it clear to all of them that it would be days before any of the dead could think clearly enough to direct their own actions. Their brains were not working properly. The ritual Enoch had taught them made it possible for others to give them direction, as if the notes the pipers played turned on some kind of motor inside them and the words of the pipers were their navigation.

Zeke wanted to believe it. He needed to believe that there was a happy ending, because having Savannah back like this was worse than having her dead. Anarosa would have cursed him for it. He could endure it if he could accept Enoch's promises, but in order for him to have that kind of faith, he needed just one glimpse of the future, one hint of awareness in Savannah's eyes to prove that she was still in there.

"Look, bud," he said. "It's Tony the Tiger. Remember him? Remember when Ginger had her kittens? She hid under the stable but you heard the mewling and you were the one who found them. You were such a big girl and when I told you that you could have one you knew right away it had to be Tony the Tiger. Remember the bows you wore when you—"

Zeke took a step closer to Savannah. The cat hissed and clawed his arms and he swore and dropped the beast. It raced the length of the stable and out the door, a rare excursion. *It knows*, Zeke thought, his stomach dropping. *Even the damn cat can see this is unnatural. It's wrong.*

"God, what have I done?" he whispered, hanging his head in the shadows.

The noise might have been the creak of a beam or the shifting of one of the other horses, but it sounded to him like a soft moan, deep in his daughter's throat. He whipped his head around and stared at her, catching his breath as an impossible hope emerged like sunrise within him.

Savannah had not moved. Her gaze remained vacant and distant.

But there were tears on her face, streaking the dry, waxy skin of her cheeks.

"Bud?" he ventured.

Nothing. No reaction. But the tears were hope enough.

"All right," he said, nodding firmly. "All right."

He dug out the pipe and began to play.

6

It was late the following afternoon when they boarded a school bus Lester had arranged to borrow from the city of Hidalgo.

Faded yellow, with no working heat or air and windows that didn't close all the way, the bus seemed the relic of another era, but it would serve their purposes. They gathered at the Vickers ranch, dust rising from the cars and trucks that made their way up the road. People parked in a fallow field, lining up their vehicles the way they would for the state fair.

The sun beat down as if it were early summer instead of the dregs of a haunted Texas winter. Zeke sat in the fifth row on the driver's side. He'd taken the aisle and given Savannah the window, but she made no effort to look out through the glass or turn away from the glare of the setting sun. He had changed her into blue jeans and high-top sneakers and a thick cotton T-shirt that hung loosely on her so as not to draw attention to the hole in her chest. The shirt had a sparkly design on it and he thought she might have borrowed it from her friend Imogene, who'd loved such things but hadn't laid claim to it after Savannah's death, either because she didn't know how to ask or because she thought it might carry some of Savannah's bad luck.

As he had undressed her, Zeke had kept expecting to feel embarrassed. His little girl had been evolving into a young woman and had all the hallmarks of that transition, and fathers weren't supposed to see their girls unclothed past a certain age. But fathers weren't supposed to see their little girls dead, either. Instead of making him blush, her nudity only made him want to weep at her fragility. Without him blowing notes on the pipe, Savannah lay there and let him do all of the work, but he didn't mind. He had changed her and bathed her and held her when fever and sickness had seized her. This was his daughter, and he would walk through the fires of hell for her.

As the last of the pipers arrived, the bus remained eerily silent. The dead did not speak and the living had nothing to say. Like Zeke, either from fear or shame, they barely made eye contact with one another. Linda Trevino sat several rows ahead of him, keeping up a constant stream of whispered endearments to her dead son. Zeke could barely breathe, watching her. Waiting for Ben to move. To reply.

"Okay, bud," Zeke whispered, turning to look at Savannah. He touched her chin and turned her to face him, noting a momentary alertness in her eyes. She had focused on him. Just for a moment, but he would take it. "We're just going for a little ride."

Enoch stood out in the road, a little man who somehow managed to look smaller with every glance. He carried a small leather bag that hung from his shoulder as if he were a college professor instead of some kind of hoodoo man, and Zeke knew that his own pipe must have been inside that bag. Aaron Monteforte moved toward the bus, playing those now-familiar discordant notes on his pipe, walking with his sister, Trish. Like Savannah's, Trish's death wounds were hidden by her clothing. If not for her complexion and the utter lack of expression, she might have been alive—just another twentysomething South Texas girl waiting for her life to really begin.

Zeke took Savannah's hand and tried not to be disheartened by the lack of any confirming squeeze from her. *Time*, he thought. *Give it time.*

People began to shift in their seats, some craning around to look out the windows of one final vehicle coming down the long, dusty drive. Zeke had been counting and knew there were forty-two people already on the bus, twenty-one dead and an equal number of those who had followed Enoch's ritual to resurrect them—the ones Zeke thought of as pipers and Vickers called proxies.

Music drifted to them, a thumping, crashing rhythm that started low and grew louder as the car approached. In the front seat, Vickers moved his considerable bulk and leaned over Martha—whose dented forehead throbbed like a newborn's fontanel—to look out at the car roaring up his driveway.

The music blared from the open windows of Alma Hawkins's little Volkswagen as it pulled to a stop forty feet from the bus. Big Tim looked absurd sitting in the passenger seat, jammed in and hunched over. Zeke recognized the music only because the deputy had tried to convert the whole town over to his love for the Dropkick Murphys. It wasn't the sort of thing Zeke could ever have enjoyed—headache-inducing stuff—but he figured if anything would get through the fog that clouded the minds of the returned dead, it would be that kind of jarring noise.

Big Tim didn't seem to notice. His wife came around the passenger side of her VW and opened the door. Her pregnant belly hung low as she bent to coax him from the car. Alma Hawkins looked pale, almost corpselike herself. Big Tim had a chunk missing out of the side of his face, but a kind of dry crust that was more like papier-mâché than flesh had begun to fill in the hole.

"Thank God," someone said, a few rows behind Zeke.

In the second row, just behind Vickers, Arturo Sanchez turned to stare into the back, looking just as pale as the revived dead.

"Please . . . ," he said. "I beg you, let that be the last time any of us mentions God tonight."

No one spoke. *What could we say?* Zeke thought.

With Monteforte and Alma Hawkins playing their pipes, they directed their beloved dead onto the bus and arranged them in the remaining seats. Enoch was the last to board. When he did, Vickers rose and offered up his place, which Enoch took while Vickers dropped his considerable bulk into the driver's seat.

"You all know the plan," Vickers said. "We're only going to get one chance."

The bus choked and then roared as he started it, coughing gray smoke out of the exhaust. Vickers drove the bus out to the gates of his ranch and turned south.

Out on the road, beyond the fence that lined his property, a couple of dozen cars were parked on either side and fifty or sixty people had gathered to watch them go. Enoch would allow the dead only one proxy apiece, but many had other family members who would have gladly taken the job.

Dressed in mourning clothes, they stood along the road and prayed, some with rosary beads and others hand-in-hand. Some held up photographs of the dead, back in their living years, and Zeke did not allow himself to focus on those pictures. He did not want to compare them to the pale, withered creatures riding on the bus with him.

Gazing out the window, he saw Skyler near the end of the line. She had swept her hair into a ponytail and wore a plain black dress. Her eyes searched the windows of the bus but Zeke could tell that she hadn't spotted him yet. In her hands she held a small cardboard sign upon which she'd written two words in large black letters.

COME BACK.

Throat dry, he forced himself to turn away. If she saw him then, at least she would not see the doubt in his eyes.

Grinding noises came from the engine as Vickers shifted into higher gear. The bus lurched forward and then they were speeding west, toward sunset, with a cargo of breathless fears and unlikely hopes.

The McAllen-Hidalgo-Reynosa International Bridge spanned the Rio Grande and connected the United States to Mexico. Though it passed through Hidalgo on the U.S. side, the bridge began in McAllen, Texas. Zeke held Savannah's hand as the bus rattled through miles of ranch and farmland all the way to Route 241, which Vickers followed straight through Hidalgo. In summertime, the sunlight seemed to linger forever, but in winter the night came on quickly, and by the time they were rolling along the bridge toward the checkpoint, it was full dark. Bright lights illuminated the short span and the four lanes going either direction. A high fence and a stretch of plain concrete separated the two, and with the towering light posts, it reminded Zeke of the time he'd gone as a boy to visit his uncle Frank in the state prison up in Houston.

"All right," Vickers called from the front. "We're almost there."

Zeke took a breath and dug out the bone pipe that had been sitting heavily in his pocket, jabbing into his thigh. He hesitated, but others didn't, and soon the whole bus was filled with a chorus of ugly notes, just a brief flurry of cluttered music that ended as abruptly as it had begun. He was one of the last to play, and once he had sounded the notes, he turned to Savannah.

"Close your eyes, kiddo. Pretend you're sleeping."

As the bus juddered and then surged forward, Vickers shifting gears, Zeke discovered he was praying. His entreaties amounted to little more than *Please, Lord, let us both come back alive,* but it surprised him to find himself on speaking terms with God again. After Savannah's death, he had all but given up prayer. Now he lowered his head and reached out with his heart, hoping to be heard, and that what they had done was not the abomination he feared it must be. *She's my baby girl, Lord,* he thought. *What else was I to do?*

And then, grimly, feeling the weight of his own guilt: *You brought your own son back to life. Can you blame me for following your lead?*

Though the air had cooled and the breeze that blew in through the partly open windows circulated well, he felt a damp sheen of sweat under his arms and down his back. It might have been his imagination, but even Savannah's hand seemed warm and clammy to the touch. He tried to take that as a good sign.

The bus idled in line for a few minutes, but it was a weekday evening and they were coming from the American side into Mexico, so the wait wasn't long. On the other side, Zeke could see headlights stretching back into the distance. Some of those people, he knew, would be waiting for an hour or two to cross the border into the States.

Vickers parked the bus and then worked the handle that rattled open the doors. Most cars were waved through, but with a bus like this, the Mexican border guards almost had no choice but to at least ask them what they were up to. The woman who stepped onto the bus wore her uniform proudly. In the dim orange glow from the tiny light above the door, Zeke could see the frown that creased her forehead.

"Some tired people," the guard said.

"We were up very early this morning," Vickers said. "I have all of the passports right here."

He offered her a small plastic container that held forty-seven passports and the guard frowned at the box, obviously not inclined to examine them.

"Where are you going?" she asked.

"Voices of Faith conference in San Fernando," Vickers said. "This is the St. Matthews Family Choir."

There were a dozen obvious questions the guard could have asked, beginning with why they didn't have any suitcases on board. Instead she frowned at them for a few seconds longer and then looked at Vickers.

"Your passport?"

He set the plastic box on his lap and handed her a single passport, which she gave only a cursory glance before returning.

"Good luck."

"Thanks so much!" Vickers said brightly. "God bless you."

The guard muttered something as she climbed off of the bus—perhaps returning the wish for the Lord's blessings—but Zeke couldn't make out the words. Then Vickers put the bus in drive, gears grinding, and they were rumbling over the bridge into Mexico.

"You said you'd made a deal with the border patrol," teenage

Tommy Jessup said from the back of the bus. "Was that a part of it?"

Vickers's face was visible in the huge rearview mirror, bathed in yellow light from the dashboard. "No. That was just them not caring. Not a lot of people sneak into Mexico. The deal we've got is with the U.S. Border Patrol, and we're going to need it to get home."

The salesman, Mooney, spoke up from two rows behind Zeke. "Let's just hope the ones you bribed keep their word."

"Yes," Linda Trevino said. "Because people who take bribes are usually so honest."

"Linda, for once please shut your fucking mouth."

It took Zeke a moment to realize that those words had come from his own lips, and then he smiled in the dark, happy to have told her off. It made him feel more alive. On a bus full of people coming back from the dead, it had begun to seem as if their presence was dragging him in the other direction.

He turned and looked at Savannah, marveling at her beauty as he always did, and he longed for morning to come, for all of this to be behind them and Enoch out of their lives forever.

The bloodstained pipe felt heavy in his hand.

And the bus rolled on.

7

Twenty minutes past the border, Enoch finally spoke up. It was strange the way he seemed to vanish when he did not want their attention, as if they had all somehow managed to forget he was among them. Zeke doubted that the Mexican border guard had even glanced at him, though he'd been right there in the front row, a little man sitting with his hands in his lap, quiet and still as a meditating monk.

"Get off here," he said. "On the left."

Vickers did not argue. Many eyes glanced out into the darkness, but no one questioned Enoch. The bus shook as they traveled along a rutted, narrow road through a small town that seemed to be nothing more than graffiti-covered shacks and a boarded-up gas station. Four or five miles farther, Enoch told Vickers to turn left again, but this time there was no road at all, only a rough dirt path that deteriorated until it vanished completely.

Moments later, Enoch said, "Okay, stop here," and the bus groaned to a halt. Zeke stood in the aisle and looked out the window on the right side. An ominous black SUV sat in the darkness, moonlight glinting off of its surfaces. As Zeke watched, all four doors opened and a quartet of grim-faced men climbed out.

Vickers opened the door of the bus and Enoch rose, turning toward them.

"Stay here," Enoch instructed. "Not a word."

Two rows up and across the aisle, Aaron Monteforte buried his face in his hands. "Jesus Christ."

Zeke took a deep breath, waited for Enoch to step off the bus, and crouched in the aisle beside Aaron. He put a hand on the young man's arm.

"Hey, brother. Take a breath."

Aaron glanced at him, swallowed hard, and nodded. "I'm trying, Mr. Prater."

Beside him, up against the window, his dead sister had left a streak of drool on the glass. Zeke had to fight to keep from recoiling at the sight, telling himself that it was good, that body fluids meant life, but his stomach roiled in disgust.

"Zeke," he managed to say. "Call me Zeke."

Through the window beyond Trish Monteforte's drool, he saw Enoch talking with one of the men as the others unloaded two heavy gray plastic boxes from the back of the SUV. Enoch reached inside his jacket and handed over a thick envelope that Zeke realized must be cash, and then two of the men carried the plastic boxes on board the bus. Neither of the men, both young and dark-eyed Mexicans, so much as glanced up at the passengers as they set the boxes down in the aisle.

And then they were gone.

Enoch climbed back onto the bus as the SUV tore away across the ragged, dusty plain, headlights popping on, brake lights like devil's eyes in the dark.

Zeke took his seat as Vickers first closed the bus door and then rose to help Enoch open the crates. Enoch had told them what would be expected of them, so Zeke knew what was to come—they all did—but the sight of moonlight glinting off gun barrels still made him catch his breath. He'd been trained to use a gun since childhood and knew the same would be true of nearly everyone on board the bus, but these were no hunting rifles or protective sidearms. The guns in the cases were Herstals, Belgian-made pistols that fired armor-piercing rounds, so popular with the cartels that they were more commonly known by their street name, Mata Policias. Cop Killers.

Either Enoch had just bought guns from the same people who supplied the Matamoros cartel, or he'd bought guns from the cartel itself. The little man had told them as part of the plan that they'd be picking up weapons on the Mexican side of the border—trying to sneak them across would be idiotic—but the presence of the Mata Policias on the bus gave the moment a terrible, weighty reality.

"You'll each take one of these," Enoch said, a golden glow in his eyes that could not be attributed to the moonlight. When he spoke, his upper lip curled back like a wolf's. "We'll wait until it's time for us to abandon the bus, and then you'll take one gun and give it to the person you came here for. Remember why you're here and you won't hesitate. There are enough guns that you can also take one for yourself, but if you do as I ask, there should be no reason for it. Once you've played your pipes and given instructions, you'll just wait for it all to be over."

Lester cleared his throat, sitting up a little straighter in his seat, trying to regain some of the dignity stolen by riding in a school bus.

"What happens if one of them doesn't come back?" he asked. "If I send my boy in there and they shoot him full of holes—"

"I told you, he'll heal. Whatever damage they do—"

"—heals eventually," Lester interrupted. "But what about tonight? If he's too damaged to come back to where we're waiting?"

Enoch stared at him, the glow in his eyes seeming to brighten. Zeke knew that there must have been others on the bus who had questions, but Lester was the only one who had dared to ask. This close to satiating his thirst for revenge, Enoch did not want to deal with their trifling doubts and fears, that much was clear.

"Then you go in and get him," the little man said. "The cartel members inside the compound will already be dead."

Lester started to speak again, but Enoch ignored him, turning to Vickers. "Drive."

As they started moving again, bumping across hard terrain, Zeke turned to check on Savannah, whose condition seemed unchanged. He decided that was for the best. If she started to get her mind back now . . . he didn't even want to think about it.

Glancing back toward the front of the bus, the desert moon casting the interior of the bus in a pale, ghostly light, he saw Aaron Monteforte shifting uncomfortably in his seat and caught a glimpse of the reason—a pistol jutting from Aaron's rear waistband. Zeke frowned, wondering what the hell Aaron was thinking. Bringing his own weapon could have blown the whole operation if the border guards had been more vigilant.

He opened his mouth to speak, but Aaron beat him to it.

"Turn the bus around, Mr. Vickers," he called, head bowed so that his voice was slightly muffled.

"Oh God, Aaron, don't," Linda Trevino said.

Enoch turned to glare at the young man.

"Fuck you and your spooky eyes, man," Aaron said, growing more agitated. He shook his head and turned to look at his resurrected sister, reached out to touch her cheek, and then shot a hard look at Enoch. "We can't do this. You've got to turn this fucking thing around."

"Shut your mouth, son," Lester growled.

Enoch stood but made no move toward the back of the bus. He seemed to ride the juddering rumble of the bus without needing to steady himself. In the moonlight, his eyes began to turn oil-black, gleaming with a terrible, deep malignance, as if the night itself began to glow from within him.

"You agreed to this," Enoch said. "You bled for this. The bond has been forged. You can't break it now."

"Bullshit!" Aaron barked, jumping to his feet, one hand clamped on the back of the seat in front of him. "There's no way a bunch of half-dead zombies are going to kill this fucking Carlos Aguilar. He'll have a couple of dozen guys with guns around him. My sister can't even speak! She can barely make eye contact, and she's supposed to—"

"*Sit down, boy,*" Enoch said. Three words, but they reverberated through the bus as if the metal itself had spoken, the windows rattling with the power of his voice.

In that moment he did not seem like a little man at all.

"*Sit down, or I will cut your sister into pieces the way they did my daughter.*"

Aaron sat.

No one spoke.

Enoch's chest rose and fell with barely contained fury, but at last he sat as well, turning to stare straight out the windshield. In the driver's seat, Vickers's hands gripped the steering wheel tightly. The bus's headlights showed nothing ahead but scrub brush and desert but Vickers kept driving, with Enoch quietly urging him onward.

The bus shook mercilessly, and once Savannah struck her head on the window. Zeke saw her wince and his chest ached with cruel hope. If she had felt that—if it bothered her—then surely she must have been getting better. Such thoughts were the only things that kept him from screaming.

Vickers had driven through a rough no-man's-land for nearly half an hour when, at last, Enoch commanded him to bring the bus to a creaking stop. When he killed the engine and turned off the headlights, their eyes quickly adjusted to the moonlight. Zeke blinked and rubbed at the bridge of his nose and when he looked up, Enoch had stood again.

"The compound is three miles due south, on foot. If we get any closer, they'll see the headlights," he said. "So we walk from here."

Again, this was nothing they hadn't been warned about, but even if any of the proxies wanted to complain, none of them would have dared. Not now. One by one, they took out their pipes and began to play, breaking off only to issue instructions to their broken loved ones, who staggered to their feet and shuffled off the bus, trapped halfway between the living world and the land of the dead. Vickers had gotten Martha off first and Enoch had put the gun crates on their seat, so that the proxies could each take a weapon as they climbed out into the cool night.

Zeke took one of the Mata Policias and stuck it into his waistband. He took a second gun, intending to keep the first for himself, and then blew a few extra notes on the pipe, just to make sure that he had Savannah's attention and that she wouldn't fall on the steps. For a moment, his mind went back to the hour of their departure, when he'd seen Skyler standing by the roadside with her hopeful, handmade sign. COME BACK, she'd written. But out there in the Mexican desert, home had never felt so far away. The future he hoped for, days of peace and laughter for himself and Savannah, seemed little more than a dream.

Out in the middle of nowhere, the day's heat quickly vanished. Zeke saw many people shivering with the chill and it took him a moment to realize Martha Vickers was one of them. He exhaled a quiet thank-you to whatever powers might have been watching over them—if she could feel cold, maybe she really was creeping nearer to being fully alive again.

Savannah's hand brushed his. Zeke turned toward her, heart pounding. She had been standing next to him, but had she touched him on purpose? He stared at her for several seconds as more people climbed off of the bus, guns stuck in pockets or carried in hand, aimed at the ground. It struck him that he had left her sweatshirt on the bus and he started back toward it, frustrated that he had to wait for the rest to get off and not wanting to leave Savannah alone for too long. Again, he thought of Skyler and her sign. COME BACK. Zeke stood at the bus door as Arturo Sanchez climbed off. The man stroked his graying mustache and played several notes on his blood-smeared pipe, and then Zeke found himself face-to-face with the resurrected corpse of Arturo's mother. Her glazed eyes blinked and then narrowed, focusing on him, and Zeke found himself smiling at the dead woman. She'd seen him. Was aware of him. Another hopeful sign.

He had turned to say that to Arturo when the night erupted with the roar of multiple engines. Bright lights bathed the pitiful school bus from all sides.

"Mother of God," Arturo whispered, turning and trying to push his mother back onto the bus.

Zeke tightened his grip on his second gun—the one intended

for Savannah. He spun and ran toward her, instinct kicking in, knowing the thunder of those engines could only mean danger, and he would not allow her to die a second time. People were screaming around him, some picking up the barely alive and struggling to carry or drag them back toward the bus while others drew guns and aimed at the oncoming headlights.

"What the hell is this?!" Lester shouted at Vickers.

But Vickers's eyes had gone wide like an animal's and he drew Martha to him and began to cry, surrender etched deeply into his face.

Zeke reached Savannah. He stared into her eyes for a second. He knew she was in there, fanning the spark of life back into a flame, if only he could give her the time. He kissed her forehead, put one arm around her, and waited, gun ready.

"Enoch!" Lester shouted, rushing at the little man, whose eyes were once again alight with a golden glow. "What's going on?!"

"Are you blind, Mr. Keegan?" Enoch said, his words dripping with venom. "It's an ambush."

"No," Lester said, shaking his head as he backed away, running to his son but twisting around as the five raised pickup trucks charged toward them. "This ain't happening!"

"Lester!" Zeke shouted. "Get your shit together!"

He saw Lester freeze, nod, and then raise his pistol.

"All of you!" Lester shouted. "Guns up. Shoot the first son of a bitch who—"

A bullet blew out his left temple, spraying brain and bone shards onto his dead son. The gunshot echoed across the desert as Zeke screamed his friend's name and turned to see that Aaron Monteforte had fired the shot, using the gun that had been tucked into his waistband. Sweating, eyes frantic, Aaron took aim at Zeke.

"Guns down, Mr. Prater," Aaron said. "I don't want to have to kill you."

"Aaron," Zeke said. "What—"

One by one, the pickups skidded to a halt, caging them all in a lattice of headlight beams. The men who jumped out of the backs of the trucks and climbed from the cabs carried assault rifles instead of pistols.

Zeke had watched his daughter die once, and he'd die himself before he would witness her murder again.

He raised his gun and pulled the trigger.

Nothing happened.

Around him, others had done the same. Arturo Sanchez ejected the magazine, trying to figure out what the hell went wrong, but it was too late. If there had been a moment when Zeke could have punished Aaron Monteforte for his betrayal, it had already passed.

The cartel gunmen surrounded them, gun barrels taking aim, promising death.

Zeke moved himself in front of Savannah. He could feel her reedy breath against the back of his neck and prepared to die for her.

8

Don't be a hero, Zeke told himself, thinking only of Savannah. But as they were all herded together at gunpoint, their weapons torn violently from their hands, he realized that there would be no heroes that night.

The cartel gunmen stared at the resurrected dead amongst them and he caught several of the hardened killers crossing themselves and muttering quiet prayers. A few others laughed in amazement. One poked a finger through the bullet hole in Big Tim Hawkins's neck and Alma shoved him away, leading to amazed chatter among the gunmen.

"Hold up, amigo," Aaron Monteforte said, trying to extricate himself from the other pipers, all muscle and scruff and just enough bravado to veil his terror.

Aaron held his gun with the barrel aimed at Linda Trevino, who hugged her undead son, Ben—Ben, whom Savannah had once had such a crush on—and shielded him with her body. Tears streamed down Linda's face, but she did not beg to be left alone. She was smart enough to know there was little chance of that at this point.

"Put it down, asshole," one of the gunmen said to Aaron, the moonlight making the jagged scar on his left cheek look like mother-of-pearl.

"Whoa," Aaron said. "I'm with you guys."

Zeke felt bile burning up the back of his throat and his fingers flexed, either wishing for another weapon or wanting to be wrapped around Aaron Monteforte's throat, or both.

The man with the gleaming scar raised his assault rifle, braced it against his shoulder, and took aim. "Gun on the ground, *chingado*. Now."

Aaron held up his left hand and gently lowered his weapon to the dirt. "Okay, all right. But take a breath, man. I'm with you, I said. All this shit wouldn't be happening if it wasn't for me. Ask Carlos—"

A cluster of cartel thugs scattered, parting like the Red Sea as a tall man strode amongst them.

Unlike the rest, the newcomer carried no gun, only a hunting knife sheathed at his hip. His white cotton shirt and brown dress pants had clearly been tailored to fit his slim, powerful physique and seemed out of place amongst the denim and leather of the others. The shoes on his feet were of a soft leather that must have cost a fortune. With his thick mane of hair slicked back, curling at the ends, and his beard trimmed to a stylish severity, he looked as if he had just walked out of a business meeting and into a nightclub.

"Ask Carlos what?" the man inquired.

Aaron exhaled. "Carlos . . . Mr. Aguilar . . . tell 'em, please. Tell 'em I helped you."

Aguilar nodded emphatically, spreading his arms wide as if in a spirit of generosity.

"Did he help me?" Aguilar said, turning a radiant smile on his prisoners, both living and not quite. "Absolutely, he helped me. You should *all* know that. Your friend, here . . . he's been working for me for more than a year."

"*You son of a bitch!*" Alma Hawkins cried, pushing forward to loose a wad of spittle that did not reach its target. She had one hand on her roundly pregnant belly as if she could protect the baby inside . . . just as Linda Trevino held Ben and Zeke stood in front of Savannah. Behind her, Big Tim Hawkins stood numbly, his gaze following her the way it might a hypnotist's pocket watch.

Aguilar gestured the scarred man away from Aaron, walked over and picked up Aaron's gun from the ground.

"I agree with you, lady," Aguilar said, nodding again. "He is indeed a son of a bitch. Running drugs through your town. Selling to kids. Giving up the names of the motherfuckers on the Texas Border Volunteers, the guys putting my business on video for the border patrol . . . it's just un-American."

The cartel enforcer tried to keep a straight face but couldn't manage it, and his men all laughed along with him. Looks of hatred and despair appeared on the faces of the herded pipers who were clustered together with the resurrected.

"Look at that, *hermanos*. It's true." Aguilar turned to grin at his men. "I see dead people."

More laughter raced around the circle of killers. Aguilar's eyes lit up with dark intelligence and unsettling hunger.

"I mean, I've heard of this kind of shit but never thought I'd see it," he said.

Zeke felt the others closing in around him and Savannah,

everyone wanting to move as far away from the guns as they could, and he pushed back, trying to keep her safe. He glanced up and caught Tommy Jessup gazing at him with desperate eyes, silently imploring him to do something. Zeke turned away; there was nothing to be done except ride it out.

"Mr. Vickers, please," he heard someone say, but when Zeke glanced at Vickers, he saw that the man still hugged Martha close, his eyes as dead as his wife's.

Zeke glanced around and saw redheaded Harry Boyd holding the hand of his grown son, Charlie, the way he must have done when Charlie was a boy. His expression was stern, his eyes steel, just waiting. Zeke pushed past the Jessup kid and guided Savannah toward Boyd.

"Look after her, Harry," he said, giving her a last shove. Savannah shuffled enough to get to Boyd and Zeke kissed her temple without looking at her face. If he had, he knew he wouldn't have had the courage to turn away.

"We'll make a deal!" Zeke called out, pushing his way through the herd.

Half a dozen weapons swung toward him, the dark holes of their barrels almost seeming to dare him to take another step.

"What are you doing?" Arturo Sanchez hissed.

But standing out there, outside the circle of his friends and neighbors and the risen dead who comprised all the hope they had ever mustered, he could see the corpse of Lester Keegan lying in the dirt. Lester had been his best friend—he had come out here to save his son and been murdered for his trouble.

But *we can bring him back*, Zeke thought, feeling the pipe in his pocket digging into his hip. *If we're still alive to do it.*

Aguilar stroked his narrow beard, smiling beatifically. "Well, well. Which one are you?"

"Ezekiel Prater." He kept his chin up and his eyes locked on Aguilar's when he said it.

The devil arched an eyebrow. "One of the ranchers."

"That's me. One of the Border Volunteers, too. Aaron just killed Lester Keegan. Vickers and Boyd are here, too. Cassaday didn't lose anyone back in October, but we can speak for him."

Aguilar glanced at his men and then at Aaron before turning back to Zeke.

"All right, Ezekiel. Speak."

"We never wanted to come here," Zeke said, heart pounding, trying to hide his hatred of this man and his comrades. "We knew it was crazy—suicide—but we had no choice."

"Your friend Aaron told us all about it," Aguilar said, waving Aaron's gun around. "We knew you were coming, *ese*. Knew about the guns you were buying."

"Which is why the first couple of bullets in every magazine are dummies," the scarred gunman said, grinning. "Click click. *Nada*."

Aguilar laughed softly. "Yeah, that was Guillermo's idea. Pretty funny, actually. And it helped get you all the way out here."

Zeke felt like throwing up.

"The school bus was a nice touch, though," Aguilar said appreciatively.

"Please, just let us go," Linda Trevino begged.

Aguilar shot her a hard look, so Zeke shifted to block his view of the woman.

"Hold on, here's my offer," Zeke said. "Full access to all four ranches. We'll cover for you with the Border Patrol, make it a hell of a lot easier for you to get whatever you want across the river. Guns. Drugs. People. Anything."

"Really . . . ?" Aguilar said, eyes widening, impressed. "And what about the rest of your people? They're all going to go along with this?"

Zeke glanced around at the others, waiting for an argument, but nobody dared to say a word.

"They are," he said firmly.

"Well. This I've gotta think about," Aguilar replied, a jaunty sort of amusement coming into his eyes.

He turned and shot Aaron Monteforte in the head with his own gun.

Screams burst from the herded pipers as Aaron crumpled to the ground. Zeke flinched, but somehow he found it within himself not to cry out or run back into the cluster of familiar faces. Unlike his father and grandfather, he'd never been to war, but those men had taught him a thing or two about fear and cowardice. Fear was the real enemy, the one foe that had to be defeated. For himself—for his own safety—Zeke could do that.

It was his fear for Savannah that he could not overcome.

"Ah, damn it," Aguilar said, looking down in dismay at the spots of blood on his expensive white shirt. "Messy. But . . . if we're going to make some kind of deal, we couldn't have him around. A man who will betray his friends cannot be trusted. His sister died that night in your town, you know? She wasn't supposed to be there. He thought she had gone to Hidalgo to visit friends. My men murdered his sister, and he still called to tell me what you were all planning. What a pal."

Aguilar spit on Aaron's ruined face, the second time he'd been spit on in mere minutes. Zeke saw that Aaron had fallen on his left side, baring the Reaper tattoo on his right biceps and burying the angel on his left, and that seemed only right.

"He used to work on my ranch," Zeke said, gazed fixed on Aguilar. "I was fond of him back then, but as of this moment, I can't say as I'm sorry the son of a bitch is dead."

Aguilar began to walk, gun pointed at the ground as he circled the cluster of prisoners. There were more than forty of them and half that number of cartel killers, but the gunmen were ranged about them in a circle like a pack of wolves. Aguilar moved through the open space that separated the wolves from their prey.

"I'm not going to lie to you, Ezekiel," Aguilar said, his voice carried on the desert wind though Zeke couldn't see him from the other side of the circle. "I've just been having a little fun with you. We spend so much time on business that when we get an opportunity to play, it's hard to resist. You of course know that if word got out that we let even one of you live . . ."

Prayers went up from the group, and curses followed in equal measure.

"Listen to me, Carlos," Zeke said. "If you're worried about how it'll look, what kind of message you'd be sending, think about how it will look when word gets out that you've staked a claim in Hidalgo County, that you've got an open pipeline into the U.S. Or how it'll look that you turned such a thing down."

Aguilar had made it three-quarters of the way around the circle and come back into view. Zeke glanced at the faces of his friends and neighbors and the vacant gazes of the dead and he held his breath.

"It would be an interesting experiment," Aguilar admitted. Zeke exhaled, glanced over in search of Savannah's face and did not see her. "But if we were to negotiate, there is only one place to start."

"Where's that?"

Aguilar's smile vanished and the amusement bled from his eyes, revealing only ice beneath. He turned to his prisoners with a snarl.

"Which one of you is Enoch Stroud?"

Zeke blinked several times and shook his head. It felt as if he'd just woken up from a dream in which Enoch had never existed. Until the moment Aguilar had mentioned his name, he had forgotten all about the little hoodoo man. Enoch had come to them, had raised their dead and dragged them all down here to Mexico, and yet for a few minutes it was as if he had been erased from Zeke's mind.

A ripple of confusion went through the pipers and they

began to shuffle aside, expanding the circle, nudging and guiding the blank-faced undead until a path had formed among them leading to a circle within the circle. At its center, alone, Enoch stood staring at Carlos Aguilar with murder in his eyes.

"How the hell . . . ?" Harry Boyd said. "For a minute there I didn't remember the little creep existed."

Aguilar aimed his gun at Enoch and the pipers and their dead scuttled farther away. The cartel killers raised the barrels of their weapons and barked orders in English and Spanish, making sure no one tried to make a run for it.

"You?" Aguilar scoffed. "You're the great *brujo? El nigromante?*"

Enoch said nothing, but Aguilar walked toward him, pausing to look more closely at the resurrected dead. He glanced at Charlie Boyd and Big Tim, but when he got to Martha Vickers, he reached out and ran a finger over the strange new fontanel skin growing over her head wound.

"Oh, you're going to teach me how to do this," Aguilar said, turning to stare at Enoch. "Whatever it is, I want to learn. When one of my people is killed, I want to be able to bring them back."

Enoch's gaze glimmered with a familiar yellow light, but it was as if an eclipse were taking place in his eyes. They turned black and the little man seemed to darken, as if the moonlight could no longer find him.

"*Chingate,*" Enoch muttered.

Aguilar sneered, pointing the gun at Enoch's forehead. "Fuck myself? Fuck you, *chilito.* You want revenge because I killed your daughter? Big deal. I killed a lot of people's daughters, and their sons, too. That's what we *do*, asshole. You get in the way and you get *dead.*"

He gestured toward the people gathered around them.

"Maybe you got some black magic in you, brought these people back to life. But now you got a chance to keep them alive . . . them and the rest of the idiots you brought down here with you. You've got five seconds, man. You gonna teach me, or am I going to put a bullet in your heart?"

Zeke caught a glimpse of Savannah, standing behind Harry and Charlie Boyd. He mentally urged her to retreat, to hide herself more deeply among the others. For a second, he thought she had seen him, that she had returned his gaze, but then Aguilar started marching back and forth in the gap, counting.

"One. Two. Three."

Aguilar glanced over at Zeke and shrugged as if to say he was trying his best here.

"Enoch!" Zeke shouted. "For God's sake—"

"Four!" Aguilar barked, turning on Enoch with a venomous glare. Then he sniffed, as if he couldn't quite summon a laugh, and shook his head. "Ah, fuck it."

He shot Enoch twice in the chest.

"No!" Zeke roared, rushing toward the widening gap between the two frantic groups of prisoners and then staggering to a halt, staring in astonishment.

Enoch had barely flinched. Blood began to soak through his shirt.

"You want to talk about making deals?" Enoch said, eyes so black they made the night seem bright. "I made a lot of them, Carlos—deals with every devil who would listen. You cut my daughter into pieces and I'm going to do the same to you, first here, and then down in hell, for every minute of eternity."

Aguilar shot Enoch twice more in the chest and then once in the forehead. The force of the gunshots knocked Enoch down, blood flying, as Aguilar rapidly pulled the trigger on an empty chamber.

Enoch lay on the ground, half curled into a fetal position, chuffing with laughter as blood drooled from his lips.

"Guillermo!" Aguilar shouted, and the scarred man rushed over to hand him an assault rifle.

He turned the gun on Enoch, bullets erupting from the barrel, blowing holes in the little conjuror at close range, turning his body to bloody wreckage. When the gunfire stopped, it echoed out across the desert and the smell of oil and cordite floated on the air. The good citizens of Lansdale, Texas, now so very far from home, wept and prayed, and Alma Hawkins fell to her knees and sobbed loudly, cradling her belly in both arms.

Zeke felt tethered to Savannah by some invisible umbilical. Carefully, not wanting to spook Aguilar or draw attention to his daughter, he started moving toward her. Harry Boyd stood by Savannah with his son, visibly struggling against the urge to fight back.

No, Harry. No, don't do it, please don't do it, Zeke thought.

"Damn. That's too bad," Aguilar said, scanning the faces of his prisoners and then looking beyond them, to his men. "It would've been pretty useful, being able to bring you sad *culeros* back from the dead if necessary, but I guess we'll have to make use of the dead folks we've got right here."

Ice ran through Zeke's veins. He couldn't breathe, could only stare at Aguilar's grinning face.

"Nothing like slave labor," Aguilar said, admiring the size of Big Tim Hawkins. "Especially when the rest of the world thinks they're dead anyway and nobody's gonna come looking for them."

Aguilar's grin turned sly. He approached Harry and Charlie Boyd and Zeke froze, trying to will the killer away, wishing him upon anyone else, damning any of the others to whatever suffering might be in store as long as Savannah could live.

Not again.

But Aguilar waved Harry aside with the assault rifle and— eyes downcast with shame—Harry gave Charlie a shove and let the devil pass.

"Beautiful," Aguilar said. "Some of them might be more useful than others." He reached out with his left hand to caress Savannah's brown cheek, tracing a finger along the freckles on the bridge of her nose.

Zeke was sure he saw her wince. It felt like a trigger in his heart.

"*Don't you fucking touch her, you son of a bitch!*" he roared, rushing at Aguilar. "*You killed her once! Isn't that enough?!*"

A big hand grabbed his arm, holding him back, and Zeke whipped around to see that Vickers had finally woken from the fog of his grief. Vickers shook his head, eyes pleading with Zeke to say nothing more. But Zeke knew nothing he did would make a difference in the end.

"Enough?" Aguilar said. "I guess not."

Zeke screamed as Aguilar shot Savannah in the chest and belly. As she crumpled to the ground, he tore free of Vickers's grasp and lunged. Aguilar turned and the gun barked again, three or four rounds stitching across Zeke's chest; the pain searing through him was nothing compared to the anguish in his soul.

He fell face-first, kicking up dust as he skidded in the dirt on his stomach. The smell of his own blood filled his nostrils, his vision already dimming.

Unable to do more than twitch and loll his head to one side, he watched as Aguilar backed out of the gap among his prisoners. The rest of the cartel killers tightened the circle, wolves finally drawing near at the scent of blood.

"Fuck it," Aguilar said. "Kill them all."

The gunfire seemed almost quiet compared to the screams.

9

Zeke drew a long, gasping breath, eyelids dragging open. He could feel the chilly night air on his face but nothing else, save for a dreadful heaviness, as if his body had been submerged in fresh cement. His breaths came at long intervals, wet and ragged, each of them a chore. His mouth opened and closed and he forced himself to take a single breath through his nose.

The copper stink of blood filled his head and he squeezed his eyes shut, trying to clear his vision, only to discover that the blurriness and the blackness that seeped in at the corners of his eyes would not go away. The stars above him were dimming, the moonlight fading. A rush of sound filled his ears and he felt himself flinch, but when he took another breath, he realized the barrage of thunder was nothing but the memory of gunfire, that the bullets were now only ghosts, their voices echoing across the desert.

Dying, he thought, the cold weight on his chest heavier. Zeke strained to move and succeeded in shifting his body just enough to feel things tearing inside him. He didn't have the strength to scream.

Savannah, he thought. *My baby girl. I'm sorry. I hope you're with your mother now.*

The cold weight of his flesh began to lift and he felt a lightness spread through him. His head lolled to one side, the shadows that veiled his eyes deepening. Yet he saw the bodies that lay around him and recognized the long bone pipe clutched in one ruined hand. The blood smears originally painted onto the pipe had been obscured by a new flow of blood, and the hand-carved pipe seemed to soak it in.

So much for the hoodoo man.

But then the bloody hand twitched. Enoch had been torn apart by bullets, body a blood-soaked mess, but now his fingers gripped the pipe and he sat up. Through darkening vision, Zeke watched Enoch bring the pipe to his lips. A portion of the little man's skull had been obliterated, but his eyes glowed with bright golden light as he began to play a variation on those same ugly, powerful notes.

Zeke felt nothing.

He forgot to breathe.

He did not close his eyes, but they went dark, nevertheless.

10

When his eyes open, his first reaction is relief. The ceiling over-head is the ceiling of his bedroom, with the frosted glass dome light fixture that Anarosa chose for the room. He closes his eyes again, just for a moment, and lets out a wheezy breath of grat-itude before opening them again.

Not dead.

But then he tries to move and cannot manage it. Not a twitch. Fear floods through him and he thinks about where the bullets struck and realizes that he is paralyzed, that one of them must have severed his spine.

Someone moves off to the left of his bed. He hears a soft female sigh and thinks for just a moment that it must be Sky-ler . . . and then she moves toward him, standing beside the bed, filling his field of vision, and he sees that it is not.

It's Savannah, whole and beautiful, alive and well. Her hair is tied back tightly and she wears no makeup, but she is so pretty that it fills his heart just to see her. His baby girl. Tears spill from her eyes as she gazes down at him and he wants to take her hand, to hold her and speak a father's love for his daughter, but he is frozen.

"Oh, Daddy, I'm sorry," she says, voice breaking. "It was the only way."

Only when she lifts it to her lips does he see the small bone pipe in her hand, his name scrawled upon it in her blood.

A figure moves to the foot of the bed and he realizes that it is Enoch, also whole and healed.

And Savannah begins to play.

A Bad Season for Necromancy
DAVID LISS

Few, perhaps, are the children who, after the expiration of some months or years, would sincerely rejoice in the resurrection of their parents.

—Edward Gibbon

It would happen, from time to time, that my father would offer me advice that, while not precisely wise, was neither altogether foolish. Given that he was a man who enjoyed boxing my ears, bloodying my nose, kicking me in the arse and testicles, sticking me with needles, on occasion branding me with an iron, or otherwise causing pain, misery, and scarring, advice was always more pleasant than other sorts of fatherly attention.

The last such morsel of wisdom was proffered perhaps three weeks before I rebelled against his tyranny by striking him in the face with a hammer and running off with his fortune. My father, having learned that he had not, in fact, been clapped by the whore he currently favored, had been in a reflective mood, and with his mustaches only moderately flecked with beef and pudding crumbs, he turned to me with something not entirely unlike paternal regard. Spitting upon the floor, by way of introducing a new topic of conversation, he observed that there are but two sorts of people in the world, villains and victims, and that a man must be determined to be one lest he make the error of becoming the other.

I prefer not to embrace so dark a view of the human nature, but a man in my condition might easily fall into the habit of hedging his bets and living as though these words contain at least a hint of truth.

The fortune I took from my father that memorable day of hammer-swinging was in excess of three hundred pounds, the greatest quantity of money he had ever possessed, and certainly the greatest he would ever be likely to possess. I knew that I would never have a better opportunity to escape his clutches, for the prize was tempting and the enthusiasm of his celebration was, if not without precedent, at least unlikely to be exceeded.

We were staying in a delightfully indifferent inn in Nottingham at the time, notable for the beauty and business sense of its serving girls. The very day I set my mind to do this thing, my father was kind enough to offer me an excellent opportunity. While he completed a vigorous bout of drinking and whoring, I lay upon my bed with my eyes open, awaiting his return. At last I heard him fumble with the unlocked door, until by some miracle of coordination he managed to operate the machine as its designers intended, cause the door to—behold the miracle!— swing open. Further advertising the likely success of my venture, my father dropped to the floor and, after a moment of careful consideration, crawled drunkenly toward his bed, resting himself at last upon a spot very near his intended destination. He lay still for a moment, then raised his head and vomited cathartically. This jetsam then served as a most agreeable pillow on which he could lay his weary head as he contentedly embraced oblivion.

For all his faults, my father was a patient man and a perceptive one, and I was haunted by the fear that he knew precisely what I intended. I am inclined toward the impulsive, but I made myself wait perhaps a quarter of an hour before making my move. I might have waited longer, but the stench of vomit was an encouragement not to be ignored, and his snoring was loud, gurgling, and undeniably convincing.

In the dim glow of the rushlight, I managed to collect his recently acquired sack of bank notes, coins, and jewels. I donned my inferior set of boots and had just begun to turn the door handle when, like a mythic creature rising from its grave, my father shot upright and rushed toward me. His teeth shone from the darkness, and I saw chunks of his vomitus clinging to his three days of beard. His hair, still long and thick though he was upwards of forty years of age, was wild like a demon's, and his eyes were wide with rage. Some instinct, perhaps a preternatural sense of avarice, had informed him of what I intended, and nothing could induce him to embrace sleep when his hard-won money was about to bid him farewell.

I was prepared for violence, if not specifically from my father. One does not commence to take a fortune out into the night without considering the possibility of assault, and I had hung a mason's hammer on my belt. My mind driven now only by fear, I unlooped the hammer and struck my father in the cheek. It was a blind swing and a reflexive impulse. I have never loved violence. Much to my father's disgust, I have shrunk from it and endured his mockery while I refused to beat or cut or stab our victims. Yet, so great was my will to preserve my life and money, I did not hesitate to strike him now.

He squeaked like a mouse in a cat's jaws, and he fell to the floor. Then, without thinking, I bent over him and philosophically considered the merits of striking him in the face once more. It was as much as he deserved, you may be sure. A thousand memories of closed-fist blows to the gut, of sticks and canes against my buttocks and sacks of walnuts to the back of my head, came rushing at me. Another blow—a disfiguring blow, even a killing blow—would have been no more than justice, but as a parting gift to the man who had sired me, I spared his life and did not strike him a second time. He had, after all, taught me the importance of filial duty, and while, like him, I am apt to be vengeful, I am unlike him in my inclination toward mercy.

All of this excitement took place in December of 1712, when I was but two and twenty. I fled Nottingham with a staggering sum of money, an amount that would have kept my father in drink and whores and gaming for more than six months. Had I so chosen, I could have taken that same amount and rented some property in a quiet village somewhere. In such a state, I might have lived out my days in moderate comfort. I might have cultivated land and raised cattle. An investment of that sort would have left me with half my stolen wealth in hand and set aside for unplanned contingencies so that I might never fear want or deprivation.

That would have been the best course, but I knew I would not be happy. Though I despised my father, I was his son. Since I was old enough to wear long pants, I had been raised a schemer and a rogue, a trickster and a thief. I knew no way of living but stealing and cheating and deception. I did not want to continue to live thus, but I certainly did not wish to grow old planting crops and shoveling manure. I was too clever and too handsome for such a fate. A life of blistered hands and an aching back was not for the likes of me. It was a mode of living that struck me on the one hand as honest, but on the other as unpleasant.

As I strode away into the cold countryside, warmed by the memory of having finally escaped my father, I realized that what I wanted was to become a gentleman of leisure. I would be willing to set aside all inclination to steal and cheat and deceive if, in exchange, I did not have to endure the indignity of hard labor and long days and a meager living. I thought it a rather decent sort of compromise.

Despite my father's pernicious influence, however, I was a far more moral person than he, and certainly more moral than he had wished me to be. Before the sun had risen, I knew I had found my course. I would do the moral thing. I would use my stolen money to pretend to be a gentleman and win the heart and hand of a young lady of property. Or, if absolutely necessary, an old lady of property. I hoped it would be a young one.

I now wave the magic wand of narrative and transport my reader nearly a year into the future and scores of miles to the south. These miles were not traversed directly, however, for before turning my attention to London, I spent several weeks in Cardiff. Why should I venture to so remote a corner of the kingdom, you may wonder. In part, because I wished to set aside my impulsive nature. I wished to plan my actions with care. In Cardiff, I kept my ears and eyes open that I might construct a plausible story, so when I came to London, I would come not as myself, but as Reginald January, son of William January, an Englishman who had made his home in the remote fields outside the Welsh capital.

There was no William January, but his sort most certainly existed, the man who wished to retreat from the world and took up residence in the obscure countryside, where his quiet was disturbed only by the song of birds, the barking of his dogs, and the occasional marble-mouthed utterance of his Welsh servants or neighbors. This species of gentleman rarely wished to be troubled by his own children, and so he would send his sons to England for their education.

My story, then, while not a common one, was nevertheless plausible. My father was a wealthy landowner, having made his fortune trading in the Dutch colonies and in the Japans. He had seen and, if rumors were to be believed, done many terrible things in those years, and so as soon as circumstance permitted, he retired to live out his years in quiet. I, his far less rusticated son and heir to his considerable wealth, had come to London to enjoy the fruits of my father's melancholy years of robbing, raping, and murdering brown savages.

I obtained fine clothes, rented a lovely home on the fashionable side of Charing Cross, and commenced my new life, just in time for the season, as a single gentleman with more time and wealth than purpose. I dedicated myself to establishing a reputation as a man who enjoyed the arts and theater and opera, who attended church with regularity and proper, though never excessive, piety. Other than religious nonsense, these things were true of me. It had suited my father to raise me to impersonate a child, and later a man, of means, and so I had received an education. As a result, I had an appreciation of the arts, and those first weeks in London, when I had the opportunity and the silver to indulge my interests, were some of the happiest of my life. At long last, I was where I belonged. I filled my eyes and my mind with delights of the intellect and artistic wonder. I needed only to make certain I could remain there.

For that to happen, I had to establish the most advantageous connections, and so I attached myself to young men much like the one I pretended to be. I was, however, slightly superior to all of them. I might accompany some of my new friends to a gaming room, but while I never gamed myself, neither did I priggishly lecture or condemn those who did. I regularly, but not frequently, gave to the needy upon the street. I subscribed to several books of sermons and a few volumes of poetry, but only those written by reputable scribblers and never the scandalous ones. And to my new friends I hinted, in half-muttered and blushing confessions, spoken only on those rare occasions when I'd had a glass too many, that I was of a mind to marry. I wanted a wife, and children to dandle upon my knee, and the quiet comforts of domesticity. My friends would then blush for me, for I was young and rich and handsome—far more handsome than they—and I ought to enjoy these years of liberty. There was time enough for marriage when I was grown old and fat. They mocked me for my tender heart, but the unmarried ladies paid attention.

I truly hoped this scheme would work, because three hundred pounds is spent very quickly in fashionable London, and I was now accumulating debts at an alarming rate. I believed I had two months at the most before I could no longer politely dodge bills, at which point my creditors would grow restive and my reputation begin to crumble. It was marry well and marry soon, or give up the scheme as a bad job.

It was during this period, as I began to worry that my investment would yield nothing, that at a small gathering I was introduced to the ladies known about town as the Four Widows. These were the most prized women in London, a quartet of fashionable charmers, joined by the common fate of being young and rich, beauties whose husbands—all considerably older—had done them the great favor of dying early in their marriages.

No hundred women in London were pursued as energetically as these four, each of whom was worth at least six or seven thousand a year. Their every social activity was reported upon by the newspapers and magazines. The clothes they wore, the food they ate, and the plays they attended became instantly fashionable. Their very desirability made them unobtainable, but my father had taught me—perhaps another piece of anomalously good advice—that the more an object was believed unobtainable, the more accessible it was to a man of daring.

I chose to be a man of daring. I would make one of those widows my own, and I cared not which one.

*   *   *

Or so I said. I selected for my prize Lady Caroline Worthington, because while I wished to be a man of daring, I did not choose to be a man of excessive daring. Lady Caroline was the least pursued of the widows because she was judged the plainest by a critical world. I certainly thought her not very pretty when I first met her, and when I first set my sights upon her, but how wrong was the world and how wrong was I. Lady Caroline was, in fact, the most beautiful of the four, perhaps the most beautiful of women, but hers was a subtle beauty, the sort a man did not notice at first but that crept upon him at a slow and steady pace until, one day, he found that this was loveliness of a species so powerful, so overwhelming, it froze the air within his lungs.

I shall spare you the details of the courtship. Suffice it to say that I made a point of finding myself in Lady Caroline's way. Shortly after we met, events conspired so that we had mutual friends and we moved in mutual circles. We found ourselves near one another at gatherings, at balls, and at operas. We would talk and I watched her lovely gray eyes light up as she discovered that her views on religion and politics and literature were mirrored by mine. Yes, I conducted researches to make certain I knew of her opinions, that she might discover we were of like minds, but we *were* of like minds. I might have anticipated her views, because, indeed, I shared them with her, and conversation with Lady Caroline was always a true delight.

We would spend hours together, talking upon subjects about which she cared so passionately, and she would sometimes catch herself and blush at her enthusiasm, which I found charming beyond words. Nowhere could a man find a woman more clever and modest and kind. Had she been penniless, I would have done anything to possess her. But she was rich, and that was ever so much better.

The enormity of my love would amount to very little, however, if the lady did not love me in return. My first hint that I might meet success came on a brisk Sunday afternoon in September of 1713, as we strolled with the bon ton through St. James's Park. The air was cool but not cold—winter had announced its imminent arrival, so all of London was out, enjoying the weather while the opportunity allowed it. Here were great lords upon their horses and ladies in their carriages. Everyone wore their finery, and those of us who chose to display ourselves on foot walked in easy satisfaction, the sun upon our faces. There were suits and dresses in every color of the rainbow, and silver and gold thread sparkled like the stars of the heavens. Lap dogs merrily chased peacocks. It was a glorious day to be a man of means, or to be masquerading as one.

Lady Caroline looked particularly resplendent in a gown of exquisitely pale yellow and embossed with elaborate floral embroidery. Her hat, wide brimmed and feathered, sat atop her piled hair, which some fools called mousy in color but I thought the most charming shade of brown. More than anything, however, Lady Caroline smiled with the pure pleasure of being in good company and in good health and in fine weather. She glowed in her joy and vitality, and there is nothing more alluring than the proximity of a woman who feels alive, and, I fancied, in love.

I flatter myself that I looked quite well in my own red velvet suit with large silver buttons, beneath it a sky-blue waistcoat, and beneath that a shirt that erupted with frills like the froth of the ocean. My newly made queue periwig showed off my face to its finest advantage, and not a few women stopped to look at me, but though they might have regarded me as the finest specimen of manhood in the park, I had eyes for none of them. I did not so much as notice when they stared or gestured toward me with their fans or giggled behind their gloved hands. I was aware of none of it, but Lady Caroline saw it all. She watched them notice me, and she watched me ignore them. She saw that I looked at no woman but her, and she smiled.

We walked in easy and, I imagined, libidinous silence for some time, surrounded by our companions. Then fate handed me a great favor. The other widows strayed hither. The other suitors strayed yon. Lady Caroline and I were alone—no one within fifteen feet of us in that great Sunday throng. It was as close to privacy as the St. James procession would afford.

"Mr. January," she said, casting those lovely gray eyes downward. "I hope you do not harbor any misconceptions about our friendship." Her cheeks turned pink, and she pressed her red lips together until they were as pale as her lovely skin.

"If you are my friend," I said, "then I am the happiest of men."

She smiled and blushed more deeply and took a moment to collect her thoughts. "Sir, I will be plain with you for the regard in which I hold you. I do not seek to marry again. Not now. Perhaps not ever."

"And that is what you think?" I asked her. "I seek out your company because I wish to marry you? Are you so certain that I have no interest in your ideas and your conversation and your taste?"

"I know you and I are very companionable," she said, looking less certain of herself. Perhaps she had hoped I would not wish to discuss this topic at length but merely take my marching orders. I was too clever for that. "It is because we are so companionable that I must be direct with you. I cannot allow you to think I would lead you where we cannot go. My marriage to Lord Albert was not a happy one. I am not so naïve to think you have not heard the rumors."

Of course I had heard the rumors. Sir Albert was some thirty years Lady Caroline's senior, perhaps fifty or fifty-five. He was greatly fat and inclined to excessive perspiration and flatulence and the stench that accompanied such leaky vessels. Beyond his lack of personal charms, Sir Albert was said to be a demon of a man. He was not, like my father, inclined to violence, but he was cruel, delighting in humiliating and insulting his wife, mocking her before her friends and his. I had heard that he would sometimes come home drunk with whores and rut loudly within her hearing. This, however, was preferable to the times he turned his slobbering attentions upon his wife. I had heard it all. Sir Albert had been a vile brute, and his death had been a gift of the heavens to Lady Caroline.

"I do not listen to gossip," I told her.

"Then listen to me," she said with a resoluteness I could not but admire. "I see marriage as nothing but a state of enslavement. My father sold me to a horrible man because Sir Albert was a baronet and he wished his family name to rise in the world through his daughter. Only once my husband died did my own inheritance come into my possession, and now that it is mine, that I am a free and independent woman, I shall never enslave myself again." She now stopped and looked at me directly. Her face was red, but with anger now, not embarrassment. Her eyes were moist with tears, and she looked like a being divine. "I shall always enjoy your company, Mr. January, as long as you enjoy mine, but there can be no more than that. You are a gentleman of fortune, and perhaps you are too modest to see how women admire you, but they do. You can have your pick of them."

I reached out to take her hand but then pulled it back—a calculated move of tenderness and restraint. Ladies always find it affecting. "The admiration of women I do not know is of no importance to me. You, however, are of the utmost importance. But understand that I am not a predator, Lady Caroline, and you are not my prey. I seek nothing but to be in your presence in any capacity that you will have me. I shall be content with as little as you choose to offer, and I shall never ask you for anything more."

She nodded and we walked on. Her face, I observed from the

corner of her eye, changed moment by moment—satisfaction, relief, sorrow, pride. She had made her wishes known. She would not marry me. She would not marry anyone.

For my part, I showed no expression, certainly not my true one, which was joy. This was a woman with a pure soul and a good heart. She was as unblemished in her character as a creature of flesh could be, and she had made her wishes known—both those of which she spoke and those which she did not intend to reveal. I believed she and I would be married within the month.

Only one week later, I exited the Drury Lane theater with Lady Caroline and nearly a dozen others, including the other members of the widows' quartet. We had just seen Addison's *Cato* and stood upon the street, taking in the power and pathos of Mr. Booth's performance while we waited for our servants to fetch our carriages. It was a cool night, cloudless and bright with stars. About us, peddlers cried out their pies and oysters and apples to the emerging crowd. Whores beckoned to gentlemen. Street acrobats walked upon their hands. Legless beggars walked upon their hands as well, dragging their stumps through the refuse. Hungry children wept for food. It was a London night in all its beauty and chaos and misery.

There, upon those magical streets, shivering in the cool air, Lady Caroline stood next to me in easy silence. We did not speak, but it was not for lack of words, but rather for their unimportance. She looked at me and I at her, and I sensed that my devotion, my kindness, my compatibility, and my apparent willingness not to seek her hand had all done their work.

Here she was, this marvelous woman with her broad face and narrow eyebrows and heavy jaw—all features that should have made her unlovely, and when I looked at her, I thought her lovelier than anything imaginable. And here was I, in all my manly beauty, oblivious to my charms, with eyes only for her. She reached out, her fingers crooked and tentative, and took my hand in hers. I felt the smoothness of her glove against my own, and my heart was carried aloft upon the delicious entangling of our satin-clad fingers. I knew that we were meant to be together, and that we would be together, and that any difficulties our love might face—such as her inevitable discovery that I was a penniless charlatan—would be both temporary and easily sorted.

That was the moment my father appeared before us.

He was not there, and then he was, a horrifying mask of ugliness with his flattened nose and broken teeth and crooked jaw, courtesy of my hammer blow. Before I had time to fully understand what I gazed upon, he reached out and gave one of Lady Caroline's breasts a hard squeeze. She cried out, and as I turned, he struck me in the face. He did not use a hammer, which was a kindness to be sure. I was horrified and terrified and in no inconsiderable amount of pain, but I was also a little bit grateful. When my father was involved, things could always be worse. And then they often were.

I lay upon the ground, mud and horse shit upon my clothes and in my hair. My jaw ached where my father had hit me. He stood over me like a colossus, waving his fist in the air while my good-hearted Caroline and our friends watched.

"Someone do something!" cried Mr. Langham, a gentleman who had never much cared for me, for he had had designs upon Lady Caroline himself. "Someone stop that man!" Who that someone might be, if not himself, he did not suggest, though I doubt he intended one of the ladies ought to take on the fury of my father. I do believe he would have preferred such an outcome, however, than be forced to throw himself into the fray.

While I readily condemn him for his cowardice, I am not entirely without sympathy. My father was a tall man, broad in the shoulders and thick in the arms. He wore his hair natural and long and wild, and while he had never been what might be called handsome—I was fortunate enough to take my looks from my mother—the recent reordering of his face, courtesy of my mason's hammer, had rendered him something of a grotesque. Beneath the scruff of his negligent beard, his face was like that of a smashed statue, put back together with some pieces missing.

"Reginald January, is it?" my father demanded to my prostrate form. "Son of a wealthy gentleman in Wales, is it? You thought I would not discover you? This is no gentleman's son, but my own," he told the onlookers, including the horrified Lady Caroline. "His money is but a fantasy, cobbled together with debt and the rhino he stole from his own father."

Here was the undoing of all my work, and for nothing more than petty revenge—though, it was true, it was a sentiment I knew well. My father, like me, was a man inclined to indulge the need for vengeance, but he had always valued money over justice, so I knew that he must have been truly enraged. If he had not been, he would have found me in private, demanding that I turn my scheme into his scheme. He would have insisted I steal from Lady Caroline or my new friends and deliver to him my takings, or he would expose me or kill the woman I cared for or some other terrible thing. That he thought nothing of money, and only of ruin, meant that I had taken the most vicious and dangerous man I had ever known and turned him into something far worse.

I was dazed, in equal parts by the surprise of seeing him there, with my refined new friends, and partly by the blow to my jaw. However, my senses were now returning to me and I knew that I could not let him continue. If I could make him stop talking now, this moment, then perhaps I might undo the damage he had done. I could claim he was a madman, one I had never before seen and hoped never to see again. I needed that

he would say no more, or better yet, say other, equally preposterous things—makes accusations about Mr. Langham or the
widows or anyone else besides me.

I began to push myself off the ground. My jaw and my head
both pounded, but there would be time later for pain. Now I
had to do something.

"Look here, fellow," I managed to say. "You mayn't attack total
strangers upon the street, nor speak of absurd accusations to
me—or to *anyone else* here."

I hoped he would take my meaning, but he only cackled a
broken-toothed laugh. "My son, my own son, who I raised without his whore mother, has embarked upon a scheme to trick you
all," he explained to everyone, and to Lady Caroline in particular.
He had evidently observed my particular interest in her. "I should
love him for it if he had but included me in his plans, but he is
a fiend, worse than his own father, from whom he stole. And
now, out of bitterness, I will set his own plans to ruin."

"Mr. January . . . ," Lady Caroline managed to say. She put a
gloved hand to her red mouth. "Can it be?"

"Of course not," I croaked. I pushed myself up into a sitting
position, but my father rewarded me with a kick to the side of
my head, and down into the mud and shit I went once more.

"He lies, you silly tart," my father said. "I raised him for just
this purpose, to be the sort of cove what could insert himself
among you rich arse-lickers and not be sniffed out. Though I'll
reckon he's sniffed you where that dress don't show."

My Caroline, my beautiful, lovely, sweet, and charming Caroline, gasped as though struck. She looked at me in horror, and
what was worse, far worse, she looked at my father as though
he were a savior. It was beyond what a man could be asked to
endure.

"Look here, you horrible stranger!" I said. "Flee while you
can!"

I reached to my side and drew my blade as I tried to rise from the muck. My hand, however, slipped and I fell back down. With unstoppable speed, my father reached down, grabbed the hanger from my hand, and wielded it himself. Now he stood above me, my own sword at the ready, prepared to skewer his own son.

"Were you prepared to use a sword as well as wear it, you would not be here tonight, for if you were less a coward, you would have stabbed me back in Nottingham. But you weren't man enough. You dared not do the deed, and so your half measures come back to ruin you. I will show you how it is done, so that the matter is final."

I looked at Lady Caroline, who stood frozen in fear and horror. I told myself I could still survive this encounter and restore my name. I needed to think. My father had always been stronger than I and more reckless and brutal, but I was by far the cleverer. Now was the time to prove it. I needed a scheme, but none came to me.

"I shall endure you no more!" cried my father. His face was the color of freshly spilled blood, and his eyes were as round as coins. He raised the sword above his head, holding it in both hands as he prepared to bring it down—only not yet. He had a bit of speechifying to do first. "I am this wretch's father, and he is a rogue who has nothing and wishes to steal what is yours. He struck me, his own father, in the face with a hammer, and he stole my money, recently stolen itself from a knave such as one of you. As I lay there, in a pile of my own blood, coughing up my own teeth, I vowed revenge. I would not rest, no, not for a minute, until I had ruined him as he ruined me. I would work tirelessly—"

This was as much of his moving address as we were to be allowed to enjoy, for at this point, my father stopped and staggered backward, releasing his grip upon my hanger. He clenched his jaw and set his right arm upon the left portion of his chest, clutching at the flesh upon his heart as though he wished to tear that organ from his breast. He then vomited forcefully upon Lady Caroline, dropped to his knees, and then fell, face-first, into the street kennel.

Only minutes after ruining my life, my father, the worst and most dangerous man I had ever known, was dead, destroyed from the inside as his own body rebelled against him. Given the damage he had done first, I could take no joy in it.

I would say that I will spare my readers the scene that followed, but in truth, I would prefer to spare myself. I cannot recall without wincing the sight of Lady Caroline covered with my father's dying expulsion. Far worse was the more metaphorical expectoration that had landed upon my lady's ears. She now stared at me with shock and horror. I had, at last, made it back to my feet, and while any lady of quality would have been disgusted to see the man with whom she had just held hands now covered with mud and horse excrement and his own blood, her revulsion was not for my appearance. She did not ask if the accusations were true. She did not have to.

Perhaps we would have spoken more, but Susan Harrow, one of the other widows, pulled her away. Mrs. Harrow had always been skeptical and contemptuous of me. Perhaps she had doubted what I claimed to be, but more likely, she considered the son of a merchant, lately of Wales, to be beneath her friend's dignity. Now she rejoiced that her suspicions were confirmed and that I was even more low than she had originally considered.

My time, I now knew, was limited. It would be only a matter of days, if not hours, before news of this incident spread through the city. Mr. Reginald January, so lately seen with the Four Widows, gentleman of fashion about town, was an imposter and a schemer. Word would pass from tea garden to coffeehouse. Notices would appear in the newspapers and then, of course, would come the creditors, scrambling upon and over and under and around one another like beetles to be first to claim what little they could of my ersatz estate. It was all coming unmade.

But if collapse was imminent, it was not immediate. I yet had time to return home, clean myself, and collect as much of my ill-gotten property as possible before the bill collectors began to spring up like mushrooms. No one would be by that day, and perhaps the next. Certainly, I did not have to let anyone in, and as today was Friday, I had only to hold off my creditors until the end of the next day, for no debtor could be arrested upon the Lord's day. Come Sunday I might, with impunity, march out of my boardinghouse with clothes, my sword, and all that I could carry, every item obtained upon credit. I might, if I chose, stroll past my creditors, and there was not a thing any of them could do to me.

Where would I go? I had but two choices. I could either flee the city or I could settle within the Rules of the Fleet, that most peculiar of neighborhoods, where a man would never be arrested for debt. Such a residence was as much a jail as the Fleet Prison itself, the massive house of gloom in the neighborhood's center, for a debtor who lived within the Rules could never depart its borders—except, of course, on Sunday, when there was so very little to do.

I passed most of the next day upon my bed, staring at the ceiling, bemoaning all I had lost—my status, my friends, my chance at fortune, and, most of all, my Caroline. I loved her, truly loved her, and she was lost to me forever. At least I was now spared the discomfort of revealing to her, after we were married, that everything I had told her about myself was a lie, but she would have understood the true man behind the fabrications, and in due course we would have been happy.

As I indulged in my misery, my landlady called to me from

downstairs, informing me I had a visitor. She was yet civil to me, for I had paid through the entire quarter, and though she had smirked at me from the early morning hours on, she had not demanded I leave, and nor could she reasonably do so. If, however, circumstances were to conspire that I must leave, and she might rent out the room that had been paid for once already, I did not believe she would shed many tears.

Awaiting me in the parlor was a boy of perhaps eight years, neatly enough dressed though dirty from the street. He handed me a folded piece of paper and withdrew.

The note was simple enough. It was from my father's landlady. Having received word of his death, she wished for me to be made aware of his possessions, which were, by all rights, my own.

Nothing could have surprised me more. My father had never been overly nice in his paternal duties, and his care of me had only ever been motivated by keeping around first a boy, and later a young man, who might be of use for his schemes. Moreover, that this note found me so soon after his death suggested my father had known where I lived for some time. It seemed, then, that he had been watching me, plotting his revenge, awaiting the moment he could do the most damage. Did the woman who now contacted me mistake his interest in me for fatherly devotion, or did she wish to pursue his revenge now that the monster himself was no longer of this world?

I was suspicious, but I feared no landlady, and I told myself— now, I see, foolishly—that my father could do little enough harm now that he was dead. Thus the next day, which was Sunday, I followed the instructions upon the letter and made my way to his house in Covent Garden.

The street was none the best, and from the exterior, I supposed the house too would be in a state of decay, but the interior was clean and neat, if spartanly furnished. A girl of perhaps fifteen—an ugly thing with a horsey face and boney frame—led me into a parlor of sorts full of mismatched furnishings. The walls were decorated with pictures torn from magazines and chapbooks. There, however, was a woman of middle years, stout and tall, with dark eyes and hair, and a handsome face that radiated kindness.

She took my hand at once. "I am Mrs. Tyler," she said. "You must be Reginald."

I nodded, for though January was a fabrication, Reginald was my Christian name. My father had always believed in keeping lies simple. He also believed in knocking children unconscious and raping chambermaids, so some of his beliefs were better embraced than others.

Once we were introduced and seated, and the horsey-faced girl brought us wine, Mrs. Tyler began to explain her business. "Bernard told me that you and he were estranged, so you may not have known that he was to have been my husband."

I made every effort to conceal the depth of my surprise. Mrs. Tyler hardly seemed like the sort of woman my father sought. Her kind disposition was evidenced in her every word and gesture. Was it possible that my father had changed? I then recalled an image of him standing over me, shouting like a madman while I wallowed in pain amid puddles of horse shit. Change, I believed, was not likely. In all probability, my father had simply wanted what Mrs. Tyler had—her house, some jewelry, or other movable.

The longer I spoke with her, however, the more I began to doubt myself. She spoke of a reformed man, a man who wished to put his evil ways aside. More importantly, she spoke of a man who had brought more property into the house than he wished to take from it, and this was the crux of Mrs. Tyler's business with me.

"I know you had difficulties with your father, and he with

you," she said. "His anger toward you was something he could not relinquish. He learned where you lived and he spoke often of teaching you a lesson, of taking you down a peg, but I take comfort that he died before he could so debase himself."

On this score I kept quiet. The bruise upon my face was big and black and ugly. If she did not suspect my father of having placed it there, then she had not truly known him.

"But though he had much anger, he also had much love. He was a man with a big and generous heart."

I chose not to comment on this subject, but I forced a nod in the interest of good manners.

"For that reason, I wish for you to take his belongings, or at least as much of them as you wish for yourself. We will go to his rooms, and you may, in private, look through his things. All that you wish for is yours."

I could not understand how my father could have conducted even a single conversation with so genuinely kind a woman, but I would not cast aside such good fortune. I finished my wine and allowed her to lead me to my father's room. When I stepped inside, she stood in the doorway, a wistful look upon her benevolent face. She wiped a tear from her eye but did not follow me within.

It was a simple room, with but a few chairs near a fireplace, a table, and several chests. One of these was open, and I could see within it linens and some cheap jewelry of indifferent value, and, most surprisingly, a single volume, bound in cracked leather. I turned to Mrs. Tyler. "Did my father take up schooling late in life? Because I have never known him to read a word or to write anything but his name."

She shook her head and smiled. "No, he brought these several items with him. They were . . ." She turned away for a moment. "They were things he acquired in his previous life."

I nodded. Evidently she knew he had been a thief, and she believed, or pretended to believe, that he had put his wicked ways aside for the love of a good woman. "Why did he keep this book? It could be of no use to him."

She smiled and shook her head. "I did ask him about the book once, and he would neither tell me nor let me look into it. He said he had a feeling about it, but would say no more. He was a man of great sentiment, as you certainly know."

"He was subject to strong emotion," I conceded.

"He did not wish to part with some of his things, and I saw no reason to make him. There would be plenty of time. You may find some jewels or other gewgaws of value, but I hardly know for certain. He was a private man, and I respected that privacy."

"And you do not want these things for yourself?"

"I want to honor his memory, and I do not need his possessions for that."

He had clearly deceived her like few people had ever been deceived in the history of deception, but I gave her my most sympathetic smile. She then closed the door and said she would give me time for my grief.

I found much to interest me. A silver chain, a few pieces of fine linen, and a purse containing almost fifteen pounds in small coins. Perhaps twenty-five pounds' worth of goods in sum. It was not nearly enough to pay my debts, but it was more than enough to secure me new lodgings.

I was almost ready to leave without examining the book, but some impulse made me inspect it more closely. On the surface it was nothing remarkable—merely a thin quarto, bound in old brown leather, with no writing upon the front or spine. I thought it must be a diary or journal of some kind, though not my father's. He had made certain I knew how to read and write—he had even extorted a Latin tutor into providing me three years of instruction on how to act and speak like a young gentleman, the better to pull off his schemes—but he had never troubled with such matters himself. So if the journal was not his own, then whose?

I reached out and touched the book, and I knew at once that I had found something of import. I am not a superstitious man, nor one inclined to believe in the hidden world, but this book's gravity was unmistakable. I felt a heat radiate from it, as though it had been sitting near a burning fire. I yanked my fingers away and then touched it again. It was still hot. Not warm, I say, but hot, like a loaf just pulled from the oven. I looked about the room, as though the chairs or the walls might offer me some explanation, but they were silent. I own that I was afraid, for a man who is not fearful of ghosts by nature will, I suspect, fear one if he sees it. I was not terrified, as a matter of course, of hot books, but I had experienced enough of the world to tremble when I encountered the unknown.

A wise man would have fled, but I am my father's son, and something unique may be frightening, but it may also be valuable. I swallowed hard, glanced about the room once more, and picked up the book more firmly, holding it in both hands.

I will not say the sensation of heat disappeared, but as I glanced through the pages, it was matched by an accompanying numbness. That is to say, I still felt heat, but I discovered I did not entirely mind it. If it had been pure searing pain, I'm not sure it would have mattered either, for what the volume contained so held my attention that all the world was forgotten. Written upon the pages, in a faded calligraphy of beautiful intricacy, were words such as I had never seen, never imagined. I gasped as I struggled to comprehend what the book explained.

My reader will forgive me if I am vague about the contents of the book or how I knew them to be true. There are things that, when you gaze upon them, convey no doubt, and this was indeed of that species. One does not question light or darkness, pain or delight, moisture or aridness. Nor could one deny truth when presented with it so forcefully.

The book contained many truths, not simply the one that

would alter my course. Some of them were of little use to me, and some I did not understand, while knowing them to be true all the same. But one section grabbed my attention, and I knew at once what I would do. I did not think that I would do it if the process worked as the book described. A man does not throw a brick from the roof of a house and consider what he will do if it strikes the ground. The brick will fall. Nevertheless, I felt compelled to test out the principles outlined in the book before I attempted them in the real world.

As I continued to read, my desire to initiate the process redoubled, because the book explained that the methods contained within worked only for the tome's true owner. It could not be stolen—only given of free will. That my father had truly given the book to me, via his lady, was a thing I doubted. That my father had acquired the book by fair means himself was a thing I considered unlikely. And yet, the book made clear that the words contained within would appear as garbled nonsense to any but its rightful owner. As I could read it, I concluded the book was indeed mine, but I had to know for certain.

I do not recall departing Mrs. Tyler's house. But evidently, I did so with the book's warmth glowing under my arm, and the rest of the inheritance as well, for even in my stupor, I did not leave the items of value behind. On my way back to my own boardinghouse, I saw a dead bird in the street, and I scooped it up in my handkerchief while a trio of middling women watched in disgust. What mattered to me their opinion? I would never see them again, and the world was about to change under my ministrations.

I ignored their disgusted stares as I examined the dead creature with its torn wing and twisted leg and missing eyes. Could it be what the book promised would come true? I could not see how, and yet I could not make myself doubt it, not after what I had read.

I went to my room and set the book down upon my writing desk. I then opened my volume to the pages that had so drawn my attention and proceeded to follow the simple instructions outlined therein. The necessary ingredients were to be found in my room and in any ordinary kitchen, and so I stealthily raided the kitchen of the very house in which I roomed. With the needful ingredients in hand, the actions were not overly complicated. Indeed they were fluid and intuitive and ever so easy, and it seemed to me as I went through the procedure that it was the most obvious thing. How had this not occurred to me—to anyone? It was as though no one had ever thought to douse a fire with a bucket of water or to brush a coat to remove lint. Were I to outline the procedure here, in these pages, and those words were to retain their shape in your eyes (which I doubt), you would think much the same, but I shan't. It is not information you need to possess.

When I finished, there was no delay. The bird hopped upon its feet and began to flutter wildly. Its wing, which before had been torn and half gone, was now whole. Its twisted leg was straight. The missing eyes were returned. It was, for all the world, a healthy and robust creature, chirping with great fury as it flew about my room as would any bird suddenly trapped within doors. I ducked and dove and swatted at it, protecting my eyes and my hair until I was able to open a window and drive it away. Then I laughed, relishing the wonder of it, not seeing the mayhem and chaos as anything at all like an omen.

The Four Widows had made it something of a habit to gather each Wednesday evening to entertain one another and sometimes guests, though they preferred such time to themselves. Other suitors would often invade these gatherings, but I never did. My father taught me far better than to insert myself where I was not wanted. Sadly, I had no choice but to do so now.

The streets were turning dark as I exited my new lodgings in the Rules of the Fleet, to which I had moved the day I obtained the book. I ducked down several alleyways, crossed streets, ran into taverns and out their back doors, all to make certain no creditors were trailing me, ready to grab me the moment I left the Rules. If that happened, I would be sent to a sponging house and given a day to find friends who could pay my debts. As I had no friends remaining to me, I would then be sent to debtor's prison and rot there until Parliament passed its next general amnesty for debtors. It could come next month or in ten years. Upon my arrest, my property would be seized and auctioned off, the proceeds split among my tailor and jeweler and brewer and chophouse and sword maker and all the others I owed. The book, at least, would not be among those items, for I had it upon me, but it would do me little good in prison. All of this was to say that I had no choice but to make my scheme work, and quickly, for I could not dodge my creditors forever.

I had seen their agents standing outside my new boarding-house, waiting for me to leave, waiting for me to wander outside the Rules. Such men did not have endless patience, and they had other clients, other men to hunt, so I did not think it impossible that I might elude them, but even I could be unlucky, as you have already observed. The only cure for poverty, it seemed, was wealth, and I had no choice but to obtain it by any means I could devise.

With the prison looming up upon my left shoulder, and the majesty of St. Paul's Cathedral before me, I moved along Ludgate Street and then headed back toward Blackfriars, slipping into the darkness of Stonecutter's Alley toward the wretched stink of London's great thoroughfare of piss and shit, the Fleet Ditch. My plan was to follow the ditch's loathsome path back to the bridge, cross over to Fleet Street, and then head to west.

My plan was a success. By the time I entered Stonecutter's

Alley, I knew I had lost any followers. I then followed the course of the ditch, all too aware that I might face more dangers, for only the most wretched and desperate of men haunted such a place. Luck was on my side for once, as no one troubled me. I, however, could not say that I traveled untroubled. As I made my way to the Fleet Bridge, I saw three girls, not twelve years old, shirtless and huddled before a fire built of dried turds. I passed a man in rags, rocking back and forth as he held up his hand, filthy and bloody bandages marking where three fingers had recently been lost. Upon the shore of the Fleet Ditch itself, where its contents had overflowed, I saw a thin man and fat woman rutting like animals, she bent over, he entering her from behind. Neither of them cared a jot for the human excrement and dead rats that pooled about their ankles.

All of these terrible sights steeled my purpose. I would not be like these people. I would not be poor and wretched, little better than a beast in my brutish desire for food and warmth and physical release. I had the means to make my desires a reality, and I would use those means. The cost of refusing to do so was displayed all around me.

I moved with care, avoiding danger and dirt, and so appeared unruffled at Lady Caroline's house off Golden Square, my box tucked under my arm. I looked like a gentleman, I told myself. I looked far better than most gentlemen. There was no reason I could not be a gentleman. I rang the bell, and I presented a tall and fair-haired young man in livery—the sort of handsome fellow whom widows employed but married ladies did not—with my card and waited.

It was very true that I might be sent away. I even considered it more likely than not. If that were the case, I would follow this visit with a letter, requesting in the most persuasive language a private audience. That was a more dependable course, but I did not wish for these events to unfold so very slowly.

I was made to wait for some time, and I had no doubt that a debate raged within. At last, the handsome servant reappeared and directed me into the parlor, where the Four Widows sat, along with Mr. Langham. All of them stared at me—all but my lovely Caroline, who looked away, her face quite red.

I observed them all, and the beauty of the room, lit with its roaring blaze in the fireplace and dozens of tallow candles in their silver sconces upon the walls and those of the chandelier, interlaced with sparking crystal. Light too danced from the silver and gold of the jewelry around necks and fingers. There were bowls and trays of food and goblets and decanters of drink. There was a fine Turkish rug upon the floor and portraits of friends and ancestors upon the wall.

What a journey I had made that very night, I thought. From the Rules of the Fleet, in the shadow of the Fleet Prison and bathed in the stench of the Fleet Ditch, to this fine town house, off Golden Square, full of fine people and fine things. Which of these lives did I want? There could be no question.

Susan Harrow cleared her lovely white throat. She sat primly in her chair, her hands upon the lap of a sea-green gown that matched the precise shade of her large and startling eyes. "We were not certain we ought to admit you," she said, "but we believed you were owed an opportunity, at the very least, to explain yourself."

"I very much doubt that," I said, bowing to all of them. "I imagine you admitted me because you thought it would prove amusing. I suspect this decision was made over the objections— spoken or merely silent and obvious—of Lady Caroline."

She turned away at the sound of her name.

"It is a bit late to trouble yourself with Lady Caroline's feelings," said Mr. Langham.

"I hope that it is not," I told him.

"Then you believe you can clear your name of the charges

laid upon you by your father?" said Mrs. Harrow, her tone rich with derision. "Perhaps you will claim that they were lies, and he was not your father at all. Perhaps the fact that no one had heard of you prior to your arrival a few weeks ago is nothing to concern us."

"He was my father, and they were not lies," I admitted.

Lady Caroline put a hand to her prim and pretty mouth. She had, I saw now, hoped that I had come to say something that would make all the unpleasantness vanish. Of course I am not a poor scoundrel, I would say. I have merit because I have money, I would say. I loved her because she wished for it, but I began to feel a growing seed of resentment as well. She had money, and I did not, so what did my poverty matter if she loved me? Why must equivalent wealth—or at least family or name or title or some other form of prestige—be of such import if she truly cared for me? I had thought her good and pure and generous, but I began to see she was no so very different than the rest, not even than that harridan Susan Harrow.

I smiled at them all and bowed once more, and thought of the terrible things I had seen on my way to this house. I had seen such things before, of course. Indeed, I had always seen them, but the contrast between that former life and this one filled me with purpose. "The world is a terrible place for those without means, and I hope you will understand that when you consider the deceptive tools I used to attempt to obtain the comforts of life you believe to be yours by right. My feelings toward Lady Caroline were genuine, and they remain so. I fear I could never have attracted her notice had I presented myself as who I am. Perhaps this does not excuse what I did, but I hope it will explain my motives."

"Then what is your motive for coming here now?" asked Elizabeth Benton, one of the Four Widows. She was a woman of great beauty, but she resented with all her heart that Susan Harrow was considered more beautiful. She might oppose her friend if she believed it could gain her notice and acclaim within her circle, but she would not take a risk unnecessarily. "Surely you did not hope to convince us to readmit you to our society merely because you wish to be among us."

I had been poor all my life. Money that my father acquired disappeared with astonishing rapidity. I was used to hunger and filth and cold and skin raw from lice and flea bites. I was used to be being beaten and run off and fired upon by pistol and musket. I was used to having nothing in a world where many had something and a few, a golden few, had more than they could ever need. That was the way of things, and it had always been so, and while I might have hated my father for the pain he inflicted upon me and the reckless way he spent our money, I had never before hated the ordering of the world in which I lived. But now, in that parlor, surrounded by their lavish furnishings and their paintings upon the walls, their crystal decanters of wine and their trays of white toast covered with mayonnaise and anchovies, I hated the world for what it had done to me. I hated the way of things. I hated the rich and their opulence and plenty and their disregard for the rest of us. Life, I now saw, wasn't merely cruel or terrible or painful. It was unfair, and it meant there was a fairness that might be achieved. I could be a force to bring about that fairness. I would make them pay for the greed and selfishness. At that moment, I believed in the justice of my cause, and that made me very dangerous indeed.

I took a moment to collect myself and then I addressed the small gathering. "For you to understand why I have come, I must demonstrate something. I hope you will forgive me and indulge me. What I will do next may seem surprising, but you will soon understand."

I took the box which had been under my arm, opened it, and dumped upon the floor a lap dog that I had found in the street the night before, perhaps a week dead. It had not been a good week of death, either. Rats had been at the little creature, and they have a particular fondness for eyes. The gray tongue of the beast fell from its lips. Its stomach had been ripped open, and its rotting entrails draped out of it. The stench, I might add, was unlovely, and all hurried to press their handkerchiefs to their faces as the sound of coughing and gagging filled the room.

The ladies gasped. Mr. Langham rose to his feet.

"What do you mean by this?!" the gentleman shouted.

"You will see in a moment," I said.

"Have you no decency shocking ladies in this manner?! Collect your rubbish and depart!"

I turned to him and met his gaze. "Do you propose to make me do so?"

He said nothing, only glowering at me for a moment before looking away.

"As I suspected," I said. "Now, I shall proceed."

Elizabeth Benton now rose to her feet, cloth still pressed firmly to her face. "No you shall not!" she cried, though the force of her words was muffled by a piece of embroidered linen dyed the most exquisite shade of sky blue. "You have abused our hospitality long enough. You have lied to us and played your tricks upon us, and now you come here and behave in a manner so shocking I can scarce believe it. Leave—and never return!"

"Sit down!" I shouted at her. And she did. I did not love to be so forceful with her or with any lady, but I had no choice. Given that I was a thief and a liar, and I had deposited a rotting animal carcass before her, I expected a certain amount of indignation. It was, I believed, only natural. However, I could not allow that indignation to metamorphose into something like authority. Another piece of wisdom I had learned from my father was that when a man took command, others naturally obeyed. I therefore took command, so that they might see what I had come to show.

With the opposition now properly subdued, I smiled most charmingly and cleared my throat. "I am truly sorry you must witness so terrible a thing, but it will not remain terrible for long. You will see the wonder of it soon, and you will forget the horror. Indeed, the sad sight before you will make your surprise and delight all the more exquisite."

So saying, I crouched over the poor animal, which I had found in the street the night before. I proceeded to work upon it the method I had discovered in the book. I muttered the words and sprinkled the ingredients and followed the procedure rapidly so as to obscure what I did. The more mystery the better, I thought.

In a trice, the dog was upon its feet, yapping happily and dancing about in excited circles. It was no longer decayed and rotting. Its eyes, in their sockets once more, were bright, its limbs whole, and its movements fluid. It was still covered with filth, but there was no helping that. The unpleasant odor that had filled the room was gone as well. All was converted to sprightly, happy things.

The company stared at me. Mr. Langham attempted to say something several times but stammered. At last he managed actual words: "It is a trick. Some kind of terrible trick. You think we wish you here to perform legerdemain for us?"

"It is no trick," I said. "I have discovered the means to return the dead to life. You all saw the beast, you saw what I did. I could not have smuggled a live creature in here and replaced the dead one. It was dead, and now it is alive. The change was affected by my own hands."

"And what?" demanded Susan Harrow. "You wish us to pay you for your secret? You think you can perform a parlor trick and we shall shower you with coins? Go see the theater managers. Perhaps they will employ you for the after-show."

The dog yipped at this. It attempted to jump into Mrs. Harrow's lap, but she pushed it away as though it were a thing of revulsion. The dog ran away to a corner, hiding behind a divan, and curled up, falling asleep almost at once. Apparently it found the business of revival a tiring affair.

"I do not wish to be paid to perform this act," I said. "I wish to be paid not to perform this act."

Lady Caroline, who had been silent throughout all this, now faced me. "What do you mean, precisely, Mr. January? Speak plainly." Her voice was cold and hard.

"For your sake, I shall. I wish your friends to pay me what I ask, or I shall return their dead spouses to life, and their property shall revert to those returned husbands. You shall be widows no more, but wives, ruled over by your rightful lords. You shall have such money and such things as they see fit. You shall go where they permit, and no other place. You shall enjoy the company only of those acquaintances that they approve. So then . . . should you like to revert to your former states, ladies? If not, I suggest you think what price you would affix to your liberty."

They stared at me in horror.

"See here," began Mr. Langham. "You must be mad if you think—"

I held up my hand to interrupt him. "You inherited your fortune from your father, sir, a rather tyrannical and unyielding man. Believe me, you have my sympathies, for I know what it is to have such a father. I have been told by men who know you that you waited all your life for him to die so you could take possession of his estate. When he returns, that money shall be his once more. Now, all of you, excepting Lady Caroline, must present me with five thousand pounds each or you shall lose everything you have to those from whom you've gained it."

"You don't really expect us to hand you a fortune because of your bit of mummery, do you?" said Mr. Langham.

"If I do not have the money in twenty-four hours," I said, "then one of this company will see what I can do, and the rest of you will pay quite willingly. It is truly that simple. I assure you, it is no trouble for me to bring a husband or a father back from the grave. A bit of digging, of course, but a life of poverty has the advantage of providing a man with a strong back and no fear of exertion. None of you have such things to fear, of course. All you need worry about is having someone else control the purse strings. If that is no matter to you, then so be it. I shall, sooner or later, find ladies willing to pay to keep what is theirs. And your examples shall prove a better advertisement than a notice taken out in *The Gentleman's Magazine*."

Lady Caroline stood upon what I supposed to be unsteady legs. "I know not if this is trickery or truth, but either way, you are a scoundrel for bringing these threats to people you once counted as your friends."

"My friends who spurned me because I had not the money they believed," I countered.

"Your friends who spurned you because you *lied* to them," she said, her lovely face now turning red with anger.

"And if I had told the truth, they would not have been my friends at all," I said. "You cared for me, Lady Caroline, and I for you. Yes, I own I was first drawn to your circle because I wanted money, but within that circle, I was drawn to you because of who you are. The belief that I had money made me a member of your set, but it did not change how you felt. I honor you too much to believe you would have loved me half as much if I had claimed to have half my fortune, or twice as much if I had doubled it. You cannot be so shallow. I cannot allow it possible."

Lady Caroline's eyes narrowed. "Whatever I felt for you was an illusion fed by your lies. And now you come here to extort money of my friends. I do not wish for any special exemption, sir. Either you are a villain or you are not. I am not your accomplice or your partner in any venture. What you do to my friends, you do to me."

"I should never harm you, Lady Caroline," I said.

"That is your concern," she said, "but it shall not be on my account. I shall hate you forever for what you do this day, and regardless of the consequences, I could not hate you more."

"You do not mean that," I said, feeling that seed of anger blossoming within me. "If I were to vent my anger upon you, you would wish you had been kinder to me."

"Nothing you could do to me would be worth the price of treating you as anything but a rascal!" she snapped back.

I opened my mouth to offer a reply but thought better of it. The dog was now awake and alert once more, and had begun yapping. The room had descended into cacophony and chaos. I should accomplish no more by continuing to press my point. My words meant nothing. My actions would show them.

Determined to make Lady Caroline regret her harsh words, I bowed once more and departed, leaving the once-dead dog to their care.

My readers will not be surprised to learn that none of them offered payment. They all believed or hoped that it had been a trick, and they chose to gamble that it was so. They also likely hoped that if it were not a trick, it would be another of their number who would be used as the example. Perhaps the widows believed Mr. Langham would pay the price. It would have been far better if he had, for the senior Mr. Langham had been a successful factor of little note. He might have returned from the grave and escaped attention as any man might hope, causing no one but his own son any grief, and then the widows would have paid. How different things would have been if I had chosen to pursue that course.

I did not like Mr. Langham, it was true, but when I left the house in Golden Square, my animosity was reserved especially for Lady Caroline. It was an irrational anger, but one born of love, and so it was a kind of madness. Her fury and contempt, which I told myself were a sign that she valued money above all else, tapped into my desire for revenge. I called it justice, but my vengeful nature had me in its grip. I sat in my rooms in the Rules of the Fleet and awaited word from one of Lady Caroline's circle that my demands would be met. I told myself if one of them, it mattered not who, bowed to my wishes, it would be enough to assuage my anger. None of them did. They all defied me, and so they would be made to pay. But Lady Caroline, who hated me because I had been born poor, who allowed that poverty to eclipse all of the things she had once loved about me—she would pay the most, and she would pay first.

That night I went to the churchyard at St. Anne's, where I knew Lady Caroline's husband, Sir Albert, to be buried. Spade in hand, and fearful of being arrested for grave-robbery, I was nevertheless resolute. I stood over the grave where the vile Sir Albert had been buried only two years before, and I considered carefully what I was about to do. Once I revived him, Lady Caroline might well regret her actions, but there would be little I could do then—I had already lost her forever. But I also wanted someone to pay as a grand gesture for all I had suffered in my life . . . for what all the poor continued to suffer. I wanted there to be a reckoning for the world's unfairness, and while I knew bringing Sir Albert back to life would not change anything, I nevertheless believed it would bring me no small measure of satisfaction.

I raised my spade, and when its blade took its first bite of the cold earth, I was committed. There was no turning back. I did not see that I could stop at any moment. I pressed forward, each little mound of earth a blow for righteousness, each drop of cold sweat that fell upon the ground a sign of my determination. I dug and I dug and I dug, and I did not stop until I struck the wood of his casket, and then I pried it open and set myself to my task.

I had come prepared. I did not want to interact with Sir Albert, but I did not want to leave him to wander about the city in ragged clothes, with no money. I knew that anyone claiming to be a two-years-dead baronet would not get very far in this world, and so I purchased an appropriate set of clothes, used but not terribly shabby, from a ragman. Generous soul that I am, I also left Sir Albert six shillings in a purse. He would have enough to make his way home, and perhaps buy some oysters for the journey. It could be the dead are hungry when they are revived. I imagine I would be if I had not eaten in two years. Perhaps he would wish to buy his wife a present, though from what I had heard of him, I very much doubted it.

Birds and dogs are one thing, but a man, with the gift of speech and thought and reflection, is quite another, and part of me did not believe the process would work upon the most noble of beings. I completed the ritual, attempting to set my doubts aside, and when it was completed, I was rewarded with the sight of this long-decayed pile of bones beginning to grow new flesh that knitted together with rapidity and purpose, like a great swarm of ants traveling across a discarded apple.

I leapt from the grave and took shelter behind a tree, surprised and delighted and not a little terrified by what I had done. I had restored human life, and not the best human life to be found either.

From my sheltered vantage point I watched him struggle from his own grave and stagger upon the earth. He wore only the tattered remnants of his funerary garb, but he clutched the clothes I had left him in his hand. Perhaps, I thought, he would now sniff the air like a beast, and I would see I had brought back

not a man but a diabolical revenant. But no. He merely looked
up at the stars, let out a laugh, and began to brush the dirt from
his body. "By Jove!" he cried. "I am back."

It was as much as I needed to see. I did not wish to meet him
or speak to him or become his aid and his confederate. He was
Lady Caroline's husband, and so he was my enemy. He was,
nevertheless, what she had chosen over me, and so she would
pay the price. I very much wanted to see it happen.

I went to Lady Caroline's house and to the back door, where
I spoke with one of the kitchen girls, a sweet thing of fourteen
whom I had always found charming and who had always seemed
to regard me in the same light. I found that for a few pennies
she was willing to admit me to the kitchens and to lurk in the
hallways, that I might observe events in the household. I did not
inform her what those events would be. I only related that her
household was about to undergo a most remarkable transfor-
mation, and she thanked me for the intelligence. She did not
wish to miss it, and she knew she would be held in high esteem
by the rest of the staff for being the first to spread the word.

I did not see all that happened. Lurking in dark hallways has
both advantages and disadvantages, but what I did not observe,
I heard, and the details were later provided by eyewitnesses. Here
is what I know: at approximately nine-of-the-clock that morning, the front bell rang and the handsome serving man answered
the door. He inquired what business the gentleman visitor in the
ill-fitting suit might have, and the gentleman visitor told him
that this was his house and his business was none of the concern
of a molly like himself. The serving man harrumphed and ob-
jected and assured the gentleman of many things, but the gentleman was not to be harrumphed or assured. He struck the
serving man in the nose and shouldered past him.

Sir Albert, I should point out, was a tall man, broad and gen-
erally built upon a larger frame than most mere mortals. Indeed,

I could see, from my darkened hallway, that the suit I had provided was rather short in the breeches and sleeves, giving him a somewhat comical look—or a look that might have been comical had he not appeared so frightening. In life, the gentleman had been inclined to corpulence, or so word and portrait had led me to believe, but the process of reviving appeared to bring great vigor and health, and now he was nothing but lean and powerful. In the darkness of the graveyard, and in my haste to leave, I had not observed it. The return had not conferred youth upon him, for he was still an elderly man, but he was one in great health. He wore no wig, for I had not had one to spare, and his hair flowed wild and long. He reminded me, in his power and fury, of my father. The perceptive reader may now begin to suspect that I began to wonder whether love and anger and rejection had led me down an erroneous path.

Sir Albert now made his way past other servants, who rushed forward upon hearing the ruckus. Some stared in wonder and, no doubt, servantish pleasure at the sight of this strange man storming his way into the house on the way to make a truly excellent story to tell at the tavern. Others, who had been in service longer, recognized this hulking creature, and swooned or dropped to their knees to seek the protection of Jesus. Lady Caroline, who was at breakfast, arose from her table and went out to the front hall to investigate the mayhem for herself, for she was no coward.

Now this part I did witness myself. I lurked like a thief in the shadows while Lady Caroline strode out like a lady knight, ready to protect her home and those in her charge. She wore a gown of the purest white, and it flowed behind her as she took mighty and forceful stride, perhaps afraid but unwilling to show her fear. Yet when she stepped into the hallway and stood face-to-face with the horror of a husband she had buried two years previous, her resolve left her. Her knees buckled, and she reached out to the wall to steady herself with one hand. The other she pressed to her mouth.

"Dear God," she said.

From my cowardly lookout, I saw her eyes fill with tears, and I felt my own moisten in kind. The enormity of what I had done now struck me with all its terrible force. I had truly forever lost the woman I loved. More than that, I had condemned her to her very own hell.

In my misery and self-loathing, I must have made a noise, for Lady Caroline turned and spied me. My teary eyes met her own, and I expected to see all the rage and anger and resentment that was my due, but all I saw was concern for us both. She blinked away her tears, swallowed hard, and mouthed one word at me: *Go.* At that moment, she thought only of my safety. I understood then that, in her goodness, Lady Caroline might have been angry with me, and she might have felt betrayed, but she still loved me. If only I had spared her and her friends, if I had chosen other victims for my scheme, things might have gone very differently, but instead I cultivated resentment and pursued revenge. I had given in to my basest side, and even in knowing that, she did not wish to see me hurt.

She looked once more at me. *Run,* she mouthed. And then she stepped forward to greet her husband, a man who made her existence a misery, whom I had brought back into her life.

I retreated to the servants' entrance and slinked out the back door. I made my way to the Rules and to my boardinghouse and to my rooms. I slammed the door shut and cursed my foolishness and my petty weakness for revenge. I did not leave my room for food. I did nothing but lie upon my bed and weep.

The next day I received four separate packages of five thousand pounds each. Twenty thousand pounds. I was rich. I had enough to live in luxury the rest of my life.

My troubles were just beginning.

*   *   *

I wasted no time, delivering for safekeeping the bulk of my money with a reputable goldsmith. I then proceeded to pay off all my debts; take a new house on Upper Brook Street, close enough to Grosvenor Square to be fashionable and close enough to Tyburn Lane to be a good value. I ordered several suits of new clothes, a few new wigs, and various items of personal and domestic furnishing, and began my life as a man of leisure.

In a matter of days, I had gone from being worth less than nothing to having as much as I could desire. I was hardly the wealthiest man in the city, but a man of my sudden fortune would never need to work again. I would never want, never suffer, never lie and swindle and thieve for my next meal. I had achieved success beyond anything my father would have thought possible.

This success was, admittedly, soured by the fact that it had come of a gift from my father and that I had consigned the woman I loved to misery, but I tried not to let those two things bother me. For the first, my father had possessed the book, but not the skills or wit to use it. I had therefore bested him quite fairly. As for Lady Caroline, I told myself that she had made her choice, she had rejected me, indeed had instructed me to do precisely what I had done. Perhaps that would have sustained me had she not seen me hiding in her house, had she not, in her moment of terror and sorrow, worried about me.

A noted baronet with political ties and influence had returned from the dead. How could I have believed such a thing would not cause a stir? I suppose I hadn't thought that part through, but soon Sir Albert's revival was the talk of London. I was no better than one of the curious, for having returned him to life gave me no particular intimacy with the man. Indeed, it was my hope that he would never find out who it was who revived him or that I had enjoyed a particular connection with his wife.

So it happened that I had no choice but to learn what I could the same way every outsider did, from newspapers and chatter in coffeehouses. Sir Albert, it seems, was unable to tell the curious anything about what lay beyond this world. If he had gone to heaven or hell, he could not say, for none of his experiences had left an impression upon him. That he had been *somewhere* and doing *something*, he was certain, for he had hazy memories of other people and movement and places, dynamic shadows and strong feelings, but beyond that he could say little. As for the means of his return, he was similarly vague. He knew that he had been brought back by a person who had discovered a method of returning the dead, but he did not know who this person was. If he had learned of my scheme to extract money from his wife's friends, he said nothing of that. I suspected he had not been told, and I was quite content that he should never learn.

So while Sir Albert's return was all Londoners wished to speak of, they knew nothing of my involvement. Indeed, the world had conspired to hide my presence well, for on every street corner there were now peddlers selling pamphlets that claimed to contain the secret method of restoring life. I purchased one of these and found it contained utter nonsense, just as I had supposed. I felt a moment of anger that dullards were profiting from my work, but I let it pass. I had profited enough.

Some readers may suspect that a man such as I might grow greedy, demand more money from the widows or seek out new victims to threaten. Anyone with whom I chose to share the secret that I was the city's only true necromancer—and a quick demonstration with a dead creature would prove I was—and who did not want a husband or father returned would pay me what I wished. However, I was not greedy. I was not my father.

I was not a man whose appetites could never be satisfied or a man incapable of keeping hold of his money. I now had all I required in the way of physical and material comforts, and I did not wish to tempt fate by seeking more. I was determined never to touch the book again unless some disaster should strike and I found myself in need.

I joined a new club and made new friends, and though I was not out and about quite as much as I had been before, I was nevertheless seen in public. Once or twice, after some dramatic coughing, a gentleman might bring up the unfortunate subject of rumors that circulated about me. He might say that he heard I had been exposed as charlatan and an imposter, a man with no wealth and ample pretension. To such questions, I would blush and hang my head. I would say that it was true that I had misled the world about my family, because my father was a lout and a drunkard. Not only had I been ashamed of him, but I had been in fear of him, for I knew once he had discovered that I had made my fortune in trade, he would seek me out and demand that I make my wealth his own. I had hidden my origins not only from the world, but from my parent, and he had discovered me all the same.

"As for the other matter," I would say, "I can promise you I am upon a very sure footing. I invite you to speak to any merchant with whom I do business. You will only hear that I pay my bills promptly and with good cheer. I haven't a debt in the world, and I know of many a gentleman, some with far more wealth than I, of whom the same cannot be said."

The facts, therefore, bore out my claims, and while having had a drunken oaf for my sire might have tarnished my reputation in some circles, my evident fortune, which I displayed with tasteful reluctance, sufficed to compensate. At the theater, at the opera, and through the rambles, I rarely saw any of my old acquaintances, and when I did, nothing more than an uncomfortable bow passed between us. Good manners and embarrassment, not to mention fear of my wrath, prevented any of that set from disclosing my necromantic secret.

I had taken on my father, and I had won. I had taken on death, the king of terrors itself, and made it my servant. In doing all this, I had betrayed Lady Caroline, and that mistake still haunted me. Do not think otherwise. Not a day went by, not an hour in each day, nor even a minute in each hour, that I did not think of what I had done with regret. If only I had chosen one of the other widows to torment, how much better, how much easier, would have been my life. Perhaps Lady Caroline would not have forgiven me, but at least she would have been safe and well and happy.

I set about in an effort to erase the mistakes of my past and enjoy my new life. I took pleasure in my new friends, in being a man about town. I flirted with some women, and more, you may be certain, flirted with me. If I was not serious in any of these encounters, I managed to take some small pleasure in them. In sum, I could not change the past, and so I made it my business to enjoy the present that I had labored so hard to achieve. In this pursuit, I was successful.

But that was before the queen began to search for me.

I was dining at my club when I overheard the conversation between two older gentlemen I found intolerably fatuous.

"It is most unusual," said Mr. Fallows, a man of about fifty with a long face and an enormous nose, the tip of which pointed down, almost touching his upper lip. Indeed, it wiggled when he spoke. He also had enormously wide eyes, and his wigs were inclined toward the frizzy. Taken as a whole, he gave every impression of being a man who had just been startled unto his death.

"I agree with you there, sir," said Mr. Christopher, some five years his friend's senior. He was less grotesque in his face, but far more so in his person. Rarely did one see a man of Mr. Christopher's rotundity. He required a cane to walk, and often the assistance of two or three servants to rise from his chair. No one liked these two save each other, but despite their disagreeable personalities and appearances, they were always remarkably well informed. It was something of a mystery how men no one was inclined to speak to somehow knew everything.

"A unique series of events," said Mr. Fallows, continuing.

"No precedent, sir. None at all," agreed Mr. Christopher.

They had become something of a fixture in the club. They were apt to speak thus loudly until someone inquired of their subject, for they loved nothing more than to demonstrate their knowledge. I was walking past, quite prepared to continue on, when I heard something I could not ignore.

"It's a deuced bad time for some jackanapes to start pulling people from their graves," Mr. Fallows said. "And Sir Albert, of all people. That pot has been stirred, sir. Stirred very much indeed."

"To overflowing," agreed Mr. Christopher, nodding so that the flesh about his chin and neck jiggled like aspic. "The Germans have certainly noticed."

I paused and turned to them, raising my glass of wine in salute. "I beg your pardon, gentlemen, but I could not help but overhear."

At this, they both smiled.

"All of London speaks of the necromancer, but what concern is this of the Germans?" I asked.

"Have a seat, Mr. January," Fallows said, pointing toward an empty chair. "And we shall tell you."

"With great pleasure," agreed Mr. Christopher.

I had hardly touched breeches to upholstery before Fallows began. "The queen wishes to employ the services of the necromancer. She proposes that we have a former corpse sit upon the throne."

In retrospect, I should have seen that my skill would be of interest to Queen Anne and her court. She was known to be ill, and it was widely rumored that she was dying, which was always a complicated thing for a monarch without an heir. More than ten years earlier, Parliament, determined that no Catholic monarch should ever rule the kingdom, had passed the Act of Settlement, requiring that the succession pass over dozens of more closely related relations—all of whom were of the Romish persuasion—to descend upon the queen's extremely distant cousin Sophia, electress of Hanover. This would be the end of the house of Stuart and the beginning of an England ruled over by German louts. No one was pleased about this prospect. At least, no one but the Whigs, for they had worked tirelessly to ensure that England would have a Protestant monarch. Better a Protestant foreigner than an Englishman with Papist leanings.

Queen Anne, as my readers well know, had many miscarriages and brought more than a few children to term only to have them stillborn. Only once did a child of hers survive infancy, but much to the nation's collective sadness, William, Duke of Gloucester, had died of a fever just after his own eleventh birthday.

Mr. Fallows leaned back, swirling a glass of wine in his hand. His frizzled wig sat askew on his head. "I suspect there will be much arguing about this in Parliament, but I'm not sure there is anything to be done. I've never heard of a bill forbidding formerly dead men from taking the throne." He sipped his drink, and wine stained the tip of his nose.

"There can be no such law passed," said Mr. Christopher, "for such a bill would prevent Jesus from being king."

"I'm not sure He has the right to be king of England, savior or no," said Mr. Fallows. "Let Him prove his bloodlines first, I say. Ha ha. And in any case, if there were to be such a bill, Jesus as an exception could be written into it."

"Very true," his friend agreed. "We can always make an exception for the messiah."

"One moment," I said. "What precisely is the queen offering the necromancer?"

"Land," said Mr. Fallows. "Wealth and title. He would be a duke, I should think. The man who can return her son to her will become one of the greatest men in the kingdom."

I took a drink of my own wine and considered this. I had not wanted to pursue more wealth, but a man could hardly refuse the will of his rightful monarch. I would not have my readers suppose this is mere posturing on my part, either. I was not looking for an excuse to accept this offer. The truth was, I would rather have been an obscure and comfortable gentleman than be thrust into notoriety by returning a dead prince to life. My own life should have become miserable. Perhaps I would have been a duke, but half the kingdom would have been pounding upon my door, begging me to restore this person or that. The other half would have been begging me to refrain from doing so. It would have become impossible for me to live the kind of quiet life I most enjoyed.

On the other hand, I could ask the queen not to reveal my name. I did not need to have a title, did I? If she wished to reward me with property and gold in secret, I would accept such terms. I would be very reluctant to make it a public matter.

"I would think the necromancer, if he is a patriot, would have to obey this summons," I said.

"If he is a Tory," said Mr. Fallows.

"A Tory who has taught his technique to a friend," added Mr. Christopher, "for he will be a dead Tory the moment he steps forward."

"What do you mean?" I asked, trying to conceal my alarm.

"It is inevitable," said Mr. Christopher, "that this offer has been met with very little delight from the Whigs. They have invested in the Hanoverians, and they mean to have their German monarch. The Whigs will not allow their chance at power to escape them. Far easier to slit the necromancer's throat, I should think."

"Surely they would not murder to advance politics," I said.

Both men laughed. I do not recommend gazing upon such men laughing. It is unpretty.

"No, sir," said Mr. Christopher with a slap upon his massive thigh. "Not politics. *Money.* There are contracts, positions, sinecures to be had once the Hanoverians take the crown. They have been waiting for Anne to die, and now that she is upon the threshold of the abyss, they will not allow some petty magician to ruin their chances."

"It is so very ironic," said Mr. Fallows, "that the most dangerous enemy this necromancer will have is the one man he is known to have returned from the grave."

"Sir Albert Worthington?" I asked.

"None other," said Mr. Christopher. "You must know he was pivotal in the passage of the Act of Settlement and is said to be one of the electress's most vital agents here in England. At least he was when he was alive."

"And now he is again," said Mr. Christopher.

"Indeed," agreed Mr. Fallows. "Alive once more, and so an agent once more, I must think. He has been rumored to say, and in the presence of the greatest men in the kingdom, that this necromancer must be stopped at all costs, that to sit a corpse upon the throne would be an abomination, and it would lead to another civil war. Do you know what these great men replied, Mr. January? Can you guess?"

I could not, and said as much.

"I shall tell him," volunteered Mr. Christopher. "They replied, behind closed doors, mind you, so no one would know—"

"No one!" cried Mr. Fallows with nose-wagging mirth.

"No rumors would spread!" laughed Mr. Christopher.

"*What did they say?*" I demanded with a severity that seemed to shock the two men.

Mr. Christopher sharply looked at me. "No need to be so animated, Mr. January. I shall tell you. Be patient."

"No rush," said Mr. Fallows. "The club is not on fire, I trust."

"I smell no smoke," agreed Mr. Christopher.

With great effort, I refrained from speaking another word.

At last, seeing I would not allow them to extend the conversation further, Mr. Christopher sighed, as if having lost something of enormous value, and proceeded. "They told him that, as he had a nearer connection to the necromancer than any person in London, Sir Albert must do all in his power to prevent the man from granting the queen's wish."

"It is a bad season for necromancy," said Mr. Fallows.

"The worst I can recall," agreed Mr. Christopher.

The two commenced once more to laughter and I excused myself.

I returned home in a state of agitation that evening, and my servants informed me that there was a guest awaiting me in my parlor. I rarely received guests in my home, and so this surprised me, but not as much as when I saw who it was—Lady Caroline.

I stared at her in surprise. She stood by the fire, her back to me, holding a glass of wine in her hand. Her velvet gown, the color of the wine she drank, highlighted the perfection of her form. Her hair was piled high under her hat, and delightful curls slipped loose.

I was filled with love and desire and loneliness and regret. She had been wrong to reject me—that much was certain—but for all that, I would have done anything to undo my terrible act. However, even I, granted by fate the godlike power over life and death, could not change the past.

"I am surprised to find you here," I said. My voice was dry and brittle. I hated sounding weak, but if there was a person to whom I would gladly submit, it was she.

She turned to me, and I could see that she had been crying. Is there anything more melancholy than tears upon the face you love?

"You are a villain," she said, "but you are not the worst kind of villain. No, that title is reserved for my husband, whom you have returned to the world."

"I ought not to have done it," I told her. "I acted out of anger."

"I know," she said, casting her eyes upon the floor. "You wronged me, but there was some truth in what you said, and I own I can understand your motives and I believe that you do—did—love me in truth."

"I did and I still do," I said, stepping toward her.

She held up her hand to stop me. "It is too late for that. In bringing Sir Albert back from his grave, you have not only made me miserable, but you have endangered yourself."

"I have heard he intends to harm the necromancer, but surely he cannot know who I am."

She swallowed the remainder of her wine and set the goblet down upon the mantel. "He has long suspected I know who returned him from death, though I denied it. I think Susan betrayed me. It would be like her, I think. It hardly matters. He demanded I tell him who had returned him. I tried to refuse. I tried to appeal to his better nature, but there is not such a thing. He hurt me, Mr. January. He hurt me where he knew the world would not see the bruises."

Again, I took a step toward her. "Caroline," I said.

"No." She backed away, as though I too would bring her harm. "Do not touch me. I am sorry, Mr. January. I hate you for what you've done to me, but because I know I played a part in this, that I could have been kinder, I come to bring you warning. My husband has always been loyal to Sophia of Hanover, and he has always been a staunch Whig. He would have done anything to end the Stuart succession, and he will not allow you to bring the prince back from the grave. And, he is altered."

"What do you mean?"

"He is not the same as he was before," she told me, her voice now sounding wild. "He is worse. He is crueler and more hurtful. He was always unkind, but not this bad. Death and resurrection, I fear, have heightened what was worst in him and dulled what little there was of good."

I took a moment to consider what she said. I had not only brought a bad man back from the grave, but in doing so, I had made him worse.

"I am sorry, Lady Caroline," I said.

She shook her head. "Sorrow will get you nothing. You cannot fathom how you hurt me, and I have hated you for it, but I will not see you murdered because of me. You must know that he will come here before night's end, and he will have his particular villain with him. He will force you to reveal your secrets, and when there is nothing more to be learned from you, he will kill you."

I smirked. I was my father's son, after all, and I was not afraid of the baronet, recently returned from the dead. His particular villain, indeed. I should have liked to have the opportunity to teach this fellow a thing or two about villainy.

"Let him try," I said.

"You do not understand."

"No, you do not understand. I am no coward to be threatened. I shall be waiting for him with sword and loaded pistols, and, if necessary, I shall send him back to the grave from which I so foolishly plucked him."

"He will have you outnumbered."

"Numbers do not signify. They will have to gain the house to fight me, and I shall happily dispatch any lackey Sir Albert cares to bring with him."

"You underestimate his resolve," Lady Caroline said, growing exasperated by my failure to quake in fear. "If Sophia takes the throne, he stands to be one of the most powerful men in the country, and his return from the grave has emboldened him. You must flee. Tonight. Take what you can carry and leave London. If you do not, you will be dead before morning, and your secrets will be in Albert's hands."

"I will not flee," I said. "I would have to abandon my home and my wealth."

"Leave your damn wealth!" she shouted at me. "You stole it from my friends once they saw what you had done to me. The money is as vile as your terrible secret. Besides," she added with a sneer, "I have no doubt a man of your stripe can always procure more."

I did not love that she should judge me so, but I knew I was not entirely undeserving of her rebuke.

Indeed, I was prepared to tell her as much when my serving man—James, I called him, though I did not know his real name—came into the room to tell me that there were two men outside, one of whom could not be called a gentleman, and they both insisted upon seeing me at once.

Lady Caroline gasped. "I did not think them to come so soon."

I turned to my man. "In a few moments, I will ask you to lead Lady Caroline out the back way and to safety. I shall deal with these men myself."

"No!" Lady Caroline exclaimed. "They will kill you!"

"Perhaps they believe they will," I replied.

I asked the serving man to hold them off for a few more

minutes. When he left the room, I turned back to Lady Caroline. "I will not run from my own home, and I will not see you hurt. He cannot know you were here."

She nodded, and then, to my surprise, she reached out and took my hand. She yet wore her gloves, but my own hand was naked, and the smoothness of the satin was exquisite.

"I will never again allow you to come to harm," I said.

She took away her hand. It was like having my heart torn from my chest. "I wish things might have been different between us," she said.

I wanted to tell her that they still might be, but I did not think she would want to hear those words just now, so I nodded and sent her on her way. I then directed my man to admit Sir Albert. My orders were that my man would show him the way to the parlor but not enter it himself.

When Sir Albert entered a few minutes later, I was prepared. I stood in my parlor, goblet of wine in my hand, sword at my side, prominently displayed. My suit was very well cut, emphasizing my own handsome physique—the strength in my shoulders and calves was quite evident. Sir Albert might have been a large man himself, but I fancied I made an imposing figure.

Sir Albert walked through the door, and I began to wonder if I had been overly optimistic. I had forgotten just how tall, just how fit he had been that day at his house. He strode into the room like a giant entering a village he was prepared to crush under his boots. And he was not the worst of it. By his side was a nasty-looking fellow in rough clothes, though neat. He was not as tall as Sir Albert, but he was brutish in appearance, animal-like, with a low brow, long hair, a protruding muzzle, and scars across his face. He grinned at me, showing a set of uneven teeth, ranging in color from yellow to black.

Should the situation descend to physical violence, I had no doubt that I would be bested, but I would not allow others to

determine the manner in which events unfolded. I made those
determinations for myself. There would be no violence but upon
my terms. These men would leave, and have gained nothing for
their efforts.

"You're January?" Sir Albert said without ceremony.

"I am Mister Reginald January," I agreed. "Who addresses me?"

He walked over to my decanter of wine and casually knocked
it over, allowing it to spill upon my very expensive Levantine
rug. The stain spread out like the creeping fog. "Don't assume
airs with me. You know damn well who addresses you. I may
owe you a debt of thanks for bringing me back from death, but
you never intended it as a favor. And you are no gentleman,
despite what your stolen money suggests. I know precisely what
you are, for my whore of a wife told me."

"One moment," I said. "You shall not insult Lady Caroline."

The brutish companion stepped forward and, before I had
time to react, struck me across the face. I reeled backward, wine
goblet flying from my hand. My head struck a painting upon
the wall, tearing the canvas. The portrait did not dislodge, but I
slid down, feeling as though I might lose consciousness or
vomit, or perhaps both. It was not a good showing.

"This is Hubert," Sir Albert said, gesturing toward the brute.

"A pleasure to make your acquaintance," said Hubert as he
unbuttoned his breeches and began to piss upon my divan.

While Hubert indulged in a long and forceful urination,
waving his penis up and down to create a dramatic arc, Sir Albert
proceeded with his discourse.

"I am being gentle with you thus far," he said, "because I
wish you to consider my terms. I will possess the means of raising the dead from you. You will provide me with this knowledge,
and then you will flee. I prefer you flee the kingdom entirely, for
if I receive word of any necromancy in England, I shall be forced
to respond as the threat warrants. Perhaps you house the means

to bring yourself back, and killing a man who can raise the dead suggests its own set of difficulties, does it not, Hubert?"

Hubert was still pissing. "It presents a bit of a dilemma, Sir Albert."

"Indeed it does," Sir Albert agreed. He scratched his chin thoughtfully, as though considering the matter for the first time, though this presentation smelled to me of the lamp. "It is a curious question, do you not think? How can I sufficiently threaten a man who has no fear of death?" He snapped his fingers and grinned, as though an idea had just struck him. "I have it. What think you of this, January? If you do not vanish from the kingdom, I shall cut off your hands and feet. And, for good measure, I shall tear out your tongue. Yes, that does sound quite good. It should certainly keep the necromancy to a minimum, I should think. A man who cannot speak or gesture or hold anything cannot raise the dead, I suspect. It should be a pleasure to watch him try at any rate. But I doubt he would. A man maimed in the most terrible way, rendered a prisoner within his own body, I imagine he would give up on life entirely."

Hubert, who had finally emptied what I could only presume to be the world's most capacious bladder, had tucked away his unwelcome organ and was in the process of buttoning his breeches. "But such a man could not look after himself, Sir Albert. Surely he would die, and you would have accomplished nothing."

"Right you are, Hubert." Sir Albert looked at me. "He's cleverer than you thought, isn't he?"

Looking at the piss stain upon my divan, I could not but reflect that I did not share Sir Albert's opinion, but I chose to keep that fact in reserve.

Sir Albert continued. "We must then keep Mr. January alive. Here's the very thing. I shall have him transported to St. Bartholomew's Hospital in his incapacitated condition, where I shall pay to have him kept alive for as long as can be effected. What think you of my solution, Hubert?"

"Very elegant, sir," Hubert said as he picked his teeth with his thumbnail.

"And I would, from time to time, pay him a visit, to remind him who had done him this terrible service and who was committed to keeping him alive and in a state of utter misery and sorrow for as long as human ingenuity could contrive. Is that not an eloquent punishment?"

"It is like a poem built of flesh, Sir Albert."

Sir Albert smiled at me. "You were once a penniless rogue, and because I am, at heart, generous, I offer to you the opportunity to return to that existence. The alternative, such as I have set before you, is a grim one. What say you?"

"You must count your blessings to receive such a proposal," Hubert offered, helpful fellow that he was. "I've heard him be less generous with them what he didn't like. You want my opinion, dying and coming back made him a bit sentimental."

"We all mellow with age, Hubert," Sir Albert said.

"Very wisely observed, Sir Albert," said Hubert. "Time was, I'd have taken a shit on that divan."

Lying upon the floor of my own house, my head aching, and threatened with violence beyond measure, I was not entirely certain what I could say. I was determined not to let Sir Albert have what he wished. I did not want to lose the book and its power to generate money and comfort. I also did not want to allow its power to fall into the hands of a rogue like Sir Albert, a bad man made worse by my very own machinations. I cared little if the Stuarts or the Hanoverians ruled the kingdom—the poor would remain poor and the rich would remain rich. I cared little if Whigs and Tories traded places at the table of power, for they were all one to me. What I cared about was not letting Sir Albert win.

"Now, tell me your secret," said Sir Albert.

"I cannot." The words tumbled out of me. "You see, there is a book—a magic book. It is how I learned my method, and only the owner of the book can affect the revival of the dead."

"A magic book, indeed. That sounds like a lot of hokum to me," he answered.

"I did raise you from the dead," I said, trying to sound both reasonable and sincere. "That also sounds like hokum."

Sir Albert allowed the point, but it did not cheer him. "Then give me the book!" he cried.

"I don't have it," I told him. "I would be a fool to keep such a thing upon my person." It was, in fact, in my waistcoat pocket at that very moment, but there was no reason to let him know such a thing.

"Then where is it?" said the increasingly impatient baronet.

"I don't know," I sputtered. My nose began to run, and tears ran down my cheeks. "Please don't cut off my hands and feet! I swear to you I don't know!" It was a good performance, if I may be my own critic. The fact that I was, in truth, quite frightened added to the verisimilitude, but I do not want the reader to think I had given way to panic and despair. I always have a plan. Or at least I often do, and this was one of those occasions when I nearly did. I was, in fact, working on a plan, and I was determined that it would be a good one.

Hubert took a step toward me and I raised my hand in protest. My thinking was rapid and erratic, but I believed I could come up with something if no one struck me again for a few moments or pissed on any of my furnishings. Such things make it so very hard to concentrate. "Once your return from the beyond became so well circulated a story . . . I feared someone would find me and demand my secrets, but I was determined to protect the book. The only solution was to keep it where even I could not get it. I . . . I gave it to a friend, who was told to give it to a friend, who was told to hide it." I hoped this many layers of obscurity would dissuade them from seeking out these friends themselves. "I can get the book, but I need a day. Perhaps two."

Hubert stepped toward me again and I pressed myself against the wall, feigning more fear than I felt. Growing up with my father had given me a certain indifference to physical pain. I did not care for it, but I knew a few blows about the head would not do me much harm.

"All right! One day, then!" I said, thrusting out my hands defensively. "I will bring it to you by tomorrow evening."

"Very well, then. See that you do," said Sir Albert, sounding a little bit placated.

Hubert punctuated this command by kicking me in the side twice, but as I said, this did not trouble me overmuch.

Once my two guests departed, I pulled myself to my feet and called for my man, demanding a fresh glass of wine and some clean clothes. After a refreshing drink and a change of wardrobe, it was time for me to put my plan into effect. If Sir Albert wanted the book not to fall into the hands of his political enemies, then that was precisely where it would go.

I hired a coach and set out to Kensington Palace without further delay. We crossed at Westminster Bridge and made our way through the dark at St. George's Fields at night until I was at last outside the gates of the queen's residence. The great red brick palace stood on the other side of those iron rails and across a few hundred yards of garden illuminated by moon and torch-light. Within those walls I would find Anne herself, or someone very near to her, who would offer me protection and provide to Sir Albert the punishment he deserved.

It was a curious thing, as I gazed across the grounds to the palace. Therein was the queen of England, surrounded by some of the most powerful and influential people in the kingdom. All of them desperately wanted to see me, and I had the power to alter the nation, not simply today, but for all time. In my hands was the means to preserve a moribund dynasty, and while I had been uncertain if I should use that power, now Sir Albert had driven me to my destiny. Just as my desire for vengeance had led me to return him to life, now that same desire would lead me to thwart his plans. I rather liked the symmetry of it.

Content with my sense of importance in the unfolding of global events, I approached the cluster of perhaps a dozen palace guards, who stood eyeing me with bored hostility.

"Good evening," I said to the guards. "I should like an audience with Her Majesty, Queen Anne."

Only one of these men turned to look at me with slow and reptilian contempt. "Is that so?"

"I understand that you must not be in the habit of admitting anyone who wishes, but the queen has sent for me."

The guard held out his hand and twitched anxiously the fingers of his studded leather glove. "Let's see it."

"I have no formal invitation, for she did not know my name. I am the necromancer for whom she has called, and now I arrive to offer my services to Her Most Royal Majesty and the benighted house of Stuart." I placed my fingertips gently to my chest and bowed.

The guards burst out in guffaws. "We've had a score of you lot already today," one of them replied.

I stepped forward, rising to my full height, thrusting forth my chin, and locking eyes with the saucy fellow who had addressed me so. He would know by the steadiness of my voice, by the authority of my bearing, that I was not a man to be sent off like a peddler with a pie cart. "I care nothing for your charlatans and imposters. I say I am the necromancer."

He deigned to blink in my direction. "Be off, or you'll be a necromancer in chains."

I laughed the laugh of the aggrieved and tolerant, and I tried not to allow my authority to deflate. "Certainly I understand that you have been troubled with fools and madmen who claim they can do what I can, but I assure you I am the true necromancer, and the queen will wish to see me."

"And I said be off!" the guard snarled.

"Look, if I could but find a dead bird or rat, I can assure you—" I stopped talking because the guards were now drawing their swords and stepping forward. Apparently they had already taken their fill of men who claimed to do what I could, in fact, do. No amount of persuasion on my part was going to gain me entrance. I thought to ask how the true necromancer could ever hope to see the queen if they behaved thus, but I chose not to press my point, as the value of a Pyrrhic victory enjoyed from prison struck me as minimal. I therefore retreated to my hired coach and headed home, wondering how I could possibly gain the protection I desired before I was due to surrender the book to Sir Albert.

Once in my house, I called for more wine and retired to my parlor, from which the divan had been removed. I sat on a chair before the fire, only a few feet away from where Sir Albert's tough had knocked me against the wall, and there fell asleep.

Perhaps a few hours later, my serving man hurried into the room to inform me that the house, to his regret, was very much ablaze. A quick sniff of the air revealed the presence of smoke, and a peek down the hallway displayed a terrifying wall of flames. Having no choice but to concur with James's analysis, I fled, very much hoping that the rest of the staff was able to do the same. Anyone burned to death, I decided, I would do the kindness of reviving. It seemed to me a safer course than running about the house looking for kitchen maids huddled in corners.

A quarter hour later, I stood in the distance, watching neighbors and volunteers pour water upon my house. I'd had the good sense to keep the book on my person, and so it was never in more danger than was I, but I had little more reason to rejoice. My house was in ruins, a charred shell. No doubt Sir Albert knew where I had stored my money, and he would have effected plans to make it impossible that I should retrieve it. I was now backed into a corner, and if I were to survive this ordeal intact, I would have no choice but to deliver ownership of the book to Sir Albert. I would have to set aside my need to win, my desire for revenge, and capitulate. As Sir Albert had observed, I had been a penniless rogue before, and no doubt I could be one again. Indeed, I could see myself, in my mind's eye, only a few days or weeks hence, riding upon a mail carriage to some nameless inn, paying forth my last few coins for a room and a chance to swindle or cheat or trick or bed some stranger out of his or her small purse.

"No," I said aloud. I would not do it. I would not surrender. I would be maimed and defeated before I would hand him that victory, but how I would thwart him, I could not say. If I could not simply enter Kensington Palace, I would need to find a sponsor. A visit to the House of Lords, perhaps, might be the first step to gaining an audience with a sympathetic and connected Tory. It was a wise course but a slow one. It would no doubt take days, at the very least, to find and convince the right person to introduce me to the queen. I only had hours, and I could not think how best to use them.

As I stood there, considering my options, a boy approached me, letter in hand. "Is you January?" he asked.

"I is," I assured him, snatching the letter out of his hand.

It was from Sir Albert. He wrote in threatening and somewhat colorful language, but his point was succinct. He had taken the precaution of having me watched, and so he knew about my abortive venture to Kensington. And now, for my perfidy, there would be consequences. My house, I already knew, was destroyed, but that was not the whole of my punishment. Lady

Caroline was dead. He had, in response to my double dealing, taken her life, strangled her while she struggled beneath his grip in wide-eyed terror. However, as I was the necromancer, there was no need that her death should be a permanent condition. If I were to bring him the means of revival, he would allow me to return her to life before relieving me of my abilities.

I stared at the words on the page, illuminated by the light of my burning house, and I felt rage and sorrow and pathetic self-pity. I had been lazy and sloppy. I had treated my power lightly and not considered its consequences. I had been content with a life of leisure while, all around me, my enemies had planned and concocted stratagems. I was, in short, outmatched and out of time. I could not preserve my wealth, my power, and the woman I loved without having a stratagem of my own. I could not repay Sir Albert for his crimes unless I possessed the means to defeat him. I therefore turned my back on my ruined house and set off into the night. It was time I showed Sir Albert that I was not a man with whom to trifle. I had wrought these terrible things. Lady Caroline was dead because of me, and I swore then and there that I would make things right. I would do anything to revive her and punish Sir Albert.

Several hours later, spade in hand and covered with sweat in the cold night air, I stood over the open grave and performed the ritual. I held my breath, regretting my decision even while I understood that I had no choice. And then I watched while he sat up and looked about, confused.

"Was I dead?" he asked.

I nodded.

"And I ain't no more."

I shook my head.

"You done it?"

I nodded again.

With closed fist, my father struck me in the face, knocking

me against the freshly dug earth of the grave from which I had rescued him.

My father remained sitting in his coffin, like a man roused from a refreshing nap. His clothes were in reasonably good shape, for he had not been in the ground overlong, and he was not excessively dirty. In point of fact, his odor was less offensive than on any occasion I could recall. His face had been restored, and the damage I'd done with the mason's hammer was but a memory. He was back, only, like Sir Albert, more powerful and potent than ever.

"Don't go thinking you're Jesus Christ," he said. "I'm sure if you done it, a monkey could do it." He pushed himself to his feet and began to bend and unbend his elbow. "It ain't felt so good in years. Now, to celebrate my return to life, I aim to get myself good and drunk. Then I want a whore. And then we'll deal with your problem."

I rubbed my jaw, which hurt, but nothing was broken and no teeth had been dislodged. I suppose such a blow might serve as the equivalent of a hug or a handshake for a normal man. "How could you know I had a problem? Have you been observing my activities from the next world?"

"I don't recall nothing of the next world, but if I'd had the ability to watch this one, I wouldn't have wasted my time by looking at you. I know you have a problem, and I know it's a big one, because otherwise you'd have left me in the ground. Whatever you're up against, it has to be mighty scary for you to recruit your old pa to your side."

That was true enough.

"Now," he said, "let's get going. Drinks and whores."

"Very well," I said. I supposed there was no hurry. Lady Caroline was not going to get any more dead than she was already.

*   *   *

We went to a bagnio toward which he felt a particular fondness, and soon he had his arms around a pair of scantily dressed beauties. The proprietress of the establishment appeared astonished to see him alive and healed in his face, but my father dismissed her questions. Rumors of his death were false, and his face was recovered. He then disappeared to a room with his two girls, and left me alone at a table with a bottle of wine and a healthy dose of regret.

I had no interest in the temptresses employed within those walls, for my heart and my mind were absorbed with Lady Caroline, lying cold and dead somewhere, waiting for me to come to her. A foolish romp with a stranger had no charms to offer me. But as I continued to drink the very indifferent wine, and as I grew increasingly inebriated, it became difficult to fend off the advances of the charmers who sought my attention.

At last I determined I could hardly be blamed for seeking comfort and release, and so I followed a fair-haired creature called Julia to a private room. There, in the near-darkness, broken only a single flickering candle, she began to kiss me, and for a moment I forgot my troubles and, to a lesser extent, the fact that Julia smelled most distressingly of other men.

This lovely oblivion lasted but a moment, for soon the door burst open with a terrifying crash, and I jumped back, prepared to explain the misunderstanding. Of course, there was none. This was not some middling man's wife or daughter, but a whore, and I had no need to explain my actions.

However, it was no angered spouse come into the room, but my father. He was drunk and staggering, and held a bottle of wine loosely by its neck. He gestured at me with it, and its contents sloshed out upon the floor.

"You like this one, do you?"

"Well enough," I said. "A bit rank, but I'm not inclined to fuss."

"Then I'll have her," he said.

I opened my mouth to object but thought better of it. My conflict was not with my father. He was, again, alive, and no doubt that conflict would be coming, but until Sir Albert was dealt with, I was best served by staying out of my father's way.

"Very well," I said. I moved toward the door.

"No." With his free hand, he shoved me hard. I staggered backward but did not fall. "You watch. You watch me do what you cannot."

"I could," I said. "I simply choose not to. I also choose not to witness your intimate moments."

"You've spent so much time among these mincing danglers, you've come to speak like one. Now you watch how a real man takes a woman, and you sit there like the eunuch you are. You do what I say, or I leave you to your problems. Maybe I'll even stick a knife in your back, like you never had the guts to do to me. A hammer to the face, indeed. A real man takes his weapon and thrusts it in, as I'm about to demonstrate."

There was no point in objecting. There was no point in refusing. I would indulge my father for the few hours it was necessary to indulge him, and then I would consider my next moves. And so I stayed. I shall spare the reader any more details of this scene. I am forever scarred by it. There is no reason you should be, too.

When he had taken his fill of drink and women and humiliating his only child, my father and I sat in a private room of the bagnio to discuss my situation. He leaned back in his chair, fire behind him, a mug of beer in his hand, and closed his eyes at the pleasure of it all.

"Swiving whores beats the piss out of being dead," he told me. "So tell me. How exactly did you, of all people, learn to raise the dead?"

"There was a book. I found it among your possessions, in fact."

He narrowed his eyes. "I think I know the one. I always wanted to keep it, and I never could tell why. Figures though, don't it? The only worthwhile thing you've ever done, and you got it from me."

I sighed. "You had the power to do worthwhile things, and you never knew it. I hardly think that is something worth bragging about."

He slammed his mug down on the table. "Don't give me sass! You wanted me, and you got me. Keep your tongue civil, or I'll beat you until you recall what it is, exactly, you got. Now, you tell me your problem, and don't leave out none of the details, and I'll figure out just what I'm going to do about it."

And so, I proceeded to tell him everything. I told him how I had found the book, and used it and brought Sir Albert back to life. I told him how I had extorted money from the others and how all of this had attracted the queen's attention. Finally, I told him how Sir Albert had threatened me and killed Lady Caroline. With only a few hours left before Sir Albert sent his man Hubert after me, I needed a resolution that was both speedy and sure.

"So, this Sir Albert is a thorny branch up your ass," he observed, "but you can't do nothing about him because he's richer, stronger, smarter, and more ruthless than you."

It was not how I would have framed it, but my best course here was to make my father feel like he needed to show me up. "That is correct."

"And you want to bring this rich slut of yours back to life. Let me give you a little bit of advice. If you find her soon enough," he told me, "before she starts to decay, you might want to have your way with her before you bring her back." He set his feet up on the table. "It's a pleasure few enough men sample, but I've never heard of a one who didn't enjoy it."

I stared at him indignantly. "I shan't violate her corpse!"

"No, not a gentleman like you. You only lied to her, brought her dead husband back to life because you knew it would make her miserable, and then took all her friends for what they were worth. But a man's got to draw the line somewhere, don't he?"

I made no answer to this.

"Aren't you going to ask me my price for helping you?" he said.

"I thought, perhaps, bringing you back to life would be sufficient."

"You thought wrong," he told me with a disturbing grin. It was the one he showed when he was pleased to demonstrate his power over me. "I want the method of resurrection. I want the power for myself."

"Only the owner of the book may possess the power," I told him, repressing a smile of triumph. "And you cannot read."

"I'll rip the lips off your face if I think you're laughing at me, boy," he said. "As for reading, I can learn, I suppose. But you will have to give me the book, and teach me the method. That will do for the nonce."

"Why do you want it?" I asked.

"Power," he said with a shrug. "And you met Mrs. Tyler."

"Yes," I said, thinking of his landlady and wondering why she would make him wish to own the book.

"She changed me," he said wistfully. "She made me into a different kind of man."

"I haven't seen any evidence of that," I said.

"Well, it's all mixed up now, isn't it?" he said. "I'm darker than I used to be. I can feel it. Coming back did something to me. And if she and I are going to be together, we need to even things up."

"So," I summarized, "you wish for the book so you can kill the woman you love and then bring her back in the hopes of her being more like you."

"That's it, exactly."

It seemed to me a very poor sort of idea to grant the power of life and death to my father, particularly as the first thing he would do is murder an innocent woman in the hopes that she would come back less good-natured. Nevertheless, I was not certain I saw an alternative. I needed a man such as he was, and such a man did not come without his price. I had to choose between saving Lady Caroline and granting godlike power to someone without pity or remorse. I chose to save Lady Caroline, and so I agreed to his terms.

"It is a power you must handle with respect and the utmost concern for the good of all mankind," I said.

"The devil take your respect and your care," he said. "If you want to save your highborn bitch, you will give it to me. If you care about all mankind, you will not."

"Then I shall give it to you."

He took a long drink from his mug. "Grand."

The next morning, we visited a series of stores that my father might purchase the items he required. We then proceeded at once to visit Sir Albert Worthington. My father stood there in his rough clothes, looking like a rustic. I was in my fine suit, a bit worn from escaping flames and a night in a whorehouse, but otherwise intact. My collar was clean, my buttons glittering, and my sword hung by my side. In sum, I looked ineffectual, and my father looked like a poor sort of servant. It was just the sort of impression I wished to make.

It was Hubert who answered the door, and it rather surprised me that he would take upon himself so menial a task, but then I suspected I understood the meaning. Given that Sir Albert was going about killing his own wife and such, he had almost certainly sent the servants away. This was so much the better.

Hubert said very little, perhaps not wishing to perform for

us without the audience of his master. He merely led us to the parlor and vanished. Nearly an hour later, he returned, now with Sir Albert, and this time, Hubert appeared far more animated. That both men were amused by our presence, there could be no doubt. Each wore an easy, good-natured smile, as though they were chums freshly returned from an errand of mischief.

"Well," said Sir Albert, "you've come to pay me a visit. And you've brought an old ruffian who stinks of whores and drink. Very kind of you. Now, are you prepared to give me the book?"

My father cleared his throat and rose to his feet. "Begging your pardon, Sir Albert. I am Mr. January's father, and he has asked me to come here and speak a few words on his behalf."

"On his behalf!" cried Sir Albert. "I've never heard the like. Have you heard the like, Hubert?"

"I have not, sir," answered Hubert. "On his behalf indeed. This ain't a funeral, nor nothing like one."

"If I may be so bold as to disagree," said my father. "It is rather like one."

So saying he removed his pistols, one from each pocket, and proceeded to shoot both men in their respective heads.

A few minutes later, I revived Sir Albert. He lay on the floor, and when I was finished, he hopped to his feet with astonishing vigor.

"How dare you!" he cried.

My father stabbed him in the heart.

I shan't bore the reader by rehearsing each separate murder. My father bludgeoned, asphyxiated, and beat Sir Albert to his death. He smashed his face into the fireplace stones until his head was a bloody pulp. He gouged out his eyes. He stuck a burning poker down his throat. In short, he died and was revived perhaps a dozen times. I lost count. He might have been garroted twice, though the details are hazy. I can assure my readers that my father rather enjoys garroting.

I noticed, and this detail was not lost on my father, that after the sixth revival, Sir Albert appeared to have a marked decrease in energy. I did not know if that was a temporary effect or if a person can only be revived a certain number of times before his life energy begins to dissipate. The truth of it hardly mattered, because my father meant to make good use of this fact.

When I revived Sir Albert after my father had killed him for the final time, I first propped him into a sitting position, and my father placed Hubert's severed head in his lap, for he had decapitated that worthy, and had made clear that I would, under no circumstances, revive him. Sir Albert opened his eyes and stared in horror. He tried to get up, but he was apparently woozy. He rose and fell down to the floor twice, finally clawing at the wall to gain purchase. He slipped in Hubert's blood, or perhaps it was his own, but did not fall over.

"You ain't what you were," said my father. His face, his hands, and his clothes were now stained with Sir Albert's and Hubert's blood. All of this endless murder had filled him with a manic energy. His eyes were wide, his cheeks flushed, and he breathed heavily. He looked like the embodiment of terror that he, in fact, was. "The effects nibble at you. You don't feel it the first time, and maybe not the second neither, but as many as we done you, you begin to feel it. Next it will be worse. Might be you don't have the use of your mind rightly, or your legs don't work. Can't put you down for another go neither, since you might well come out the worse for it."

"This is preposterous," said Sir Albert, his voice now slow and somewhat slurred. "How . . . dare you treat me so. Are you in the queen's service? I demand . . . you tell me."

"You don't demand nothing," my father said. "Though I'll tell you because it pleases me to do so that I don't give a turd for Tory or Whig, Protestant or Papist. I'd take the queen's coin if she were offering, but it's too hard to get to at the moment, so I'll take yours instead. Tell me where you put your wife's body, and then tell me where you got your valuables, and in exchange, I'll let you live."

"Do you . . . think you can use violence . . . to force my hand?" Sir Albert demanded.

"You burned down my son's house and killed your own wife, so I'd say violence is the order of the day."

"Your son," Sir Albert sputtered with contempt. "He can't . . . he can't even fight his own battles. He needs . . . his papa to save his precious book."

My father laughed. "That's true enough, but because he needed me, it ain't his book no more, it's mine. You have to deal with me now, my popinjay, and you've already wished you hadn't forced my son's hand, I'll wager. So now, here's how it is going to transpire. You will tell us where you put your wife, and if you then run as fast as your legs will carry you, and I never see you more, I shall let you live out your days as best you can without name or money or influence. That's all there is. You ain't going to get a better offer. Say no if you like. I'll just keep on killing you until you say yes. I haven't yet tried to kill you by cutting off what little you got between your legs. Now that sounds like a right good time."

Sir Albert stared at him, and he seemed to know he had been bested. "She's upstairs . . . upon her bed."

"Now, that wasn't so hard, was it?" my father said, and he cracked Sir Albert over the head with a fire iron.

"I thought you weren't going to kill him again," I said.

"I don't think I did. I just put him to sleep while we make certain everything is as he says."

We went upstairs and searched through the various rooms until we found Lady Caroline, upon a bed, cold and still in the grip of death. Her skin was pale and waxy, her lips blue. Her eyes, which were open, looked like clouded marbles. Around her neck, a ring of black bruises told the tale of her brutal murder. I stood in the doorway staring at her, full of hatred for the monster who could have done this to her. There she was, dead, but within my power to restore. And yet, might she be different? Might she be vile? Would the Lady Caroline who came back be the same as the one who died?

My father appeared behind me. "Now's your chance," he told me. "Lift her skirts and have yourself a little taste."

I chose to ignore this bit of advice. Instead, I went to work upon her at once, bending over her and beginning the procedure. I had only just started when I felt my father's rough hand on my shoulder, yanking me back.

"If you won't take your fill, I'll do it for you." He grinned at me. "Let's just say there's one more payment to be made for my services. You can have a go at her or I can. But she ain't coming back to life until one of us does."

I stared at him. "Why?"

He laughed. "Because that is how I like it."

I shook my head. "Why must you be like this? For what possible reason do you wish to torture and crush your own son? Have you no capacity for love or joy or sentiment?"

He snorted. "This from the boy who struck me in the face with a hammer and stole my money."

"You had it coming, as you most certainly know. And, as you say, I might have stabbed you. Will you punish me for showing you that mercy?"

"For being a coward, you mean," he said with a derisive laugh. "Don't pretend to be a saint when all you are is a boy who can't ever be a man. That's all there is to it. You're afraid of me, and I have nothing but contempt for a coward. If you can't do things as you like, then you'll damn well do them as I like. Now, will you have a tumble with this dead woman or no?"

"I will not," I said with a noble dignity certain to fill him with disgust. "What would Mrs. Tyler say of you if she were here?"

"Don't you speak of her," my father said, jabbing a finger into my chest. "Besides, once I break her neck and bring her back, she'll be the first to cheer me on. Now, if you are not going to have at her, you shall see it done." So saying, he began to unbutton his breeches.

"No," I said, my voice hardly more than a whisper.

He continued to unbutton, but he looked at me with a wolf-ish grin. "What are you going to do about it, boy?"

I said nothing.

"That's what I thought." He turned away from me, having pulled down his breeches, laughing, no doubt, at the juvenile delight of thrusting his bare buttocks at me. He grabbed Lady Caroline's skirts and began to lift. Then his eyes went wide, in surprise. He staggered backward, one hand straight out, the other reaching frantically for the waist of his breeches, that he might pull them up. He could not grab them, however, and he tripped over his own clothing, falling facedown onto the cold floor.

After inserting it into his neck, I had pulled out my hanger at once, and now there was a gaping hole in the flesh, which bled copiously. My father, still lying facedown, raised one hand to the wound, but blood flowed freely past his fingers.

"You wouldn't dare," he said. "You don't have the courage to take a blade to me."

"Apparently, I do," I observed.

"You'll . . . bring me back," he muttered.

"Of course," I said. "You are my father, and I shall restore you. And next time, you will be better behaved."

I had no intention of doing any such thing, and I briefly considered tormenting him with that knowledge, but better safe than sorry, I decided. If he thought he would be revived, he would be content to lie there and bleed. If he knew I would never return him from death, he might find a hidden pool of strength. My father ought not to be underestimated. And so, in the service of my survival, and so Lady Caroline's survival, and indeed Mrs. Tyler's survival, I swallowed my love of revenge. I like to think this demonstrates my moral growth.

Once the old monster was properly dead, I took Lady Caroline's body, which was uncomfortably stiff, in my arms and carried her to another room. This was an awkward procedure, for a dead body is a heavy thing, and there may have been some unmanly dragging at certain points. She did not appear to mind. Once I had her in a guest room, away from the sight of my father's corpse, I commenced once more to break the shackles of mortality, as only I know how, and used my remarkable skills to restore breath once more to those sweet lips.

In a moment, her eyes fluttered and she shot up from her bed. She looked at me, and she gasped, putting a hand to her now-milky throat in the memory of what that beast had done to her. And then, to my surprise, she flung her arms around me.

"You came back for me, Reginald!" she cried. "I knew you would!"

The warmth of her body against mine, the wet of her tears against my neck—how can I describe the joy of this moment? I held her close and told her I would always save her, always take any risk for her. I told her I loved her, and even death could not keep us apart.

"I am sorry I doubted you," she said to me, still crying against my neck. "I know now you love me."

I studied her. "Do you feel any different, Lady Caroline? More . . . evil, perhaps?"

She cocked her head as she considered the question. "I don't believe so . . ."

That was good enough for me. "I have seen to everything," I said. "Sir Albert is no more. He shall never trouble you again."

She pulled away from me and looked at me, her moist eyes locking with my own. "You killed him?"

"You needn't concern yourself with the details," I told her. "When I met you, he was dead. The dead should remain dead."

"Excepting me?" she asked.

"Excepting you," I answered. "And me. I shall leave you the book in my will, and you shall do the same for me, and we may be immortal and together."

She wrapped her arms around me again. I was not quite certain that I wished to be with her for all eternity. I loved her absolutely, but can a man ever love a woman that much? I supposed I would find out, and it was clearly what she wished to hear, so the plan would do for now.

I then excused myself, explaining to her that there was a bit of cleaning up to do, and that she might not wish to see what damage that necessity had wrought in her house. She told me she was content to remain closeted until I told her otherwise. Lady Caroline closed the door behind me, so she would not have to listen to the sound of me disposing of the bodies.

My man James was yet in my employ, and he proved useful in helping me to collect bodies, parts of bodies, and other detritus. I could think of no better place to deposit them all than in the Fleet Ditch itself. How fitting that so foul a pit should be the final resting place of the worst man I had ever known, along with one more who had proved surprisingly good competition for that title.

Since he had arrived on the scene and then disappeared so suddenly, Sir Albert's return from the dead proved to be a short-lived sensation. Most people presumed he had wandered back to his grave, or what had appeared to be a corporeal Sir Albert had merely been a spirit. Those who had not seen him with their own eyes might have guessed that the entire story was a hoax.

All of these theories were well with me, for Lady Caroline was never legally declared unwidowed and her property remained her own.

I should say that it continued to remain her own after we wed, for she arranged that her wealth should be held as separate property, but since I now had money of my own, I was in no way distressed. We wanted one another, not one another's silver, and that is a much better foundation for a happy marriage. We did choose to vacate London, however, for it was uncomfortable encountering, upon a regular basis, those people from whom I had, by means of necromantic extortion, obtained my wealth. No matter. As it turned out, neither Lady Caroline nor I was particularly attached to London society. We removed ourselves to the north, from whence Lady Caroline's family originated, and bought a beautiful house in York, in the shadow of the minster. It has proved to be a happy home for us.

As for the book, and its powers, I have set these aside. I want nothing more to do with them and I have vowed never again to use them unless financial distress or some other inclination should convince me otherwise. It is but a surety of my happiness with Lady Caroline, there to bring her back should some tragedy befall her, assuming we are still, at the time, living in a state of felicity.

Perhaps it was so that Lady Caroline was a bit darker after her resurrection. Perhaps it was this darkness that allowed her to forgive me my crimes and to marry a man who had blackmailed her friends and taken such liberties with the lives of others. I could not say. I do feel that a little bit of darkness might have made her even more compatible with me, and nothing that re-sulted from her death and revival harmed our love. As to whether or not it strengthened it, I shall leave that to better minds than mine.

As one last note, I should mention that business takes me,

from time to time, to London to meet with bankers or lawyers or suchlike people, and while I am there, I always make it a habit to pay a visit to St. Bartholomew's Hospital. It is a wretched place, mostly full of the housed dying, but there are a few longer-term patients, paid for out of donations. There lies such a terrible case, a man who lacks feet and so cannot walk. He lacks hands, and so cannot write. He lacks a tongue, and so cannot speak. Some unknown benefactor pays for his upkeep, and I must say, I find it a touching experience to visit this unfortunate, whose eyes are wide and expressive, as if he has something to say to me. What could it be? No one knows. Perhaps he wishes to express gratitude to those who care for him. Perhaps he wishes to say that it was a mistake to cross a man so disposed to feed his inclination for vengeance. Perhaps he wishes to plea for death. I can offer no informed guess as to what this poor fellow wishes to communicate. I suppose it is a secret he will take with him to his grave.

Alive Day

Jonathan Maberry

Author's Note
This story features Captain Joe Ledger, the lead character from
my series of science/action thrillers. It is not necessary to have
read any of Ledger's previous adventures in order to read this
story.

1

RATTLESNAKE TEAM

Ten Days Ago . . .

He lay there, crushed inside a fist of darkness.

Unable to move.

Barely able to breathe.

"I'm sorry," he tried to say. "God . . . I'm so sorry."

There was no answer from the darkness.

The Afghan desert that surrounded this abandoned town had been so hot before . . .

Now it was cold.

So cold.

Sergeant Michael O'Leary—combat call sign "Finn"—tried to move his legs, but they were dead and distant things. He could barely feel them. His toes were cold, though. Icy. He could feel that much.

He tried to move his arms.

Nothing from the left side except a dull and nonspecific ache.

Finn's arm moved, though. Just a little. He tried to will it to respond with speed and strength and dexterity, but there was nothing like that. He couldn't actually feel the limb as he raised it. Only its weight, where it pulled on his shoulder muscles.

His wrist bumped against something, and despite the overall numbness he could feel that. Some of it. Enough to know what it was.

Rock. Or maybe tumbled stone from when this cave was part of a market stall in some ancient time. Either way it was cold and unyielding.

In the shadows, Finn tried to remember the terrain of this place. Whoever lived here once had smoothed the floor and chipped back the walls, but it had all been abandoned long ago. Now the walls were cracked and debris lay scattered.

He'd been running through darkness; he remembered that easily enough. Running to get in position so his team could launch the ambush. All he had to do was reach the end of the tunnel, kneel behind a pile of old rough-cut sandstone blocks, and use his first shot to signal the attack. That was all. Simple. He'd done it so many times before, on battlefields around the world.

So easy a child could have done it. Something his experience and training should have guaranteed was smooth and without a hitch.

Except . . .

Except.

"God . . . I'm sorry. Please, please, please . . ."

Running. Stumbling. Tripping over obstacles that weren't where he remembered them being. He should have used his night vision. Finn knew that now. Knew that it was his fault that he'd tripped and fallen.

And accidentally fired that shot.

It was so stupid a move that if they walked off this, his men would never trust him again. If any of his team got killed because of it . . . ? His best hope would be court martial and discharge. That thought was a ladder that climbed down into some very dark places.

When he'd tripped, he'd hit something and lay stunned, sprawled and groaning, while his men died.

The darkness around him still seemed to echo with that single fucking shot.

And the screams that followed as all hell broke loose outside.

When Finn closed his eyes, he could still hear it.

The deep bass of Bear's voice strangled into a piercing shriek.

Jazzman's voice, begging and pleading and crying.

Cheech Wizard's unbroken, inarticulate gargle of wet agony.

Were they still screaming now? Was that real or was he going out of his mind?

Finn stopped moving and listened to the darkness.

All he heard was his own shallow breathing. He held his breath, listened harder.

Then he heard the screams again. All three of them. Bear, Jazzman, and Cheech Wizard. Screaming with raw misery.

But the screams were far away. Down the corridor, or outside, or somewhere else.

How could they still be real? How could his men still be screaming?

Finn had no way of knowing. He was sure that he'd badly hurt himself. This could all have been a dream. The product of shock and injury and blood loss.

His men couldn't still be screaming.

Not after all this time. Not after all these hours.

No one could yell that loud for this long.

"I'm coming!" Finn cried.

Or thought he did.

But his throat felt dry and dusty. Had he managed to even make a sound?

The echoes of the screams faded. First a little, then more and more until the last warped and broken fragment rebounded from the wall and struck him like an accusing arrow.

After a long time, Finn realized that he was weeping, but even his tears were dry and cold against his cheeks. The sobs hurt his chest.

"I'm sorry," he whispered, and this time the words were dragged past the stricture in his throat. "Oh . . . God . . . I'm so sorry . . ."

There was a time of absolute silence, and then the echoes of the screams blasted him in the face. Finn could feel their breath as if each of his men crouched over him. He could feel the heat of their breath and the wet wrongness as their screams spackled him with spit.

Or blood.

The screams were of pain so big, so hideous, that words could not express them. These screams were shrieked in a language known only to the dead and dying, to the tortured and the damned.

But Finn, shivering in the dark cave, knew that language.

He could understand every accusation. Each derisive shout. Each curse.

"I'm sorry," was all he could say.

Then there was another sound.

Distant, small, rhythmic.

The screams faded for a moment.

No, that was wrong. They paused. The echoes of the screams paused as if they were listening to the new sound.

Into the silence, Finn said, "I'm sorry."

In his despair he thought he saw a figure in the cave, even though there was no light to see anything. A slender figure in loose clothes. A boy, or maybe a small woman. Moving without sound, turning first to look at him and then away as if realizing that he could see her and not wanting to be seen. Then he blinked and there was nothing there. Nothing to see. No way to see anything even if it was there.

I'm losing it, he thought. Christ, I'm going to go out of my mind in the dark . . .

The sound in the distance was growing stronger, becoming distinctly what it was. A sound that seemed to be as old as these mountains even though it belonged only to the last century.

Whup-whup-whup.

"God," breathed Finn.

The echoes were still there, but faint. They bounced around through the dark air the way echoes will, but they didn't fade the way echoes should.

Whup-whup-whup.

Finn raised his hand, feeling its solid deadness as a weight supported by the muscles in his shoulder. He tried to raise his hand, as if signaling would matter with him lost inside a cave, wrapped in shadows and blood.

Finn felt something brush past his fingertips.

Something that was colder than his dying flesh.

Something that, at first, shied away from his touch.

Something that came back, though.

As the echoes came back.

Whup-whup-whup.

The helicopter was coming.

"Please," whispered Finn. He said it to the darkness and to the pain. He said it to the illusion of the furtive woman that his madness had conjured. He said it to the awful possibility of the helicopter drawing near and then going past him and away. He said it to the shadows.

"Please . . ."

Finn suddenly felt something near his ear. A bug?

No.

Breath.

The soft, warm exhalation as someone crouched behind him, out of sight, out of reach.

"Who's there? Cheech? Jazz? Is that you? C'mon, Christ, I'm hurt and—"

Another breath exhaled against the side of his face. God, it stank. Like meat left out in the sun.

Was it an animal? Something living in this fucking cave?

"Get away!" yelled Finn.

But with the next breath he heard a voice.

Soft. So soft, like sands blowing over the desert in the deep of night. A whisper of a woman's voice.

"You come to my town speaking a foreign tongue. Are you a heretic and defiler?"

The woman seemed to speak in a language he didn't know or recognize, and yet he understood every word.

I'm really losing my shit here. Oh God . . .

It was so strange a question under the circumstances that it took Finn a moment to organize an answer. Was this one of the Taliban, lost in the dark? If so, then the question was framed in an awkward and old-fashioned way.

In Pashto, Finn said, "No . . . I'm a friend."

"You are no friend of mine," spat the woman. "No friend of ours. You are a foreigner. You come to my town and take what is mine. You take what is sacred—"

"No," Finn said quickly, defensively.

"I want back what was stolen," whispered the woman. "You damn yourself by taking it."

That's when he felt her presence. Actually felt it. Not a touch, not the breath. A presence.

It was aware, intelligent; somehow Finn knew that. Sensed it. Finn's mind resisted as he tried to define what this was. Even though he knew this was a person, somehow it didn't feel like that. Not anything like that. Even if he could have seen who spoke to him, even if everything had looked totally normal, he knew that it wasn't. That it couldn't be. With everything Finn was, he was certain of that. This was—different. In the way that blood is different from paint, even if not to the eye. In the way a dead child is different from a sleeping one, even at a glance through the open bedroom door. This was that kind of difference. Not really human. Something else. This was like—sickness. As if the woman who crouched breathing at his ear was sickness. Not a sick person, but a person who was sickness itself. It was the worst thing Finn had ever felt.

"You can have the opium," Finn said quickly. "We don't want it."

In the darkness, the woman spat and Finn felt a searing pain on his cheek.

"You have taken what is mine."

"No, we haven't," Finn said insistently, desperate now to make some kind of deal, a bargain that might give him a lifeline. "Look . . . all I want is to get my guys and get out of here. We don't want anything. Nothing, okay? I just want to get my guys and then the four of us are gone. We'll leave you alone and you can do what you want with the—"

"There are four of you?"

"Yes . . ."

The next sound he heard was so strange that it took him a long time to make any kind of sense of it. A series of soft, abrupt moist sounds.

Was this woman . . . sniffing him?

Yes.

The sniffing stopped and there was silence for a while.

Then he heard a small and ugly laugh. He had never heard a woman utter a laugh like that before. It was the way an animal might laugh.

"You are telling me the truth," said the woman. "You have not defiled the shrines of the lilitu?"

"The what . . . ?"

Another pause, more chuckling.

"Then we are at a place," said the voice, and suddenly it sounded less alien and more human. Even the feel of it changed. Now it seemed as if it truly was a person squatting over him. The nightmarish delusion that it was a monster began to recede. Not all the way, but enough to keep the terror just beyond reach. "It seems I have taken something from you."

Soft laughter. Mocking and ironic.

"What do you mean? What did you take?" But Finn thought he knew what had been taken. "Wait, do you . . . do you have my men?"

"They are with us," said the voice.

"No!"

"Do you know where we are?"

"W-what?"

"This tunnel . . . long ago this was where vendors set up their tables. Spices hung from these walls; the rocks echoed with the cries of sheep and lambs and goats. Men and women dickered and sold and bought. This was where bargains were made for all of the things that offered sustenance and comfort and pleasure."

"No . . . this is just a bunch of old ruins."

"'Ruins,'" echoed the voice, and for a moment there seemed to be a flavor of sadness there. "I can still hear the voices of the thousands who came here. Them . . . and those who lived here after the old times had passed. This place has had a dozen names. A hundred. Even in times like these when the desert sands and the fires of war turn these caves and caverns into a realm of ghosts, I can hear those old voices. Such . . . deals were struck here. For a string of camels. For lambs to sacrifice. For a knife in the dark. For the return of something lost."

Finn waited, muscles tensed, not sure how to respond, or even if he should.

He could feel the person bend closer. A rustle of clothes, the creak of joints. "And now, here in my town, a town I saw built, a town I saw carved from the living rock, we are well met to bargain once more."

"What . . . kind of bargain?" he asked cautiously.

"What will you give me for what you want? What bargain will you make for what you want?"

It made Finn suddenly furious that this fucking thing—man, woman, whoever or whatever it was whispering to him in the dark—had his men. Had them and wanted to trade them like beads at a bazaar. Like sacrificial lambs.

God.

It made Finn so furious. He summoned all of his flagging strength and, with one vicious growl, twisted around and lashed out with a balled fist.

His hand found nothing, struck nothing.

As if there was nothing there. But Finn could hear it breathing. He could hear it laughing softly to itself.

That laugh . . . that was the worst thing of all.

2
ECHO TEAM

My name is Captain Joseph Ledger. Former Baltimore PD, former Army Ranger. Currently drawing pay from one of those alphabet organizations that the public never hears about.

Ever.

The DMS. Short for Department of Military Sciences. Only we're not military. Not in any way I could explain.

We're certainly not regular army.

Guys like me aren't regular anything.

We're not even regular Special Forces. You won't find a single mention of a DMS field team on any list of JSOC crews, not even on those eyes-only black-ops lists. We operate off the radar because there are times someone has to. Plausible deniability will only take you so far and the president has to either lie or tell truths that—believe me—nobody wants to hear.

You know that saying, about how the truth will set you free.

It's true most of the time.

It's not that we're out there being bad guys. Nothing like that.

It's just that there are some things that will never fit into a newsfeed. Some things would make very bad TV. Disturbing TV. The kind that wouldn't just shake Joe Public's faith in the political powers that be but that would put serious cracks in his fundamental view of the world.

You can't sum up an after-action report with "There are more things in heaven and earth, Horatio," and nobody can stand behind this stuff in a press conference.

I know it's fucked, but it is what it is.

Some of this stuff has really screwed with my head. I'm not the same guy I was when I was recruited by the DMS.

How could I be?

How could anyone?

We were in a Black Hawk cruising low and fast through a series of rocky passes that looked like the ruins of some ancient castle. Afghanistan is like that in areas. It's a bleak, broken, and desolate place. I know of at least two video games that used scans of the landscape as the design basis for inhospitable alien worlds. Personally, I think the surface of Mars would be cheerier and more welcoming.

I didn't have my whole team with me. Most of my guys were taking some R and R after a cocksucker of a firefight we had in North Carolina. Yeah, that's right. The homeland itself. The DEA had been working a joint op with the FBI, something about a rumor that terrorists were backing meth production. Meth is not really an export drug—it's mostly screwing up people at home, and in increasing numbers. The joint task force got themselves into a firefight with a distribution team, and in the process, a lot of bags of crystal got torn apart by live rounds. Worst case should have been contact highs. Instead, every single man there—DEA, FBI, *and* the bad guys—died within twenty-four hours.

Cause?

A brand-new strain of synthetic anthrax that had been mixed with the meth during the cool-down stage. Stuff had a contagion factor of 94 percent and a 100 percent kill rate. The Feds shut down the hospital and the site of the gunfight, and my guys were called in. I'm top-kick of Echo Team, a crew of first-chair shooters based out of the Warehouse in Baltimore. We took over the operation from the DEA and backtracked the meth to a major supply depot in a hangar of a bankrupt private airfield. Forty guys on the deck, mostly Russians with a few Cubans there for variety. They were in combat hazmat suits and everyone was armed for bear. We had our own protective gear—the latest generation of Saratoga Hammer Suits, which are designed for combat in the age of extreme bioweapons.

Echo Team was joined by Riptide Team out of Florida and Bronco Team out of Atlanta. We hit the place in a coordinated strike that started with a total lights-out thanks to a low-yield e-bomb that fried all their electronics. Then, with our night vision online, we raided from three points and cut them down.

They made a fight of it. Not sure if I admire that or not. Soldiers are supposed to respect their enemies, but that math gets skewed when your enemy is a terrorist who's trying to unleash a plague on a big chunk of the nonmilitary population. Junkies aren't the only ones who smoke meth. Lots of kids do, too. And lots of ordinary citizens. With that synthetic bacterium in there, it only needed one puff for a death sentence.

Of the forty bad guys and the eighteen of us, there was a big butcher's bill. Twenty-six thugs went to the morgue. I've blocked out two seconds sometime next year to give a shit about that. Three DMS guys went down, all from Bronco, when they raided a Quonset hut our intel said was cold storage and it turned out to be a lab. The bad guys were in the middle of a cook and everything blew. The three shooters from Bronco never knew what happened. Apart from that, there were nonfatal gunshot wounds and some shrapnel cuts. Anyone whose Hammer Suit got so much as a nick in it was washed down with antimicrobial soap and medevaced to a quarantine facility at a hospital a few blocks from the CDC in Atlanta, where they were given a cocktail of antibiotics. The only bright spot was that the synthetic anthrax responded really well to treatment.

So, that left me with two gunslingers—First Sergeant Bradley Sims, known as Top, and a giant of a kid from Orange County whose real name was Harvey Rabbit. No surprise that everyone called him Bunny. Top and Bunny had been with me since I joined the DMS. They'd been through almost everything I'd been through, and even between us, there were things we didn't talk about. Even though I had no way of knowing it, an itch between my shoulder blades told me that the situation we were flying into was going to be one of those.

I looked out the window and saw the Black Hawk's insectoid shadow fly up and down the sides of the austere Afghan mountains. Here and there, I saw a few small flocks of sheep, and in the hollow between two almost-vertical mountains was some burned-out wreckage.

"Dead crocodile," murmured Top.

I nodded. The debris was that of an old Soviet Mi-24 assault helicopter, known as a "crocodile" because of the scale-like camouflage paint job.

"Thought the Russians always recovered their downed birds," said Bunny.

"When they can find 'em," said Top. "Too damn many places out here to get lost."

That was true enough. These mountains were so remote and in many parts inaccessible to anyone but a goat or a goatherd.

"Besides," said Top, "sometimes an area's too hot for a recovery, and I can see at least fifty pocked-out cave mouths up the sides there. Taliban could have put a single shooter in each, and maybe two or three guys with RPGs, and half the damn Russian army couldn't smoke them out. It'd cost too much."

Bunny and I nodded, knowing that Top wasn't referring to a price tag in dollars.

That was really the story of the Afghan wars right there. The landscape favored hit-and-run guerilla fighters and was a total pain in the ass to a heavily mobilized ground force. Air support was good when the winds were right, but one eighteen-year-old kid with a rocket-propelled grenade and a six-foot-deep cave to squat in could turn the five-million-dollar fully armed and loaded UH-60L Black Hawk into flaming debris as useless as the old Russian crocodile that was now dwindling into the distance behind us. In the modern age, unmanned Predator technology was giving us a marginal edge. Yeah, marginal, against guys in sandals and robes. War wasn't war anymore.

I knew that if my team went down, someone else would pick up the mission, but no one would come looking for us. Our helo was equipped with a telemetric response system, which is a fancy way of saying that if the entire crew and all authorized passengers died, the cessation of our telemetry from the chips we all had under the skin would trigger a self-destruct package.

Boom. No evidence bigger than a paper clip. Our bodies? Vultures would pick us clean and the desert winds would strip the clothing from our bones. It was a chilling thought. If we died out here, our transport would die with us and all official records would be deleted. We'd cease to exist.

The men we were looking for were *almost* at that point.

It spilled out like this . . .

We were on an off-the-books search-and-rescue for an even deeper off-the-books infil team composed of four members of Rattlesnake Team. That team was one of four DMS groups on semi-permanent loan to the CIA for operations here on the Big Sand. Rattlesnake Team was hunting a very special Taliban convoy that was reported to be using opium transport to cover a much nastier cargo. Some kind of new pathogen that either had been weaponized or was on the way to a lab to be weaponized. That was about as precise as the intel got, but it rang the right bells all the way up the chain of command. The CIA deals with WMDs, but when it comes to bioweapons, they pick up the phone and call us.

Here's where it got complicated in a freaky kind of way.

The CIA had gotten a tip about the caravan from a village headman named Aziz, who was a known Taliban sympathizer. And the tip was not the result of a bribe, threat, or any enhanced interrogation. Aziz went into Kabul, bought a disposable cell phone, and called a guy who knew a guy who knew a guy who was in the CIA.

Yeah, chew on that for a moment.

Why'd Aziz make the call? Turns out that, despite digging the money the Taliban paid him to smooth some details for the drug caravans, this guy's regular gig was facilitating archaeological digs all through this part of the country. He knows who to bribe to get permits, and he makes arrangements with the local bad guys not to shoot the university types who risk their asses to collect Sumerian potsherds or ancient dinosaur poop. In the middle of a war.

I know, right?

Understand, most Muslims, especially those with college educations, are fiercely protective of anything historical. They treasure and preserve culture, partly because most of them are civilized folks who don't have their heads up their asses, and also because Islam contributed a hell of a lot to art, science, and math. After all, "algebra" is an Anglicized version of the Arabic word "al-jabr." They invented it.

However, there's this small group of total fundamentalist dickheads who think that Allah wants them to blow up anything that wasn't created for or by Muslims. They already destroyed some of the most profoundly beautiful Buddhist temples and statues. They want to destroy the Sphinx and the pyramids, too. The kind of stuff that would make Indiana Jones go totally postal.

Well, apparently some of the local Taliban have been messing with dig sites, shrines, and old ruins that predate Islam. People of one kind or another have been living in the region since the Middle Paleolithic era—call it fifty thousand years, give or take a long weekend. Islam's been around since the seventh century. These bozos wanted to erase any evidence that a civilized or enlightened culture existed before Muhammad founded the religion.

Aziz dimed the Taliban partly because, from the CIA intel reports, he was more of an opportunist than a villain, and partly because the destruction was cutting into his main source of income, which was greasing the archaeology network.

Or so we thought at the time. We found out more later, but I'll get to that.

So, Aziz contacted the CIA to tell them that the Taliban had royally screwed the pooch in two very distinct and related ways. First, they had taken control of a series of caves that were scheduled for excavation by a twenty-man team from the Institut National de Recherches Archéologiques Préventives in France, thus preventing Aziz from exacting his inflated fees to provide on-site safety for the team. And, second, in their downtime between ferrying tons of opium through the region, they were amusing themselves by destroying one of the world's most pristine lilitu, a kind of female Semitic desert demon related to the Lilith legends of the ancient Jews. Part of the shrine's uniqueness was that it was in Afghanistan at all—the lilitu were Mesopotamian monsters, and Afghanistan was not part of that empire.

Point is, the desecration of the site—and the clear loss of income for Aziz—turned him into a CIA informant. He'd have rather seen this band of Taliban get whacked than lose the university trade. The next link in the chain was that the CIA determined that this was the *same* Taliban group running the caravans that were likely hiding the bioweapons.

Nothing in the Middle East is ever simple and straightforward. Not a goddamn thing.

So, my boss, Mr. Church, sent Rattlesnake Team in to take out one of the caravans and kick-start the process of reclaiming those caves. None of this was in the name of archaeology or the preservation of antiquities.

In retrospect, maybe it should have been. Don't ask me. I'm just a shooter.

Ten days ago, Rattlesnake Team went dark.

No telemetry at all.

The team leader, Sergeant Michael O'Leary—combat call sign "Finn"—was a friend of mine. We'd walked through fire more than once since we joined the DMS. Finn was a stand-up dude and a certified badass, but he was one of the good guys. He'd walk on his knees through broken glass for his friends and his team. And though he was patriotic, he wasn't one of those empty-brained "my country, right or wrong" assholes who are an embarrassment to genuine patriots. Finn was smart and resourceful, too. So were all three of his men.

Rattlesnake went in, using intel from the CIA and some ad-ditional stuff from a friendly among the villagers. The Taliban convoy was due to pass through a dry valley that used to be a town way back when. Great place for an ambush, so Finn wanted to get there first. The job should have taken nine hours if it all went like clockwork, and maybe double that under worst-case scenarios.

They'd been missing now for three whole days.

I opened my tactical laptop, which was the size and weight of an iPad, but with a much stronger router and battery. The thing was snugged into a ruggedized case that clipped to the front of my chest. The screen still showed the same thing.

Four telemetric signals. Three here in this valley, and one eighty klicks away. That one was bright and green—theoretically proof of life—but it was in a fixed position and hadn't moved since the anticipated time of engagement, ten days ago. The other three signals were weird. Every operative in the DMS has a radio-frequency identification chip the size of a rice grain sur-gically implanted in the fatty tissue under the triceps. Unlike the passive chips used to store medical information, these RFID chips are true telemetric locators. They're late-generation mod-els manufactured by Digital Angel, and as long as GPS tracking satellites circle the earth, the chips will locate the wearer and send a continuous feed to establish location and proof of life. The battery is charged by blood pressure. If the heart stops, the chip immediately begins losing its charge. That diminished sig-nal is read as what it is—the death of the wearer.

Now, here's the kicker—the other three chips went dark for almost ten hours. Totally dark. Then they started back up again. None of them were transmitting at anything like full strength, but they were sending signals that made a case that the wearers were alive.

Both our computer geek, Bug, and Dr. William Hu, head of

our science division, say that this would only be possible if the
three soldiers wearing those RFIDs were so deep inside the earth
that the collective iron-rich rock of these mountains blocked the
signal—and that was a hard scenario to construct. Or all three
of the RFID chips malfunctioned in exactly the same way at
exactly the same time. The likelihood of that was somewhere
around .000087 percent. Bug did the math.

The only scenario that was more plausible was the presence
of an EMP. That might have explained why the chips all went
out at the same time. Unfortunately RFID chips don't simply "get
better" after an electromagnetic pulse. If they were blown out,
then they should still have been dead.

That's the point at which we stopped speculating. No other
scenario made a lick of sense.

Not one.

We flew on.

3
RATTLESNAKE TEAM

Ten days ago . . .

Finn had no breath left for screaming.

All he could do was lie there in the darkness of what had once been a
market stall and was now a wind-blasted cave. He was curled like a beaten
dog, bleeding, sweating, his pants soaked with piss and heavy with shit, his
mouth cracked with a paste made from snot and tears.

Blowflies had found him, and Finn could hear their buzzing wings and feel
their threadlike legs as they walked over his face.

In the darkness around him, the laughter was still there.

Less, though. It only came once in a while.

It wasn't as loud.

It was a softer sound. Softer, but somehow worse than anything he'd heard before.

This laughter was different.

It was sneaky.

It was as if something big and hungry crouched just above him where he couldn't see. Sat there, waiting for something to happen, and delighted at the prospect.

It was an ugly laugh.

Finn realized at some point that it was also female. But there was nothing about it that fit his definition of feminine. It was earthy and raw, and oddly sexual in a way that made Finn feel ashamed.

"I'm going nuts," he told himself. "Jesus, I've finally fucking lost it."

The words tumbled out of his mouth and fell into the darkness.

The breath whispered across the unprotected upper curve of his lip, and against all possible sense or reason, Finn felt himself grow suddenly hard. His cock swelled and pressed against the fabric of his soiled pants.

Then the voice murmured again.

"What will you give me for what you want? What bargain will you make?"

"I don't know what you mean," Finn lied. His voice broke in the middle and the rest of the sentence came out in weak little chunks.

The woman—if it was a woman—laughed her ugly laugh.

"You know," she said. The tips of fingernails caressed the edge of his throat, running along the line of his throbbing artery. "You know what you've lost."

"No."

"Yes. You know what has been taken, and you want it back."

"No."

"It's a gift," she said. "You are the enemy of my enemy, but you are not my friend."

"We didn't do anything to you. We didn't hurt you or—"

"You are in our town. Men like you have been coming to our towns—here and elsewhere—to take what is ours. Our sacred relics. The images of us that people—a precious, precious few—still worship."

"Relics? Who cares about relics, for Christ's sake? We're trying to stop terrorists from killing innocent people. Your people, too. My team . . . we came to protect everyone and everything from the Taliban. We don't want to take anything."

A subtle touch of fingernails on his cheek.

"Everyone wants to take something."

"No."

"Everyone wants something. Everyone wants to barter and trade."

"All I want are my men, damn it. That's why we came here. Please . . . believe me. That's the only reason we came to this goddamn place."

"This is our home. No one comes here unless they want to make a deal. To get back what has been lost."

"Get back . . . ?" His voice trailed off.

"Yes," she said, "I can smell your desire. You do want to make a deal. You want what I have."

"Then give them back!" he shouted.

Soft, soft laughter. "They belong to me now. To us. To the sisters of the desert wind, to the lilitu. They shed blood in our streets, on our ground. Your men are ours by right. Body and soul, flesh and blood. And we will use them. Oh yes. You say that they are soldiers come to fight? Then fight they will. They will be our knights, our champions."

"No. It's not fair. It's those Taliban fucks who are your enemy. If anyone's stealing your stuff, it's them. My men killed them. They're heroes."

"They will be heroes. Our heroes."

"No. You had no right to take them."

"As I said . . . they became ours when they drew blood on our streets."

"You bitch, that's not fair!"

The unseen woman made soft shushing sounds, the way a mother would soothe a hysterical child. "Listen now. Listen. We are cruel, but we are not dishonest. We repay our debts." There was a long pause, then she spoke again, her fetid breath moist on his cheek. "We took from you because we claim the right to do so, and that is fair. But you are here, in our market stall, and you beg for something we have that you want. That is as it should be, for it is in keeping with this place. And so we will barter honestly with you."

"*What are you talking about? Barter for what?*"

"*You know.*"

"*No . . . this doesn't make any sense.*"

"*Oh, yes,*" she cooed. "*You want something returned. Restored. Brought back.*"

"*Yes, but—*"

"*But we must have something in return. Something to replace it. This for that. Something of value for us, and something you value for you.*"

"*Please,*" he said, and even he didn't know if it was an entreaty or an acknowledgment that the dickering could begin.

"*What will you give me for what you want?*" she asked.

Finn began to cry.

4
ECHO TEAM

The pilot's voice crackled in my ear jack.

"Coming up on it."

Bunny pulled the door open and I peered out at the shattered gray landscape.

"Oh, what fun to be back," muttered Bunny.

He'd done a couple of tours each in Iraq and Afghanistan with Force Recon before he was scouted for the DMS. Whenever he mentions Afghanistan, it's by the name "that fucking place." Iraq is "that *other* fucking place."

Not a lot of love.

But I knew the other side. Bunny had bonded pretty heavily with a bunch of villagers. Even one or two who worked in the opium fields. Most of them weren't bad guys, and for the most part, they'd have been happy if the Taliban were all eaten by rats. But the Taliban provided work. Granted, sometimes it was forced labor, but there was a paycheck, and for a lot of these villagers that was the only paycheck they'd seen in years. Bunny, like a lot of soldiers, didn't heap blame on the blameless. He just hated the goddamn country.

Can't blame him.

I was out of the Army Rangers when 9/11 changed the world. I was a street cop with the Baltimore PD, working on getting my detective's shield. However, since taking charge of Echo Team, I've been here three times. Short missions, but when you do what we do, short is long enough. Top and Bunny were with me for two of those road trips, and I did one solo gig that still gives me nightmares.

I tapped my earbud to get Bug on the line. He was back in the DMS main headquarters at the Hangar on Floyd Bennett Field, but he was wired into a network of surveillance databanks, so he was on tap to give us real-time intel.

"We're two klicks out," I said. "Status update?"

"Same as before, Cowboy," he said, using my combat call sign. Bunny was Green Giant, Top was Sergeant Rock. "One strong signal and three intermittent beeps."

"What about hostiles? Who's making trouble in the neighborhood?"

Bug snorted. "Thermal scans show a lot of heat up there. You have a couple of villages in the lowlands and a shitload of four-legged critters. A bunch of two-legged signatures, too, but no one's flashing me their Junior Terrorist Club badge. CIA says that the locals are heavily infiltrated by the Taliban, so don't take chances."

"Not a chance," I said.

The pilot slowed the helo and we spent a little time doing visual recon as he made a careful circle of our landing zone. Bunny had the minigun locked and loaded in case somebody stuck an AK barrel out of a cave mouth. He was sweating and his eyes looked jumpy. An RPG could come out of nowhere and it would probably hit us. We all knew it.

From the air you could hardly tell this had ever been a town. Bug's intel said that over the last ten thousand years this town had been occupied by dozens of different groups, ranging from the Achaemenid Empire to the Sassanids. However as we circled we could pick out some eroded ruins, cave mouths that had been chiseled out to form orderly doors and windows, and a rough symmetry to some of the humped hills where buildings might have been hiding under a thousand years of sand and dirt.

"Looks calm," I said, giving that the irony it deserved.

The pilot brought the helo down to just above the deck. One of the chopper's crew took over for Bunny as we all clipped ourselves onto fast-ropes.

"Eyes open," I said. "Top, me, and Bunny. Nobody fires unless you have eyes on a hostile. I'd rather not start something until there's something to start."

"Hooah," they said, which is the Ranger equivalent of everything from "copy that" to "fuck yeah."

Then we were out.

We stepped into the late-afternoon air and rappelled down the ropes, pushed by the rotor wash, eyes trying to take in absolutely everything, guns ready, fingers laid tight along the curved steel of our trigger guards.

Top hit first and moved away from the bird, tracking in a full circle with his M14, eyes hard and face as calm as if he was sitting in a lawn chair. Top is always the scariest when he looks calm.

I hit the ground a second later and then Bunny was on the deck. We broke apart and took cover behind tumbled rocks as the helo lifted away from us. It took away the noise, the blown-up dust, and the rotor wash—which gave us back our sense of hearing and a chance at stealth—but it took with it the hellfire missiles and minigun, and any hope of an immediate withdraw if this was a trap.

The sun was a white hole in the sky and it threw weird black shadows over the landscape. We waited in the relative safety of cover, not knowing if we were being observed or if gun barrels were being aimed at us from any of the countless cave mouths that pocked the entire mountain range. The fact that no one was shooting at the moment was not a source of comfort. They could have been waiting for the helo to be totally out of range, or they could have been calculating our size, probable designation, and overall value as targets. Hell, we might even have lucked into finding cover that didn't offer any of the bad guys a clean shot, which meant that as soon as we broke cover, they might make their move.

In these situations, you really discover what being afraid means and what paranoia means. It's that way because you know damn well that anyone out there might be a hostile, might be armed, might be strapped to explosives, might be waiting for the exact moment when it bests suits them to end everything that defines you.

But you can't hide forever, either.

I hand-signaled to my guys, then I broke and ran for a standing rock fifty yards up the valley, heading into the ruined old town. I did all the zigging and zagging the trainers drill into you.

No one shot at me.

I hit the wall, crouched, and turned in time to see Top duck and dodge his way across. Then Bunny.

I tapped my earbud.

"We're on the ground, Bug. Give us a route."

I pulled up my tactical computer and watched a circuitous route appear that wound us through the west end of the valley and up into the shallows of the foothills beyond the town limits. The colossal mountains in Afghanistan are riddled with tunnels, caves, shafts, and deadfalls. The consistent and pervasive irregularity of the rock made it difficult for the eye to latch on to specific landmarks, and even Bug's topographical maps didn't quite jibe with the terrain. We'd have to do this like a treasure map: fifty feet this way, twenty that way, in through there and out through here.

And so we did.

We got exactly one kilometer before they started shooting at us.

5

RATTLESNAKE TEAM

Nine days ago . . .

The woman's voice was gone.

Her touch was gone, though Finn could feel the cold echo of it on the flesh of his throat.

The feeling of being in the presence of something whose very nature defined overwhelming sickness was gone.

And yet the horror of it lingered.

The experience had sent creeper vines of atavistic dread deep into the vulnerable fabric of Finn's soul and they had taken root, but the source—the unknown thing that had spoken to him—was gone.

She had wanted to barter with him.

Barter.

Finn had refused. Even here—whacked out with pain and out of his damn mind—he wouldn't barter with some unknown and invisible thing whispering to him in a cave. Right? He demanded answers of his own fractured memory.

What will you give me for what you want?

That had been her question. Over and over again.

No, he'd told her. I won't make any bargain.

That's what he'd said. Right?

Right?

As he thought that, pain flared on his chest and he cried out.

Had the woman-thing cut him? No . . . it felt more like a burn. Had it been there before? Had she put it there?

Finn tried to pry open the memory of the last few minutes—hours, days?—to remember what he'd told her. Wanting his memories to be of nothing but ferocious denial.

But the hinges on the vault of his memory were rusted shut.

He needed to get the fuck out of there. Right. Fucking. Now.

With a growl and a sob and a surge of every muscle, Finn O'Leary tried once more to move his body . . . and this time he could. He rolled over without restriction.

Without pain.

It was so abrupt, so different than all the other times he'd tried to move, that it actually frightened him, and he froze there, turned halfway, waiting for a flare of pain or damage or wrongness.

The moment stretched and stretched . . . but nothing, externally or internally, tried to stop him.

The old market-stall cave was still as black as pitch, but Finn was able to roll all the way onto his chest without bumping into anything. He paused again, belly down on the cold rock. When everything up until now had been a heartbreak or a cruel trick, Finn expected only those things.

The darkness around him was as still as death.

No screams.

No echoes.

Just the irregular rasp of his own breathing.

He slowly placed his hands on the ground—aware that he could now actually feel his hands, and his arms. Everything felt normal. He lay like that for a moment, searching inside his body for the pain of injuries. For shrapnel cuts, for bullet wounds. For any of the damage he'd felt after the ambush.

But there was nothing to feel. Just a deep, abiding weariness that seemed to blow like a cold November wind through the empty chambers of his heart.

Finn took a slow, careful breath and then pushed against the ground. He expected it to be like jacking up a truck. It wasn't. The hard muscles in his arms responded with more than enough strength to push his chest and stomach up from the rock. His upper body peeled away from the ground with no resistance at all.

He paused again, took another careful breath, and got to his knees. To his feet.

There was no trace of light in the tunnel, and that was weird, because there should have been some bounced light from around the curved bends. The channel simply wasn't long enough to be this dark.

He ran a hand across his cheeks. He'd always had a heavy beard, and back in the world, he had to run an electric razor over his face twice a day. He'd shaved this morning. Now his cheeks were heavy with stubble. A day's worth at least.

Shit.

Finn slid one foot along the ground, found no holes, then did the same with the other foot. Moving like someone doing tai chi. Moving in slow and silent motion, like a blind mime. Part of him thought that was funny and a weird little laugh bubbled from between his lips. But the laugh was ugly and strange and it scared him. You don't want that kind of laugh coming from your own mouth.

The laugh hitched his chest, though, and that triggered a flare of pain. Surface pain. Something on his skin that he'd somehow not noticed. Or been too dazed to react to.

Finn stopped and plucked at the buttons of his shirt. His body armor was gone; his shirt was torn. Beneath it, his scrabbling fingers touched his skin and he hissed.

He'd been burned. Nothing else feels like a burn. But the weird thing was that this burn felt old. A day or two old. He gingerly probed at it and realized that it was big, and when he traced the outline of it the whole world seemed to go suddenly cold.

There was a wide, flat central burn with five thick lines running outward from it.

Put all that together and the shape became obvious.

A handprint.

Someone had branded him with a burn in the shape of a hand, fingers splayed.

God, he prayed, let it only be that. Evidence of torture, a rude gift from the Taliban.

Only that.

Only that.

Otherwise . . .

Finn had a vague, buried memory of the woman placing her hand on him. Whispering to him in the dark and touching him.

Right. Here.

Like she'd been marking him.

He reeled sideways until he crashed against the wall. She put her mark on me. Christ Jesus on the cross.

And then the realization of that wound tugged at a thread of memory stitched into his mind. With the memory came her voice.

We are agreed then. Here is my seal upon it.

"No way, you fucking bitch," he said through gritted teeth. "I didn't agree to nothing. You hear me? Nothing!"

Only the wind and the shadows and the rocks heard him.

Desperate to escape the cave, he shoved himself forward, staggering through the shadows with awkward steps. Expecting pain, expecting hands or worse to tear at him, but he didn't trip, didn't bump his head.

Five paces. Ten.

A dozen.

Then . . .

He had to blink several times to make sure that his eyes weren't lying to him.

"Light," he said aloud. The word "light" floated in the darkness and for a few terrible moments, he didn't know if it was a lie or the truth. The light was a ghost of a thing. Only enough so that the shadows weren't a uniform black, but rather pieces of a greater darkness.

He licked his dry lips and took another step, moving in the direction of the light.

Four tentative steps later he was sure that there was light down there. He could see the faint outlines of rocks rising from the floor or hanging like fangs from the ceiling.

Eight more steps and he could see his own hands. A sharp cry burst from between his clenched teeth. He was covered with blood.

Was it his blood?

Finn stopped and touched his chest, his stomach, his limbs.

If he was hurt, then where was the wound?

If he wasn't hurt . . . ?

"God," he breathed, and the word sounded too loud in the dark tunnel. It echoed badly and took on different meanings as it ricocheted past him.

He took a few more steps, and now the light began peeling the shadows back in layers. The palette of the moment changed from black to brown. The color of the desert, except for the sheer walls of gray rock. However, in that light, he could see that the blood was the brightest of reds. A garish scarlet from a cheap paint box.

He tried wiping his hands on his thighs and on the walls, needing to clear his skin. To clean his hands. He spat on the stubborn spots.

He got a little of it off.

Not much.

And that made him want to move faster. He stumbled forward, falling into a clumsy run, his boots barely lifting from the ground. He left smudged and elongated footprints in the sand behind him.

His breath came in ragged gasps as if he was running uphill.

At the end of each inhalation, there was a little squeak of a sound. Almost a whimper.

"Stop it stop it stop it," he told himself, but his voice lacked conviction.

The light was stronger just around the bend ahead. He could smell the air, too. Clean air. Not the stale air of the tunnel. There was wind, too, whispering past the mouth of this motherfucking tunnel.

His stumbling run turned into a sprint as he bolted for the light.

He burst from the mouth of the cave, a smile carving its way onto his filthy face, a sob breaking in his chest as he flung off the last of the shadows.

He stopped and leaned against a boulder to catch his breath. There was movement to his left and Finn spun, drawing his pistol, raising it, pointing it.

A boy stood there, his face turned away. He wore a loose kameez over shalwar—the loose pajama-like trousers—with a kaffiyeh wound around his head and simple pair of dusty kabuli sandals. His clothes were streaked with dust but the only bloodstain on them was an oddly shaped splash of red over his heart. It looked like a desert rose.

"Boy . . . ," said Finn in Pashto.

The child did not respond, did not seem to hear.

Finn said it again in Dari.

The boy stiffened and suddenly began running away. As he did so, he pressed the wrappings of his kaffiyeh to his face as if trying to conceal his features. Finn tried to run after him, but he was too weak and dizzy. He snaked out a hand and caught one trailing edge of the kaffiyeh and pulled. It jerked the boy almost to a stop and made him half-turn—and that revealed more of the boy's face.

Only it was not the face of a boy.

It was the face of an ancient woman. Withered beyond belief, scarred, ugly, almost bestial. Her skin was a livid red, almost the color of blood, and her nose was caked with clay. She opened her mouth to hiss at him, and Finn saw that instead of teeth she had a pair of razor-sharp tusks. The woman spat at him and tore the cloth from his hands. Then she spun and ran as lithely and quickly as a young, athletic child.

Finn could never hope to keep up.

He stumbled along and finally ran down to a sloppy stop, bent over, hands on his knees, panting, confused and terrified and sure that he was losing his mind. Minutes dragged past and the world around him seemed to steady itself down to become nothing more than mountains and sand and a hot wind.

Finn pushed himself erect and began walking along the path that led through the old town square, looking for answers, for the thread of sanity he'd lost. Looking for the sight of the ambush. Looking for his men.

He found nothing for a long time, and he was beginning to think that there was nothing to find. That he was irretrievably lost out here. Or that he was mad and imagining all of this as he lay dying somewhere. He gave up trying to make sense of it. He summoned what strength he had and began to run in the only direction that promised any hope of an answer—back the way he'd come.

But the day was not done with Sergeant Finn O'Leary.

He took five steps, but each one was slower and less steady than the last. His final step was broken and he realized that he was falling. Not onto his face again, but down hard onto his knees. His body weight collapsed as the air flew from his lungs in shock and defeat. Finn knelt there, slumped like a despairing supplicant. His hands hung slack at the ends of his arms, palms up, fingers curled like the legs of some pale, dead spider.

Spit glistened on the rim of his lower lip and as his unblinking eyes took in the things that lay tangled in the dust, the drool broke over the edge of his lip and ran in a crooked line down his chin.

Tears burned into his eyes and they fell, too, cutting like acid down his cheeks.

He looked at the things that lay scattered around the clearing that had once been a town square.

Red things.

Ragged things.

Torn and broken. Defiled and discarded.

Three of them, lying in broken humps that did not add up to the orderly shapes of men. There were too many bad angles. There were parts that should have been connected and stubbornly, stupidly were not.

Bear was the closest.

Or at least Finn thought it was Bear.

But his eyes . . .

His eyes were gone. The flesh around the holes burned to blackened leather. Smoke curled upward from each socket, but the smoke seemed to glow as if fires still burned inside the dead man's skull.

It was the same with the others. They lay on their backs, faces pointed to the sky. Fiery smoke rose from their eye sockets.

You know what has been taken, and you want it back. That's what the woman said.

Yes. He knew.

What will you give me for what you want?

What indeed.

God . . . what had he told her?

How had he answered that horrible question?

There was a rustle and he spun around. Bear had turned his face toward Finn.

Finn stared in horror, trying to understand this. *Was* it rigor mortis? *Was* the heat from the fire shortening the tendons in Bear's neck? *Was . . .*

Jazzman and Cheech Wizard turned their heads, too.

All three of his men stared at Finn with eyes that were nothing but fire and smoke. With the eyes of hell.

All Finn could do was scream. It was the only reasonable response to this. It was the only choice left to him.

6
ECHO TEAM

The shooter was so close that I heard him racking the bolt a split second before the shots started banging their way through the day. That little bit of warning saved my ass, because as soon as I heard it, I threw myself off the path and behind a heap of fallen rock. The bullets hammered a line along the ground where I'd been standing. I saw that much as I scurried like a lizard into the smallest crevice I could find. The impact points walked up the path a yard from my nose.

I realized that it was only a single shooter and started to breathe a sigh of relief.

Then I heard other guns open up from back the way I'd come.

I heard someone yell: "It's more of them! Kill the unholy! *Allahu akbar!*"

We'd walked into a nice trap, but then I heard Top and Bunny open up with their M14s set on rock 'n' roll and immediately the valley was filled with thunder. There were some yells amid the thunder. Screams of pain and curses in Pashto.

I had my own worries.

I rolled sideways and peered around the corner of the rock and saw a man firing an AK-47. He stood with one foot braced on the boulder he must have been hiding behind. His clothes were streaked with blood and dirt, and his eyes were completely wild. His turban was in disarray and the ends of it flapped in the hot wind. He burned through an entire magazine, shooting the whole landscape around me, and all the time he screeched prayers to Allah. Calling me a demon. Begging for protection from Allah.

The bullets ricocheted all over the damn place. One plucked at my sleeve, which made me yank my arm in tighter and utter another in a long string of promises to Jesus I knew I'd later renege on. I meant them right then, though.

When he stopped to reload, I leaned out with my Beretta in both hands and put three rounds into his chest. He fell back and the AK dropped onto its stock, stood for a moment, and then fell over with a clatter.

Dangerous guy, but a stupid guy.

Now a dead guy.

I got to my feet and ran in a low, fast crouch across the path and knelt by the man I'd killed—and then did a double take as I looked at him. He was a mess. When I'd seen the bloodstains on his clothes, I'd thought that it was somebody else's blood. Survivors get like that after a battle, and we had to presume that these guys were the ones who ambushed Rattlesnake Team. But this guy's clothes were torn, and when I poked around I could see long lacerations—days old—that were festering with pus and crawling with maggots. This guy was more than half dead before I shot him. He had to have been in agony and probably out of his mind with fever.

The wounds were a mix. Long slashes in parallel lines that looked like they might have been done by a rake. Or a set of claws. A big hunting cat might leave marks like that. But there were also burns in weird segmented sections around his face and throat.

I had no idea what could have caused marks like that.

The gunfire abruptly stopped.

I tapped my earbud. "Cowboy to Echo Team. Give me a sitrep."

"All clear, boss," said Bunny. "Three up, three down."

He was right. As I rounded a shoulder of the mountain, I saw Bunny standing over three bodies while Top knelt between two of them. He used the tip of a knife to lift sections of torn, bloodstained clothing, then glanced up at me as I approached.

"Looks like Rattlesnake Team had some fun with these jokers before we got here," said Bunny, nodding to the bodies, which were all as torn as that of the man I'd killed.

Top nodded, but he didn't look convinced.

"My guy, too. Cuts and burns."

None of us said what all of us were thinking. Those marks might have been the result of some prolonged torture. I knew Finn pretty well, and his boys. They were rough and they were hardasses, but I was sure I'd have pegged them as guys who couldn't do this.

On the other hand, I'd been wrong before.

I tapped my earbud for the command channel. "Cowboy to Bug."

It took a few seconds before I got anything but static.

Then, "Cowboy? Jeez, man, what happened?"

"What do you mean what happened? We just got ambushed

by four Taliban shooters. I thought you said this valley was empty."

"I think we have a satellite malfunction. And sat phone is acting funky, too. NASA tells us it's sunspots."

"Fuck NASA."

"Thermals tell me no one but Echo, then a whole bunch— thirty or forty—then no one at all. It's weird."

"Go bang the thermals with a hammer then, goddamn it. We nearly got our dicks handed to us."

"It's in space, Cowboy," he complained. "Only so much we can do. Shit, wait, the board just lit up again. Counting six—no, ten—jeez, fourteen signals coming to you from the west. Satellite's only giving us grainy crap, but it looks like three vehicles. Jeez, Cowboy, you've got a Taliban team zeroing your twenty." He read the map coordinates. "Four klicks out and coming fast."

"Swell."

"Hey!" he yelped, but it wasn't at me. "Cowboy, be advised, RFID tracking chips for Cheech Wizard, Jazzman, and Bear have come back online. Intermittent but . . . no, the signals are strong. Four klicks to the southwest. Looks like they're on an intercept course with the Taliban, all three."

"What about Finn?"

But the line dissolved into static.

We looked at each other. Top had the coordinates up on his computer and he pointed the way. Straight down the valley we were in. There was a sluggish breeze coming from that direction, and as he listened, we thought we heard thunder. Way off in the distance.

We all knew it wasn't thunder.

"Rattlesnake," said Bunny.

And then we were running.

7
RATTLESNAKE TEAM

Six days ago . . .

Finn didn't remember walking away.

He didn't remember much of anything.

All he knew was that when his mind started becoming aware of things, there were no bodies on the ground. No cave. No voices. He was miles and miles from where he'd deployed with his team.

His team.

Cheech Wizard. Bear. Jazzman.

This morning, they had been so full of life. Big, covered in the scars they'd earned fighting genuine threats to the world. Men who had saved the world. The actual world.

Now . . .

He closed his eyes—his real eyes and his inner eye—in hopes of shutting out the image of those things that had been scattered across the valley floor. Those impossible things with their impossible eyes.

Things that could not have been his men.

His friends.

They call it being "brothers in arms," but it went so much deeper than that. He and those men were brothers, more so than if they'd been born of the same mother.

Brothers.

Finn loved them more than anyone he'd ever known. More than his wife. More than his two kids back home. More than his actual brother, who was a fat accountant in Des Moines and would never have believed what Finn did for a living. Did for his country, for the world.

Bear, Jazzman, and Cheech Wizard understood.

Bitter tears filled his eyes.

The kind of love a soldier has for his battlefield brothers can't really be defined. Maybe "love" is the wrong word. Maybe there's too much romance and bullshit hanging off that word, and there's none of that here. It's not about that kind of shit. This was a fundamental thing; it went down to the DNA. Down to the soul.

Finn knew that if he could have dialed the clock back, he would have done anything in his power to keep from failing his men. He'd have done anything—any damn thing in the world—to save them.

To spare them.

To take their place.

He blinked his eyes clear and stared at the landscape. There were people on the road. A man and two boys leading a string of goats. Beyond them was an old truck, wheezing along the road away from him, and with dull astonishment, Finn realized that it must have passed him while he was walking.

Finn stopped and stared at it. Far beyond the truck was a cluster of huts, and beyond that . . .

A town.

A hot wind blew past him and he held a hand up to shield his eyes. Buried deep inside the wind was a voice.

Her voice.

What will you give me for what you want?

8
ECHO TEAM

Guys like Bunny, Top, and me, we live in a landscape of war. Our lives are defined by it. As a result, we are almost always in a high-alert state. It's a bitch, it wears at you after a while, but it is what's required of us and we know that we have the option of turning in our badges and hanging up our guns.

As if.

We ran straight along the valley for two klicks, then split and began climbing the slopes on either side, running from one cover position to the next. We had no idea if the Taliban had scouts or spotters out here and we didn't want to find out the wrong way.

With every step, the noise sounded less like thunder and more like what it was. Heavy-caliber weapons. Grenades.

As we passed the three-kilometer mark, the sound of the battle suddenly changed.

Fewer gunshots.

More screams.

And soon, all screams.

We poured it on for another half klick and then slowed to a predatory crawl, weapons ready, minds and hearts ready.

The screams continued.

Then the last scream dwindled down to a wet gurgle and faded.

Black towers of oil smoke curled up over the lip of the ridge directly ahead of us. And there, strewn among the rocks, I saw sunlight glinting on brass.

I signaled that I was going ahead and that Bunny and Top should cover me.

The path climbed a short hill that was shaded by the shattered remains of a fig tree whose trunks had been comprehensively chewed apart by gunfire. I ran to the trunk, crouched momentarily behind it, then went over the rise.

And stopped.

The scene below was a tableau in a museum of hell.

Two of the three trucks were burning. From the driver's window of the lead vehicle, a charred arm protruded, the fingers slowly curling into a fist as heat contracted the tendons.

Men lay everywhere, like islands in a lake of blood. Blood was everywhere. On the ground, on the surrounding boulders, even splashed high on the walls.

Fourteen of them.

The ground was littered with thousands of shell casings and spent magazines. All of the magazines were the banana clips of the AK-47. As I moved down the far side of the ridge, I bent and picked up a shell casing. It was a 7.62 round. From their guns. I didn't see any shell casings from M14s or M16s.

Nothing moved except smoke wandering on a sluggish breeze.

I heard Top and Bunny coming up on either side of me, fifty yards out. I held my fist up to signal them to stop and hold.

Letting my gun barrel lead, I moved forward, walking among the corpses, looking for signs of life, finding only death.

Then I heard a sound behind the rear truck. I froze, then hand-signaled my guys to move in fast and wide so we could circle the truck from two positions. I ran forward on cat feet, and as I reached the back of the truck I yelled, "Freeze!"

Or something like that.

Whatever I said never got out.

The tailgate of the truck was down and an Afghani was sprawled on the bed, arms and legs wide, eyes wide, chest torn wide. Three men were bent over the corpse. Their arms were crimson to the elbows. Their faces were smeared with blood. Pieces of raw meat hung from their teeth. They heard me and turned.

Their eyes . . .

God almighty, *their eyes.*

Where eyes should have been were holes torn into their faces and inside those holes . . .

Impossibly . . .

Fires burned inside of them.

Fires.

They froze there, lumps of red pressed to their mouths. Then they hissed at me, showing red teeth that had been filed to dagger points.

Somewhere, a million miles away, I heard Top and Bunny running, yelling.

The three men—if that word even makes sense anymore—dropped the red chunks of meat they held. They straightened. The biggest of them reached past the dead man to a wooden crate that had been smashed open and removed a piece of rock. Then I saw that it was a fragment of carved stone. The fleshy, rounded figure of a woman with a huge belly and breasts. The man pressed his bloody lips to the feet of the figure, then shoved it inside his jacket.

All three of them were staring at me with burning eyes.

In a voice as cold as death, the man with the statue said, "*We return what was stolen. We honor the bargain.*"

Then I felt myself falling backward with no memory of why I'd lost balance.

Someone was yelling my name. Top? Bunny?

I hit the ground hard on my ass and the shock snapped me out of my stupor. Bunny was right there, catching me under the armpits and hauling me to my feet. Top had his rifle out and was turning to cover the area.

But nothing moved.

There was nothing that could move.

It was the three of us and fourteen dead men.

Absolutely no one else.

"Boss!" yelled Bunny. "Yo, boss, what's wrong?"

I pointed numbly at the dead man sprawled in the back of the truck. But when they looked all they saw was a corpse.

The world seemed to be falling off its hinges, and I was dangerously close to losing my shit. The three men—things, whatevers—were gone. I could not have imagined them. On the other hand, let's face it . . . I couldn't have seen them.

So . . . what the fuck?

Before I could organize my brain so that I could say something that made sense, we all heard a sound behind us. A cough, a soft grunt.

I pushed myself free of Bunny as we all whirled, weapons coming up.

A man knelt on the ground twenty feet behind us, in the midst of all that blood. He wore a cotton shirt in a rough local weave over faded camouflage pants, but the pattern was from the First Gulf War. He was drenched head to toe in blood.

The kneeling man looked down at the ground in front of him.

He slowly raised his head and stared at me with eyes that had grown huge and round with shock. Or maybe it was madness.

He looked at me for a few distorted seconds, then opened dried, cracked lips and said, "Joe . . . ?"

Sergeant Finn O'Leary fell face-forward onto the dirt, making no attempt to break his fall.

9
RATTLESNAKE TEAM

Four days ago . . .

The town was barely that—just a desperate cluster of a few tents, mud buildings, and the open mouth of a cave inside of which was the local bazaar.

Finn O'Leary barely remembered coming here. There were tattered memories of a goatherd and his wife taking him in, cleaning him, washing his body, forcing mutton stew down his throat. Praying over him. Or maybe near him; Finn couldn't be sure.

When he could speak—sometime during the second day—Finn croaked, "Where am I?"

They told him. A place called Haykal. He'd never heard of it.

"My sons found you walking on the road," said the father, then he hesitated.

He was a stick of a man with light brown eyes filled with shadows. Living as a simple farmer in a country that hadn't known peace in his lifetime probably aged him beyond his years. He said, "You were in a fight, yes? A battle?"

Finn didn't ask how the man knew. Finn was aware enough to remember that his clothes had been covered in blood.

Even so, he didn't answer. Soldiers don't answer those questions, and the little farmer didn't push it.

"You are not injured," the farmer said.

"Yes," said Finn, "I am."

He opened his shirt to show this old man the hand-shaped burn on his chest.

The man did not look at it. He turned his head, closed his eyes, and began to pray very quickly and fervently.

Finn pulled his shirt closed.

"I'm sorry," he said, though he didn't quite understand what he was apologizing for.

Without turning to face him, the old man said, "The person you need to talk to is here."

"What person? What are you talking about?"

"He is a black marketer," said the man, still not looking at him. "A criminal. A bad man who has forgotten the name of God."

Finn said nothing.

"His name is *Aziz*. He knows about such things." The old man stood up. "When you are well, I will take you to him. He can be found in a very bad place, a place where criminals meet. I cannot ask such a man into this house. I am poor and worthless, but we live according to the teachings of the Prophet, and we cannot have such a person here."

"You brought me in here."

The man finally turned. "You were hurt and God requires mercy of us."

Finn nodded. "Thank you," he said.

The man nodded but said nothing.

Finn touched his chest. "Do you know what this is?"

The man looked away.

"Look, I don't know what happened to me. I don't know how I got this. I was attacked and I've been out of my head for days. If you know something, then you have to tell me."

It took the old man a long time to answer. Finally he said, "There are things in the desert older even than Islam. Older than Christianity. Older than the Jews." The man made a sign against evil. "There are things older than the world. These things are evil. They are demons who trick and seduce. But . . . no man's heart is ever corrupted by them if his faith is strong, if his faith is real." He shook his head. "I will pray for you."

And that was all he would say.

10
ECHO TEAM

"Jesus H.T. Christ, Esquire," muttered Top as he rolled Finn onto his back. He pushed two fingers against the side of the man's throat. "He's got a pulse. Don't seem to be hurt. Got a weird burn on his chest, but it's a coupla days old. Nothing else. Been in the sun too damn long."

"The fuck did he come from?" asked Bunny, glancing around.

Finn slowly opened his eyes and blinked up at us, and it was clear that he didn't see us. Or at least didn't quite understand who—or perhaps *what*—we were.

"Finn," I said again, then repeated it more firmly.

He blinked again.

Finn's eyes locked on mine and I could see them gradually begin to clear. He tried to speak; his lips formed my name, but all that came out was an inarticulate croak. He licked his lips, swallowed, winced at the pain in his dry throat, and tried again, forcing it.

"Joe . . . ?"

I slung my rifle and knelt in front of him.

"Jesus, Finn," I said, "where are you hurt? How bad is it?"

"Hurt?" he asked as if he didn't understand the word. I pushed past Top and began checking Finn myself. I saw the burn and pulled Finn's shirt completely open to look at it. Finn tried to stop me, his fingers quick and nervous.

"Finn," I said, helping him sit up, "what the hell happened?"

He shook his head and looked past me at the blood. "My men," he whispered. "Bear . . . Cheech Wizard," he said slowly, his voice barely a whisper, "Jazzman."

I took him by the shoulders and tried to steady him. Gave him just a little shake, maybe put some of his marbles back into their slots. "Finn, what happened here? Where's your team? Where are your men?"

I almost said what are your men. My pulse was still hammering.

Finn's eyes roved around the town square, from one patch of blood to the other.

"Here," he said hollowly. "Joe . . . they were all just here."

Top and Bunny glanced at me, but I let nothing show.

"What happened out here?" asked Bunny.

But Finn's eyes rolled up in their sockets and he pitched forward into my arms.

I took his weight and, with Bunny's help, carried him out of the big pool of blood and onto unmarked ground. We propped him up with his back against a rock wall. Top watched and I could tell from the calculating look in his eyes that he was doing the math on all this and wasn't happy with the numbers.

Top gave me a small sideways tic of the head, and I rose and walked a dozen yards away with him. We stood there, surveying the carnage. Top took a pack of gum from his shirt and we each had a piece. He saw my hands trembling as I unwrapped mine.

I tapped my earbud. "Cowboy to Bug."

It took five tries to get a static-filled connection.

"Go for Bug."

"Give me a rundown on thermal and satellite feeds."

"Satellites are a negative. They went offline ten minutes ago. NASA's working on it."

"Balls. And the thermals? We getting any signal?"

"We got lots of signals, Cowboy. We got four signatures right now—Echo and Finn. All clustered together. That's cool that you found him. How is he?"

Bug had never been great at the formality of tactical radio chatter.

"Alive, minimal injuries but disoriented. Unable to debrief at this time. What about Rattlesnake?"

"Their signals are weird, Cowboy. One minute they're here, the next they're not. Then they're up in the mountains, then somewhere else. The telemetry is totally fritzed."

"Okay. We're returning to the LZ. I need exfil for four now and then air surveillance. Screw the satellites, get me some helos."

There was a squawk of static and we lost the signal again.

"Shit," I said, and picked up a rock to throw it as hard as I could. I stopped midthrow, weighed it in my hand, and dropped it.

Then I gave the order to make a stretcher and carry Finn back to the ancient town built into the mountain, back where his team had gone missing. There were enough slats from the un-burned stake-bed pickup, and we used the jackets of dead men for a sling. Top and Bunny carried while I walked point.

"Why not wait here?" asked Bunny, and Top nodded.

Fair question.

"Because this shit started back by that small cave," I said. "I want to figure it out in some kind of order."

As explanations go, it was lame as hell; but they were ser-geants and I was a captain and this wasn't a democracy. The truth . . . ? This place spooked me more than I could express. Those faces with the burning eyes had been too real, but I didn't want to talk about it with them. I've had some psych issues in the past, and I'm pretty sure my guys know about it. This was not the time to shake their confidence in me.

When we were back at the abandoned town, we placed Finn in the shade of pair of withered trees. He was still unconscious.

"I'm going to walk the scene," I said to Top.

He glanced around, not liking it. "This is a weird place, Cap'n."

He left it there in case I wanted to say something. I didn't.

"Call me when Finn's awake."

I stepped back from them, moving to the edge of the town square so I could see the whole thing. I used to be a pretty good homicide cop back in West Baltimore. A lot of what I know about working a crime scene comes from three reliable sources. The first was my dad, who was a cop before me, and he'd worked his way up from the street to a gold shield to commissioner before finally jumping ship to run for mayor. None of his promotions were purely political. He'd been a cop's cop—he'd done his time and closed a big share of his cases. He taught me a lot.

The second source was my own time on the job. Baltimore has a lot of crime and never enough cops, so the guys on the job have to do the job. .

My third source was a cop from DCPD named Jerry Spencer. He was a grumpy son of a bitch, but he could work a crime scene like Sherlock Holmes. He didn't just see, he *observed*. And he kept his opinions in neutral until he had enough facts to build a reasonable supposition. Even then, he was never sold on a theory as long as there was a potential for a decent competing theory.

So I stood there and I let the scene speak to me.

Here were the things I could tell for sure.

Rattlesnake Team had come into this valley from the west. As I walked around a clearing that must once have been the town center, I found the trail of their footprints at a few hundred yards, and then the faint brush marks from where Finn and his boys erased the signs of their presence as they prepared to lay a trap. The four of them separated. Finn went through a short tunnel that curled and rose to a flat rock on the far side of the town, almost certainly to set up a good elevated shooting position. Personally, I thought it was a questionable choice. A good shooting position should be in can't-miss range, but even for a sniper as good as Finn that spot was at the outer edge of safe range. Its only virtue was an element of absolute surprise, but there were better choices he could have made. Maybe that was part of whatever went wrong here. One bad choice can shove everything else downhill in an avalanche of consequences.

The other three guys from Rattlesnake skirted the edge of the town square and found concealed spots to set up an ambush. There were the distinctive marks in the sand of men sitting, lying prone, and kneeling. That spot was thick with their shell casings.

I went upslope and that's when I found the caravan. Or what was left of it. From ground level, it looked like an empty trail because of a raised lip of ragged stone. But as I drew near, I heard blowflies and smelled the stink of rotted meat. A dozen of the corpses were adult men, and one was a boy of about ten. My heart twisted for the kid. It's insane how many cultures drag their children into the middle of a war, often literally putting guns in their hands and metaphorically painting bull's-eyes over their hearts. Bastards.

There were also three dead horses, their bellies swollen from internal gases and crawling with flies and maggots.

The ground all around them was littered with shell casings. The men had made a fight of it, but they all went down.

There was a sudden rasp of static in my ear. "Bug to Cowboy."

"Go for Cowboy. Good to hear you, kid."

"Hey," he said, "we might only have this connection for a few seconds. NASA's now saying that there might be some combination of minerals in the mountains where you are that's screwing up the signal. Nothing else seems to make sense."

"You have any useful intel?"

"We got a couple of good thermals and some clean satellite images and your whole area is clean. Just the same four signals—Echo and Finn."

"No one else?"

"No."

"Bug, see if you can take another look at the area we just left. The convoy ambush. I thought I spotted the rest of Rattlesnake Team there, but I lost them."

"We've scanned it. No life signs, no thermals, no visuals, and no telemetry from the RFID chips. There's nothing out there but dead Taliban guys and lizards."

"Look again."

"Okay."

"And get me some frigging choppers. I want to get the hell out of here."

But he was gone. The timing was really pissing me off. And . . . scaring me, too.

A lot.

I sucked it up, though, and went back to studying the dead caravan, and that's when the scene got suddenly very weird.

On and around the three horses were heavy cotton sacks. Most were still tied shut, but all had been pierced by rounds so that white opium powder spilled out onto the rock. Hundreds of pounds of it. Hundreds of thousands of dollars' worth.

It was still there. No one had touched it.

One bag, however, had been cut open with something sharp and a parcel had been removed. The wrappings of the parcel—

green silk—lay discarded on the ground. Whatever had been wrapped in the silk was gone.

From my perspective, it appeared that Rattlesnake Team had ambushed and killed the Taliban caravan, then someone—either a member of Rattlesnake or someone else—targeted one bag, cut it open, and removed something that had been hidden among the drugs. That item, and now three members of Rattlesnake Team were missing, and there were no footprints in the spilled blood of the Taliban to indicate how anyone had approached the bag without leaving a mark.

Curious, I drew my rapid-release folding knife from my pocket, snapped the blade into place, and systematically cut open the other bags. I made sure to keep a cloth pressed to my nose and mouth. Getting stoned was not part of the agenda.

There was a green silk parcel in each bag. They were heavy, too.

None of them felt like the kind of vacuum-packed metal cylinders that would be used to transport a pathogen. They felt like rocks, maybe carvings.

I collected them and retreated down the slope, but I noticed that as careful as I had been, I left a trail of bloody footprints. How had someone looted that first bag without doing the same?

At the bottom of the slope, I found a table-sized rock and placed the parcels there, then unwrapped each one. The first one was a small statue of a snooty-looking little man with an enormous dick. Fertility symbol from some culture. The second was a broken statue of one of the Egyptian gods. The one with the cat face, can't remember the name offhand. The others were similar. Small idols of gods from several different cultures, including one that was of a very nice carving of a bull. That one really caught my eye and I spit on it and rubbed the dirt away. What I at first thought was brass was something else entirely.

It was solid gold.

The fucking thing had to weigh four pounds.

I whistled, long and loud.

I have some stocks and I have some commodities. I keep a lazy eye on the price of gold because I have some that my grandfather left me. Some coins and stuff. Last time I checked the price per ounce, it was hovering around seventeen hundred bucks.

Times four pounds?

I was holding about a hundred grand in my hand.

Not to mention the value of the statue. That was probably ancient.

The other objects? If they were all as old, then maybe they were equally valuable in their own way.

So . . . why did someone leave all this shit behind? What was so valuable in that other parcel? Was that the container of pathogen that Rattlesnake Team had been sent here to intercept?

My instincts were telling me no. I thought it was another one of these statues.

But why take that one in particular and not the rest?

What was it about that one?

Then I heard a sound behind me.

Soft. A scuff of pebbles sliding down an incline.

I immediately whirled and brought my rifle up as I threw myself to one side. My finger slipped inside the trigger guard and I almost fired.

Almost.

The barrel pointed straight and steady and my finger was curled around the trigger.

A boy stood there.

He was dressed in the robes of an Afghani villager. He had an oversize kaffiyeh on his head with the scarf pulled around to hide everything but his eyes. The kid must have come down the same slope used by the caravan.

His clothes were dusty and there was a bloodstain on his

chest that I thought at first was a bullet hole. It was right over his heart.

He took a step toward me, hands out in a pleading gesture, and in good English said, "Please . . ."

As much as I hated to do it, I pointed my gun at him. "Hold it right there, kid."

The boy stopped and stood his ground. His eyes were big and dark and they darted nervously from my face to my gun and back again.

"No one's going to hurt you if you just stay right there," I told him.

He nodded.

I tapped my earbud. "Bug . . . ?"

I got static for a moment, then I heard his voice.

"—ug to Cow . . . you copy . . . ?"

"Bug, you're breaking up. If you can hear me, we have a civilian boy who may be a witness. I need evac right now."

There was no answer.

I tapped my earbud again.

Listened.

Heard static.

I switched to the team channel. "Cowboy to Sergeant Rock."

A burst of static was the only answer.

"Cowboy to Green—"

A sudden scream of unbearable intensity ripped through the earbud and into my head. It hit me like a punch, as if it were coming from an inch behind me. The shriek was male but piercingly, insanely loud. The shock knocked me forward onto my knees and I clawed at the bud, tearing it out of my ear.

All the while the boy stared at me, his face twisted into a grimace that almost looked like a smile.

The scream instantly stopped.

Just like that.

But it seemed to echo faintly inside my head. My eyes teared up and my nose was running. I pawed at my face and the back of my hand came away slick and wet. And red.

I gagged and coughed dark blood onto the sand.

The boy was still standing where I'd told him to, but he touched his face beneath the rippling scarf. There was a weird look in his eyes. Like he was smiling. Or crying. I couldn't tell.

Behind me, off somewhere at an incalculable distance, I heard other voices. Men's voices. Not screaming. Yelling.

Calling my name.

I swung my rifle around on its sling and brought it up as blood continued to pour from my nose.

"Cowboy!" called a voice that was muffled and distorted. "Cowboy, on your nine. Friendlies. Lower your weapon."

I turned to my left to see Top and Bunny coming toward me. Both of them had their weapons in their hands. Top's was pointed up to the sky and he held out his other hand in a calming no-problem gesture. Bunny's barrel and eyes were both pointed at the small boy.

"Freeze!" he yelled, and through the pain and disorientation in my head I thought that was strange. The boy hadn't made a move, though now there was no expression except fear in his eyes.

Top pushed my rifle barrel aside as he knelt in front of me.

"Where are you hurt?" he said, asking me the same question I'd asked Finn.

I touched my nose. The bleeding had stopped.

"Jesus Christ," I snapped, "what the fuck was that scream? Was that Finn?"

Top blinked. "Scream?" he asked.

"Yeah, that goddamn scream. You telling me you couldn't fucking *hear* it?"

Top's dark gaze roved over my face. "Didn't hear nothing, Cap'n," he said. "Just you yelling."

I turned to Bunny. "What'd it sound like to you?"

"Yeah," said Bunny, "I heard you scream, boss."

"No," I snapped. "Not me. Over the mic."

Top shook his head. "Radio's dead."

We stared at each other and then we turned and looked at the kid. Bunny still had him at gunpoint and the kid looked terrified. Bunny told the kid to open his robes, and when it was clear the kid wasn't wearing a C4 vest, Bunny stepped cautiously toward the boy and took a long reach to pull the scarf away from his face. The kid's face was badly burned. Not sunburned, either. Flash-burned. He had some kind of gray clay caked over his nose. Maybe a local pain remedy.

"You okay, kid?" asked Bunny gently.

The boy said nothing.

Bunny patted him down and pushed the kid toward where I knelt. "He's clean, boss."

Top helped me to my feet and the whole world did a drunken jig for a moment, but I stood still for a few seconds and it passed. Then I leaned on Top and together we staggered back to where Finn lay in a semiconscious stupor.

He raised his head as we approached. "I thought I heard something," he said in a muzzy voice. He sounded like someone who'd just woken up after a heavy nap.

Top cut a look at me and I gave him a tiny shake of my head.

"It's all quiet on the western front," I told Finn. "But we have a visitor, so maybe we can get some answers to—"

As I spoke, Finn looked past me to where Bunny stood with the boy.

His eyes snapped wide and a look of total horror wrenched its way onto Finn's face. He threw himself backward, raising an arm to shield himself from the sight of the kid.

"Oh God! That's her!" he cried.

"That's who?" asked Bunny.

Finn made a grab for my holstered pistol, and he was so damn fast that he had it in his hand before I could stop him. Made a dive for it, but Finn clubbed me in the face with his free hand.

Bang!

Bunny shoved the kid behind a rock and dove for cover in the opposite direction. The bullet whanged off the rock, missing the boy by an inch. Even in his panic, Finn was a hell of a shot.

Finn managed two more shots before Top kicked the gun out of his hand. Finn was still yelling and he dove for the weapon. I shook off the punch to the head and tackled him. We rolled over in the sand, him bellowing about some woman while trying every dirty trick he ever learned to shake me off. He head-butted me, drove his elbow into my ribs, hoof-kicked me in the nuts, and was about to bang my head against a rock when Top stepped in front of him, grabbed a fistful of Finn's hair, and hit him with three short punches that were so fast the impact sounded like one.

Finn dropped flat on his face and I rolled off, coughing, wheezing, and feeling like shit. Top caught me under the arm and hauled me up, but I could only manage a hunchbacked bend. My balls felt like they'd been mashed flat and then set on fire. Finn was one of the toughest guys I'd ever known and I did not appreciate the reminder.

"Get that fucking kid over here!" I snarled. "I want some fucking answers right fucking now!"

Bunny stood by the rock and he had a look of total perplexity on his face.

"What?" I demanded.

I already knew.

The kid was gone.

He couldn't have been.

But he was.

Fuck.

11
RATTLESNAKE TEAM

Two days ago . . .

Finn O'Leary entered the tiny café and sat down across a table from a wizened little man with a smile like a bamboo viper and eyes the color of cow shit. He was the kind of man you'd distrust on first meeting and probably never feel the need to alter your opinion. The kind of man who knew that this was how people perceived him, and instead of trying to ameliorate that gut reaction, he cultivated certain qualities within him to more strongly engender those feelings. It worked very well for him.

"Sergeant O'Leary."

"You're Aziz?"

The reptilian smile widened a fraction.

"People in town . . . they said that I should come talk to you," said Finn. "Why?"

"They said you were pretty well connected, that you had resources. And contacts."

"So does the Red Cross," said Aziz. "What of it?"

A greasy waiter came and Finn ordered coffee, wishing he could get something stronger. But booze was hard to come by in Muslim towns. Even in shitholes like this where probably nobody within a day's ride had been to a mosque in years. Guys like Aziz, who was probably Muslim for convenience's sake and no other reason.

When the coffee came, Finn sniffed it, winced, drank some, and nearly spat it against the wall. But he forced it down.

"Let's cut the tap dance," Finn said. "I'm not in the mood for three hours of cryptic bullshit and I don't banter. I was told to see you. If that's the case, then someone told you I was coming here to find you. So, can we get right down to it?"

Aziz's smile flickered and dimmed by half. "You take the fun out of things," he said, then waved that away. "Sure. Let us talk plainly."

"Good. Do you know why I'm here?"

After a long pause, Aziz said, "Yes. Do you?"

"No."

Aziz folded his hands and waited.

"Why I'm here doesn't make sense," Finn said. "But I'm here anyway."

"Yes."

"So . . . you tell me. You know what the fuck's going on, so you tell me. Otherwise I got nowhere to go with this thing."

Another pause, then Aziz nodded to Finn's chest. "Open your shirt."

Now it was Finn's turn to pause.

"Open it," said Aziz insistently, "or I walk away."

Finn sighed, and with trembling fingers, he pulled up the rough cotton shirt to show the hand-shaped burn on his chest.

Aziz sat there with his eyes wide and small fists balled into knuckly knots on the tabletop. Then he rattled off a long prayer in a mix of languages. Like most SpecOps field agents, Finn had a passing familiarity with a number of them—he caught words in Pashto, Arabic, Hebrew, and Egyptian. There were many blessings overlapping one another, most of which Finn couldn't understand clearly, and a handful of names repeated over and over again.

"Lilitu."

"Al-bashti."

"Iblis."

"Lilith."

No mention of Muhammad or Allah. No mention of any other god, prophet, or saint. Aziz removed a small stone statue from his pocket. It was an earth-mother statue, one of the fertility idols, with pendulous breasts, an enormous stomach, and tubby legs. It also had a hideous face that was painted red and a wide mouth filled with sharp teeth. The stone looked ancient but in excellent condition. *Aziz* put it to his mouth and kissed each breast and then the feet. Then he put the idol back into his pocket.

The smile he gave Finn was truly appalling. It was filled with awe and worship, but also with a naked, undisguised sexual lust that made Finn's stomach churn and his testicles contract into his body.

"You have been touched by her. Touched."

Finn pulled down the front of his shirt.

"I wish I could kill you so I could carve that from your chest and sew it onto my own skin," *Aziz* continued. "You have been touched by her. Flesh to flesh."

"You're fucking nuts."

That changed *Aziz's* smile back to something closer to what it had been. *Aziz* drew a breath and let it out slowly. Finn's chest shuddered as he did that, as if with the aftershock of a prolonged orgasm. He wanted to vomit.

The wizened little man leaned across the table, head bowed and voice low. "You want something back that's been taken from you?"

"Yes."

"But they are already at work," said *Aziz*. "They found her idol out there in the desert. They took it from the thieves who desecrated her temple. She has taken them as her own and they are already doing what they must do in her service."

"I don't give a fuck. I want them back."

"You know the price?"

"Listen to me, shitbag, I can make one call and have a platoon of marines in here kicking the ass of you and everyone you've ever met. I can firebomb this shithole into the next dimension. I told you already: do not fuck with me."

Aziz contrived to look hurt. "I am not 'fucking' with you, Sergeant Finn. I am required to ask this question, and I am asking it. Do you know the price? Do you understand it? What it means?"

"Yeah, yeah, fuck you, I understand. Now let's get this done."

Aziz stood firm on his point and his lip curled in a sneer. "We are not haggling over a rug, you arrogant asshole. You came to me—me—bearing her mark. Who do you think I am? A cheap gangster? Sure, that's what everyone sees. But I protect her."

"She seemed able to handle herself," Finn said, and he was surprised he could manage that sarcasm.

"You don't understand. There are proper ways to do these things. Prayers and rituals. Why do you think shrines are so important? They focus, Sergeant. They allow. Without doing everything the right way, the precise way, it all falls apart."

Finn said nothing.

"Even now, the old bargain—the one she made with your men—is falling apart because things were not done properly. She took them after they were already dead. Their souls are being torn. Worlds are breaking apart." He shook his head and made to stand up. "Ah, why am I lecturing a fool?"

Finn caught his arm. "No," he said quickly. "No . . . I'm sorry. Look . . . just tell me what I have to do."

"Are you sure? Because what we do now is to make the actual substance of the bargain. What you will do, what you will get, how it will all play out." Aziz leaned forward and his face was alight, intense and vicious. "Are you sure?"

Inside Finn's chest, his heart was hammering dangerously hard.

"Yes," he lied.

12
ECHO TEAM

With the radio out, there was no way to call in our helo. Protocol allowed for a flyby six hours after we'd rappelled into the LZ, and there were still four hours on that clock.

So we used the time to locate and secure a safe spot to use as a base camp. It was a tunnel near the ambush point. It was shaped like a croissant and ran maybe sixty-five feet from one end to the other. Bunny rigged one end of the tunnel with booby traps.

No explosives, just a couple of flash-bangs that he hid so cleverly that a mountain goat wouldn't see them. Bunny is very good at that sort of thing.

Top used flex-cuffs to bind Finn's ankles and wrists. Once he was secure, Top used the first-aid kit to fix the damage to the man's face. The three punches had cracked his nose and bruised the orbit around Finn's right eye. He'd have a headache for a month. Better than a bullet, though.

For my part, I had aching balls, scattered bruises, and some wounded pride. And I was more confused than I'd ever been in my adult life. I swallowed a couple of painkillers—wishing I could wash them down with Jack Daniel's—and took up a position at the other cave mouth while Bunny did a quick recon of the area. I motioned for Top to join me out of earshot and told him about the statues, and he brought them back and stood them in a row on the sand. Except for the gold bull. That one he held and stared at with goggle eyes.

"Is this . . . ?" he breathed.

"Yes," I said.

"Solid?"

"I think so."

"Holy monkey-fuck! This has to be worth a fortune."

"Call it a hundred grand, give or take." And I explained about the fight, the massacre, the opium, and the parcels. They worked it through and came to about the same conclusions I had . . . that it didn't add up. Not in any way we could see.

At my direction, Bunny buried the statues and marked the spot so we could find them again. None of us wanted to hump all that weight around.

"Even the gold bull?" Bunny asked, reluctance showing on his face.

"All of it."

When he was done, I asked, "What's the status on the radio?"

"Still out," said Top. "This is hinky as shit, Cap'n."

"I know." I didn't mention to them that it seemed to go out every time I tried to arrange for a helicopter evac.

"And here's something else you ain't going to like," he said.

I just looked at him.

Top flipped up his tactical computer. "This is dead, too. Went out the same time as the radio. Ditto for every other gadget we have. Sensors, meters, all of it. Now, I know that sounds like an EMP, but the Taliban don't have anything that can send out an electromagnetic pulse. Not unless someone dropped a nuke somewhere and we ain't heard about it."

"Maybe an e-bomb?" I ventured, but it was a lame suggestion. The Taliban didn't have hardware like that. And no one in their right mind would have sold it to them. That would have been a ticket to a military escalation that nobody on either side wanted. "Okay, Top, drop the other shoe. What's the rest of it?"

"I got no shoe to drop, Cap'n. I'm standing here in my socks ankle-deep in some weird shit."

We looked up at the mountains.

"Bug said NASA thought it's something in the rocks," I said. "Some metal or ore that's creating a field of interference."

When I looked at Top, I could see how much of that he believed. "You really trying to sell that?" he asked.

I didn't bother to answer.

When Bunny returned, we three hunkered down around Finn. I said, "I'm tired of watching Finn get his beauty rest. Let's see if we can get some straight goddamn answers."

Top produced a syrette filled with a stimulant and cocked an eyebrow at me. I nodded and he jabbed.

Finn twitched and groaned, and in a few seconds his eyes fluttered open. He blinked his vision clear and looked at the three faces ringed around him. He wasn't seeing any smiles. Then the pain from his face registered and he winced.

"What . . . happened?" he asked thickly.

I told him.

He winced at that, too. Then his eyes popped wide and started darting around, looking past us as his whole body went rigid with tension.

"Is she *here*? Did you get her?"

"Whoa, whoa," I said soothingly. "Who are you talking about?"

"*Her*, goddamn it. Did I get her?"

"Finn—you grabbed my piece and started taking potshots at some local boy. A *kid*, for chrissakes."

He shook his head. "That was no boy, Joe. It only looks like one."

We stared at him.

"We searched him," Bunny finally said. "Definitely a boy."

Finn kept shaking his head. "No, you're wrong . . ."

I snapped my fingers in front of his face. He blinked and stopped shaking his head. His eyes were bloodshot and there were dark smudges under them.

"Hey—listen to me, Finn," I said, pitching my voice low and calm, "you're in shock and you're not making a lot of sense. You've got to calm down and—"

"No, I—"

"Shhh," I said. "It's cool. We're clear and we're safe. We searched the area. It's just the four of us, and help is on the way."

He gradually calmed, but only halfway. "What's . . . what's our status? Why is there all this blood on my clothes?"

"We're piecing that together. We found the spot where Rattlesnake Team ambushed the opium convoy. All of the Taliban are dead, the opium's there, but there's no sign of your guys."

Finn gave me a sharp look, penetrating and unblinking. "You're sure about that, Joe? You haven't seen them?"

Before I could respond, Bunny said, "Nah, we ain't seen hide nor hair. But we think they ambushed another convoy a couple hours ago."

Finn stared at him. "You're sure it was them?"

"Not sure of anything today," said Top. "But whoever did it used M14s. Classic SpecOps ambush scenario, too. How many teams of gunslingers you think are out here? There's us and there's your boys."

Finn's eyes shifted away. He looked toward the town and then he looked down between his knees at the dirt.

"My team is gone," he said softly.

"Gone . . . ?" prompted Bunny. "You mean they been capped?"

Finn shrugged.

"Where are the bodies?" asked Top.

Another shrug.

"Excuse me," said Top, "you may be top-kick of that team, Finn, but I'm still a first sergeant and you're a master sergeant and I asked you a question. Where are the bodies of your team?"

Finn closed his eyes. "Gone," he said again, but then he added, "They've been taken."

"Taken by who?" demanded Bunny.

"I—don't know," said Finn. I had the weird impression that he was hiding something but not actually lying to us. When I made eye contact with Top, I could see that he was in the same place as me.

I placed my hand on Finn's shoulder and gave him a reassuring squeeze. "Listen, brother, you've been out here for ten days and it's pretty clear you've been through some shit."

"I've been through hell," he said without looking at me.

"If we're going to help you, then we need to know everything that happened."

Finn shook his head. "It's too late for that, Joe."

"What do you mean?"

"Telling you won't make it better. My guys are lost."

"Maybe not," I said, putting some edge into it.

He gave me a pitying look like I was a naïve idiot who didn't have a clue about how the world worked.

"I . . . ," he began, then stopped and swallowed. He brushed a tear from his eye. "Joe, I don't know why I'm even here. I should be dead, not them. I thought that was how it was supposed to work. Me, not them. It wasn't their fault."

"What wasn't their fault?" I asked gently.

"That they . . . that they were lost."

I noticed that he kept avoiding the word "died" or "killed." He called it "lost." He said they were *gone.*

It troubled me in ways I couldn't quite explain.

"Look, Finn, just start from the beginning. There was a firefight here, and there's a hell of a lot of blood, but there are no American bodies. The only other person we found is a kid, maybe ten years old. And it was definitely a boy, that's not even a discussion."

"Hooah," said Bunny.

I continued. "So, I need you to take a breath, get your shit wired tight, and tell me what happened. And I mean everything."

I can't know what Finn was thinking, but I watched his eyes and I could see the process of the frightened and disoriented man yielding all control to the trained soldier—the top-of-the-line SpecOps gunslinger. Top handed him a canteen and Finn took a sip, swallowed, took some breaths through his nose, took a longer sip, and nodded thanks to Top. Finn blew out his cheeks and nodded.

"Okay," he said.

He told us everything.

As he spoke, I tried to get inside his head and see it all the way he saw it.

13
RATTLESNAKE TEAM

This is how his story fit into my head . . .

The heat.

The fucking heat.

The heat was a hammer, a fist.

Finn pinched sweat out of his eyes with thumb and forefinger and saw that his fingers were dry. The desert had leached the moisture out of him.

You'd think the desert would leave enough for tears, he thought as he blinked his eyes back into focus and fitted the monocular back into place. The rubber gasket was hot and soft against his eye socket. The heat made the rubber feel like flesh, like some curled length of worm.

He was stretched out on a flat shelf that was jabbed into a cliff wall too high above the jagged rocks below. He had a camo blanket over him and a smaller one over the barrel of his rifle. The blanket didn't do a fucking thing to deflect the heat and Finn felt like he was slowly being broiled alive. But it was better than being without cover, because his Irish skin didn't tan worth shit. He'd gone from freckle-white to skinned-knees red the first day here in Afghanistan. Since then he'd kept out of the sun, but being in shade didn't seem to offer so much as a splinter of relief. Nothing did. Not unless his team had to follow this mission into the higher mountain passes, and then it went from hellish heat to mind-numbing cold.

You couldn't win in Afghanistan.

Not with the weather.

Not with the people.

Not with the son-of-a-bitching Taliban.

Finn knew he couldn't beat any of it, so he did what he always did. He did what everyone else did. He did the only thing he could do.

He ate his pain.

He swallowed it whole, feeling it slide down his gullet like a bundle of barbed wire. That was the only way you got through the day, and the week, and the month, and the whole tour. You ate your pain, knowing that the more you consumed, the more poison it would release into your system. After a while, that poison ate away at your nerves, your patience, your tolerance. Sometimes your humanity.

It drove some guys right over the edge. Finn knew—knew for fucking sure—who was collecting fingers from the Afghans. Maybe two-thirds of them were Taliban fingers. The rest? Well, when a guy had that much poison in his system, he sometimes said fuck it and took a trophy wherever he could find it.

A few guys had gone on trial for that.

Most didn't; most never saw the inside of a military court. No one caught a whiff of the madness cooking inside of them.

Finn hadn't eaten that much poison yet. But, day by day, he found it harder to hate and revile the guys who went off the reservation. Day by day, that seemed to make more sense.

He ground his teeth and stared through the monocular, feeling the seconds and minutes catch fire around him in the burning afternoon air.

The rocky path below was empty.

All morning it was empty.

Well into the afternoon it was empty.

Not a mule. Not a sheep farmer.

Not a stray dog.

Empty.

Until it wasn't.

From two hundred yards, the man who stepped out of a shadowy cleft and onto the path looked like a goat farmer. He was dressed in cheap clothes that were visibly patched. He leaned on a crooked stick. His face was elaborately bearded and seamed like lizard skin.

Finn adjusted his focus and studied the man.

A farmer.

Definitely a farmer.

Then the man turned and beckoned behind him.

Ten men came up the slope out of the shadows. Ten men leading six horses.

Each of the animals staggered under the weight of heavy burlap bags hung from leather straps.

The men were all dressed as farmers. One of them was a boy who couldn't have been more than ten. The oldest of them was probably sixty, sixty-five.

Just a bunch of shit-kicker dust farmers from the middle of no-fucking-where.

Finn followed them with the monocular, watching them, studying them, looking for a tell that would give them away. Sometimes it was American boots. Or Russian boots. New ones, not old discards. Sometimes it was an iPod or iPad. The Taliban loved that high-tech shit. Sometimes it was a top-quality cell phone or a satellite phone.

Not today. There was none of that.

But, Finn asked himself, what's in those bags?

This was goat and sheep country. Nobody around here raised cotton. There was no real blanket industry in this corner of the region.

So what was in the bags?

The CIA intel expressed a very high confidence that the next few caravans of opium would include sealed biocontainment flasks filled with a virulent pathogen. Rumor control said that it was a new twist on the seif al-din prion-based thing from a few years back. A new generation of the bug that terrorists had tried to release at the Liberty Bell Center on the Fourth of July. That stuff did something to the metabolism and rewired the brain so that the infected went apeshit nuts and started chomping on each other like they were extras in 28 Days Later. Not actual zombies, but the real-world science equivalent.

If it was that, then Finn knew that the caravan couldn't be allowed out of this valley. Even if it was one of the other pathogens, stuff that wasn't 100 percent lethal, the Taliban had to be stopped here. If something with any kind of significant communicability was allowed out, thousands could die. Maybe hundreds of thousands. If it got to the States or to Europe, the potential loss of life was unthinkable. Imagine releasing an airborne pathogen in Times Square on New Year's Eve. Or at the Wailing Wall in Jerusalem. Or at a crowded airport like Heathrow.

The orders Rattlesnake Team had been given left no room for error. And it had no provision for mercy.

The caravan moved quickly along the path. In four or five minutes, they'd be out of range of Finn's rifle. He tapped his mike.

"Cheech Wizard," murmured Finn, "they're coming your way."

"Got 'em," replied the voice in his ear. Cheech Wizard was the machine gunner of Rattlesnake Team. He was tucked into a nook formed by two slabs of rock that had tumbled down the side of the mountain. A sheer wall at his back and the only exit was covered by the other two members of the team, Jazzman and Bear. They had shadowy niches with good elevation.

"Tell me what you're seeing," said Finn quietly. He didn't whisper. The sibilant "ess" sounds traveled more when you whispered; quiet voices faded out into nothing. Besides, their team radios had excellent pickup. That wasn't SOP. The stuff that was usually issued was often beat-up, the works ruined by heat and sand; but there was a gal in supply that Finn had been banging for a couple of months. It wasn't love, and they both knew it, but he didn't give her the clap and didn't trash-talk about her to the other guys, and she made sure his team had gear that was in good working order. Pretty good swap. Everybody came out on top, nobody got hurt.

Bear had the best vantage point and the best eyes.

"Count ten. Eight adult males, one teenage male, one kid—could be boy or girl," he reported. "No, correction, not a teenager. Kid's maybe ten."

Finn's lip curled. He hated this part of it, but it was something you couldn't avoid. The Taliban were heartless fucks, and they knew their enemy. They often brought kids along with them—kids, and sometimes women—knowing that most of the allied forces would hesitate to pull a trigger if there was a chance of capping a youngster. Partly because it was a cultural thing with the allies, and partly because the Taliban used their propaganda machine to fry the Americans in the world press for killing civilian children.

Which was total bullshit.

The Taliban, al-Qaeda, and a lot of these other asshole terrorist organizations put a lot of those civilians in the crosshairs. It was part of their strategy. In the towns, they put their supply depots and main meeting places in schools or in apartment buildings. Then they more or less shook their dicks at the Americans to take the shot, knowing they had to take the fucking shot. More than once they'd even sacrificed one of their own low-level people or slipped some intel through back-alley channels just to guarantee that a strike would be made. Then, before the smoke cleared, they'd trot out the screaming, weeping parents of the dead children. Somehow the Red Cross and the world press were always tipped off first. Or some "neutral" would capture bloody children on their iPhone. It was all theater, and it turned a knife in Finn's guts.

"What's your read?" Finn asked.

The others knew what the question meant. It had become a common thing for him to ask.

Were these Taliban drug runners? The presence of guns didn't prove anything. After the Russians had their asses handed to them a couple of decades ago, there was a lot of stuff lying around. Plenty of AK-47s. A villager could buy an old one for a male goat.

Bear said, "Four of the men have new boots."

"Confirmed," said Jazzman, "and I'm seeing some serious hardware. I count six . . . no, seven confirmed AKs. Shit, they're armed to the teeth. These aren't villagers. No way."

"Look at the second horse," said Cheech Wizard. "Something long and hard strapped onto the side closest to the wall. I think it's an RPG."

"Affirmative," said Bear. "I see it, too. These fuckers came to play."

"Damn," breathed Jazzman.

"Okay, they're bad guys and it sucks to be them," said Finn. He studied the path the caravan was taking. The trail wound through patches of intense shadows, gray wash, and bright sunlight. The longest sunlit path was forty yards from where they were. It meant that his team would have better angles for a three-point shooting box, but it would put the caravan partly behind an upright stone, effectively hiding half of the targets from Finn's rifle.

He surveyed the terrain. There was a much better shooting position sixty yards around the rim of the same mountain on which he lay. But it would mean breaking cover, and the only two paths to get to that spot either made him a bug on the sandy wall of the mountain or required that he go through a short tunnel. The second choice of the tunnel was smarter, but it meant losing sight of the caravan for a few seconds.

"I've got no shot." Finn told his team the situation and explained what he was about to do. "Hold your fire until I'm in position."

They acknowledged and he wormed his way backward off the ledge, mindful of every sound, every ripple of the sandy-colored camouflage tarp that covered him. He knew the others would keep their eyes on the caravan, watching to see if they reacted to anything.

To Finn, it seemed like it took forever to get to the edge of the shelf. He let gravity pull him over and he dropped down to the path behind the ledge, bending his knees to take the shock, exhaling, hands mindful of his gear.

He froze and listened for the telltale sounds of reaction and response.

Nothing.

He dropped the tarp, turned, and threaded his way quickly through the cracked stone spikes and wormhole tunnels that honeycombed this side of the mountain. Mountains were like echo chambers—every noise seemed amplified, and moving in total silence was maybe possible for ninjas and mimes, but carrying forty pounds of gear made it impossible. They didn't call it battle rattle for nothing.

The mouth of the curving tunnel was dead ahead and Finn moved toward it with lots of small, even steps—a pace designed to cover ground while preventing the hard jolt of regular footfalls.

The tunnel was only sixty-five feet long and curved. There was one brief section in the middle of the curve where it was pitch-black, but the rest was lit well enough by reflected sunlight. Finn had walked it several times. If he kept to the center of the path, the flat sand would see him through. The obstructions were all near the walls.

He moved into the cave and the shadows closed around him.

Within ten paces, the light faded from a dusty tan to purple-gray, and as he rounded the bend the tunnel plunged into total darkness. It was so much darker than he thought it would be, darker than it should have been, but that didn't matter. He stuck to the path and ran.

And slammed into something—a corner of rock, a stalagmite, something—

and rebounded hard. A yell of pain and surprise escaped his throat before he could stop it, and the finger of his right hand, with all the efficacy of a deliberate Judas, slipped inside the trigger guard and jerked.

The single gunshot sounded louder than all the bombs in the world. Magnified by the cave's acoustics, bounced and banged around, it sounded like a barrage.

Finn dropped to his knees, both dazed by the impact and aghast at what he'd done.

After the last echo faded, there was one second of absolute silence, and Finn prayed with all of his might that the Taliban hadn't heard the yell or the shot. It was a stupid prayer, without any possibility of being answered. There were no gods that tolerant or forgiving.

Outside there was a chorus of yells in Pashto, and the world was shattered by the sound of AK-47s opening up.

And then the screaming began.

14
ECHO TEAM

He told us the rest, too.

About crawling through the darkness. About the pain of wounds he was positive had torn him nearly to pieces.

About things that crouched around him in the shadows.

Things that laughed at him.

And he told us about the woman dressed like a village boy, but who revealed a hideous and monstrous face when she pulled away her scarf. Flesh that was livid red and a nose that seemed composed of clay.

At this, Bunny glanced at me over Finn's head. The boy we had encountered had been flash-burned and his nose was covered with mud. Bunny's raised eyebrow questioned this. Had Finn, dazed as he was, also come across this boy and misunderstood what he was seeing?

I gave Bunny a small nod. Had to be a mistake.

What else made sense?

"How's that explain the shell casings?" I asked.

Finn looked perplexed. "I . . . don't know. I didn't see any of the fight. But they had to have fought back. The fight went on and on. Fifteen minutes at least. Maybe twenty. Christ, Joe, the guns never stopped. Neither did the . . ."

His voice trailed off.

"Neither did what?" I said, prompting him.

Finn shook his head, and for a moment I didn't think he was going to answer. One emotion after another crossed his features, each giving his facial muscles a twist and leaving some damage behind. There was doubt and anger and deep uncertainty there, but the most dominant expression was that of fear.

"Joe," he said in a wretched voice, "I don't know what happened. I only know what I told you."

The wind was picking up and blowing like a tribe of banshees through the high mountain passes. It was a cold and terribly lonely sound, and I could have done without the chill it sent crawling up my spine.

"And your men, Finn?" I asked. "You said they were gone? Gone where?"

Tears were running down Finn's face now. Instead of answering my question, his story jagged in a different direction. "I tried to find them. I did a one-man ambush and killed two Taliban drug runners and took their Jeep and some clothes. Drove all over. Looked everywhere. I was in a dozen little towns. There are places you can go, you know? The CIA spooks showed me last time I was in-country, and I knew some from my own tours here. Back-alley places. Off the radar. Black marketeers, all sorts of brokers and wheeler-dealers. I put the word out that I was looking for my men. I guess . . . I guess I made it pretty clear that I'd do anything to get them back." He paused. "Couple of times I had to hurt some guys. Informers who worked for the Taliban who tried to sucker me."

I nodded.

"Then I wound up in this little town and found the right guy. He said he could get my guys back."

"And . . . ?"

The tears rolled down his face.

"He took me to someone who offered a deal," he murmured.

"What kind of deal?" asked Top.

"Me for them," said Finn. "Blood for blood, bone for bone, heart for heart."

It was at that moment that I realized Finn O'Leary was insane. As he spoke these words, I was looking deep into his eyes and there was absolutely no doubt that he believed what he was saying.

"What's that mean?" asked Bunny. "Blood for blood and all that shit? What's it mean?"

Finn didn't answer him. He stared vacantly into the dirt. "The funny thing is . . . I used to think that you had to be dead in order to go to hell. But . . . that's not true at all."

We tried to ask more questions, but Finn was done for now. He went away somewhere deep inside his own head. Top cut him loose, and he lay down on his side, drew his knees up to his chest, tucked his head down, and closed his eyes. Like a terrified child going to sleep.

It was one of the most chilling things I've ever witnessed. It was so inappropriate a thing in so odd a place that it scared the hell out of me.

And saddened me.

I nodded to Bunny to keep watch; Top and I stood up and walked a few paces away to where we could speak privately.

"What was that all about?" asked Top. "Beginning to wonder if our boy's lost some muscle tone." He tapped his forehead as he said this.

"I think so. PTSD or something. I don't know if it's worth trying to get anything else out of him right now. Clearly, though, he's tearing himself up with guilt about the mistake he made in the tunnel."

"If he got three men killed, then it's going to be a damn hard mistake to live with. He was tight with those boys."

"I know."

It was tragic, but we'd both been at this game long enough to see it happen before. Sometimes a guy can be Captain Terrific for five years, then the next day he wakes up and all his marbles are in the wrong bag. It happens, even to guys as tough as Finn.

But seeing him like this was hard.

And I still had the other thing to deal with—maybe evidence of the mental lease expiring on my own acre of sanity. The three things I'd seen tearing the man in the truck apart. Creatures in the shapes of Rattlesnake Team, but with eye sockets filled with fire devouring the guts of an enemy combatant.

Did I tell Top or keep it to myself?

If I was losing it, would that mean I'd get my own guys killed?

Tough questions.

The sun was tumbling through the sky toward the western mountains.

Finn said, "Can I have my gear back? This deep in Indian country, I feel naked without at least a sidearm."

"Listen, brother," I said to Finn. "You're acting freaky, so let's keep things in neutral for a while. If you act cool, then we can talk about guns."

He considered me for a moment, then nodded. "Yeah, sure, Joe, whatever you want." Then he snaked a hand out and caught my arm. "But . . . please find my guys. I can't leave them out here. I can't."

I hesitated, because it was a hard promise to make. If the Taliban had taken them, and if somehow their RFID chips had shorted out, then it could have taken a hundred men a thousand years to search all these caves. We've been looking for the Taliban for only a dozen years. You know how we find them? Informants tell us. Or we spot a caravan, something like that. But when they go to ground inside these caves? They can hide there without being seen until the mountains crumble to dust.

I gave his hand a reassuring squeeze. "We'll do our best, Finn. You know that."

With that, I got up and walked away. After a few minutes, Top followed me. He made sure we were out of earshot before he spoke.

"Earlier," Top said, "you heard a scream through the radio, right?"

I hesitated. "I heard something."

"And right then, the radios and all the electronics went dead."

"Yup."

"Kind of weird," he said.

"Uh-huh."

"The timing of everything, I mean."

"Uh-huh."

"It'll be night in a couple hours. No radio. Hallucinations and shit."

"You going somewhere with this, First Sergeant?"

He spat into the dust. "Cap'n, I got nowhere to go that makes any sense at all. And that is the problem." He cocked his head sideways at me. "Finn's lost his shit. Now you're hearing stuff Bunny and me ain't. Look me in the eye and tell me I don't have to worry about you, too."

This was the conversation an NCO and an officer can only have where there's a lot of history, a lot of trust, and no one close enough to hear.

I turned to him. "Whatever I heard, I heard," I said. "Maybe it came over my mic and not yours, but I heard it. We're going to leave it at that. I'm not going over the edge."

And yet I didn't tell him about seeing Rattlesnake Team.

Why not?

Top studied me for a five count, then he nodded.

I said, "I think I want to take another look at the town square and the cave while there's still enough light to see."

He was still looking at me. "Want company?"

"No. Stay here with Bunny and keep an eye on Finn."

I left him there with Finn and Bunny and went back to the valley. I stood for a long, long time looking at the blood. The placement and amount of the blood fit the scene as Finn had described it. Except that it didn't explain the missing bodies, the lack of any evidence of return fire, or what happened to Finn in that cave. I slung my rifle and drew my sidearm, turning on the small light that was mounted forward of the trigger guard.

The open mouth of the cave was only rock and sand and some dead snarls of creeper vine, but I paused just outside, still in the sunlight. But the sunlight was growing weaker as the day ground on toward twilight. I did not want to be out here past sunset, but the best ETA for our helo was still two hours and change.

Would Bug pass along a request for that timetable to be moved up in light of the electronics and communication being out? Maybe. Knowing him, he'd pass along a recommendation that our mission was way off the radar, even for our own military. My boss could send in more black-ops shooters, and then only if he had anyone on deck. When we'd set out for this mission, we were the only backup. The mission sensitivity made it less likely there would be any standard military assets deployed to save our own asses. If we failed, that would mean that the canister of pathogen was unaccounted for. Best clean-up option then would be to carpet the area with fuel-air bombs and turn this region into the valley of the shadow of death in point of fact.

I clicked on the flashlight and the narrow beam rose in

harmony with the barrel of my gun as I pointed them both into the cave. With slow and very deliberate steps, I moved out of the down-slant of sunlight and stepped into the shadows under the mountain.

The cave was already very dark, and I moved the flashlight beam over everything—sandy floor, boulders, crenellated walls, craggy ceiling. No motion—not a bat, not a sand mouse, not even blowflies.

At ten yards, the cave still had enough light for me to see, but with every step beyond that point, visibility diminished to only those things the flashlight's beam picked out. Until you're in the dark, in a place you know to be dangerous but whose nature you aren't sure of, you really don't appreciate the fear of the dark. So many things can hide so easily there.

I moved forward and the darkness closed around me.

It was surprisingly cold, surprisingly damp. Like the way you'd imagine a dungeon would feel. Clammy and wrong.

Immediately, a part of my mind said, Fuck this.

Seriously, I wanted to turn right around and run the hell out of there.

Yeah, I said run.

Understand something here—I don't spook easily. Usually when something's weird and violent and mysterious, I want to go grab it by the throat, wrestle it to the ground, and wail on it until it makes sense. A somewhat Neanderthal approach, I grant you, but it's worked for me in a lot of very bizarre situations.

This one, though, had a different feel to it.

I didn't get the impression that a mixed group of Taliban and al-Qaeda thugs were lurking behind a rock ready to spring on this blue-eyed, blond-haired agent of the Great Satan. Nor did I have the feeling that Doctor Doom or Lex Luthor was watching me on video cameras from the safety of a secret lair, one hand stroking a white cat, the other holding a detonator that would send Mama Ledger's favorite son to see Jesus on a mushroom cloud.

Without understanding a single thing about what was going on—or what was inside that cave—I knew for sure that this was not going to be anything I'd faced before. Don't ask me how I knew that. But I was absolutely sure.

And that scared the living shit out of me.

Icy lines of sweat trickled down my back and my mouth kept going dry.

I moved deeper into the cave, leaving all traces of daylight behind. We'd brought night vision gear with us, but the electronics on that were as fried as the computers and radio.

The path was more obstructed than I expected, with rocks thrusting out over the sandy walkway and a few unexpected deadfalls. A man running in the dark would be in serious trouble.

Sweat stung my eyes and I dragged a forearm across my face.

And that's when the voice spoke.

"You won't find what you're looking for."

15
ECHO TEAM

I spun and crouched, bringing the pistol around in a two-handed grip.

A figure stood five feet behind me.

"Freeze!" I bellowed. "*Show me your hands . . . show me your fucking hands!*"

The figure slowly raised its arms to either side, standing cruciform in the stark white of my flashlight.

It was the boy.

Dressed in the same clothes, with the same small bloodstain over the heart and the same kaffiyeh on his head with the scarf wrapped all the way around so that all I could see were his eyes.

But that's not what was making my heart pound like thunder in my chest.

The voice hadn't been a boy's.

It had been the voice of a woman.

An old woman.

"Turn around!" I snapped. "On your knees! Now!"

The figure—boy or woman, in this light I could no longer be sure—did not move.

I took a single threatening step forward. "Turn around, or so help me, I will kill you."

"You must listen to me, Captain." The words were spoken in a whispery and uninflected English. No trace of an accent.

It took a full second for the impact of that to hit me.

The boy still spoke in that old woman's voice, but she'd called me *Captain*.

I don't wear captain's bars. None of my team wears a rank or unit patch. No one in the DMS ever does when they're in the field.

So how in the wide blue fuck did this little freak know what I was?

I made sure my voice was controlled. "Who are you?"

"I need to give you a message, Captain."

The figure stood there, arms still out to the sides. I ran the light over his face. The eyes were as dark as holes. The burned flesh around them was puckered and raw.

"I won't tell you again," I warned him.

"I have something you want. You have something I want. I wish to complete my end of the bargain."

"You are going to shut your fucking mouth," I said sharply. "Right now."

I took another step forward and reached a careful hand out

to do a gentle pat-down. It didn't matter that Bunny had already searched the kid. It didn't take all that long to pocket a pistol or strap on a C4 vest. The body inside the robes was as thin as a scarecrow, and dust plumed out from the dry cloth.

The flesh between my shoulders twitched and contracted, because even though the shape my eyes saw was a boy, the shape my hand touched was not. The hips were wider, the waist narrower, and there were breasts. Huge, pendulous, drooping nearly to her waist.

My hand recoiled as if it had a mind of its own. Recoiled in horror and disgust.

"What the . . . ?"

I raised the pistol and pointed the barrel ten inches from the dark eyes, and with my other hand, I tore open the front of the robe.

There was a flash of something.

The world seemed to go red, as if the whole cave was washed with a crimson floodlight. I had a split second's look at the body revealed beneath the robe.

Definitely not a boy.

It was a woman's body. Bloated in spots, emaciated in others, with those huge breasts and skin that was puckered and blistered from furnace heat. Her eyes flared wide and she swiped at me with one hand.

Or . . . with what had been a hand.

The fingers were wrong somehow. They'd . . . changed. They were too long, each joint stretched to an unnatural length, and there seemed to be an extra joint. Or . . . segment. Like the segmented legs of some disgusting pale bug.

I saw—but in no way could prevent—that elongated hand from slapping my pistol. The gun went flying, end over end, and struck a wall.

Then the second hand wrapped itself around me—around

my face and throat. The segmented fingers seemed to be able to completely encircle my head so that I was caught in a net of bony fingers weirdly hot to the touch. I heard my own skin sizzle; I could smell it burning.

I screamed, but then the woman . . . thing . . . whatever in God's name it was . . . lifted me completely off the ground and yanked forward so that my face was an inch from hers. She tugged away the scarf, and I now saw what Finn must have seen—the face of an ancient woman, hideous and disfigured, with a nose either covered in clay or composed of it. Small fires seemed to ignite in her dark eyes, and when she smiled, her lips curled up and wide—wider than is possible—until row upon row of jagged teeth were exposed in a leer.

I saw all of this from the reflected light of the fallen gun.

When she spoke, her voice was a rasping wrongness. If a reptile tried to force human speech from a mouth that had never been constructed for it, I believe that's how it would sound.

"*We have what you want,*" she said, and her breath stank of rotting eggs. Like methane or sulfur. It made me want to vomit, but I fought it back. Just like I fought back the scream that wanted so badly to burst from my chest.

"Christ!" I whimpered. "What *are* you?"

"*The bargain needs to be completed,*" she said insistently.

I hit her as hard as I could, hooking a left over the top of the arm that held me and catching her on the temple. Her head snapped around just like it should have, but then it whipped back to center. Just like it shouldn't have.

I hit her again, and again.

Kicked her, too. Real goddamn hard. In the stomach, the thigh, the chest.

I might as well have been dipping my toes in a cool pond. She took it all and I could see her body sway slightly from the impact of foot-pounds. Those kicks would have put Bunny down.

Bones should have splintered, the jagged edges tearing through muscle and veins and organs. These were of lethal intent, delivered with steel-tip shoes by someone who knows what the hell he's doing. I've killed people with such kicks before.

She ignored them.

No, that's not quite right.

They really pissed her off.

A snarl of irritation rumbled from her chest, and she shook me violently. It was then that I realized that she was holding me completely off the ground. I'm a big man. Two twenty, six two, all muscle. Maybe—*maybe*—someone like Shaq or Hulk Hogan in his prime might have been able to do something like this, but I didn't think so. But she stood there, so small and sickly, one hand wrapped around me, her arm raised straight above her so that I hung there by my goddamned head, toes inches off the ground. It was impossible. Even if everything else that was happening was some kind of trick or illusion, this was actually impossible.

And it hurt like a motherfucker.

She shook me again, and I could feel something slip in my back.

Then, without warning, she dropped me to the ground so that my feet hit hard, my knees buckling.

"*The bargain needs to be completed. He is holding on to you and to false hopes,*" whispered the woman's harsh voice, "*but he has already made his promise.*"

"Wh-what . . . ?" It was all I could manage. Pain was exploding up and down my spine, and my head felt like it was half pulled off.

Burned and mangled lips leaned close to my ear. As she spoke, those lips brushed my ear in a way that was the most appalling parody of sensuality I could imagine.

When I said nothing, she grabbed me again and added, "*You can have them back. All three. You can have their flesh and bone and breath.*"

"What the fuck are you talking about?" I growled as I fought to break free.

"He asked to come back and confess his failure. He wanted you to know that it was his mistake that led to his men being taken. I do not care, but it was part of the bargain. Confessions belong to the infant son of a false god."

I kept struggling.

"But it is time for the deal to be closed. If you stand in the way, you will be consumed. The only grace you have is what your friend bought for you. Break his deal, and you are mine."

She growled that last word, loading it with a pernicious delight more avaricious than anything I have ever heard. Her grip was so strong that it was getting hard to breathe. I fumbled at my pocket for the rapid-release folding knife that was clipped there. It sprang into my hand, and with a flick of my wrist, the three-and-a-half-inch blade snapped into place.

"Fuck you!" I yelled, and rammed the knife into the fire of her eye.

And the red world turned black.

As I plunged down into the pit, I wanted to hear her screams. I wanted to hear a howl of agony.

All I heard was the mad laughter of an old woman.

And something else.

The screams of men in terrible, unbearable, unending pain.

16
ECHO TEAM

It was Top who found me.

He later said that I was standing alone in the center of the ancient town square. Just standing there.

He tried calling my name. Tried shaking me.

In the end, he had to slap me. That apparently had pulled me back from the edge of wherever I was. But only halfway, so he belted me again.

I came all the way back and very nearly kicked the shit out of him, purely by reflex. Top knows me, though, and as soon as I began to react, he danced out of the way, hands up in a no-problems gesture, staying well out of range of my hands and feet.

"Cap'n . . . *Cap!*" he yelled.

That part I heard.

My eyes then cleared, and I saw that it was just the two of us there in the town square. It was dark, but Top's flashlight was propped on a stack of old building blocks. Above us was a field of stars so saturated with white lights that it looked fake.

"What . . . ?" I asked, my voice thick, my head numb and stupid.

"You hurt?" asked Top. "You okay?"

"I . . . don't know," I said, answering both questions at once. "Where am . . . I mean, what the fuck happened?"

Top stepped forward, and there was a strange look in his eyes. He was also bleeding from one nostril. One eye was puffed nearly shut.

I didn't ask what happened to him. He didn't ask what happened to me. We looked into each other's eyes and knew. It had been the same for both of us.

He helped me to my feet and we leaned on each other and half-ran, half-staggered back to where we'd left Finn and Bunny.

Bunny was there.

Bruised and bleeding, sitting on the ground, weeping like a child and holding his face in his hands.

Finn, though, was gone.

There was a burned spot on the ground where he'd been sitting, and that was it.

But I don't think that's why Bunny was crying.

On the ground, laid out in a row, were three men. They were dressed in the same uniforms as us.

Cheech Wizard.

Jazzman.

Bear.

All dead.

Their bodies were as fresh as if they had expired a moment ago.

But their eyes.

God almighty.

God save us all.

Their eyes.

Smoke curled upward from the blackened pits where their eyes should have been. We scrambled over and poured water on them and smothered the fire with sand and our hands, but it was far, far too late.

17
ECHO TEAM

We stood there for a long time, staring at the three dead men from Rattlesnake Team. We all felt lost, confused. Damaged in ways that resisted identification and definition.

Top told me that after I'd left earlier to walk the scene, he'd checked the perimeter of our camp while Bunny made some food. A figure cut right in front of Top. The little boy, running at full speed. Top immediately gave chase and caught up to the kid three hundred yards down the valley. However, when he grabbed the boy's shoulder, the robes tore away and a woman was there. For just a moment, Top thought that it was a young woman.

"Really friggin' beautiful, too," Top told me. "Dusky skin, and built like Beyoncé. Naked and all shiny like she was covered in oil. Got to admit that it floored me. Absolutely fucking floored me. Then I blinked and she wasn't like that at all."

The creature who stood facing Top was the same one—or

same kind of thing—that had attacked me. Wrinkled, emaciated, with sagging breasts, jagged teeth, and hands that made Top shiver as he described them.

The thing knocked the rifle out of Top's hand, slammed him against a wall, and kept saying the same thing.

The bargain needs to be completed.

Top didn't try to figure out what that meant. All he did was try to fight, but the woman slammed him face-forward into the rock.

When Top woke up, he ran back to the camp. Bunny was on his hands and knees, his face covered in welts, coughing blood from a split lip. His story was the same as Top's.

The same as mine.

It was an impossible story. Bunny is six foot seven and can bench-press four hundred pounds in sets of twenty. And he's a top SpecOps shooter trained to kill in every way known. Nobody ever manhandled him. Not without a lot of help.

Until that day.

He was no more effective against this thing than me or Top.

All three of us had been defeated easily. Mastered, humiliated. Discarded.

But Sergeant Michael "Finn" O'Leary was gone.

And Rattlesnake Team had been returned.

What was left of them, anyway.

We all wanted to compare our stories, to sit down and work out what it meant. Hallucinogens. Some kind of spore in the air that was screwing with our minds. Maybe an electrical field from some kind of science fiction gadget.

We wanted to make sense of it.

There wasn't time.

We had to find Finn.

For a moment, though, we stood there, back-to-back in a defensive circle, weapons in hand, looking out at the vast darkness around us.

"Fastest way to cover the area is to separate," said Top.

Bunny looked at him. "Fuck that."

After a few seconds, I said it, too: "Fuck that."

Top just shook his head.

So, we stood our ground.

We are three of the toughest, scariest fighters around. That's not a joke. The DMS scouts the top players from the SEALs, Delta, and other groups. We are actually the best of the best.

But all we could do at that moment was stand there, huddled together for the warmth and assurance of human contact, holding our guns and praying that the night would end.

We tried very hard not to look at the three dead men who lay nearby.

Thirty-six minutes later, we heard the distant whup-whup-whup of our helicopter returning to find us. We popped flares, but we still stood together while we waited.

When we saw the Black Hawk pop its landing lights, I very nearly broke down and cried.

18
ECHO TEAM

They flew us out. Five hours later, we went back out there, this time with three Black Hawks full of SpecOps guys and CIA shooters. A day later, the rest of Echo Team was in-country and they joined us. We scoured the area, searching every inch. The blood was still there, along with the shell casings and footprints.

We found absolutely nothing else.

Not a goddamn thing.

When Bunny went to dig up the artifacts . . . they were gone as well.

And of course, no Finn O'Leary.

We were out there for two whole days. Finally, the word came down to call it.

Oh, was the debrief a bitch.

My boss, Mr. Church, personally flew over and brought along the DMS's top shrink—who is also my personal therapist—Dr. Rudy Sanchez. They interviewed us separately and together, multiple times. They took blood and urine samples. They did MRIs and CT scans. Rudy hooked us up to lie detectors and ran through a minefield of questions. In the privacy of my session with him, I told him about seeing Rattlesnake Team at the site of the Taliban convoy ambush. About how they were eating one of the terrorists. How their eyes were on fire. When I was done, except for the faint whir of the machine and Rudy's shallow breathing, there wasn't a sound in the room.

A lot of the people involved in running those tests, and all of those who'd been out there scouring the ground where we'd been picked up, began avoiding eye contact with me, Top, and Bunny. They didn't find the right kind of evidence to support our stories, and we sure as fuck weren't changing our stories. Not one word.

I cornered Rudy one afternoon after he came out of Mr. Church's temporary office at the Forward Operating Base Delaram, one of the Marine Corps bases there in Afghanistan.

"Talk to me about those polygraphs, Rude," I said.

I expected the usual obfuscation he gave when pressed about anything clinical, but he shrugged. "All three of you believe your stories . . ."

He'd pitched it as a straight answer, but I could hear some reserve in his voice and called him on it.

Rudy smiled. "Come on, Cowboy," he said, giving me his best Gomez Addams smile. "You know how these things work. As I said, the tests verify that you believe your stories, and the lab work is clean. But that's not the same as saying that the stories are believable as described."

After I gave him three or four seconds of a stony face, he sighed.

"Joe, in the absence of physical evidence or some workable theory that would explain the kinds of things you three claim to have seen—"

"'Claim to have seen'?!" I said, jumping on it.

"Yes. Claim. There is nothing I know of that can provide a useful framework for constructing a hypothesis that explains it. A tiny woman beating all three of you up, and apparently doing it all at the same time? A woman who was invulnerable to physical assault by trained special operators, including a knife attack to the face? C'mon, Joe . . . give me a scenario that covers that, and I'll be glad to put it in my report. Hell, I'll lead with the theory in my summation."

He knew, as I knew, that there was no theory that could cover it.

"What about the autopsies on Rattlesnake?"

"They've been sealed in freezers and shipped back to the States. Mr. Church wanted the top guy at Mount Sinai to do the post."

And that's where we left it.

For the next couple of weeks, I was completely obsessed. I took teams of various sizes out there whenever I could to continue the search, the specter of the pathogen always being the primary excuse. Through our CIA contacts, we put feelers out through the various intelligence and criminal networks that are everywhere in Afghanistan. A lot of black-budget money changed hands. I'd like to think that we kept up this level of intensity because three Americans were dead, one was missing, and something— something—was happening out there on the Big Sand that didn't make any kind of sense. Top and Bunny always went with me, but they'd now become moody and silent. Off the clock, we were all drinking too much. And Top had been seeing the chaplain a lot.

After three weeks, we packed up our toys and prepared to fly home. The CIA took over to try to discover what Plan B was for the Taliban and their bioweapon.

Which is when my boss called me into his office.

Everything was packed except his laptop, which was open on his borrowed desk, the screen turned away. Mr. Church is a big, blocky man, past sixty but looking a fit and brutal forty. I don't know his past, but there are a lot of wild tales and even wilder rumors. I wonder how he would have fared in that cave.

"Sit," he said, and like a good dog, I did. Mr. Church had an open package of Nilla Wafers on his desk. He selected one and nibbled it thoughtfully while he studied me through the nearly opaque lenses of his tinted glasses. "An Israeli intelligence officer working undercover in this region captured a series of photos and video with his phone. They were taken last night around twenty-two thirty. I want you to look at them and give me your opinion."

He spun his laptop and pressed a key. The screen was dark for two seconds and then a grainy image popped up.

It was clearly recorded at a dark and seedy coffee shop in what had to be a dangerous part of some local town. The people at the table—nearly all men—were extravagantly bearded, grim, wary eyed. They sat in a tight cluster, sipping small cups of black coffee and bending their heads close in order to talk quietly to each other. The place was crowded, and when the image shifted, I estimated forty or more men and a couple of women with chadors.

Church kept tapping the key to go from frame to frame. At first, it was clear that the Israeli agent was using his phone camera to take pictures of as many of the men as possible. A cataloging process that I've seen with field agents dozens of times. You do that when you're trolling for someone who is a genuine person of interest. Then there were fifteen shots of three men at a distant table, their heads bent together in earnest conversation.

"Our contact identifies these men as known Taliban drug

traffickers," said Mr. Church. "But they're also active in the black market for looted antiquities."

Then the camera settled down solidly enough that it was clear the Israeli agent had laid his phone down on his table. The lens was pointed at another table against the far wall. Mr. Church then started the video component. Three men sat there. One was an Afghan villager wearing a kaffiyeh with tribal markings. He sat and listened, clearly not a major player in the conversation. The second man was also an Arab, but I couldn't tell anything specific about him except that he was old, hawk nosed, and wore a turban that was so thick that the wrappings cast shadows down over his deep-set eyes. This man appeared to be doing all of the talking. Unfortunately there was too much ambient noise to pick out any of the conversation.

However, it was the third man who was the real story here. He was dressed in Afghan clothes, including a kaffiyeh, but he was clearly not an Arab. He wore sunglasses and a faint smile that was very strange—sensuous to the point of being almost overtly sexual. He sat with hands folded on the table as he listened to the older man.

"Jesus Christ," I said.

Mr. Church said nothing.

"That's Finn."

"Without a doubt. Sergeant Michael O'Leary."

"Where was this taken?"

"A small town named Tekleh."

"Never heard of it."

"Nor had I until today. It's an unincorporated town ninety-four klicks from here, used mostly by smugglers. A few small buildings outside made to look like a sheep camp, and a few dozen furnished chambers built into a series of caves. The CIA is aware of it, and they've been working to get a man inside. The Israelis already have a man there, as do the Russians."

"Can we pick up the guy Finn was talking to? What's his name? Aziz? Encourage him to tell us where Finn is?"

Mr. Church tapped the key again, and we were back to still images. The next picture showed the mouth of a small cave. There were equipment boxes around and the kind of gear you expect at archaeological digs. In front of the cave lay six bodies. You could tell they were men and that their clothing was typical of the fighters in the Taliban drug trade. But that was it.

"This is one of several archaeological sites that were hijacked by the Taliban and used as a base. It's one of several sites rich in artifacts of some of the oldest religious cults in the area. The lilitu, among others."

The Taliban fighters had been torn to pieces. Their chests and stomachs were ripped apart. Pieces were clearly missing.

"In previous cases of a similar nature, all of the artifacts were missing from the site. Not one of them has turned up on any of the black markets the Taliban typically uses to peddle such materials. Not one piece."

He tapped another key. "This was taken an hour ago. It's a newly opened shrine."

"So . . . ?"

"Reliable witnesses claim that Sergeant O'Leary was seen in the area moments before the Taliban team was hit."

I stared at him.

"Finn? But . . . why? I don't understand. Why would he . . . ?"

My question trailed off into the dust. I didn't want to finish it. Mr. Church said nothing.

19

Last two things I want to say about this, and then I'm closing this report. I'm going to seal it and make sure that it gets buried someplace that sane people won't ever look. I'm sure as fuck never going to look at it again.

We buried Staff Sergeant Albert "Cheech Wizard" Sandoval, Staff Sergeant William "Bear" Pulaski, and Gunnery Sergeant Treyvon "Jazzman" Walker back home in Arlington National Cemetery. Mr. Church fixed it so that they were given official military status again and it was noted that they'd died honorably in combat. All of the proper awards and flags were given to their families. Before they were buried, a team of forensics experts and pathologists from Mount Sinai did full autopsies on them. They confirmed without any doubt—based on the degree of tissue decomposition and other factors—that all three men had been dead at least thirteen days.

The autopsy was done three days after Echo Team brought their bodies home. That means that they had to have died during that ambush in the old town.

Explain that to me in a way that doesn't make me scream at night. Because that's what I do now. Maybe I will for a long time. I'm still drinking more than I should. Rudy's on me about that, but he knows what really happened, so he doesn't push too hard.

So that's the first thing.

The second thing is that we've started getting reports of hits on certain Taliban teams in the region around Tekleh. Not all of them, not most. The hits aren't interfering with those assholes fighting us and the Afghan regulars, and it sure as shit hasn't done much to slow down the opium caravans. But since that day in the hills near Haykal, every attempt by Taliban forces to occupy or desecrate the old shrines hidden in the mountains has been met with armed resistance.

The stories are always exaggerated, of course. The Taliban blame it on drones, on CIA kill squads, on U.S. surges. And, who knows, maybe that accounts for some of it.

Call it 1 percent, overall.

For the rest?

I've been to three of those sites, and I've seen photo documentation of eight others. The Taliban at those sites haven't just been shot—they've been torn apart. Even if you put the pieces together, it doesn't add up to whole bodies.

I've walked those three scenes. You can read a firefight by shell casings and footprints.

In all of them there was only one set of footprints going in, and one coming out.

Just one.

American military combat boots.

I'm a reasonable guy, a rational man, so I guess there are a lot of very reasonable and very rational explanations for all that.

But, go ahead . . . name one.

Acknowledgments

The authors would like to thank the ever-ebullient Ed Schlesinger for his keen eye and his enthusiasm, the dashing Howard Morhaim for his agent-ly shepherding, and NECON, where this book was dreamed up.

David Liss would also like to thank his Gemini Ink novella workshop, and Jonathan Maberry sends out his gratitude to the fans and supporters of the Joe Ledger thrillers.

About the Authors

Kelley Armstrong is the *New York Times* bestselling author of the *Cainsville* modern gothic series, *Otherworld* urban fantasy series, *Darkest Powers* and *Darkness Rising* teen paranormal trilogies, and the Nadia Stafford crime trilogy, as well as coauthor of the *Blackwell Pages* middle-grade trilogy. She grew up in Ontario, Canada, where she still lives with her family. A former computer programmer, she's now escaped her corporate cubicle and hopes never to return. Visit www.kelleyarmstrong.com.

Christopher Golden is the *New York Times* bestselling author of such novels as *Of Saints and Shadows* and *The Myth Hunters*. He has cowritten three illustrated novels with Mike Mignola, the first of which, *Baltimore, or, The Steadfast Tin Soldier and the Vampire*, was the launching pad for the comic book series Baltimore. His current work-in-progress is a graphic novel trilogy collaboration with

Charlaine Harris entitled *Cemetery Girl*. Golden was born and raised in Massachusetts, where he still lives with his family. Visit www.christophergolden.com.

David Liss is the author of seven novels, most recently the historical urban fantasy *The Twelfth Enchantment*. His previous books include *A Conspiracy of Paper*, which was named a *New York Times* Notable Book and won the 2001 Barry, Macavity, and Edgar awards for best first novel. *The Coffee Trader* was also named a *New York Times* Notable Book and was selected by the New York Public Library as one of the year's 25 Books to Remember. *A Spectacle of Corruption* was a national bestseller, and *The Devil's Company* has been optioned for film by Warner Bros. Liss is also the author of numerous comics and graphic novels. Visit www.davidliss.com.

Jonathan Maberry is a *New York Times* bestselling author, multiple Bram Stoker Award winner, and freelancer for Marvel Comics and Dark Horse. His novels include *Extinction Machine*, *Fire & Ash*, *Assassin's Code*, *Ghost Road Blues*, *Patient Zero*, and many others. Nonfiction books include *Ultimate Jujutsu*, *The Cryptopedia*, and *Zombie CSU*. Jonathan's award-winning teen novel, *Rot & Ruin*, is now in development for film. Since 1978, he's sold more than twelve hundred magazine feature articles, three thousand columns, two plays, greeting cards, song lyrics, and poetry. He teaches the "Experimental Writing for Teens" class, is the founder of the Writers Coffeehouse and cofounder of the Liars Club. Jonathan lives in Bucks County, Pennsylvania, with his wife, Sara Jo, and a fierce little dog named Rosie. Visit www.jonathanmaberry.com.